THE STORY OF
THE STONE

石

Also by Barry Hughart

BRIDGE OF BIRDS

Barry Hughart

THE STORY OF THE STONE

A Master Li Novel

A Foundation Book
Doubleday
NEW YORK   LONDON   TORONTO   SYDNEY

All of the characters in this book
are fictitious, and any resemblance
to actual persons, living or dead,
is purely coincidental.

A Foundation Book

Published by Doubleday, a division of
Bantam Doubleday Dell Publishing Group, Inc.,
666 Fifth Avenue, New York, New York 10103

Foundation and the portrayal of the letter F
are trademarks of Doubleday, a division of
Bantam Doubleday Dell Publishing Group, Inc.

This one is for the Sacred and Solemn Order
of Sinologists

石

Prologue

Jen Wu is a day Master Li sets aside for my literary endeavors, and I was pleased that it was cold and rainy and fit for little else than splashing ink around.

"Ox," he said, "the writing of your memoirs is doing wonders for your calligraphy, but I must question the content. Why do you choose the rare cases in which matters run melodramatically amok?"

I heroically refrained from saying, "They always do."

"When you allow sensationalism to do the work, you're eliminating the need for thought. Besides," he added somewhat petulantly, "you give the impression that I'm violent and unscrupulous, which is only true when there's a need for it. Why not explain a case that was calm and rather leisurely and lovely; in which the issues were philosophical rather than frenzied?"

I scratched my nose with my mouse-whiskered writing brush as I tried to think of such a thing. All I wound up with was ink in my nostrils.

"*Shi tou chi,*" he said.

I stared at him incredulously. "You want me to try to explain that awful mess?" I said in a high strangled voice. "Venerable Sir, you know very well it almost broke my heart, and I—"

"*Shi tou chi,*" he repeated.

"But how can I tell The Story of the Stone?" I wailed. "In the first place I don't understand where it begins and in the second place I'm not sure it has an ending and in the third place even if I understood the ending it wouldn't do me any good because I don't understand the beginning in the first place."

He gazed at me in silence. Then he said, "My boy, stay away from sentences like that. They tend to produce pimples and permanent facial tics."

"Yes, sir," I said.

"Begin at the beginning as you understood it, proceed through the middle, continue to the end, and then stop," said Master Li, and he sauntered out to get drunk, leaving me to my current misery.

What can I say about the affair of the stone? All I know for certain is the date when we first became involved: the twelfth day of the seventh moon in the Year of the Serpent 3,339 (A.D. 650). I remember it because I had a premonition that something dramatic was about to happen, and had been checking the calendar for auspicious days, even though I wasn't so much foreseeing but wishing because I was worried about Master Li. He'd been in a foul mood for a month. For days he did nothing but lie on his pallet and drink himself into oblivion, and when he was sober he pinned up sketches of government officials and riddled the wall of the shack with throwing knives. He never spoke to me about it, but he was old, old almost beyond belief, and I think he was afraid he'd drop dead before something interesting turned up.

I didn't like that at all, but I couldn't afford a decent fortune-teller so I had to rely on *Ta-shih* to tell me whether my premonition was favorable or disastrous, and that meant I could only get six possible answers: "grand peace and luck," "a little patience," "prompt joy," "disappointment and quarrels," "scanty luck," and "loss and death." I didn't dare tempt the anger of the gods by trying more than once a day. I took the first reading on the eighth day of the seventh moon, and my heart sunk when I saw "loss and death." On the ninth I tried again, and again I got "loss and death." My heart bounced up and down upon my sandals when "loss and death" appeared on the tenth day, and on the eleventh, before dawn, I slipped out to pray at the temple of Kuan-yin. Not even the goddess of mercy could help. "Loss and death" came up again, and I read it in the shadow of the goddess's statue as the sun lifted above the city walls, and just then I heard wails of woe drifting from Master Li's alley, and then the dread peal of the Cloud Gong.

I ran back, blinded by tears, and knocked Ming Number Six head over heels, nearly crushing the delicate tapers of sacrificial Buddha's Fingers incense that he had just bought at great expense. He didn't mind. I have never seen anyone happier, and it was only then that I realized that the wails and the Cloud Gong were coming from his house, not Master Li's shack, because Great-grandfather Ming (a loathsome tyrant if ever there was one) had finally condescended to breathe his last. Master Li was still with me, and he even felt well enough to invite a few people over that night.

It had been a spur-of-the-moment thing. The gentlemen were collected from a wineshop, and the ladies came from one of the bawdy *Yuan Pen* troupes that I far preferred to *Tsa Chu* opera, and things went very well except for the Mings' cat. They had tied the beast to Great-grandfather's coffin, hoping to chase away evil spirits that might come for the corpse's *po* (sentient) soul while his *hun* (personality) was down in Hell being judged. I thought it was a terrible idea—a dog, yes, but everybody knows that if a cat jumps over a coffin the corpse will sit up and climb out and cause all sorts of trouble—and the cat also thought it was a terrible idea and began howling its head off. Then one of the guests, a pasty-faced fellow I didn't know, started a dice game called Throwing Heaven and Nine, and the ladies got tipsy and decided to try to drown out the cat by bellowing bawdy songs from the classic lowbrow farce "The Merry Dance of Mistress Lu," and at that point a storm began moving toward Peking. A wild wind howled in counterpoint with the cat, and a hole about a foot across suddenly appeared in the roof. I fished some fallen thatching from a pot of rice and turned the cooking over to the ladies, and then I went out to the alley and climbed up on the roof to make repairs.

I checked my thatching and twine and mallet and nails, and began sliding across the ridgepole toward the hole. The ladies were catching their breaths before launching into another chorus, but the wind and the cat and the gamblers' doggerel were still going strong.

"*Red Mallet Six; easy to fix!*" yelled the pasty-faced gambler, meaning he had to beat a throw of one and five.

"*Ooooooooooooooooohhh,*" moaned the wind.

"*Yeeeeeeeeeeeeeeeeow!*" howled the cat.

"*Halfway to Heaven with the One-leg Seven, money-money-money!*" yelled the gambler, who had just tossed one and six.

I slid farther along the ridgepole and cautiously tried my weight on a bamboo rafter. It held, and I took out a length of twine and began measuring the hole. Directly below me the ladies got their second wind, and I vaguely recalled that more than one sheltered mandarin was reputed to have been sent to his grave by accidental contact with the Yuan Pen songs of the great unwashed.

"Make your pile while you're young, dear, for beauty must flee,
And middens greet maidens whose image you'll be;
Wrinkled belly and breasts, features mottled and gray,
Lurching lonely through nights while your nose lights the
waaaaaaaaaaaaaaaaaaay!"

Another two or three jars of wine, I thought, and they should really loosen up. I didn't want to miss it.

"Oooooooooooooooohhh," moaned the wind.

"Yeeeeeeeeeeeeeeeow!" howled the cat.

"Hear what I said?" the lucky gambler yelled. *"It's the Tiger Head! Money-money-money!"*

Faintly through the din I could hear the watchman crying the double hour of the rat. A new day had begun, and for some reason I automatically grabbed some nails, totaled them, added the numbers of the moon, day, and hour, and started one last Ta-shih reading. I rapidly counted across the upper six joints of the three middle fingers of my left hand, and stared in disbelief as my counting finger came to a stop on the deadly sixth joint.

"Loss and death?" I whispered.

What could it mean? Surely the prophecy had been fulfilled by Great-grandfather Ming, unless he had arisen . . . I hastily slid down and peered through Ming's window to see if that damned cat had jumped over the coffin. The lid was still securely in place, so why did I keep getting the death reading? Something was very, very wrong, and it took a moment to register what it was.

Only the cat and the wind were serenading the night. The shack was silent. Not a peep. I hastily slid back up and peered through the hole, and it was apparent that the phenomenal luck of the pasty-faced gambler who had just beaten double fives with a five and a six had run out. The lash of a donkey whip was wrapped around his right arm, jerking the sleeve up to reveal a leather tube strabbed to his forearm. The dice he had palmed and switched for loaded ones fell from the tube and rolled over the floor, and I stupidly noted that he would have won anyway: "Heaven," double sixes, gazed up at me.

The idiot decided to try something even more dangerous than loaded dice. The handle of the donkey whip was in Master Li's left hand, and surely the cheater could see that Master Li's eyes looked like narrow chips of ice, but he reached into his robe with his left hand and awkwardly pulled out a knife. He never had a chance, of course. I hit the roof between two rafters and crashed through like a water buffalo stepping upon a half inch of river ice, and my aim was good—I landed upon the idiot's left shoulder—but I was way too late. When I climbed to my feet I was dripping with red ooze.

"Sorry, Ox. The son of a sow moved on me," Master Li said, glaring disgustedly at the corpse.

He meant that the fellow should have allowed himself to be murdered cleanly, and shouldn't have turned so Master Li's throwing knife would sever his largest jugular vein. Murder was the only term for it. Master Li surely saw from the way the fellow held a knife that he was a raw amateur, and he surely knew that I was going to land on the dolt before he took two steps. The old man looked at me rather contritely, and spread his hands wide and shrugged, and then he accompanied me outside for more thatching. It's amazing how much blood the human body contains, and we were going to need at least four armloads to mop up the lake on the floor.

At least we wouldn't be bothered by guests. They had vanished like figments of dreams, and within half an hour they would have witnesses willing to swear that they had spent the night sacrificing to Chu-Chuan Shen, Patron of Pig Butchers, in West Bridge Temple on the other side of Peking.

Master Li knelt beside the body. "No idea who he was," he muttered. "Saw him in the wineshop and he looked vaguely familiar, so I invited him along."

There was no identification. The money belt yielded an extraordinary amount of gold, and Master Li examined the fellow's discolored fingernails and said he had worked with a variety of metallic acids, although he bore no other resemblance to an alchemist. In a concealed pocket was a squeeze tube made from a pig entrail that released tiny puffs of a grayish substance, and Master Li whistled.

"That's a small fortune, Ox," he said. "Powdered Devil's Um-

brella and absolutely pure, so far as I can judge. It may not be the
best, but it's far and away the most expensive as well as addictive of
all *ling-chih,* and mushrooms like that haven't grown naturally
around Peking for a hundred years."

He found nothing else of interest. Ming's cat and the wind
greeted me as I stepped out with the pallid bloodless body draped
over my shoulder. The cold air smelled of rain. Small black clouds
were skidding across the wind-whipped sky, and stars blinked on
and off like a billion fireflies, and the moon looked like the great
billowing yellow sail of a ship that was racing across a blue-black
ocean toward immense cloud cliffs in the west, where lightning
flickered.

No one saw me slip into the abandoned smugglers' tunnel that
led from the alley and under the city dump to the canal. When I
stepped back out the sky was almost completely covered by clouds,
and I could barely make out the jetty and the dark water beneath.
There were heavy rocks beside the jetty. I tied the other end of a
tarred rope around the corpse's legs, and it slid silently beneath the
surface and drifted down to join the others.*

The incident was closed. By unspoken agreement Master Li and I
erased the affair of the dice cheater, and never intended to mention
him again. The roof would have to wait until morning. I wearily
crawled into my pallet while Master Li huddled over one more wine
jar, listening to the rain patter down, sifting like a shower of silver
through the holes. A small pool formed at his feet, and the last
thing I saw before I closed my eyes was the ancient sage gazing
moodily at his image reflected in rainwater that glistened like a
mirror in the candlelight.

I awoke with the awareness that something strange had happened. During the night a weight seemed to have been lifted from
me, and while I had an even more powerful sense that something
important was about to happen, this time all the omens were good.
It was as though Master Li's moment of rage and murder had been
a necessary purgative, although I couldn't imagine why. He was
wincing and groaning under the weight of the morning light, as

---

* The meaning is unclear, although the implication is alarming. It should be remembered that volumes two through five of the complete *Memoirs of Number Ten
Ox* were seized and burned by the Imperial Censors, and while copies are rumored
to exist, none have been found.

usual, and I eased his hangover with a compress of hot sliced ginger root. Apparently he hadn't felt the same purgative effect yet, because he was sore as a boil.

The morning was drowned in mist and drizzle. Along about the hour of the goat Master Li jumped to his feet and grabbed his coat and rain hat and set out toward the Wineshop of One-Eyed Wong, which was usually a bad sign because he knows very well that the famous bouquet of Wong's wine comes from crushed cockroaches. I was more sure than ever that something of great importance was heading straight toward the old man, and I happily accompanied him to his private table.

Master Li sat there looking like ninety pounds of Fire Drug ready to explode, and that is absolutely all I know for certain about the weird affair of *Shi tou chi.* I didn't understand anything that followed. All I can do is set down events as I witnessed them, and freely admit that I missed the subtleties that could have told me what was really going on, and what was important and what was not.

Begin at the beginning, Master Li told me. Proceed through the middle, continue to the end, and then stop. That is what I shall do, and then, perhaps, a kind reader will write and explain it to me.

石

1

One-Eyed Wong and his beloved wife, Fat Fu, have worked very hard to earn the reputation of running the worst wineshop in all China. The notoriety gives them a clientele that is the envy of the empire, and the usual mix was present: Bonzes and *Tao-shih* swapped filthy stories with burglars and cutthroats, and eminent artists and poets flirted with pretty girls and boys while high government officials played cards with the pimps. All I could see of great scholars was their lacquered gauze caps, because they were on their knees rolling dice with grave robbers. Against one wall is a row of curtained booths for aristocrats, and occasionally a manicured hand would part beaded curtains to give a better view of the lowlife. The antics of the clientele could be quite dramatic, and One-Eyed Wong constantly patrolled the premises with a sand-filled sock swinging in his hand while Fat Fu sent him messages by whistling.

She knew everybody who was important or dangerous. When Master Li entered, she whistled a few bars of a popular song he had inspired: *Fire Chills and Moonlight Burns, Before Li Kao to Virtue Turns.*

As I say, I was waiting for Master Li to explode, and at the same time I was waiting for my premonition to prove itself, and at that moment a pair of curtains parted at an aristocrat's booth and I said to myself, this is it! The girl who stepped out was one of the most beautiful creatures I had ever seen. Surely she was a princess, and she was coming straight to our table. She wore a honey-colored coat of some exotic material, and a waistcoat trimmed with silver squirrel fur. Her long slit tunic was fashioned from the costliest silk, Ice White, which loses its luster after ten minutes' exposure to direct sunlight. Her blue cap was trimmed with perfect pearls, and her blue slippers were embroidered with gold. Her feet made no sound at all as she drifted toward us like a lovely cloud.

Then she came close enough for me to see that her beautiful eyes were totally mad. I jumped to my defensive position at Master Li's left side, leaving his knife hand free, but she paid no attention to us. She floated past in a subtle mist of perfume. Master Li took note of the tiny flickers of fire deep inside her wide eyes, and the hugely distended pupils.

"Thunderballed to the gills," he observed.

He was referring to hallucinatory mushrooms so dangerous that sale of them has been banned. Fat Fu reached the same conclusion and began whistling "Red Knives," and One-Eyed Wong moved swiftly. The princess was approaching a table where a bloated bureaucrat who boasted all nine buttons of rank on his hat was laying down the law to admiring underlings, and she smiled so beautifully that it took my breath away. A delicate hand slipped inside her tunic. Wong's sand-filled sock reached the back of her head just as the point of her dagger reached the bureaucrat's throat. She descended to the floor as gracefully as a falling leaf, and one of the scholars glanced up from his dice game.

"Got her again, Wong," he said.

"One of these days I'm going to miss," One-Eyed Wong said gloomily.

The bureaucrat gazed down at the lovely body and saw who she was and turned green. "Buddha protect me!" he howled, and he charged out the door so hastily that he left his purse on the table, which the underlings grabbed and divided. Wong picked up the princess and took her to the side door, and the last I saw of her she had been collected by a pair of liveried servants and was being carried away in a silken sedan chair.

"So much for premonitions," I said to myself.

Master Li was turning purple. "What a world we live in," he said, breathing heavily through his nose. "Ox, that exquisite girl is Lady Hou, who happens to be one of the three finest poets in the empire. In any civilized age she would be honored and decorated and praised to the skies, but ours is the age of the Neo-Confucians."

He smashed the table so hard that his wine jar bounced up in the air, and I caught it before the contents could spill on his robe and burn holes in it.

"Fraud, Ox!" he said furiously. "We live in a land so debased that its most valued art forms are fraud and forgery. The Neo-Confucians cannot accept the fact that a mere woman could be so gifted, and they, of course, control the Imperial Censors, who control publication. They graciously consented to publish the lady's poems, and to her amazement she saw the author's credit: 'Attributed to Yang Wan-li.' That is really quite clever. The implication being that somebody was faking a masculine classical style, and by officially classifying genuine work as fraudulent, they have, in effect, deprived Lady Hou of her identity. She's been destroying her mind with Thunderballs and slitting Neo-Confucian throats ever since, but there are simply too many of them. They'll win in the end. Eventually she'll be convinced that she really doesn't exist, and is actually a teapot or something in that general price range, and then they'll lock her up and the head Neo-Confucian will suavely appropriate her poetry as his own."

He downed his wine at a gulp, and signaled Fat Fu for some more.

"My boy," he said gloomily, "we live in the last days of a once great civilization. Dry rot has set in, so we paint it with lies and gild it with fool's gold, and one of these days the whole works will blow away in a high wind and where an empire once flourished there'll be nothing but a bunch of bats flying in and out of a bunghole."

He was depressed but I was cheered. I knew with a certainty I couldn't explain that my premonition had been correct after all, and I had simply focused on the wrong person. I suppose it had to do with the terror in the voice I heard—I couldn't see who it was, but somebody was working his way through the crowd, and he was chanting the same incomprehensible words over and over again. Even Master Li looked up from his wine jar and took notice.

"Interesting," he said, with a faint sign of animation. "One doesn't often hear ancient Sanskrit. The Great Prayer of the Heart Sutra, to be precise: *Gyate, gyate, harag yate, harosogyate, bochi, sowaka!* which means 'Gone, gone, gone beyond, gone altogether beyond, what an awakening, hail!' Nobody can explain why it should be, but the prayer has an extraordinarily soothing effect when one repeats it over and over."

Then we saw him, and I was disappointed. I had expected a wild-eyed barbarian, but he was only a bonze. He was small and pale and appeared to be frightened half to death, and he was looking desperately around the room. His eyes fastened upon Master Li like a pair of limpets, and he scuttled up and fell to his knees and began kowtowing energetically.

"Bl-bl-blpp-blppt," he said, or something like that.

"If you stopped trying to bang a hole in the floor with your chin, you might be more comprehensible," Master Li said, not unkindly. "Why not stand up and try it again?"

The monk jumped up and bowed as jerkily as a kou-tou beetle. "Have I the honor of addressing the great and mighty Master Li, foremost among the scholars and truth seekers of China?" he squealed.

Master Li brushed away the compliments with a modest wave of a hand. "My surname is Li and my personal name is Kao, and there is a slight flaw in my character," he said. "This is my esteemed former client and current assistant, Number Ten Ox. You got a problem?"

The monk struggled for some semblance of self-control. "Venerable Sir, I am the humble abbot of the insignificant monastery in the Valley of Sorrows. You have heard of our valley?"

"Who hasn't?" said Master Li.

I hadn't.

"We have lived in peace for centuries, but now one of my monks has been murdered in a terrible and impossible manner," the abbot said with a shudder. "Our library has been broken into, and something has happened to trees and plants that must be seen to be believed."

He had a fit of trembling, and it took him some time to get more words out.

"O Master Li, the Laughing Prince has arisen from the grave," he whispered.

"Well, he always said he'd return, although he seems to have taken his time about it," Master Li said calmly. "How long has the aristocratic son of a sow been in his tomb?"

"Seven hundred and fifty years," the abbot whispered.

Master Li poured himself another cup of wine. "Punctuality is not a priority of princes," he observed. "What makes you think this one has returned to his old playpen?"

"He has been seen. I myself have seen him dancing and laughing in the moonlight with his murderous companions, and when we found the body of poor Brother Squint-Eyes, the expression on his face bore witness to the presence of the Laughing Prince. We found this clutched in his hand, and a search of the library revealed that the manuscript had been stolen."

The abbot timidly offered a fragment of ancient parchment. Master Li gazed at it casually, and then he froze. Not a muscle twitched in his face, but my heart skipped a beat. I knew what it meant when his body was as still as a boulder and his eyes were almost hidden by wrinkles that could have formed a relief map of all China.

"Anything else?" Master Li asked calmly.

The little monk was close to fainting. He was being squeezed by a memory that made his eyes bulge from his head, and his voice was strangled.

"There was a sound," he whispered. "I cannot describe that sound. It turned half the monks to jelly, yet the other half couldn't hear it at all. Those who heard were forced to follow the sound. We had no will of our own. It led us to a scene of destruction that cannot be described in words. It was a sound that seemed to come from Heaven yet had the effect of the worst fires of Hell, and I knew at once that I must come to the greatest resolver of riddles in all the empire."

Master Li turned the fragment over and examined the back of it. "What do you know about the stolen manuscript?" he asked.

The abbot blushed. "I am no scholar. I couldn't read a word of it," he said humbly. "Brother Squint-Eyes, the murdered monk, was our librarian, and he said it was ancient but not valuable. A curiosity that was probably intended to be a footnote to a history."

"How large was it?"

The abbot formed the shape of a scroll with his hands, about a foot high and a fifth of an inch thick.

"What has happened to the body of Brother Squint-Eyes?"

"There is some ice left in our cold room, so I had the body placed upon it," the abbot said. "Venerable Sir, ours is a poor order, but you will have heard of Prince Liu Pao. I have written him, and he is on his way, and I assure you he will pay whatever—"

Master Li held up a hand. "That may not be necessary," he said. "Suppose I were to offer my services, including all expenses, in return for this fragment of the manuscript?"

"Done!" the abbot cried.

The thought of having Master Li take over did wonders, and the little fellow was instantly twenty years younger. It was settled in a matter of minutes. The abbot had to return to his monastery at once, and Master Li promised to set forth toward the Valley of Sorrows the following day. The abbot got a bad nosebleed from banging his chin against the floor as he crawled backward from the table, but his face was joyful when he hopped up and ran out to bring the good news to his monks. Master Li watched him go like a fond grandfather.

"Well, Ox, what do you make of this?" he said.

He meant the fragment, and he knew very well I couldn't make anything of it. I can read only the simplest script, and this was scholar's shorthand, and ancient shorthand at that. I answered by shrugging my shoulders.

"It's a forgery," Master Li said happily. His eyes were almost reverent as he gazed at it. "That's the understatement of the millennium. It's a forgery so great it should have a temple built around it and be worshipped with prayers and gongs and incense, and the monk who discovered it has been murdered, which is precisely as it should be, artistically speaking. Blessings on that ice!" Master Li exclaimed. "If this is any guide, the left lung of Brother Squint-Eyes is sure to be packed with yak manure, and his right lung will contain volcanic ash, and the sheared pigtails of novice nuns will be wrapped around his lower intestine, and engraved upon his liver will be the Seven Sacrileges of Tsao Tsao. My boy, we're going to perform the most delightful autopsy in history."

I wasn't sure that any autopsy could be delightful, but I didn't care. The old fire had returned to Master Li's eyes, and I felt like a war-horse who was being called back to battle. In fact, I very nearly whinnied and pawed the floor.

石

2

The rain had almost stopped and the sky was clearing rapidly. It
was going to be a beautiful afternoon with enough clouds left over
for a glorious sunset, and I reveled in fresh air after inhaling the
reek of raw alcohol in Wong's. The rain had left the streets slippery,
so I carried the old man on my back as we came back up the Alley
of Flies, as I always do when the going is difficult. His tiny feet fit
comfortably into my tunic pockets, and he weighs no more than a
schoolboy.

The streets were nearly empty. That suited me very well because
we were in the part of the city called Heaven's Bridge, where every
alley is usually filled with scar-faced gentlemen who converse in the
silent language of the Secret Societies: fingers wriggling rapidly inside the sleeves of their robes. Heaven's Bridge is also the place for
public executions, and it is said that at the third watch one can see
rows of ghosts perched like vultures on top of the Wailing Wall
behind the chopping blocks. (Decapitation has not improved their
dispositions. Kindly strangers who hear the sobs of a child or the
pleas of a woman and step into the shadows will never be seen
again.) Heaven's Bridge makes me nervous, and I was pleased that
the only person we encountered was a bonze who was dutifully
banging his wooden fish even though it wasn't subscription day.

"The double hour of the goat!" he bellowed. "The Governor's
Banquet has been canceled, but there will still be a recital of the
stone bells in the Temple of Confucius! West Bridge is closed to

traffic, and drivers will be fined! A new storm is approaching from the east, but the western horizon is clear!"

I looked around. "He's crazy," I said. "The east is clear, and the clouds are in the west."

Master Li nudged my ribs and pointed. A patrol of the City Guard was approaching from the east. He pointed up, and I spied some gentlemen who were perched on top of Meng's Money Exchange. The burglars waved to the bonze and slipped out of sight, over the western ridgepole.

"Heaven's Bridge," I sighed.

Master Li was gazing at the bonze as we passed him. "Alibi Ah Sung, from Chao-ch'ing," he said thoughtfully. "That's the Purple Flower, and what are they doing . . ."

His voice trailed off. Then he began to chuckle.

"Ox, what do you smell in the air?" he asked.

"Wet earth, pine needles, pork fat, donkey manure, and perfume from Mother Ho's House of Joy," I said.

"Wrong. You smell destiny," Master Li said happily. "Destiny that appears to be approaching with the delicate tread of an overweight elephant. Do you recall what I was talking about in Wong's before we were interrupted?"

"Fraud and forgery, Venerable Sir, and something about our decadent civilization blowing away with the wind."

"And last night I was impelled to assassinate a fellow and examine the body, which led to the fact that he had a peculiar pattern of metallic acids on his fingers and a tube of Devil's Umbrella in his pocket. Then somebody slipped a few Thunderballs to Lady Hou, and the darling girl decided to slit a mandarin's throat, and then a monk popped up with a forgery to end all forgeries, and now some crooks from Chao-ch'ing are burglarizing Meng's Money Exchange. Add it up and it totals destiny," Master Li said confidently, if somewhat enigmatically. "Let's make a detour."

Peking is not beautiful the way big cities like Ch'ang-an or Loyang or Hangchow can be beautiful, but Fire Horse Park is very lovely, particularly after a rain, when the air is filled with the scents of pine and poplars and willows and locust trees. Master Li told me to head for the Eye of Tranquility, which is not my favorite place. It's a small round lake set aside for old sinners who are grabbing for salvation at the last moment, and the conversation is not exactly inspiring. For some reason the codgers confuse sanctity with senility, and the dialogue consists of "goo-goo-goo," accompanied by drooling and coy little glances toward Heaven. I think they're trying to prove how harmless they are. They also follow the example of saintly Chiang Taikung and sit on the banks with fishing poles, carefully keeping the hooks three feet above the water. (Chiang Taikung loved to fish but refused to take life, and he said that if a fish wanted to leap up and commit suicide, it was the fish's business.) Venders do a brisk business with worms. The old rogues buy bucketfuls and cast more coy glances toward Heaven as they ostentatiously set them free. Frankly, the place gives me goose bumps.

Master Li had me circle the lake until he found what he wanted, and then he slid from my back and walked up beside an apprentice saint who strongly resembled a toad. The fellow had two small leather cups over his ears, secured by a headband, and Master Li removed the headband. I took one of the cups and held it to my own ear and listened to the lovely *linn-linn-linn* sound of Golden Bells, the little insects from Suzhou who sing so sweetly that dowagers keep them in cages beside their pillows to soothe them to sleep.

Golden Bells are also said to induce pure thoughts, and the toad looked like he could use some. I politely picked up and moved a couple of codgers so Master Li and I could sit down flanking the toad.

"Goo-goo-goo?" said the codgers.

"Goo-goo-goo," I replied.

The toad's pale bulging eyes slowly moved toward Master Li.

"I didn't do it," he said.

"Ten witnesses," said Master Li.

"Liars. You can't prove a thing."

The toad turned back to his dangling fish hook. His mouth was set stubbornly, and I doubted that even Master Li could get another word out of him.

"Hsiang, I envy you," Master Li said rather sadly. "Such is your seraphic vision of the life hereafter that you can turn your back on this one, and forgo such worldly pleasures as watching your family flourish. Your nephew, for example. What's his name? Cheng? Chou Cheng of Chao-ch'ing, and what a promising lad he is. I hear he's risen right to the top of the ling-chih trade, and has practically cornered the market on Devil's Umbrellas and Thunderballs."

The toad continued to stare straight ahead.

"I also hear he's put up part of the profits to buy a full seat on the Purple Flower council. Such precocity!" Master Li said admiringly. "I predict the lad will go far, not least because he knows what to do with his assets. Last night, for example, I met a delightful fellow who had a full tube of Devil's Umbrella, and it just occurred to me that the odd stains on his fingers might come from the coiner's trade, and that I had seen him slipping in and out of Meng's Money Exchange. A fellow like that might know all sorts of valuable secrets—what's in the basement, for example—and do you know what we saw on our way here? The Purple Flower Gang, opening up Meng's Money Exchange, and I rather suspect they don't intend to steal anything. They intend to draw the attention of the magistrates to some rather peculiar paraphernalia."

The fishing pole was beginning to tremble.

"Everybody knows that Meng's Money Exchange is merely a front for the counterfeiting business," Master Li said thoughtfully. "It is said that the ringleader is the Second Deputy Minister of Finance, and can you guess what we saw at One-Eyed Wong's? Some bright young man who had access to every kind of ling-chih presented a few choice Thunderballs to Lady Hou, and then he whispered something into her lovely ears, and—well, you know Lady Hou. Guess who she approached with her little dagger? Right! The Second Deputy Minister of Finance, that's who, and I rather suspect that his position as king of counterfeiters is temporary. I wouldn't be at all surprised if your precocious nephew and his friends take over, unless somebody decapitates them first."

The toad dropped his pole into the water. "Li Kao, you wouldn't do that, would you?" he said pleadingly. "He's only a boy."

"And a delightful one, so I'm told," Master Li said warmly.

"A trifle wild, perhaps, but that's the way of the young," the toad said. "You have to allow for a little excess in boyish ambition."

"Youth will be served," Master Li said sententiously. "Sometimes after having been stuffed with truffles and basted in bean curd sauce," he added.

"Li Kao, if you're working for the Secret Service, I can give you a few tips," the toad said hopefully.

"No need," Master Li said. "All I want is an expert opinion, and no evasions." He pulled out the manuscript fragment and passed it over. "Do you know anyone capable of doing this?"

The toad looked at the fragment for no more than five seconds before his eyes bulged even farther and his jaw dropped.

"Great Buddha!" he gasped. "Do I know somebody who could do this? Nobody but the gods could do this!"

He held it up to the light, oblivious to anything else, and Master Li took the opportunity to continue my education.

"Ox, there are no more than ten great men in history whose calligraphy was so prized that kings would go to war to get a sample," he said. "Such calligraphy is unmistakable, and no connoisseur could look at that fragment without crying, 'Ssu-ma Ch'ien!' Surely you studied some of his texts in school?"

Surely I had, and surely I was not going to give Master Li a frank opinion. I used to love history class. I can still quote whole passages by heart: "When the emperor entered the Hall of Balming Virtue, a violent wind came from a dark corner, and out of it slithered a giant serpent that coiled around the throne. The emperor fainted, and that night earthquakes struck Loyang, and waves swept the shores, and cranes shrieked in the marshes. On the fifth day of the sixth moon a long trail of black mist floated into the Hall of Concubines, and hot and cold became confused, and a hen turned into a rooster, and a woman turned into a man, and flesh fell from the skies." Now, that is grand stuff, just the thing to give to growing boys, and then we were old enough to read the greatest of all historians. This is what Ssu-ma Ch'ien had to say about the exact same subject: "The Chou Dynasty was nearing collapse." Bah.

"Nothing is harder to forge than calligraphy, and the calligraphy of greatness is nearly impossible," Master Li explained. "The writer's personality is expressed through every sweep of the brush, and the forger must *become* the man who's hand he's faking. Somebody has done the impossible by perfectly forging Ssu-ma Ch'ien, and the baffling thing is that he made the forgery pathetically obvious."

"Sir?" I said.

"Would you write down your father's name unless you were directly referring to him?"

"Of course not!" I was appalled at the idea. "It would be grossly disrespectful, and it might even open his spirit to attack by demons."

"Precisely, yet in a fragment supposedly written by Ssu-ma Ch'ien, he refers to a minor government official named T'an no less than three times. T'an was his father's name."

That stopped me. I couldn't for the life of me imagine why a forger would produce a masterpiece that would be unmasked in an instant. Neither could the toad.

"This is both unbelievable and incomprehensible," he muttered. "Have you seen the entire manuscript?"

"No," said Master Li. "I understand it's quite brief, and was perhaps intended to be attached as a footnote to one of the histories."

The toad scratched his chin. "The parchment is genuine," he said thoughtfully. "When one thinks of forgery, one thinks of modern works, but what if the forger was a contemporary? Li Kao, we know that Ssu-ma was castrated by Emperor Wu-ti, but are we sure we know why? The official reason has never seemed very persuasive to me, and this forgery is so superb that Ssu-ma would have a hell of a time proving he *didn't* write it. One can imagine sly courtiers pointing out to the emperor that the Grand Master Astronomer Historian was so impious he would write down his own father's name, and if the text also contained slighting references to the throne—"

At that point his voice was drowned out. One of the reprobates looked at Master Li's venerable wrinkles and decided that somebody might be challenging for the title of Saintliest of Them All, and he took three or four deep breaths and raised his gaping mouth toward the Great River of Stars.

"*Hear me, O Heaven, as I pray to the six hundred named gods!*" he bellowed. "*I pray to the gods of the ten directions, and the secondary officials of the ten directions, and the stars of the five directions, and the secondary stars of the five directions, and the fairy warriors and sages, and the ten extreme god kings, and the gods of the sun and the moon and the nine principal stars!*"

The venders perked up. "Worms for sale!" they cried.

"*The gods who guard the Heavenly Gates!*" the champion roared. "*The thirty-six thunder gods who guard Heaven itself, and the twenty-eight principal stars of the zodiac, and the gods for subju-*

gating evil spirits, and the god king of Flying Heaven, and the god of the great long life of Buddha, and the gods of Tien Kan and To Tze, and the great sages of the Trigrams, and the gate gods, and the kitchen gods, and the godly generals in charge of the month and the week and the day and the hour!"

"Worms!" cried the venders. "Take pity upon poor helpless worms, most unfairly condemned to cruel death upon hooks!"

"The gods of the nine rivers!" the saint shrieked. *"The gods of the five mountains and the four corners! I pray to the gods in charge of wells and springs and ditches and creeks and hills and woods and lakes and rivers and the twelve river sources! I pray to the local patron gods! Chuang huangs and their inferiors! The gods of minor local officials! The gods of trees and lumber! The spiritual officers and soldiers under the command of priests! The spirits in charge of protecting the taboos, commands, scriptures, and right way of religion!"*

"Gentlemen, think of your poor old white-haired grandmothers who may have been reborn as worms!" an enterprising vender shouted.

"Boy!" Master Li yelled, and to my astonishment he bought a bucket of worms.

"I pray to the gods of the four seasons and eight festivals!" screamed His Holiness. *"I pray to—"*

Master Li reached up and pried the gaping jaws even wider apart and dumped the contents of his bucket inside. Silence descended upon the Eye of Tranquility. The toad was holding the forgery no more than an inch from his eyeballs.

"Forgery of a forgery," he muttered. "Someone's made a tracing of this, and recently. The oaf left marks where he pressed down too hard."

He handed the manuscript back to Master Li. "Tracing is an amateur job," he said contemptuously. "A freak forgery that can make scholars doubt their sanity is worth a fortune, but a tracing of it couldn't fool an illiterate baby. If the idiot tried to sell it to the wrong man, he'd soon be contemplating the pretty fish swimming around his solid stone sandals."

I had a sudden queasy feeling in the pit of my stomach, but if Master Li was thinking of a dead dice cheater at the bottom of the canal, he gave no sign of it.

"How very interesting," he said mildly. "Hsiang, the manuscript has apparently been stolen. Any word on the grapevine?"

"Are you serious? Li Kao, if a collector allowed word of something of this quality to get out, he'd have a visit from the emperor's agents inside of a day. There can't be another fraud as good as this in the whole world," the toad said. "And don't bother looking for the forger. The August Personage of Jade has lifted him to Heaven, and he's now handling the divine correspondence."

Master Li scratched his forehead and tugged at his beard.

"One last question. I can think of any number of men who would kill to get their hands on the manuscript, but the murder I've been handed appears to have been rather gaudy. Can you think of a man who would use methods suitable for the worst excesses of Chinese opera?"

"One," the toad said promptly.

"Who?"

"You," said the toad. He turned to me. "Boy, do you realize that entire cemeteries are dedicated to this antique assassin? How many corpses did he leave behind during that weird fling you had with the birds?"*

"Well, maybe twenty or thirty," I said. "But that was only because—"

"Begone!" the toad yelled. "Begone, and let an old man die with dignity."

"Old?" said Master Li. "If my oldest grandson hadn't eaten an untreated blowfish, he'd be about your age."

"The problem with you is that you *refuse* to expire from old age," the toad snarled. Then he quoted Confucius. " 'A fellow who grows as old as you without dying is simply becoming a nuisance.' " He turned back to me. "I, on the other hand, shall succumb with serenity, secure in the sanctity of my soul. Boy, just look at the soul shining through my eyes! It's like a goddamned flower!"

It is dangerous to play the quoting game with Master Li. " 'When I return from trampling flowers, the hooves of my horse are fragrant,' " he said softly.

The toad turned pale. "Now, look here, Li Kao, there's no need to find offense where none was intended. All I seek is the True Path that will lead me to the Blessed Realm of Purified Semblance." The thought of his newfound purity emboldened him. "Begone!" he cried. "Begone, you animated accumulation of antiquated bones, and take the sulphurous scent of sin with you."

He turned and glared back at me.

"Also," he added, "take this walking derrick."

Master Li stood up and bowed, and I followed his example, and we turned and walked away over the grass, and a gentle bubbling chorus of *goo-goo-goos* faded behind us.

---

* See *Bridge of Birds* (St. Martin's Press, New York, 1984).

石

3

The journey to the Valley of Sorrows was not a long one, and three days later I climbed to a ridge overlooking the valley. It was quite early in the morning. I mopped the dew from a large flat rock, and we sat down and waited for the mist to clear. As it did I realized that the Valley of Sorrows was like a bowl with a chip in it, the chip being the gap to the south that opened to other valleys in the distance. Winding around and down the sides of the bowl was a lovely path of trees and flowers—too lovely, from my point of view. No peasant in his right mind would waste that much arable land on flowers when something useful could be planted. Conspicuous waste is the boast of wealth and power, and it makes me nervous.

"The peasants are paid not to plant it," Master Li said, reading my mind. "It's called Princes' Path, and the reason for it lies in a fairly long story." He swept his hand across the valley. "Rich or poor?" he asked.

I mentally dug my toes into the earth. "Neither," I said. "The soil seems to be good, but there isn't much of it. Too much rock and shale on the hillsides, and the marsh at the west side is salty. The valley probably supports a small population quite well, but there can't be much left over."

"Excellent," Master Li said. "The first feudal lord of the valley discovered how hard it was to make money from the place and set an admirable precedent by drinking himself to death. His successors followed his esteemed example, and every few years the peasants could look forward to the banquet that accompanied a noble funeral. What do you think their reaction was when a certain Prince Chou turned out to have a cast-iron liver, and lasted thirty years?"

Peasants are the same everywhere, and I said confidently, "They have never forgiven him to this day. They tell their children nasty stories about Callous Chou the Pinchfist Prince, and strangers can tell where he was buried by watching the direction when farmers pee in the fields."

"Right you are, although Callous Chou stories are rare today," Master Li said. "Somebody came along to replace him, and he cornered the story market. Ox, one of your most endearing qualities is the ability to keep your mouth shut when you are dying to ask questions, and it's time to answer one of them. Who was the Laughing Prince? Why are the peasants and the monks and even the abbot terrified at the thought that he may have come back from the dead?"

I settled back to listen, and this is a brief summary of what I learned about a gentleman whose merry spirit still haunts me to this day.

Emperor Wu-ti had a younger brother, Prince Liu Sheng, who was something of a problem. He was a brilliant student of Taoist science, but undisciplined, and it was said that his affability was matched only by his laziness. At court his merry jests kept the nobility in stitches, but it was time for him to do something useful. When Prince Chou finally succumbed the emperor sent his feckless sibling to rule as Lord of Dragon Head Valley. (It was not then called the Valley of Sorrows.) The peasants looked forward to such a fun-loving fellow, and in due course the headmen were summoned to the prince's estate.

"My dear friends," said the prince with an enchanting smile. "My dear, dear friends, I beseech you to plant gourds. Lots and lots of gourds."

Then he broke into an irresistible little dance step, while he chanted, "Lots and lots and *lots* and lots, lots and lots and *lots* and lots . . . of gourds!"

Well, a prince is entitled to a few peculiarities. The peasants planted lots and lots of gourds, and the question was where Prince Liu Sheng was going to find the pigs to eat them. As it turned out, he didn't want the gourds for the meat. The dried seeds of the calabash have the peculiar property of burning for a very long time and shedding a brilliant white light, and the prince had brought in experts who had discovered a substantial deposit of salt beneath the marsh at the west end of the valley. By placing calabash seeds inside rhinoceros horn lanterns, Prince Liu Sheng was able to establish the world's first twenty-four-hour-a-day salt mine.

The peasants were chained to enormous horizontal wheels. Overseers whipped them around in circles as they powered drills that bored more than a thousand feet into the soft soil. Bamboo casing was installed, and ropes and windlasses replaced the drills, and buckets lifted the brine to a pipeline that ran clear across the valley to a large patch of shale at the east side. An odorless gas seeped up through the cracks, and it was easily ignited. The brine was dumped upon iron plates and heated, and the salt was extracted and carried away to market. Day and night the whips lashed the peasants around in circles, while Prince Liu Sheng rode through the works on a silken litter with a merry quip and friendly wave for one and all.

Eventually the salt gave out, but the prince had also discovered a narrow but rich vein of iron ore. The male peasants were chained into work gangs that dug endless tunnels, and the female peasants remained chained to the wheels. Now they powered huge bellows at blast furnaces, and in no time at all the Iron Works of Prince Liu Sheng was the talk of the empire. That was when he became known as the Laughing Prince. His sense of humor almost finished him, because he nearly guffawed himself to death as he watched the comical capers of the ladies at the wheel. Their chains were red hot, you see, and for a time "The Dance of the Peasants of Prince Liu" was all the rage at court.

The Laughing Prince called upon his scientific genius, and somehow devised a treatment of acids and other agents that made his iron less brittle than any other. The acid plant was on top of the eastern hills, and the waste trickled down in a steaming path that circled almost the entire bowl of the valley, and sages and scholars gathered to observe the astonishing effect when the waste reached the marsh. The water turned bright yellow. By day it steamed and bubbled, and at night it emitted an eerie violet light, and fish and frogs floated on their backs with horrified dead eyes lifted to the billowing black clouds from the ironworks. By then the trees were all dead, and no birds sang, and the Laughing Prince made some marvelous jokes about the smell. There were some who protested, but protests ceased when the prince opened the books. The profits were enormous.

Then something happened which nobody fully understands to this day. Prince Liu Sheng abruptly lost interest in making money. He returned to his first love, and he had his field of science picked out. He was going to revolutionize medicine.

"I shall strip the veils of ignorance from the healing art, and display the very nerves and tissues!" he proclaimed.

The assembled sages and scholars were appalled when the prince explained some of his proposed experiments, but their protests abruptly ceased when he pointed out that he would need lots and lots of subjects. "Lots and lots and *lots* and lots," he chanted, breaking into his little dance step, "lots and lots and *lots* and lots . . . of subjects!" The sages and scholars danced right along with him.

Close to his estate was a grotto. He transformed it into his Medical Research Center, and sages who came to observe the experiments either applauded and praised—and then staggered outside to vomit—or protested, and became subjects for the next experiments. Nobody argued about the prince's expertise. Unquestionably he was the world's greatest expert on the effects of stretching, compressing, slicing, dousing in acids, burning, breaking, twisting—seldom if ever has the human body been so carefully studied. People who enjoy such pastimes need never be lonely. The Laughing Prince gathered like-minded fellows around him. He called them his Monks of Mirth, and he dressed them in robes made from clown's motley, and they danced and laughed beneath the moon as they capered through the valley with a brigade of soldiers to gather peasants for more experiments.

The Laughing Prince was hopelessly, homicidally mad. Some say that his imperial brother finally had enough and sent the yellow scarf, which is the imperial command to commit suicide. Others deny it. At any rate, the prince fell ill. He tossed and turned in a delirium of fever, screaming and swearing, and in his lucid moments he gazed out the window at the ruins of the valley and swore to return from the grave to finish the job.

He died. He was placed in his tomb.

"Seven hundred and fifty years later, capering monks in motley have been seen in the Valley of Sorrows," Master Li said. "Brother Squint-Eyes has been murdered, and it appears that part of the valley has been destroyed in a way that is worthy of the Laughing Prince."

"*Whoof,*" I said.

"*Whoof* indeed, although in such cases the poetic promise almost always turns out to be pathetically prosaic," Master Li said, rather sadly. "Let's go see what the body of Brother Squint-Eyes can tell us."

The monastery was very old, and quite large for such a small valley. The abbot had his monks lined up like an honor guard, and he was disappointed when Master Li declined a tour of inspection. Master Li also declined to begin with the scene of the crime, stating that it was unwise to come to a corpse with one's mind crammed with preconceptions, and we were led down a long winding flight of steps to the lowest basement and the cold room.

Lanterns were hung all over. The room was very bright, which meant that the shadows were very dark, and the play of light and shadow over the body on the block of ice highlighted the head. I stopped short and caught my breath. Never in my life had I seen such terror on a human face. The bulging eyes and gaping mouth were permanently fixed in the expression of one whose last view has been of the most horrible pit in Hell.

Master Li said that the expression was interesting, in that three or four drugs could have caused it, but none of them was common to China. He rolled up his sleeves and opened his case, and the blades glinted like icicles in the cold musty chamber. The abbot appeared to be on the verge of fainting, as did his four assistants, who hovered on the staircase. I myself will never get used to it, and I had to force my eyes to watch. The minutes passed like molasses dripping in winter. After ten minutes Master Li straightened up, and the murderous expression on his face was not entirely a trick of shadows.

"Bat shit," he said.

He bent back over the cadaver, and his knives moved angrily.

"No yak manure, no volcanic ash, no nuns' pigtails, and no Tsao Tsao," he muttered. "Nothing but another corpse."

He went back to work, and various pieces of Brother Squint-Eyes landed on the ice beside the body.

"Our departed friend was recently in a large city," Master Li said matter-of-factly. "His death occurred not more than four hours after his return."

The abbot stepped nervously backward, as though fearing witchcraft. "Brother Squint-Eyes went to Ch'ang-an," he whispered. "He died within a few hours of his return."

"He had also been playing fast and loose with his vows," Master Li remarked. "I would rather like to know how he could afford thousand-year eggs."

"No monk can afford thousand-year eggs," the abbot said flatly.

"This one did. At least three of them."

"Eggs can last a thousand years?" I asked skeptically.

"Fraud, Ox! Fraud and forgery," Master Li said disgustedly. "Paint slapped over the rot of reality and gilded with lies. They're simply duck eggs that have been treated with lime. The lime works through the shells and slowly cooks the contents, and after eight or ten weeks the treated egg is billed as being a thousand years old and is sold for a ridiculous price to a credulous member of the newly rich. Delicious, actually. Certain barbarian tribes grow a fruit that tastes quite like it. It's called avocado." He deposited some revolting stuff in a bucket on the floor. "Constipation is a godsend to a medical examiner," he said. "Abbot, you might also consider the fact that in addition to the eggs, Brother Squint-Eyes regaled himself in Ch'ang-an—it had to be a large city to get the eggs—with carp and clam soup, lobster in bean curd sauce, pickled ducks' feet smothered with black tree fungus, steamed shoats with garlic, sweetmeats, candied fruits, and spiced honey cakes. I estimate the cost of his last meal at three catties of silver."

The abbot reeled. "Check the books!" he screamed to his monks. "Take an inventory of the candle holders and incense burners! See if there have been any reports of highway robbery!"

"While you're at it, somebody find out if Brother Squint-Eyes ordered an unusual amount of ink for the library," Master Li said. "The type called Buddha's Eyelashes. Also parchment of the type called Yellow Emperor."

The monks galloped up the stairs, and the abbot lifted his robe and wiped his forehead with it. Master Li displayed another gory object.

"Ox, you should learn a lot more about physical sciences," he said. "This thing is the spleen. It isn't a very good spleen; functional, but not completely reliable, which is unfortunate because the spleen is the seat of good faith."

He detached another unpleasant object and waved it around.

"The same applies to the heart, the seat of propriety; the lungs, the seat of righteousness; and the kidneys, the seat of wisdom. The only first-rate organ Brother Squint-Eyes possessed was his liver, which is the seat of love, and I would suspect that the late librarian led a somewhat tortured existence. It's damned dangerous to walk around overflowing with love when you're deficient in wisdom, righteousness, and propriety."

"That was Brother Squint-Eyes," the abbot sighed. "He was something of a specialist in abject confessions."

I closed my eyes tightly, education or no education. Sawing sounds echoed from the stone walls. When I opened them Master Li had removed the top of the corpse's skull and was fishing out the contents.

"You know," he said conversationally, "in the days of my youth I once visited the court of Muncha Khan, who had just destroyed another enemy army and was celebrating with a banquet. It was held on the field of battle, and servants casually dropped priceless rugs over corpses so we could sit on them. Muncha's tree was trundled out—I never did learn the symbolism of it—and a couple of fellows with pumps were concealed inside. The tree was silver, with jeweled leaves, and four silver lions at the base held their jaws over four silver basins, and at a signal the lions' mouths began spurting mare's milk. Four jeweled serpents wound up toward the top of the tree, and two of them began spouting carcasmos, which is fermented milk that can take your head off. The other two spouted bal, fermented honey, and when we were nicely drunk the chefs rolled out the main course. Turned out to be the brains of the slaughtered soldiers. They were delicious. I cornered one of the chefs because one never knows when a good recipe may come in handy, and he told me it was simplicity itself. You just grab somebody and chop off the top of his head and pull out the brains and wash them in salt water. Then rub them with garlic, pan fry them briefly, stuff them into rolled cabbage leaves, and steam them for two minutes with onions, ginger, and a touch of turnip sauce."

Master Li held the brains up to the light.

"Never do for a banquet," he said. "Tuberculosis, although in an early stage. I doubt if Brother Squint-Eyes noticed anything more than an occasional headache." He tossed the brains down on the ice and turned to the abbot. "No trace of poison," he said. "No sign of violence. No exotic disease from a place he couldn't possibly have visited. In short, no proof of murder. Brother Squint-Eyes died from a heart attack."

The old man gazed thoughtfully down at what was left of the corpse. "It could be murder if he was intentionally frightened to death, but it would be hell to prove. Abbot, when we catch the fellows who stole the manuscript, you might consider suing for damages rather than insisting upon a murder trial. We'd have to be able to demonstrate the precise method, and an out-of-court settlement might make more sense. How about settling for having your roof fixed? There has never been a monastery that isn't selling subscriptions for a new roof, and never will be."

The abbot seemed cheered at the thought. Master Li washed his gory hands and we began walking back up the stairs while the abbot explained that in ages past the monastery had been used as a fortress against bandit armies, which was why the lower stories were fashioned from huge blocks of solid stone, and why thick iron bars were set in the windows.

"It was just after the third watch," he said. "I was awake, listening to see if Brother Pang had finally got the bell rings right, and I heard a terrible scream. Other monks joined me as I ran toward the library. The doors are always open, but now they were closed and bolted from the inside. I sent monks out to get a log."

The doors had been bashed apart, and the log lay in the corridor. We walked inside to a large square room. Three of the walls were lined with tables, and the fourth was lined with scroll racks. The books were kept in side rooms. In the center of the floor was a large circular desk for the librarian, and the abbot showed the careful chalk marks where the body had been found behind the desk. The scrolls, he said, were very old but totally without value, being feudal records involving every payment to the various lords of the valley. Several times within living memory the imperial clerks had searched to see if any treasures were mixed with the trivia, but none had been found.

"Until Brother Squint-Eyes found a curiosity," Master Li muttered.

"His body lay there, and no one else was in the room," the abbot said. "One glance told us how intruders had entered, but the entry was impossible."

A side window that ran almost down to the floor opened upon a small garden. The bars in it were iron as thick as my wrist, but four of them—two on each side—had been squeezed together like soft warm candles to form entrances. Master Li raised an eyebrow, and I walked over and spat on my hands. I could feel muscles strain all over my body as I tried to straighten the bars, but I might as well have tried to straighten crooked pine trees. I stepped back, panting.

"So," Master Li said, folding his arms and narrowing his eyes. "You heard a scream. You ran to the library. The doors were bolted from inside. You got a log and broke the door down. You entered and saw nobody. Behind the desk was the body of the librarian, with an expression of extreme terror on his face. The bars of the window had been squeezed together by some incredible force, making an entrance to the room. Then what happened?"

The abbot was trembling again. "Venerable Sir, that's when we heard the sound. Or some of us did, since others couldn't hear it at all. It was the most beautiful sound in the world, but heartbreaking at the same time. It hurt us, and we wept, and then we started running after it. We had to. It was calling us."

He led the way out through the window to the garden, and Master Li grunted at the mass of sandal prints that covered any possible clue. We went out through a gate, and I realized we were on Princes' Path. It was very beautiful, and mixed with trees and flowers I had known all my life were strange ones I couldn't identify. Master Li pointed out one flower as being a golden begonia, and said there couldn't be more than three others in all China. The path was really a vast garden, and I began to get the feel of it when we reached a ridge and I could look across the valley and see the green line winding up the opposite hills. Master Li confirmed my thoughts.

"The heirs of the Laughing Prince were appalled when they saw the destruction," he said. "They vowed to set things right if it took a thousand years, and Princes' Path was planted to conceal the scars from the acid works. In fact, the only reason the peasants of the Valley of Sorrows aren't spoiled rotten is that the Liu family is land-rich but cash-poor, and most of the cash goes toward maintaining Princes' Path and countless charities."

The abbot stopped at the crest of a low hill.

"We ran to this point," he said. "Did I mention that the moon was very bright? We could not be mistaken in what we saw. Down below, down where the sound seemed to be coming from, we saw monks, but their robes were of clown's motley, and they were laughing and dancing beneath the stars. Normally we would have run for our lives, but the sound was summoning us and we had no choice but to obey. We ran on, and we came close enough to clearly see the clown robes although we could not see the faces because of the cowls. Then the monks danced into heavy brush and disappeared. Shortly afterward the wonderful-terrible sound stopped, and when we got through the brush, the dancing monks had vanished. In their place was something else."

We walked down and made our way through the brush, and we stopped in our tracks and stared. "I'll be the Stone Monkey," Master Li said softly.

Death had laid an icy finger across Princes' Path. In an area approximately thirty feet wide and five times as long, not one living thing could be seen. Trees were bare and dead and without even a trace of sap, as I discovered when I broke off a branch. Flowers were withered. Bushes might as well have been sprayed with engraving acid. Not even the grass had survived, and brown clumps broke off beneath our feet. It looked like a cemetery one might see in a nightmare, and the line between life and death was so sharp it could have been cut with a knife. An inch from a dead flower was a blooming one, and lush greenery rubbed against bare brownness, and birds sang less than a foot from a place where not even an insect moved.

Master Li threw back his head and laughed, but without humor. "Incredible," he said. "Abbot, Ox and I will have to take plant and soil samples to Ch'ang-an for analysis, and I doubt that it's worth speculating until we get a report on what caused the damage. Don't worry. Most of this affair seems clear enough, and quite simple, and I expect to wrap it up in one or two weeks."

His confidence cheered the abbot, who pointed up toward a roof-line high on the opposite hill.

"Prince Liu Pao has returned, and is eager to see you," he said. "Could you possibly stop there first? The peasants . . ."

His voice trailed off.

"Want the prince and the visitor from the big city to search the Laughing Prince's tomb and make sure that the bastard is still in his coffin?" Master Li said.

The abbot nodded.

"We will be honored to visit the living prince and the dead one," Master Li said. "I assume you have a great many things to do, so if you'll point out the way, we'll stroll up there and then on to Ch'ang-an."

The abbot was obviously relieved at not being asked to enter the tomb of the Laughing Prince, and he gave directions and bowed and trotted away, muttering something that sounded like "forty-two kettles of fish." I gathered plant and soil samples, and then we set forth to visit an aristocrat whose nerves, I hoped, were made from good material. Superstition is easily dismissed in daylight, but when the owls hoot, it's a different story. The wind sighs like ghosts whispering, and moonlight and leaves form patterns of mad monks dancing on the grass, and the house makes creaking sounds rather like the footsteps of a long-dead lunatic lord creeping up the stairs, and Prince Liu Pao's bedchamber was sitting practically on top of the maniac's tomb.

石

4

The estate was as large as one would expect for the ancestral seat of the former lords of the valley, but very little of it was still used. Weeds covered the formal gardens, and everywhere I looked I saw crumbling ruins. I suppose I was expecting a classic setting for a horror story, but that idea was dispelled the moment we walked through the gate to the wing of the mansion that was still kept up. The courtyard was rock and gravel and natural planting, and the spirit screen was simply a beautiful slab of red stone placed upon a sandalwood pedestal. We walked around the screen to the inner court, and instantly we were surrounded by a blaze of cheerful colors. Bright flowers were everywhere, and gaudy parrots and cockatoos greeted us raucously. A long vine-covered veranda led to the house, and a stack of broad-brimmed peasant hats had been provided for visitors who were allergic to bird droppings.

From the logistics of the place I decided that the living quarters had once been the kitchen. No obsequious flunkies came to greet us, but the door was open. We walked inside to a hallway, and instead of being confronted with grand family tablets proclaiming the Hall of Glory and Beautitude, we saw one simple plaque on the wall. Master Li had been obviously pleased, and now he practically purred. He said it was a classic essay by one of the ancients, Chen Chiju, and that it was one of the four pillars upon which civilization had been constructed. My education had not gone far enough to get to the pillars of civilization, and since it was in modern script, I read it with great interest.

The Home Garden

Inside the gate there is a footpath, and the footpath must be winding. At the turn of the footpath there is an outdoor screen, and the screen must be small. Behind the screen there is a terrace, and the terrace must be level. On the banks of the terrace there are flowers, and the flowers must be bright-colored. Beyond the terrace there is a wall, and the wall must be low. By the side of the wall is a pine tree, and the pine must be old. At the foot of the pine there are rocks, and the rocks must be quaint. Over the rocks there is a pavilion, and the pavilion must be simple. Beyond the pavilion are bamboos, and the bamboos must be sparse. At the end of the bamboos there is a house, and the house must be secluded. By the side of the house is a road, and the road must branch off. Where several branches come together is a bridge, and the bridge must be tantalizing to cross. At the end of the bridge there are trees, and the trees must be tall. In the shade of the trees there is grass, and the grass must be green. Above the grass plot is a ditch, and the ditch must be slender. At the top of the ditch is a spring, and the spring must gurgle. Above the spring there is a hill, and the hill must be undulating. Below the hill is a hall, and the hall must be square. At the corner of the hall there is a vegetable garden, and the garden must be big. In the garden is a stork, and the stork must dance. The stork announces that there is a guest, and the guest must not be vulgar. When the guest arrives he is offered wine, and the wine must not be declined. At the drink the guest must get drunk, and the drunken guest must not want to go home.

"I think I'd like to see the other three pillars," I said. "I like this one."

"We'll get to them," Master Li promised. He led the way down the hall to the living quarters, which were simply furnished with comfortable furniture, and our host came bounding from a back room to greet us.

Has anyone but me ever mistaken a prince for a feather duster? That was precisely my impression. He was small and skinny, but his

thin neck lifted to a huge head, and the unkempt hair that sprouted
from it in all directions could have filled a couple of mattresses. I
remembered hearing that he was a renowned artist, and paint stains
decorated his nose and chin. Brushes stuck out from his pockets,
and his favorite cup for dipping them in hung on a cord around his
neck.

"My surname is Liu and my personal name is Pao and I am
honored to greet the renowned Master Li!" he cried, bowing jerkily.
He moved in a series of uncoordinated jumps and bounces, and his
cheerful smile jerked in my direction. "Arms like logs, legs like tree
trunks, and no neck. You must be Number Ten Ox. Delighted to
meet you!"

I have seldom met anyone I liked so much on first sight. I felt
quite at ease with him, and after a few minutes I completely forgot
he was a prince and his great-great-and-so-on-uncle had been Emperor of China. We sat outside on a terrace that offered a wonderful
view of the valley and listened to chipmunks quarrel with parakeets
while we sipped tea.

"They say that my revolting ancestor has been dancing in the
moonlight with his mad monks," the prince said. "Stories like that
are scarcely new, but this time they tell me there really has been a
murder. I also looked at the destruction on Princes' Path. I saw it,
but I don't believe it."

"I wouldn't either if I weren't convinced that there's a reasonable
explanation," Master Li said. "As for murder, I can only say that
the library was forcibly entered and a manuscript was stolen.
Brother Squint-Eyes suffered a heart attack. He may have been
frightened to death, but we'd have to prove intent and method.
Have you ever seen the stolen manuscript?"

The prince shook his head negatively. "This came from it," Master Li said, and he handed the prince the fragment of parchment.
The prince was like the toad in that it took five seconds for his eyes
to pop wide as soup plates.

"Buddha," he whispered. "Whoever did this should be deified,
but why would he make the forgery so obvious?"

"We may never know the answer to that," Master Li said pen-
sively. "The rest seems fairly simple. Brother Squint-Eyes came
across a fake Ssu-ma Ch'ien in the ancient library scrolls. It probably doesn't matter whether or not he recognized it as a forgery. If

real it would be worth a small fortune to historians, and if fake it would be worth the same to collectors of frauds."

Master Li shook his head sadly.

"Brother Squint-Eyes succumbed to temptation, but he was woefully ill equipped for crime. He tried to forge the forgery by tracing, and then he took a sample page of the original to Ch'ang-an and made a deal with a collector. In order to divert suspicion from the librarian, the collector agreed to fake a burglary. The foolish monk received a small down payment with which he purchased an elegant meal, and then he returned to put his own little scheme in action. My guess is that he wanted it both ways. He would salve his conscience by keeping the original for the library, and pass off his tracing to the collector. He tried to swindle the wrong man."

Master Li turned to me. "Ox, those iron bars had to be bent by large levers, which would make quite a bit of noise. All Brother Squint-Eyes had to do was draw the bolt and run out to the hall for help, but he stayed right where he was. That means he was an accomplice."

He turned back to the prince. "I can well imagine the collector producing a knife and saying that since the good monk imagined he was Ssu-ma Ch'ien, the resemblance should be completed by castration. At any rate, Brother Squint-Eyes screamed and quite literally died of fright. The collector had forced him to produce the original. He snatched it from the dead man's hand and ran, and then he and his accomplices went into their act. Anybody who wants to steal something from the Valley of Sorrows is advised to dress as a mad monk in motley. Witnesses will probably keep running until they land in the Yellow Sea."

The prince poured more tea. Master Li added a splash of wine to his.

"Prince, your ancestor tunneled all over the valley for iron, and Buddha knows what else. He also doused the place with acids and mysterious substances of his own invention. Suppose one of the tunnels collapsed. It isn't impossible that underground echoes could have produced a strange compelling sound, and that a pocket of ancient acids—or whatever—could have been released into that particular area of Princes' Path. I don't know of any substance that retains its potency for seven centuries, but that doesn't mean there isn't one, and we'll find out at the academy in Ch'ang-an. We'll also find the person responsible for the burglary," Master Li said confidently. "The problem will be proving murder. The abbot is willing to settle for a new roof. Do you have any objections?"

The prince pointed to his chest. "Me? My family hasn't had a claim to this valley since the ghastly days of feudalism, so beloved by Neo-Confucians. All we do is go bankrupt maintaining Princes' Path, and a few other things. I have no say in it."

Master Li looked at him quizzically. "I wonder if the peasants look at it that way," he said. "Your family served as lords of the valley for almost five centuries, and I rather suspect that when it comes to the welfare of the valley, they won't turn to the emperor. They'll turn to you, and they won't ask for help. They'll demand it. Rather unfair, since you don't collect a penny of rent or a share of the crops, but there it is."

Prince Liu Pao looked at him thoughtfully. Then he turned and examined my callused hands and large coarse body and homely face with peasant printed all over it.

"Number Ten Ox?"

I flushed with embarrassment. "Your Highness, Master Li is right," I said. "Nothing will convince them that the welfare of the Valley of Sorrows isn't the responsibility of the Liu family, and as for fairness, it's like Princes' Path. Peasants can't afford it."

The prince laughed and stood up.

"It seems I have no choice but to go through the motions," he said. "I assume I'm supposed to make sure that my abominable ancestor is safely tucked in, with the famous Master Li as witness?"

"That's all for now," Master Li said.

The prince took a key from a cabinet and led the way outside and through a gate and down a winding path toward the face of a cliff. As we came closer I saw an iron door set in the rock, almost covered by tall weeds and thistles. The door was old but the lock was new, and the prince's fingers were trembling as he inserted the key.

"Nightmares of childhood," he said wryly. "You see, the Laughing Prince's successor decided to keep the famous grotto precisely as he found it, and place the family tablets inside. Every succeeding prince has been forced to pray and sacrifice inside a monument to the abuse of power. Makes it rather difficult for us to pull wings off butterflies, if our instincts run to that kind of thing."

I expected blackness, but there were fissures in the stone that let in a greenish-yellow light. The famous Medical Research Center should, I think, be part of the early education of emperors. It is hard to forget.

A long row of iron racks against one wall held the essential instruments for scientific research, such as thumbscrews and iron whips and testicle crushers and pinchers and various things for slicing and gouging. Ancient operating tables still stood in the center of the floor, and gutters beneath them ran to stone troughs for the blood. Grim-looking machines whose purpose I didn't understand lined another wall, and a third wall was lined with something I did understand: iron cages where peasants were held. They allowed the peasants a good view of what was happening to members of their families. The worst thing was the back wall.

It was naturally smooth stone, almost like a huge board of slate, and it was covered with annotated experiments, drawn with painstaking accuracy. Mysterious mathematical formulas and ancient script alternated as annotations, and Master Li was quite puzzled as he translated the script for my benefit.

"True path of the stone . . . False path of the stone . . . Stone strongest here . . . Total failure of stone . . . Stone branches three ways . . . No reaction from stone . . ."

It made no sense at all, nor did the jumble of arrows pointing to various gruesome aspects of the experiments.

"What on earth did he mean by all these references to a stone?" Master Li asked.

"Nobody knows, but his obsession appears to have been overpowering," the prince said.

He took a torch from a bracket and lit it, and led the way toward a shadowed corner. There I saw the family tablets, and I shuddered to think of small boys being led in here to pray, with grim lectures about the curse the family carried. The tablets were lined up in front of an ancient sacristy, which was empty. On the wall above it an inscription had been chiseled, and again Master Li translated for my benefit.

In darkness languishes the precious stone.
When will its excellence enchant the world?
When seeming is taken for being, being becomes seeming.
When nothing is taken for something, something becomes nothing.

The stone dispels seeming and nothing,
And climbs to the Gates of the Great Void.

The prince smiled at my bewilderment. "I agree," he said. "It has the same quality of apparently leading somewhere and then disappearing that distinguishes the very finest Taoist mumbo jumbo."

Master Li scratched his head. "Lao Tzu?" he wondered. "His third step toward Heaven was to hear the sound of stone growing in a cliff, but he didn't climb to the Gates of the Great Void on the screams of his victims." He winked at me. "He rode an ox," he said.

In the shadows of the alcove was a darker shadow that resolved itself into a narrow tunnel as the prince again led the way with the torch. At the end of it was another iron door, but this one had neither a lock nor a handle. On the wall was a large bronze plaque engraved with a map of the Valley of Sorrows, and beside it hung an iron hammer on an iron chain. The prince grimaced.

"Sense of humor," he said sourly.

He raised the hammer and smashed the plaque, and the iron door slid silently open. We stepped inside to a circular room that was astonishingly bare. Nowhere was the sickening display of wealth that usually distingushes the tomb of a tyrant. There was nothing but two stone coffins, two offering bowls, and a small altar with incense burners. Master Li was as astonished as I was, and the prince shrugged and spread his hands in an I-give-up gesture.

"My ancestor was a mystery from beginning to end," he said. "He amassed an enormous fortune, but didn't spend a catty of silver on his own final resting place. What did he do with it? He certainly didn't pass his wealth on to his personal family, and there is no evidence that it was seized by his imperial brother. For several centuries after his death the family had to spend half its time chasing away people who dug holes all over the valley, and crooks still do a thriving business in fake treasure maps. The sarcophagus on the left is that of his principal wife, Tou Wan, who predeceased him, and my ancestor sleeps on the right."

Master Li nodded to me. I stepped up and tested the stone lid. It weighed at least a ton, but it rested in smooth grooves, and I got in position and heaved. I almost broke my back before I could persuade it to move, but then it began to slide down toward the foot with a painful screeching sound. A mummy wrapped in tarred linen appeared. Part of the wrappings had crumbled away, but they had prevented the bone itself from crumbling, and a piece of a white skull was exposed. An empty eye socket gazed up at us, and I will confess that I was relieved to see that the Laughing Prince was not in shape to laugh and dance in the moonlight.

Master Li reached into the coffin and came up with a small enameled container like a pillbox. There was nothing inside but a tiny pile of gray dust, and when he cleaned off the top, we saw the picture of a toad seated upon a lily pad.

"I have heard that the Laughing Prince was expected to recover from his final fever, and this may explain why he didn't," Master Li said thoughtfully. "Even in his day it was known that tear-like secretions of certain toads are heart stimulants even more effective than foxglove, and usually Toad Elixir was prescribed only for severe cardiac disorders. An overdose can be fatal, of course, and this could have been placed in his coffin either to signify a natural cause of death, or the fact that the emperor had indeed sent him the yellow scarf and he had chosen to hop into the underworld upon the back of a toad. Not that it matters."

There was nothing else in the coffin. In death as in life the lunatic lord was a mystery. I slid the lid back in place. We walked back into the tunnel, and the prince closed the door. The grotto was as ghastly as ever, but when we stepped outside I knew it was as dead and gone as the Laughing Prince. A lovely sunset was spreading across the sky, and birds were singing their last songs of the day, and down below us we could see the Valley of Sorrows in a haze of green and gold and purple shadows. As pretty as the setting of a fairy tale, and far more alive.

石

5

There was no point in starting to Ch'ang-an with plant and soil samples until morning—besides, it was the fifteenth day of the seventh moon, and my ears had not misled me about the abbot. He had indeed muttered "forty-two kettles of fish," and the monastery smelled like Yellow Carp Pier. Smells of rice, pork, cabbage, eggs, and traditional eggplant tarts drifted up the hill from the village. Word that the Laughing Prince was safely in his tomb had spread like wildfire, and the Valley of Sorrows was ready for a festival.

"Mark my words," Brother Shang said gloomily. "Somebody will break a leg."

Master Li listened to the faint sounds of music from the village. "Peasant dancing can get rather wild," he agreed.

"Smell that pepper sauce! Every child in the valley will be sick to his stomach," said Brother Shang.

"For at least a week," said Master Li.

"Monks by the dozens will forget their vows. I'll have to mop up the vomit and brew hangover remedies," said Brother Shang, whose full name was Wu Shang and who lived up to it by always drawing the short straw. (Wu Shang means "Difficult Birth.") This time he had to stand the lonely vigil at the monastery while the other monks enjoyed the festivities.

"Somebody is sure to toss a torch into a barn," Master Li predicted direly.

"They'll be lucky if one cottage remains standing," said Brother Shang, who was beginning to cheer up. "Family feuds will erupt all over the place! Broken skulls will be beyond counting! Mark my words: This date will be marked in black in the annals of the valley."

We left the poor fellow to his self-pity, a very useful emotion, and started down the hill to the village. The Feast of Hungry Ghosts has been my personal favorite ever since I began traveling with Master Li, since I am almost certain to become a hungry ghost myself. (It honors, among others, those who have died in distant and desolate lands, or whose bodies have been mangled beyond recognition.) I was slightly surprised to see that Master Li was on his best behavior. As the visiting dignitary he was required to pass judgment on the wines of the valley, and I was prepared for the worst when he approached the reeking pots and uttered the formal *"Ning szu che hou t'uen,"* which means "I'm ready to die; I'll try it," but he only took a small sip of each vitriolic product and praised all without restraint, even the brew that spilled on the ground and killed two lizards and three square feet of grass.

The abbot kept the formal prayers and ceremonies mercifully brief, and I was delighted when the hit of the early going turned out to be Brother Shang. He couldn't attend, but he had spent the winter carving and tuning tiny bamboo flutes and he tied them to the tails of the monastery's pigeons and sent them flying over the village to serenade us with a bawdy song called "Chu Chang's Chamber Pot." The abbot said something about disciplining the impious rogue, but his heart wasn't in it.

The dancing started, which meant the fights would start shortly, and I was very disappointed when Master Li decided to slip away and walk through the hills in the moonlight. His feet led him to the destroyed area of Princes' Path, and he stood there for several minutes, rocking on his heels with his hands clasped behind his back.

"Ox," he finally said, "what was wrong with the analysis of the situation that I gave to Prince Liu Pao?" he said.

"Sir?"

"I was trying to reassure him. I wish I could reassure myself," the ancient sage said gloomily. "It's perfectly clear that crooks dressed in motley stole a manuscript and frightened a monk to death. After that, everything begins to run amok. A weird compelling sound is heard *precisely* as the crooks make their escape; some mysterious substance kills trees and plants *precisely* where they place their sandals. If it was a coincidental collapse of a tunnel and the release of old acids, as I suggested to the prince, it's the kind of coincidence that deserves priests, prayers, and an elaborate theology. If it wasn't a coincidence, why would crooks waste effects like that on the simple theft of a manuscript? They could walk off with the Imperial Treasury if they felt like it, or pilfer the emperor's undergarments while he was wearing them. My boy, this affair makes no sense at all."

I said nothing, of course, but I noted that the old man was enjoying every moment of his confusion. He had feared that all he had to work with was a simple burglary, and now he was praying for a puzzle that could baffle the judges of Hell. He wiped off a flat rock and sat down beneath the stars. Just below us on the hill we saw tiny flickers of light moving through the woods. Little girls have large maternal instincts, and they take the Feast of Hungry Ghosts very seriously, and they were making their rounds with small lanterns made from candles inside rolled lotus and sage leaves. I could feel ghosts all around us, moving toward the warmth of the sweet singing voices: You are not alone, the girls sang, you are not forgotten, we care and understand, our own lives are but a candle flame from yours:

> *"Hou tsu-teng,*
> *Ho yeh-teng,*
> *Chin-erh tien,*
> *Ming-erh ko jeng;*
> Sagebrush lantern,
> Lotus leaf lantern,
> Alight today,
> Tomorrow thrown away."

I wiped my eyes. The moonlight was shining upon Dragon's Left Horn and the ancient estate of the Lius, and I wondered how the Laughing Prince could have enjoyed torturing and murdering little girls like these. Apparently Master Li was thinking the same thing.

"I have a theory about the late lunatic lord," he said. "Ox, what occupation is most closely linked to insanity?"

"Emperor," I said promptly.

He laughed. "I can't argue with that, but I meant a commonplace occupation."

I scratched my nose. "Making felt?" I guessed.

"Precisely," said Master Li. "Felt is cured by immersion in mercury. People in certain trades—hatters, for example—practically swim in the stuff, and it's almost certain that the Laughing Prince drank it."

"Sir?"

"In his youth he had been a promising scientist," Master Li explained. "Sooner or later he was bound to experiment with the Elixir of Life. The formulas are beyond counting, but they all contain the common ingredient of cinnabar, and cinnabar is simply mercuric sulphide. For years I've been warning about mercury, but nobody listens. The reason is that the effect is cumulative and gradual, and one needs to live as long as I have to see the pattern."

He hopped to his feet and began demonstrating expressions and body movements.

"It attacks the nervous system, and eventually produces tics and twitches and spastic movements, like this," said Master Li, and he did a strange jerky series of steps that was oddly appealing. "I am most definitely thinking of the Laughing Prince's irresistible little dance step," he said. "As the poisoning progresses, it leads to outbursts of hysterical laughter and fits of murderous rage, and the final result is insanity followed by death. Ox, it's perfectly possible that the crimes of the Laughing Prince were caused by experiments intended to achieve immortality by drinking cinnabar—not very dramatic, perhaps, but more people have been massacred because an emperor's sandals didn't fit properly than because he received a sign from Heaven, and whenever I hear a high priest howl for divine retribution, I suspect acid indigestion."

He jigged around the grass some more, and then he stopped and looked closely at me. "Acid indigestion?" he asked.

It wasn't that, but I couldn't explain what was bothering me. Something was wrong with the night. I doubt that city people would have noticed it, but I am pure country, and my nerves tingled at the tiny hesitation in the chirping of crickets. An owl stopped a hunting call halfway through. There was a tentative sound to the rustling of small night creatures. Something strange and unnatural had entered the Valley of Sorrows, and I realized that I was holding my breath.

When it came, it was only a small vibration. Then the vibration grew more pronounced, and I saw Master Li look around sharply. Then the sound came. I can't describe it. Nobody could. It was like nothing on earth, yet like everything, and my whole body shuddered with an agonizing sense of loss, but with yearning and hope as well—as though I had once lost something very precious and the memory was returning, and also a hope of finding it again. Can I say that the sound had notes to it? If so, they were as simple and direct as the first three tones of the scale, with the third tone drawn out:

Kung . . . shang . . . chueeeeeeeeeeh . . .

That's the best I can do, and it hit me so hard I wept, and I held my heart as though it would break in half.

"Ox? What's wrong with you?"

"The sound!" I sobbed. "Master Li, surely you hear the sound!"

"What sound?"

Kung . . . shang . . . chueeeeeeeeeeh . . .

It was beautiful and agonizing and it was calling to me. I knew I had to reach it or die, and I was not alone. The festival was breaking up and people were running through the woods, but others were like Master Li and couldn't hear it at all, and they were shouting, "Come back!" and "Have you gone crazy?" I jumped to my feet. Three little girls ran past us, weeping, instinctively shielding the tiny flames in their lotus leaf lanterns.

Master Li swore and hopped up on my back and stuck his feet in my pockets. "Stop trembling like a hobbled racehorse and run," he growled.

I ran. The moon was so bright that the shadows might have been etched on the ground with a sharp instrument and carefully painted black, and the Great River of Stars was sparkling overhead. For a moment I wondered if the strange sound might come from the heart of a star—surely it was as hard to catch. It was like trying to find a cricket at night in a huge old barn: in front of me, then behind me, then to this side, and then to that. I finally realized I was running around in circles, and that Master Li was hauling back on my neck like on the reins of a runaway horse.

I came to a stop and stood with my legs spread and my head down, panting. Master Li held his wine flask out, and I managed to drink some of it. I choked and gasped but felt better, and he patted my shoulder soothingly.

"I can't hear whatever it is, but I know you're going at it the wrong way," he said soothingly. "Ox, at the risk of sounding like a character from the tales of Granny Shu, I will point out that a noise some people hear and others don't isn't speaking to the ears. It's speaking to the heart, and you have a hole in your heart. All young people do. It's there to catch the wonderful things of the world, and later on it gets filled up by broken things. Forget about your ears. Listen with your heart. Aim the hole at the sound and follow in the direction where it hurts the most."

The vibration was coming again, even stronger than before, and I held my breath.

Kung . . . shang . . . chueeeeeeeeeeh . . .

I was off and running, but more confidently now. Master Li was right. Run where it aches the most, and forget about the lies of the ears. I was climbing steadily, and now the night was changing as a thick mist began to rise. The distant lights of the village were blotted out, and then the moon and stars, and Master Li began swearing in a gravelly monotone as the damp blinding blanket closed around us. I could barely see a foot ahead, and I was colliding with trees and rocks. All I knew was that I must keep climbing higher and higher.

I have a vague recollection of sliding down into ravines and climbing back up the other sides. Now the mist was so thick that I could see nothing, and Master Li shouted for me to stop. I couldn't. The wonderful agonizing sound had been silent for some time and I had to reach it, before it vanished forever and I kept skidding downward and scrambling upward—I want to explain that clearly, because of the extraordinary thing that happened.

I was exhausted. All I could do was crawl, but I sensed something ahead of me. The mist was beginning to lift. I saw a pair of sandals, and then skinny legs, and then a slight torso, and then a huge head with wild hair. Prince Liu Pao was staring down at us as though we were ghosts.

"Ox? Number Ten Ox? Master Li? How on earth did you . . ."

His voice trailed off and he looked wide-eyed at the path behind him.

"I heard noises and I came outside, and nobody passed me on the path," the prince whispered.

The mist was lifting rapidly now, and with a sudden shock I realized why the prince couldn't believe his eyes.

I have not described the physical setting of his estate in detail. Dragon's Head, for which the valley had originally been named, was a tiny mountain. Ages ago some cataclysm had split it in half: Dragon's Left Horn and Dragon's Right Horn. The estate was at the top of Dragon's Left Horn, and between it and the sister peak was a sheer gorge about forty feet wide and two hundred feet deep. I had begun the climb up the side of Dragon's Right Horn, and since I was now at the estate, I had somehow managed to cross that gorge.

The prince continued to stare. I crawled back to the gorge and peered down a sheer vertical cliff to jagged rocks far below, and then I slowly raised my eyes up a matching vertical cliff to the place I had come from. It was impossible.

"Ox," Master Li whispered in a tiny voice, "you have a wonderful career ahead of you as the human fly in a carnival, but for the love of Buddha, don't do it again when I'm riding on your back."

We could hear a few faint shouts from the village far below. The wonderful sound had disappeared, and the prince said he was like Master Li in that he hadn't heard it at all. Just then there was a sound we all heard. The monastery bells began to sound the alarm, and in an instant I was on my feet and running down the path with Master Li on my back while Prince Liu Pao panted along behind us.

Villagers stood at the monastery gates, afraid to enter. We forced our way through, and the abbot met us and gestured dumbly. I ran to the library. It had been ransacked. Every book and scroll had been pulled from shelves and torn apart, and every desk had been searched and overturned, and the librarian's desk resembled a pile of kindling. Master Li slid down from my back and scanned the wreckage, and then he turned and trotted rapidly out the door and down one of the corridors.

The cell of the late librarian, Brother Squint-Eyes, was in chaos. The scant furniture had been torn to pieces. Robes had been ripped open at the linings. The pallet was shredded, and pools of congealing blood stained the floor.

Master Li bent over and dipped a finger in the blood and put it to his lips. "It's only ink," he said. "To be precise, it's ink called

Buddha's Eyelashes, and that stuff sticking to the pallet is what's left of Yellow Emperor parchment. After finishing the tracing of the Ssu-ma forgery, Brother Squint-Eyes hid the remaining materials inside his pallet."

Master Li turned and trotted rapidly back to the library. Again his eyes moved over the debris, and he walked to a huge pile of papers beside the bent bars in the window where the thieves had entered before. He began tossing scrolls aside, and then he straightened up with an angry face and cold eyes.

"Well, Ox, if I drop over dead in the next few weeks, it won't be from boredom," he said sourly.

"Buddha save us," the prince whispered, while the abbot and the monks made signs to ward off evil spirits.

Poor Brother Shang's vigil had not been as lonely as he would have liked. The monk lay on his back among the pile of scrolls, staring at the ceiling. He was as dead as Brother Squint-Eyes, and his bulging eyes and gaping mouth were permanently fixed in an expression of terror and horror beyond belief.

石

6

I have but a confused memory of the next few hours. The abbot sent out groups of terrified monks to interview equally terrified peasants, while Master Li hastened to perform an autopsy. There might be some poison that dissipated inside of a few hours, but all Master Li discovered was that Brother Shang had been in excellent shape and had expired from a heart attack. The monks returned with the news that at least eight peasants had seen mysterious monks in robes of motley who laughed and danced beneath the moon, and who disappeared as though the earth had swallowed them.

The other piece of news was that one more section of Princes' Path appeared to be destroyed.

Master Li tossed his knives down beside the corpse of Brother Shang and said we had better get a few hours sleep. It seemed only minutes before he shook me awake again and handed me a cup of strong tea, and then we set out to meet Prince Liu Pao. He was standing forlornly on Princes' Path, and once more we gazed at the impossible. Nothing lived in a swath of approximately fifty by one hundred fifty feet. Death had cut cleanly. Flowers bloomed beside withered ones, and sap dripped from healthy trees not ten feet from trees whose sap had been sucked right out of them. Again I thought of a cemetery in a nightmare, but something in the pattern of it caused me to frown and sketch shapes in the air. Both Master Li and the prince watched me with widening eyes, and I blushed.

"Do that again," Master Li commanded.

I repeated the patterns.

"Li Kao, am I losing my mind?" the prince asked. "I could swear that Number Ten Ox is sketching scholar's shorthand for antique Great Seal script, which hasn't been in common usage for a thousand years."

"Ox is capable of the damnedest things," Master Li muttered. "Right now he's capable of sketching the ancient characters for 'Love,' 'Strength,' and 'Heaven,' and I know perfectly well he doesn't understand a single Great Seal ideograph. Well, boy, are you going to keep us in suspense?"

I turned bright red. "I had a dream," I said humbly. "Just before you woke me up. Something in this scene reminded me of it, and it had strange patterns."

I had dreamed that I was sitting on the grass near a village very like my own. Somebody had attached a bamboo pole and a black flag to the gears of the grindstone at the waterwheel, as we did in my village because the gears kept slipping. Farmers could glance up from the fields and see if the flag was pumping up and down, and if it wasn't, a boy would be sent to get Big Hong, the blacksmith, to reset the gears. As the black flag rose to the apex, it flared out and hovered in the air for a moment before starting back down.

Children were playing in front of the waterwheel. One little girl was jumping up and down. Her long black hair lifted up into the air and hovered for a moment before settling down to her shoulders.

In front of the children were butterflies fluttering among some reeds. One was black, and it swooped up, paused, hovered, and then fluttered back down.

The black flag, black hair, and black butterfly formed a nearly straight line that pointed toward my feet. I looked down and saw a small round orange-colored piece of clay. My hand reached out and closed around it, and something told me to keep watching the pattern: up, pause, down . . . up, pause, down . . .

My fingers tingled. The piece of clay had a heartbeat, and it was the rhythm of the pattern, and an ache filled my heart and tears filled my eyes. Up, pause, down: *kung, shang, chueh.* I was not hearing the wonderful sound but feeling it in the pulse of a piece of clay, and then I was in my old classroom in the monastery and a bunch of boys were looking at me with eyes like owls and I was desperately trying to explain something very important.

"Don't you understand?" I said. "The life force of a round piece of orange-colored clay is like a flag and a butterfly and a little girl's hair. Up, pause, down; up, pause, down. The important thing to remember is the pause. Can't you understand that?"

The boys stared at me solemnly.

"It's the pause!" I yelled. "It isn't like the heartbeat of a person, and you'll never hear the wonderful sound it makes unless you understand the pause!"

The old abbot was shuffling toward me. Then he came closer and he wasn't the abbot at all. He was Master Li, and he grabbed my shoulders and shook me and screamed furiously, *"Number Ten Ox, you couldn't teach a banana to turn black!"*

Then I woke up.

"Sir, that's all I can tell you about the dream," I said. "Something in this scene reminded me of it, and the pattern it took. That tall dead tree, then a space, then lower dead trees, then a space, then bushes . . ."

I shrugged and sketched in the air. "And you draw ancient scholar's ideographs for love, strength, and Heaven," Master Li said thoughtfully. "Are you quite positive that the round piece of clay was colored orange?"

"Yes, sir," I said.

He scratched his nose and chewed thoughtfully on the tip of his mangy beard. "That may bear looking into when we have the time," he said. "The symbolism is obvious, but it leads to a swamp I'd rather stay away from."

Master Li started looking for traces of mysterious monks in motley, and I started gathering more plant and soil samples, and just then the drums began. Sheepskin drums, hundreds of them, pounding softly but methodically from all over the Valley of Sorrows. The prince looked at Master Li with raised eyebrows, but Master Li jerked his head in my direction. "When it comes to the ways of peasants, ask the expert," he said.

I flushed again. "Your Highness, they're going to blackmail you," I said meekly.

"Eh?"

"Blackmail isn't quite right, but I don't know the proper word," I said. "They're going to start a work song. It's older than time, and it's used by peasants when they want the lord of the valley do do something."

"*What* lord of *what* valley?" the prince said angrily.

Master Li kindly stepped in to help me. "The peasants think your ancestor is behind this, and so far as they're concerned, you're lord of the valley whether you like it or not. The headmen are preparing the chant that details the peasants' duties to the lord, and thus implies the lord's duties to the peasants. Ox, how many verses are there?"

"Over four hundred," I said. "When they get to the end, they'll start all over again, and they can keep it up for a year if need be."

I didn't add that in their place I'd do the same thing myself. Confucius thought so highly of the blackmail song that he put part of it in the Book of Odes, and it's really very effective when the drums go boom, boom, boom.

> "*In the fifth moon we gather wild plums and cherries,*
> *In the sixth moon we boil mallow and beans,*
> *In the seventh moon we dry the dates,*
> *In the eighth moon we take the rice*
> *To make with it the spring wine*
> *So our lord may be granted long life.*
> *In the sixth moon we pick the melons,*
> *In the seventh moon we cut the gourds,*
> *In the eighth moon we take the seeding hemp,*
> *We gather bitter herbs, we cut ailanto for firewood,*
> *That our lord may eat.*"

The chanting is without emotion except for the last line of every third verse, and after a few months of it the subject begins to cringe when each third verse starts. It's hard for a lord to justify chopping off insolent heads; it's just a work song.

Boom, boom, boom:

> "*In the eighth moon we make ready the stackyards,*
> *In the ninth moon we bring in the harvest;*
> *Millet for wine, millet for cooking, the early and the late,*
> *Paddy and hemp, beans and wheat.*
> *My lord, the harvesting is over.*
> *We begin work on your houses;*
> *In the morning we gather thatch reeds,*
> *In the evening we twist ropes,*
> *We work quickly on the roofs,*
> *For soon we will sow the lord's many grains.*"

"How can they do this to me?" the prince said plaintively. "They know very well that my family hasn't collected a copper coin or grain of rice for centuries."

Boom, boom, boom:

> *"In the days of the first we cut ice with tingling blows;*
> *In the days of the second we bring it to the cold shed.*
> *In the days of the third, very early,*
> *We offer pigs and garlic, that our lord may eat.*
> *In the tenth moon are shrewd frosts;*
> *We clear the stackyards,*
> *With twin pitchers we hold the village feast,*
> *Killing for it a spring lamb.*
> *Up we go to our lord's hall,*
> *Raise the drinking cups of buffalo horn:*
> *Hurrah for our lord! May he live forever and ever!"*

"They'll keep that up for a year?" the prince said. "I think I know what they want, but I'd prefer to have it explained to me."

"You and you alone have the right to dispose of your ancestor in the old way," Master Li said gently. "By the old way they mean pre-Confucian."

"Which is punishable by torment in the Eighth Hell!" the prince said angrily.

"Yes, according to our Neo-Confucian overlords, who also impose upon rivals the sacred duty of retiring from public life for three years upon the death of a father, and then they poison the father," Master Li said sardonically.

Prince Liu Pao was made from tough stuff. He turned without another word and began marching up Dragon's Left Horn toward his estate. He turned off the path and took a shortcut to the grotto. The horror of the Medical Research Center seemed even worse with the muffled sounds of drums and chanting in the distance. The prince opened the door to the tomb and marched inside to the sarcophagus of his ancestor.

"Ox, can you get the lid all the way down?"

I spat on my hands. The lid was so heavy I couldn't stop it after it slid down to the mummy's feet, and it crashed to the floor. Prince Liu Pao stood looking down at the remains of his ancestor, and Master Li beckoned for me to open the other sarcophagus.

"While we're at it, I want to look for something," he said.

The lid was easier to move, and the mummy of Tou Wan, the Laughing Prince's wife, was intact. Master Li reached inside and came up with some jewelry, which he examined closely.

"Good stuff, but not the best," he said thoughtfully. "Tou Wan was said to have been a spendthrift of epic proportions, and I doubt that this would have met her standards. One wonders whether their highnesses might not have been buried by a light-fingered steward."

He stood there scratching his forehead.

"Strange," he muttered. "The Laughing Prince apparently worshipped a stone, and possibly his wife also did, yet the stone wasn't included in either coffin. The faithful steward again?"

A sound made us turn. The prince was struggling to lift his ancestor's mummy from the coffin. The tarred wrappings made it heavy and awkward. I stepped forward to help, but Master Li held me back. Prince Liu Pao was sweating heavily, but he kept going: through the tomb, through the grotto, and outside to the path. He turned off the path and carried the mummy to a flat jutting rock overlooking the Valley of Sorrows. Every eye must have been lifted there.

The drums stopped. The prince searched for a heavy rock, and I closed my eyes. I kept them closed while I listened to ancient bones splintering, but I opened them too soon and saw the rock descend on the skull and smash it to pieces. A white cloud of crushed and powdered bones drifted down to the valley, followed by the scraps of linen from the wrappings, and then by the stone used for the sacrifice. I have seldom admired anyone as much as I admired Prince Liu Pao. He turned toward us and managed to keep his voice steady.

"According to Tsao Tsao, my next step on the path to damnation is either to violate my sister or fail to return for my mother's funeral, but I can't remember which comes first," he said.

"The mother," said Master Li, "takes precedence, but I wouldn't be so sure about damnation if I were you. Prince, this time the criminals have made a very bad mistake, and the mummy of your ancestor puts the seal on it. You and I have something interesting to talk about."

From below came one last roll of sheepskin drums: "Hurrah for our lord! May he live forever and ever!"

石

7

Before we had seen the living quarters. Now the prince led the way to his studio, and the breath went out of me as I stepped through the door into forty captured sunsets. I was in the presence of genius.

Paintings and sketches were everywhere, and they were alive. I could swear that real sap was flowing through painted trees, and real dew was dripping from flowers. The most extraordinary thing was the glowing light that seemed to come from inside the paintings, and the prince smiled at the stunned expression on my face.

"It's just a trick, Ox," he said modestly. "It's called *p'o-mo,* and it means the technique of applying dark ink over light. The effect is scarcely noticeable when you first put it on, but when it dries, it gives the effect of glowing with inner light—'like focused eyes,' my teacher used to say."

"Ah! You studied with Three Incomparables?" Master Li asked.

"Li Kao, you know everything," the prince said admiringly. "Yes, I was his student for several years, and he was without doubt the most disagreeable man I've ever met." He graciously included me in the conversation. "His name is Ku K'ai-chih, but he's called Three Incomparables because of his boast that he's incomparable in painting, in genius, and in stupidity. Unquestionably he's the greatest master of p'o-mo in the empire."

"He used to be, but you surpassed him long ago," Master Li muttered. "Prince, this is incredible work, but have you considered the likelihood of disgrace and exile?"

"Oh, I have no intention of showing my paintings," the prince said. "This is practice. I'm trying to learn, and I have a long way to go."

Being back in his beloved studio had done wonders for him. It was as though the smell of paint had wiped away the recent experiences, and his eyes were shining happily.

"Ox, Master Li means that our overlords have decreed that all art must follow supposedly classical techniques, which are set down in a manual called 'Mustard Seed Garden,' " he explained. "Rocks, for example, may only be painted using *kou* strokes for outline, *p'o* strokes for the tops and sides, *ts'un* strokes for texture, and *ts'a* strokes for expression. Any other technique can lead to a trial and exile."

Master Li laughed at the expression on my face.

"It gets worse," he said. "Ts'un strokes, for example, are broken down into the exact lines suitable for individual rocks: curling cloud strokes, axe cut, split hemp, loose rope, ghost face, skull-like, woodpile, sesame seed, golden blue, jade powder, spear hole, pebbles, and boneless. An artist who uses ghost face for painting granite instead of the officially approved axe cut faces six years in the Mongolian desert."

The prince waved around the room. "You are looking at approximately one and a half million years worth of exile," he said proudly. He was becoming quite animated, and he eagerly tossed aside paintings from a pile on the floor and came up with a simple sketch of a tree. "Laws are liars," he said. "Look here. Every single law of painting insists that the *shih,* the movement force, of a tree like this must be concentrated in the principal branch that thrusts so proudly toward Heaven. Except it isn't. I tried it the correct way eight times, and it sat there as lifelessly as a lohan. Finally I said to myself, 'Stop trying to think, you idiot! *Paint!*' So I let my hand take over, and this lovely tree came to life. Do you see why?"

He covered the proud principal branch, and gradually I saw what he meant. The energy of the tree didn't run that way at all. It spread out and up from the trunk, reached a knot in a branch, doubled back down the trunk, and then lifted up the far side and throbbed with life as it reached for the sky from a tiny insignificant branch that was barely more than a twig.

"Laws lie, the eyes see only what they have been conditioned to see, and the mind is a refuse pile of other people's ideas," the prince said. "Only the hand tells the truth. The hand!" he cried passionately. "Trust the hand, and it will never lie to you."

Master Li looked at him approvingly. "Prince, that is precisely what I wanted to talk to you about," he said. "I'm beginning to suspect that this case is one lie piled on top of another lie, but for the first time we have something to go on. You see, the criminals have told us where to look."

The prince showed me where things were, and I busied myself making tea while they moved a table out to the garden. We sat outside and after sipping his tea Master Li said, "We know that thieves broke into the library to steal a manuscript, leading to the death of Brother Squint-Eyes, but why did they enter again last night and cause the death of Brother Shang? There seems to be only one reasonable explanation." Master Li pulled out the fragment of the Ssu-ma. "This had been traced by Brother Squint-Eyes. When the criminals examined it closely, they saw the markings, and it was the copy they came back for. Thus the books ripped open and robes split at the seams and so forth. But why would they want a badly done copy that had no market value? The answer is that they weren't after the manuscript for its value to dealers, they were after it for its *content,* and possibly—just possibly—they may have come up empty-handed all the way around."

Master Li placed the fragment on the table and tapped it with a fingernail.

"It was a very brief manuscript," he said. "The odds against this fragment containing what they were after aren't as astronomical as one might think. Perhaps no more than twenty or thirty to one, and I've bet on cricket fights with worse odds than that. Prince, did Ssu-ma Ch'ien ever visit your abominable ancestor?"

The prince looked startled. "I really don't know," he said. After a moment's thought he added, "I'd be mildly surprised if he didn't. Before his fall from grace, he served as the emperor's confidant, and who better to send when a younger brother shows signs of losing his mind?"

"And is it possible that the younger brother caused Ssu-ma's fall and sentence of castration?" Master Li wondered. "The abbot tells me that among the many uses for the monastery was that of a prison back in the jovial days of the Laughing Prince, and might that explain why the manuscript was found there?"

"You mean the forgery?" the prince said, scratching his head.

"An acquaintance of mine, an exceptionally saintly soul at the Eye of Tranquility, has offered an interesting hypothesis," Master Li explained. "The forgery might have been intended to frame Ssu-ma with the charge of filial impiety. I was almost convinced of it, but now, thanks to you, I'm even more convinced of something totally different."

Master Li pointed back inside the studio at the prince's glorious paintings. "The hand. Trust only the hand!" he cried. "That very idea has been gnawing at the back of my mind for days. When I looked at the fragment and saw references to Ssu-ma's father, I said, 'Fraud!' but when I looked only at the calligraphy, I said, 'Ssu-ma!' You did the same thing. The hand is unmistakable, and I am now going to conclude that this isn't the world's greatest forgery for the simple reason that it isn't a forgery at all. Ssu-ma Ch'ien set down his father's name in order to cry out to scholars, 'Look! Look closely! Something is wrong!' Meaning that he had concealed his real message in some kind of code, and you and I are going to entertain ourselves by seeing who can be the first to break it."

Not Number Ten Ox, who couldn't decipher a single character of ancient scholarly shorthand. I got up and inwardly sneered at the fragments of dialogue that drifted to my ears. They were like children playing games, and we had serious matters to think about.

"Never seen so many errors of fact in a few brief paragraphs."

"Deliberate, perhaps?"

"Errors as starting points?"

"Interesting how many errors deal with numbers."

"Indeed yes. Here he writes, 'one hundred and forty-six scales of a dragon.'"

Even I knew that a dragon has 36 evil scales and 117 good ones, which used to add up to 153 when I was in school. I sniffed contemptuously, and wandered around looking at flowers.

"Better break it down. One, four, and six."

"Each error probably has a direct relationship to each mention of T'an, his father's name."

"He was really straining here, wasn't he? Comparing the marks on a stone to the 'two hundred fifty-three points of acupuncture.'"

Didn't they realize we had two murdered monks on our hands, and that a strange sound was driving people out of their minds while Princes' Path was being destroyed? I decapitated a few dandelions.

"One . . . two . . . three. Got it!" Master Li said happily. "Ox, stop pouting and come over here."

Pouting? Me? I walked back with dignity and peered down over Master Li's shoulder. His finger danced across the fragment.

"Coded sections begin with mentions of Ssu-ma's father's name and run to the next error in fact. The numbers give the spacing between important words, and here is what we have: 'Down stairs . . . Cold room . . . Tunnel to construction site . . . Stone in sacristy . . .'"

He leaned back happily. I stared.

"That's all?" I said incredulously.

"It's all we need, and all thieves would need, for that matter," Master Li said complacently. "Unless anyone knows of another place where a stone was kept in a sacristy, Ssu-ma Ch'ien was referring to this estate. He either went or was advising someone to go down the stairs to the cold room, and somewhere there would be a tunnel that led to a construction site and the sacristy of the stone. A cold room is as far beneath the earth as one can put it, and what could be the purpose of a construction site deep under the earth?"

Master Li reached into his tunic and took out a piece of cloth. I recognized it with something of a shock as being a piece of the wrapping around the mummy of the Laughing Prince.

"Prince, this has faded, but one can still see that the color was imperial yellow, as it should be for the brother of an emperor," Master Li said. "However, I seem to recall that Tou Wan preceded him in death by a few months. Wouldn't your ancestor still have been in mourning for his wife?"

The prince stared, and turned purple as the implications struck him. They took a good deal longer to strike me.

"Of course. It should be white. You mean I just crushed the skeleton of a total stranger?"

"Tsao Tsao built seventy-two decoy tombs," Master Li said mildly.

"I'm damned if I'll go through that experience seventy-two times!" the prince yelled.

"I doubt that will be necessary," said Master Li. He looked up at me. "Wake up, Ox. The Laughing Prince amassed an incredible fortune, which has never been found, and people have been buying fake treasure maps and digging holes in the Valley of Sorrows ever since. Now we have the words of Ssu-ma Ch'ien. Words that thieves would go to any lengths to get their hands on, because what could the Laughing Prince have been secretly constructing deep in the bowels of the earth? Dear boy, we're probably sitting on top of a tomb that contains enough loot to buy half the empire."

石

8

"These abandoned wings were paradise for a boy," the prince said
nostalgically. "Think of the hiding places. I once counted a hundred
and six rooms filled with things that nobody considered to be valuable. Not valuable to a boy? Chests filled with ancient costumes for
masquerades, for example, and love letters bound together with
challenges to duels, and portraits of beautiful concubines and sinis-
ter distant cousins."

We followed him as he confidently stepped around rotting sections of wooden floors and ducked under sagging beams. He stepped
into an alcove and began prying boards from a window. Sunlight
burst inside and glowed upon a portrait upon the wall.

"Liu Sheng, better known as the Laughing Prince."

The silk was still intact, although faded with age, and the color
was very good. The man who gazed from the portrait was quite
handsome. I judged him to be in his early thirties. His forehead was
high and broad and serene, and his thin nose had a proud hook to
it, and his mouth was firm and well formed. His eyes were quite
strange in that they appeared to be clear but somehow they didn't
focus. It was as though the Laughing Prince was not gazing out at
the viewer but at something in front of the viewer—a ghost, perhaps, or some strange vision that only he could see. His hands were
small and so gracefully formed that they were almost feminine. I
could see no trace of madness, yet something in the assurance of the
pose suggested an inner arrogance that was capable of almost any-

thing. His dress was clearly symbolic of something, but I didn't know what. Master Li did.

"Great Buddha, if his imperial brother saw him dressed like this, the yellow scarf would have been on its way inside of an hour," Master Li said. "The son of a sow thought he ranked above the emperor. In fact, he thought he ranked above most of the gods."

He explained the ornaments to me.

"Upper garment: sun, moon, stars, mountain, dragon, and the flowery fowl. Lower garment: temple cup, aquatic grass, flames, rice, hatchet, and symbol of distinction. Only the emperor of China is allowed to wear all twelve ornaments, and the Laughing Prince added a thirteenth: the peacock eye, which symbolizes the Second Lord of Heaven. One assumes he was preparing to place his throne beside the August Personage of Jade."

Now the strange unfocused eyes took on a different aspect, and I decided I was looking at a man who had found the world not to his liking and stepped outside it—like Pea-Head Chou in my village, who joined the roosters every morning and commanded the sun to rise.

When the prince led us away I found that I was tiptoeing, and the painted eyes appeared to be following me. The prince made his way to a brassbound door and unlocked it with an ancient key that was as big as his forearm. "As I said, this place was paradise for a boy," he remarked.

Paradise indeed. Inside was the old armory, and some of the axes were so huge they could only have had a ceremonial function. A thousand weapons hung in racks along the walls, and we found some that were better than anything modern. I chose a small axe and a short sword, and the prince selected a spear and a dagger, and Master Li stuck a row of knives into his belt. The next door took us outside into an inner courtyard, and in a tool shed I found a modern steel pick and bar. In the center of the courtyard was a stone building that housed an abandoned well, and a flight of steps led down to deep basements.

"The old cold room is at the bottom," the prince said. "I doubt that anyone has been down there since I played at being a hero locked in a terrible dungeon."

Master Li searched for any signs of recent entrance, and his eyes gleamed when he saw layers of untouched dust. I had brought some torches, and we lit them. The prince started forward, but I jumped ahead of him. "A thousand pardons, Your Highness, but this is what I'm here for," I said politely. I started down the stairs, clutching my axe. The prince, I decided, had been a very brave little boy, and I couldn't suppress a small shudder as I cut through thick cobwebs that hung like blankets, and dozens of spiders scuttled over my hands and arms.

Then I was assaulted by a hundred demons—no, bats—no, *white* bats—and I let out a yelp and dove to the stairs and covered my head with my hands. When I dared to peek I saw that Master Li was standing calmly behind me, regarding me with a mixture of exasperation and amusement.

"Number Ten Ox, there is not one word of truth to peasant legends about white bats," he said wryly. "They aren't even albino. They suffer from a parasitical skin disease, like the so-called white elephants of India, and they do *not* live a thousand years, and their black blood is *not* an Elixir of Life, and if you touch them, your hair will *not* fall out."

The prince smiled at me reassuringly. "As a boy I caught a few and kept them as pets," he said. "Unsanitary, but no worse than that."

He ran a hand through his wild mop of hair, and I sheepishly uncovered mine. I got to my feet and reclaimed my axe and torch and started down again, feeling very foolish. There were four landings. The last flight of stairs ended in the cold room, which was enormous, and Master Li and the prince examined the solid stone floor and walls for some sign of a secret tunnel. I began to cheer up as I watched them. Finally Master Li stepped back and clapped his hands to his hips and glared at me.

"Why are you standing there like a statue?" he growled. "You should know something about digging tunnels. Find the damn thing."

It was childish, but I had to do something to counter the humiliation with the bats. I made a great show of examining the floor. "Aha!" I said. I examined the walls. "Aha!" I said. I stood thoughtfully, posing for a portrait of The Young Genius. "Ssu-ma Ch'ien wrote 'cold room,' but not 'in the cold room,'" I said. I made my way back to the stairs and examined them carefully. "Aha!" I said, and I started climbing to the last landing.

Master Li had a smile on his face as he followed, and I couldn't keep it up.

"I saw it on the way down," I explained. "I was thinking about the labor involved in carrying huge chunks of ice up five flights of steep stairs, so I looked and found what I was looking for."

I swung my torch to both side walls to show old bronze rings set in them. "Pulleys, with center ropes hauling some kind of sleds," I said. "They're evenly spaced and neatly in line except for here." I lifted the torch to the right-hand wall and showed an arc in the line of rings that ran almost up to the ceiling. "This made it awkward to get equal leverage on both sides. The only possible reason for it is that the wall isn't solid."

"Bravo," Master Li said, and I felt much better.

He held my torch and I spat on my hands and swung the pick. It didn't take very long. Soon I had a crack I could work with, and I pried out a stone slab with the steel bar, and the torches almost went out as the flames joined the air rushing into the dark space behind. In a few minutes I had a hole big enough to pass through, and we entered a tunnel carved through stone, sloping downward.

"Be very careful," Master Li cautioned. "If this does indeed lead to a tomb, it may have been set with traps for grave robbers."

We moved slowly, testing the floor in front of us for pits and nervously examining the ceiling for things that could fall on us. The tunnel sloped even more sharply downward, with many turns. We descended for such a length of time that I was willing to bet we had reached the level of the valley, or even below it, when the tunnel finally leveled out, and then after a hundred feet or so it began to slope upward. We climbed steadily, in total silence except for the sounds we made ourselves. There were no signs of traps. Finally our torchlight reflected back to us from the surface of a brick wall that completely blocked the tunnel. Master Li examined it and found nothing dangerous. My pick and steel bar went to work again. It was a double-thick wall, but no match for steel, and with a crash and a cloud of red brick dust, a large section of it soon collapsed. We coughed and wiped our eyes and held up our torches, and the dust slowly cleared, and we stood rooted to the spot, staring in horror at what lay upon the floor behind the wall.

No wonder the tunnel had remained a secret. The workmen had never left it. We were staring at skeletons, hundreds and hundreds of them, piled almost to the ceiling. The prince was beyond speech as he gazed at the memento his ancestor had left behind. Master Li's voice was cold and angry.

"So much for the peasants. The soldiers who herded them here and bricked them up were probably rewarded with a banquet at which nobody survived the second course, and then the poisoners received their own rewards, and so on. It's estimated that Emperor Shun killed eighty thousand men to keep the secret of his tomb, and even then it was discovered and looted inside of a century. Prince, this should put all doubts to rest. Your esteemed ancestor is indeed sleeping somewhere inside here."

He stepped past me and began tossing skeletons aside, and I forced myself to move. Piles of white bones rose like mounds of snow beside a road as we slowly cleared a path down the tunnel. After an hour we finally reached the end, and it was a blank brick wall. Three swings of the pick were enough to knock bricks loose, but then I felt a shock that numbed my hands and arms. The pick had struck solid iron. I moved to different positions, knocking bricks away, and discovered that a seamless iron wall ran from one side of the tunnel to the other, and from the top to the bottom.

"There's probably another brick retaining wall behind this one, and molten iron was poured into the gap," Master Li said thoughtfully. "Ox, what do you think?"

I shrugged. "Iron is tough but it will break, and my bar is steel," I said. "If I can pound four holes in it, I should be able to crack an opening big enough to crawl through."

After that my memory of the tunnel is one of noise. The steel bar produced hard harsh sounds that echoed back and forth between the narrow walls and banged against my head and ears and made me sick. I had to stop every now and then and sit with my head down between my legs until my stomach stopped heaving. I had a terrible headache, but I got into the slow steady rhythm of a wood-cutter or ditchdigger, and cracks like cobwebs appeared beneath the point of the bar. Then small chunks of iron broke loose, and finally the bar plunged through. As Master Li suspected there was another brick wall behind, but that caused no problem. The other holes went more quickly now that I had the feel of it, and in about three hours I was able to crack the iron between two of the holes. Another hour was enough to finish the job. We crawled through the small opening and lifted our torches and looked up at a ceiling gilded with real gold. The floor was marble, and the walls were richly ornamented with silver and bronze. We were in a long hallway lined with side rooms, and we clutched our weapons nervously and stepped into the first one.

No wonder criminals would do anything to find the place. Chests were piled so high with gold and jewels that the lids couldn't close, and bars of gold and silver were stacked like firewood around the walls. Prince Liu Pao was so furious his torch was shaking like a lantern swinging in a high wind.

"Four years before my ancestor died there was a famine in this part of the empire," he said in a high tight voice. "Two hundred thousand people died, but the Laughing Prince said he was unable to help because all his money was tied up in mining equipment and debts."

The prince stalked on to the next room, which held huge jars that had probably contained rare oils and perfumes and spices. Other rooms contained weapons that were so covered with costly jewels they were quite useless for warfare, and we stopped and gaped at a huge room that contained the skeletons of forty horses. Apparently the Laughing Prince had intended to ride in style in his next life, and it wasn't only horses he rode. The prince almost approached Master Li's level of swearing as we entered the Hall of Concubines and found forty small skeletons neatly arranged on forty beds.

"No sign of panic or disarray. Poisoned," Master Li said grimly. "Timed, no doubt, to breathe their last along with their master."

After that we more or less expected to find what we did: skeletons of cooks, courtiers, dancers, actors, acrobats, eunuchs, clerks, accountants—the lunatic lord had taken his entire court with him, or so I assumed. Master Li had reservations.

"One element is noticeably missing. Where are his Monks of Mirth?" he wondered.

We had no answer to that. We entered banquet rooms and game rooms and elegant state bedrooms, and we found closets crammed with the remains of costly clothes and pantries stuffed with petrified piles of rich foods. It wasn't so much a tomb as a vast underground palace, and at the center was a huge throne room, which even had a chopping block as part of the entertainment. Behind the throne was a small door, and we entered a round room with a lapis lazuli floor,

and walls and ceiling of solid gold. Two sarcophagi lay side by side.
The one on the right bore the dragon symbols of an emperor, and
the one on the left bore the phoenix symbols of an imperial consort.

Master Li strode between the coffins to the back wall. There in a
niche was a sacristy. The two side panels of the niche were covered
with the same mysterious charts and formulas we had seen in the
grotto, and the center panel carried the same inscription.

In darkness languishes the precious stone.
When will its excellence enchant the world?
When seeming is taken for being, being becomes seeming.
When nothing is taken for something, something becomes nothing.
The stone dispels seeming and nothing,
And climbs to the Gates of the Great Void.

The sacristy was empty. Master Li swore angrily and whirled
around and gestured for me to open the coffins. I stepped up to the
one on the left. The lid was hard to move, but at last it began to
slide down the grooves, and the farther it slid, the wider our eyes
grew. I stepped back, panting, and we stood in silence and gazed at
the burial dress of Tou Wan, the bride of the Laughing Prince.

She wore a suit that could have fed a million people for a year. It
was priceless jade cut into rectangular pieces that were tightly
linked together by fine gold wire. There must have been two thousand jade pieces encasing the mummy, but Master Li wasn't interested in jade. He was interested in a stone, and he let loose another
volley of oaths when no stone was revealed in the coffin.

An inscription had been chiseled on the front of Tou Wan's sarcophagus, and Prince Liu Pao translated the old script for me.
Apparently it had been written by her grieving husband.

> *The sound of her silk skirt has stopped.*
> *On the marble pavement dust grows.*
> *Her empty room is cold and still.*
> *Fallen leaves are piled against the doors.*
> *How can I bring my aching heart to rest?*

It seemed to me that there was real feeling in that, and the prince
shook his head wonderingly. "My ancestor was quite unknowable,"
he said. "He wrote this, and then he went out with his Monks of
Mirth to capture and torture a few more children."

Master Li nodded at the other sarcophagus, and I bent to the lid. As it slowly slid down, our eyes nearly bulged right out of our heads, and when it slid all the way down I stepped back and sat down heavily on the floor. The silence was broken only by the hiss of our torches.

The coffin was empty. Prince Liu Pao sat down in a heap beside me, and I supposed that both of us were seeing a mummy dressed in jade crawling from a coffin and creeping out to join his merry monks in motley. Master Li glared down at us.

"Oh, bat shit," he snarled. "Stop trying to catch flies with your gaping mouths and start using your heads."

He sat down on the rim of the coffin and glared around the golden room. He was furious.

"Ox, what happened to your torch when you punched through the iron and brick?" he asked.

"Wha . . . Why, nothing happened," I said.

"Precisely. The flame didn't jump toward the hole because there already was fresh air in the tomb," he said. "That means there's another entrance somewhere, and it's been used recently. We're too late. The thieves have already been here, and that means we have to change our minds about their being thieves."

That was too slippery for me, but the prince looked up with sudden interest.

"They didn't take the gold and jewels, and not even Tou Wan's burial suit," he said wonderingly.

"So what did they take?" Master Li asked.

We remained silent, so he answered his own question.

"They took a stone," said Master Li. "All the inscriptions indicate that the Laughing Prince worshipped a stone. When he died he would certainly have arranged for it to be buried with him, so it was taken from the sacristy and—perhaps—placed in his hands, and then the jade suit was fashioned around him. Jade is among the hardest of materials. The stone might be damaged if somebody tried to crack the jade, so whoever it was who beat us to it simply carried the whole damn mummy away. What kind of people would pass up gold and jewels to get their hands on a sacred stone?"

"A religious order of some sort?" the prince guessed.

Master Li shrugged. "That's all I can think of at the moment," he said. "Remember that the Laughing Prince created a quasi-religious order he called the Monks of Mirth, and notice that the Monks of Mirth, alone among his court, did not die along with the prince—at least we haven't seen their skeletons. Suppose he arranged for the order to be perpetuated through the centuries?"

I finally found my tongue. "Why?" I asked.

Master Li threw his hands wide apart in exasperation. "How would I know?" he said. "We can assume that he worshipped a stone, although we don't know why. The use of laughter and dancing in place of prayer is not unknown to ancient preshamanistic religions, and I can't help but wonder about the constant repetition of the number five in his peculiar formulas. Five is a sacred number to many weird cults, ancient and modern alike. The primitive Yu-ch'ao, for example, who are said to live in five-sided tree houses and sacrifice to five-headed demons in five-celled temples."

Master Li pulled out his wine flask and offered us some, but we declined. He swilled a pint or two and wiped his lips with his beard.

"Prince, for the moment I'm stymied," he said frankly. "The idea that we may not be dealing with normal criminals throws everything out of balance. All I know for certain is that we have to get to the bottom of the strange compelling sound and the destruction of Princes' Path, and that means Ox and I will have to go to Ch'ang-an with soil and plant samples for analysis, and then get our hands on the greatest sound-master in the empire. In the meantime, you have a problem."

He waved his wine flask back toward the treasure chambers.

"Technically this stuff is yours. Do you want it?"

The prince shuddered. "Nightmares would finish me in a month if I took a single coin," he said.

"Nonetheless, if word of the discovery gets out, you'll be visited by every criminal, warlord, and greedy state minister in the empire," Master Li pointed out.

"Suppose I make a gift of it to the throne?" the prince asked hopefully.

"People tend to impute their own flaws to others," Master Li said. "The avaricious will never believe that you didn't keep the choicest gems for yourself, and the missing jade suit of your ancestor will be considered absolute proof. Are you particularly fond of torture?"

The prince turned as white as one of the skeletons. "But what can I do with this tomb?" he whispered.

Master Li turned to me. "Ox, can you manage it?" he asked.

I drew myself up proudly. "Venerable Sir, you are talking to a former apprentice of Big Hong the blacksmith," I said.

He turned back to the prince. "What tomb?" he said.

"What tomb?" I said.

The prince began to regain some color. "What tomb?" he said.

It really wasn't very difficult. The stones and bricks were easily replaced, and there were countless pieces of old iron lying around the estate. I was very proud of my makeshift furnace and bellows, and when I had finished, I doubted that anyone would notice the patch in the iron wall unless he was looking for one.

The difficult part was putting the skeletons in the tunnel back into place, and that was because I kept hearing a mad mummy in a suit of jade creeping up behind me. When I added artistic layers of dust and cobwebs there wasn't a greedy bureaucrat in the empire who would believe that Prince Liu Pao or anyone else had entered the tomb of the Laughing Prince. Then we left for Ch'ang-an.

石

9

I had never been to the capital before, but I thought I knew about big cities from my experiences in Peking. That illusion vanished the moment we passed through the Gate of Luminous Virtue. I gaped like any yokel at a raucous beehive where two million people buzzed inside walls that enclosed thirty square miles. There were twenty-five north-south avenues, and every one of them was four hundred eighty feet wide and lined with elm, fruit, and pagoda trees. The avenues rose to a high hill called Dragon Head Plain, and converged to a single road of bluish stone that wound up like a dragon's tail to the vast basilicas of the elite who ruled the empire.

I was awed and silent as we took the Street of the Vermilion Sparrow toward Dragon Head Plain. We passed through the Gate of the Red Bird just as a thousand drums pounded the three hundred beats that heralded the opening of the markets, and I felt dizzy in the atmosphere of a thousand years of greatness as we approached the legendary Brush Forest Academy, where Chinese genius is nurtured. Master Li had been one of the geniuses, and his reaction was slightly less than reverent.

"Fraud, my boy! Fraud and forgery," he said, waving disgustedly at sacrosanct landmarks. "Paint slapped over dry rot and gilded with lies. Some of the lies are rather pretty, however, and my favorite concerns the little peasant lad who's digging a ditch behind a village schoolhouse."

Master Li pulled out his flask and drank deeply, which caused outraged comments from distinguished-looking pedestrians. He ignored them.

"The urchin's keen ears catch fragments of lessons drifting from the window," Master Li said between burps. "One day the schoolmaster absentmindedly falls into the ditch and discovers to his astonishment that the boy has covered the walls with masterful drawings, flawless mathematics, and learned quotations from the ancients.

" 'Boy, are you not the scrofulous, illiterate, and lice-ridden urchin called Hong Wong?' the schoolmaster gasps.

" 'The insignificant name of this worthless one should not blemish the esteemed lips of Your Magnificence!' the lad wails.

" 'And is not your father the ulcerous, flatulent, maggot-infested fellow called Hong the Hopeless, who takes pride in the fact that he has failed the examination for village idiot sixteen years in a row?'

"The lad falls to his knees and begins banging his head against the ground. 'Seventeen!' he sobs. Well, the schoolmaster grabs the boy by the ear and hauls him into the classroom, of course, and gives him every test he can think of, and word spreads far and wide that the latest Chinese genius has been discovered in a ditch in an insignificant village eight miles from nowhere. You know the rest. Triumph after triumph, the highest awards and degrees, elevation to important office, advisor to emperors and savior of peasants, and eventual deification to become Celestial Patron of scrofulous, illiterate, lice-ridden lads digging ditches behind schoolhouses."

Master Li spat with lamentable accuracy upon a statue of K'uei-hsing, God of Examinations.

"Now let's take a look at reality," he said. "Little Hong Wong is indeed taken in hand by the educational establishment and force-fed languages, calligraphy, poetry, painting, dancing, music, chess, etiquette, courtly ritual, philosophy, religion, history, and the classics, following which he's ready to start learning something—mathematics, for example. Agriculture, engineering, economics, medicine, government, and the art of war. He passes his examinations with honors and receives his first official appointment, and then what happens?"

He actually seemed to want an answer, so I shrugged and said, "A superior who inherited the job from an uncle rams a barge pole up his ass."

"Good boy," Master Li said approvingly. "Hong Wong has just entered the world of the Neo-Confucians, to whom all innovation is anathema. His brilliant plan for a sanitation system will be rejected out of hand because it has no direct parallel in ancient times. His astronomical observations will be used as evidence in his trial for heresy, because they cannot be confirmed in the oldest texts. His paintings do not slavishly imitate the ancients, and his poetry is not plaigarism, and his essays do not deal with the three hundred thirty-three approved subjects, so all of them will be burned. Hong Wong will be very lucky if he is merely stripped of rank and possessions and kicked out to starve, and if he is truly a genius, he will not be so lucky. Lin Tseh-shu was banished to a corner of Turkestan so distant the sun hasn't reached it yet, or so they say. Su Tung-po was exiled to Hainan, whose principal exports are malaria, jungle rot, and leprosy. Chu Suilang was last seen sinking into a swamp in Vietnam, and when Han Yu stepped off the prison boat in Swatow he was very nearly devoured by crocodiles."

Wen Ch'ang, God of Literature, received the next stream of saliva.

"Ox, at an early age a Chinese genius gazes at the path that lies ahead and reaches for a wine jar," Master Li said. "Is it any wonder that our greatest men have lurched rather than walked across the landscape as they hiccuped their way into history?"

"Sir, that's the best autobiography I ever heard!" I said enthusiastically.

Master Li's reputation was still considerable, although tainted with a questionable aroma, and our soil and plant samples were given priority at the Academy of Divination and Alchemic Research. Then he set out again, climbing to Imperial City and the great palaces of the bureaucrats. Again I was overawed as I gazed to the top of the hill and Palace City, where the imperial family lived, and then the Gate of the Cinnabar Phoenix, which led to the Great Luminous Palace of Emperor T'ang T'ai-tung. Master Li wasn't going that high, however. He turned toward a building that made my blood turn cold: the Gate of the Beautiful Vista, which is the headquarters of the Secret Service and which was surrounded by straw mannequins with the flayed hides of corrupt officials wrapped around them. (The emperor had been busy cleaning house since he took over, and Master Li thoroughly approved of T'ang.)

Fortunately Master Li was heading toward a smaller palace next door, and I looked forward to meeting a legendary lady.

The Captain of Prostitutes is the most powerful woman in China, except when an Empress sits upon the throne. Her guild is the heart and soul of espionage, and almost entirely responsible for probing the mysterious minds of barbarians. Couriers constantly gallop from her palace with coded messages for the Bower of Brilliant Companions in Hangchow, or the Sun-Bright Residence in Loyang, or the Pavilion of Increasing Perfection in Peking, and many a powerful official has shared his bed and secrets with a young lady and awakened to find the lady gone, and in her place an official pouch containing the yellow scarf.

I expected a long wait for an audience, but Master Li presented his business card, and in a matter of minutes we were ushered into the presence of the great lady herself. She was tall and middle-aged and very beautiful, and her voice was an exquisite musical instrument.

"Most exalted and venerable of sages," she said, bowing to the floor.

"Most lovely of earthbound goddesses," Master Li purred, matching her bow.

That sort of thing lasted several minutes, and then we were served tea, and I sat like a turd in a truffle shop while they played the game of social shuttlecock. I have never been able to understand why perfectly sensible people waste time being wittily obscure instead of just saying what they want and going on about their business. The Captain of Prostitutes began the game by strewing a few flower petals over the golden surface of the tea.

"Dear friend, these flowers will die from loneliness, since I appear to be out of butterflies," she said ruefully.

Master Li caught the shuttlecock in midair.

"Alas! No flower can be complete unless accompanied by butterflies. Just as hills must have springs, and rocks must have moss," he said.

"What is a stream without cress in it? What are tall trees without creepers? What are men without the mind of Li Kao?" she said musically.

Master Li bowed at the compliment. "Women," he said, delicately brushing her wrist with a fingertip, "cannot be complete without the expression of a flower, the voice of a bird, the posture of the willow, the bones of jade, the skin of snow, the charm of an autumn lake, the heart of poetry, and the soul of my lovely hostess."

"Invincible charmer," she said with a sigh. Her eyes lowered to the old wrinkled finger upon her delicate wrist. "Passion, dear friend, displays but the bottom end of the universe," she chided.

"Then it is the job of the poet to give it a new dress!" cried Master Li. "Shall I sing of mountains clothed in clouds, or pines dressed in wind, or willows adorned in rain, or terraces attired in moonbeams?"

The captain served more tea and flower petals. "One must be careful in one's attire," she said. "Sometimes it is too easily removed, and at other times it cannot be removed at all. Green hills are reflected in water which borrows its color from the hills. Good wine produces poetry which borrows its beauty from the wine."

"And a beautiful woman," Master Li cooed, "is like a poem in that she is best seen when one is slightly drunk. If a mere man may appropriate a lovely lady's train of thought, pale clouds become multicolored when they reflect the sun, and placid currents become falls when they pass over a cliff. Things acquire the characteristics of associates, and that is why friendship is so valued, and why one's friends must be carefully chosen."

She caressed his wrinkled hand. "Then I shall choose as my friend an ancient unyielding rock," she said.

"And if the rock is but a dream?"

"Then I shall be a shadow in the dream," she said softly.

Master Li swallowed his tea and leaned back and did some mental addition. "Ten points each?"

The Captain of Prostitutes fined herself a slap on a cheek. "No, I misquoted," she said. "Chang Chou wrote that passion 'holds up' the bottom end of the universe, and I said 'displays.' Eight points at most."

"That means I only owe you sixty-six," Master Li said.

"Sixty-seven," she said firmly. "Well, Kao, what can I do for you?"

"Direct me to a sound-master," he said. "I hear that you play host to the best when he's in town."

She nodded. "Moon Boy," she said matter-of-factly. "Ever hear him?"

"No, but I'm told he's a phenomenon the likes of which are seen once in a thousand years," Master Li said.

"Frankly, I doubt that there has ever been a sound-master to match Moon Boy," she said. "How badly do you need him?"

"Very badly. I've run up against something that has me baffled."

She leaned back and regarded him with narrowed eyes. "Moon Boy isn't here at the moment," she said. "Nobody in his right mind would accept an invitation to perform for the King of Chao, but Moon Boy went off with a song on his lips."

Master Li whistled. The captain was all business now. "The king isn't the problem. You can handle that twelve-chinned wonder if anyone can, but handling Moon Boy is another matter."

"I've heard he's a bit difficult to control," Master Li murmured.

"Multiply what you've heard by a thousand," she said. "However, I can loan you the one person in the world who can lead him around like a little lamb."

She rang a bell and whispered to the servant who appeared, and he trotted away.

"What would you want in return?" Master Li asked.

"Your influence and writing brush," she said, and she stood up and began pacing the floor like a man, smacking a fist into the palm of the other hand.

"Li Kao, impatience is not pleasing to Heaven, but it's been nearly two thousand years since our guild received celestial signs indicating that our patron diety had been replaced, and we're getting impatient. We lost the protection of Golden Lotus, the greatest whore the world has ever known, and not one of the substitute dieties we've been saddled with could lift a customer's purse if he was dead drunk and stuck headfirst in a barrel of molasses," the captain said angrily. "Now nothing is going right! The court keeps us tied up with Secret Service work that pays practically nothing, and there have been eight outbreaks of pox in the last five months, and now the palace eunuchs are trying to divert the emperor's attention from their activities by starting another morality campaign. Golden Lotus wouldn't have stood for it!" the captain said passionately. "She'd have marched from star to star across the Great River and demanded an audience with the August Personage of Jade! We need a patron with her kind of guts, not an obsequious blob of suet."

She whirled around and swept a delicate porcelain teacup from the table and watched it smash on the floor.

"Li Kao, I'll loan you the girl who can control Moon Boy for as long as you need her, and all I ask in return is that you petition the imperial court to make a formal request to Heaven for a new Patron of Prostitutes."

"You overestimate my influence at court," Master Li said wryly.

"You underestimate my ability at blackmail," she replied. "The emperor can't ignore a petition from Master Li, and I'll see to it that an army of priests and bureaucrats falls in behind you. Besides, our candidate will be one of the emperor's predecessors, and he wouldn't want to disturb the dear lady's ghost."

Master Li sat up straight. "You don't mean Empress Wu?" he said incredulously.

"Who would be better qualified?" the captain asked. "She bounced from bed to bed all the way to the throne, and why should she fry in Hell when she can do something useful in Heaven?"

"Dear lady, you'd be asking the Emperor of Heaven to accept as a junior minister a tyrant who poisoned her sister, her niece, and one of her sons!" Master Li exclaimed. "She forced another son to hang himself, had three grandsons and a granddaughter whipped to death, executed two stepsons and had all sixteen of their male progeny decapitated, strangled thirty-six senior ministers, and wiped out three thousand entire families. In addition, she turned out to be one of the cleverest and ablest rulers China ever had, and she acquired the throne so smoothly, her rivals never knew what hit them. The August Personage of Jade will accept letters of office from Empress Wu the moment he accepts mine to be Patron of Teetotalers."

The captain looked at him in silence for a moment, and then extended her hands in a charming gesture of offering a gift.

"The guild has authorized me to take whatever steps are necessary, and I hereby pass that authorization to you," she said. "Li Kao, you have been known to occasionally catch the ear of Heaven. If the opportunity arises, you may handle the situation as you think best, keeping in mind that our patron must be tough, smart, quick, remorseless, and blessed with the moral principles of a rutting angleworm. It's a damn shame you yourself happen to be the wrong sex."

Master Li stood up and bowed. "Never have I received a greater compliment," he said sincerely.

I looked at the gleams in their eyes and groaned inwardly. They were about to begin another game of shuttlecock, but just then the servant reappeared with a young lady in tow. She was small and lithe and pretty, but not pretty enough to make me feel like a pig at a peacock convention, and the captain looked at her fondly.

"This is Grief of Dawn, who will never make a good whore," she said. "Her heart is too tender, but fortunately, it's the only tender spot she has. She's tough and capable and far too experienced for her years, and you won't need to worry about traveling with her."

She turned to the girl. "This is the notorious Master Li and his assistant, Number Ten Ox. They need Moon Boy. Prying him loose from the King of Chao will be his responsibility, and yours will be keeping Moon Boy in line until he does what must be done."

Grief of Dawn bowed. She undid her hair clasp and handed it to Master Li. "Moon Boy and I are as one," she said simply. "With me he will stay, but with anyone else he will fly away upon the first breeze."

Master Li examined the clasp and nodded appreciatively. Grief of Dawn politely extended it to me, and I saw the interlocking yin-yang motif of phoenix and dragon. She turned it over to show the interlocking names of Grief of Dawn and Moon Boy, and her hand happened to brush mine. I don't know if my reaction was visible in Hangchow, but the captain's eyebrows nearly lifted off her head.

"Is he always this susceptible?" she asked.

"Well, I've never before seen his ears emit puffs of smoke," Master Li said judiciously.

"Get a bucket of water," the captain said to the servant.

"No need," I said in a high strangled voice. "Just choking on a flower petal from the tea."

Grief of Dawn's eyes were startled and wary, but there was a hint of a smile in them. She discreetly moved to the other side of the room. The flower petal excuse fooled nobody, and here I think I should insert a tirade I have heard many times from Master Li. It's the only way to begin to explain my reaction to Grief of Dawn.

The great dream of bureaucrats and most aristocrats is to return to the best of all possible worlds: the rigid feudalism so prettily praised by Confucius. The key is the total subjugation of peasants, and some of the methods are very ingenious. One of the best has been the establishment of a dowry system that requires a bride to be accompanied into her new home with a substantial gift of money or land.

In practical terms it means that peasants who are cursed with an overload of daughters must choose between starvation or infanticide. The girls can't quite pay their own way in the fields. The parents can't afford to keep them and can't marry them off—the only thing left is to drown them at birth, which allows aristocrats to screech, "What inhuman callousness! Who can argue that mere pigs should be allowed to own their pigpens?" Peasant girls who are kept alive soon learn that they are starving their own parents and that marriage is out of the question, and if they are at all pretty, they often run away and become prostitutes in order to send a little money home. This allows bureaucrats to bellow, "Look at the immoral sluts! Who can argue that such swine should have any legal rights at all?" It's a marvelous system, without a flaw, and those who say that some of the sluts could teach the bureaucrats a few things about morality will be given a fish hook, a knife, a candle, and unlimited time in which to mend their manners in a swamp in Siam.

When my hand brushed Grief of Dawn's, I felt calluses. It would take years for the hard lines to soften completely, and from my point of view they were prettier than pearls. That doesn't explain it completely, of course, but one thing was certain. I was in love.

Master Li was grinning at me. "Ah, if only I could be ninety again," he said nostalgically. "Ox, try to keep your paws off the young lady while we're traveling. Grief of Dawn, hit him over the head with a log every now and then. He will be grateful for the attention."

"We have a pact?" said the Captain of Prostitutes.

"We have a pact," said Master Li. "I promise nothing, but I shall do my best for Empress Wu, and, should that fail, do everything possible to get you a competent patron. Can you blackmail somebody at the postal service? We're in something of a hurry."

"It shall be done," said the Captain of Prostitutes.

The sun was just lifting over Serpentine Park when Master Li and I arrived at the postal service stables. Grief of Dawn was waiting for us. She had chosen clothes that indicated experience in serious traveling: boy's tough trousers, high leather boots, a tunic made to withstand thorns as well as raindrops, and an oiled rain hat. The rest of her clothes and possessions were neatly stored in a pack on her back. Master Li approved, and his approval rating jumped ten points when she walked to her horse and slid the bow from the saddle holster and grimaced at the pull. She went through six or seven different bows before finding one that suited her, and when she swung up to the saddle, I knew she was a far better rider than I was. I'm only comfortable upon a water buffalo. Meanwhile, I was strutting around like a peacock.

Only somebody with the influence of the Captain of Prostitutes could have arranged it. I had an official cap and tunic emblazoned with imperial dragons, and a message pouch sealed with the emblem of state. Master Li showed me how to fix the butt of the flagpole into the cup beside the stirrup. The gates swung open and I managed a respectable blast on my silver trumpet and we galloped out in a cloud of dust, scattering pedestrians quite satisfactorily. I even made the turn without falling off.

Master Li let me set the pace—to get it out of my system, I suppose—and I exhilarated in the kind of speed that is only possible for those who ride beneath the flag of the gyrfalcon. The horse stations were positioned every few miles, and I would raise the trumpet and blow "alert," and then "three horses," and we would ride up to grooms holding fresh horses and swing from one mount to the other without touching the ground, and then be off again as though the fate of the empire depended upon it. That lasted one day. After that we traveled a good deal slower because my rear end was almost as sore as the insides of my thighs. Master Li could still ride with the best of them, and Grief of Dawn might have been born on a horse, and I was grateful to them for not laughing when I hobbled around our camp at night.

When the route led downstream beside a major river, we would ride our horses onto a postal service barge and let the current do the work. Those were the best times. I had a chance to talk to Grief of Dawn. She was pure peasant, just as I thought, and we learned that she had no memory of her life until she was about eighteen. She had been found by an old lady she called Tai-tai ("great-great"), unconscious and covered with blood, and the old lady had taken her in and treated her as a daughter. It had been early in the morning, so Tai-tai named the girl Grief of Dawn. Master Li examined a deep round indentation in her skull and said that somebody had certainly tried to kill her, and it was a wonder all she had lost was her memory.

He had no objection to my telling her about the case we were on, so long as I made no mention of the tomb, and she was fascinated to hear about Lady Hou, the Thunderballed princess in One-Eyed Wong's, because she knew and loved some of her poems. The bargemen always had musical instruments. At night we would play and Grief of Dawn would sing peasant songs so old that not even Master Li knew them, and one night she adapted one of Lady Hou's poems to our circumstances and sang it for us. I will include it here as a matter of interest for those who may not have encountered the deceptively simple art of Lady Hou.

> *"Tonight no wind blows on the river.*
> *The water is still and dark,*
> *No waves or ripples.*
> *All around the barge*
> *Moonlight floats in air;*
> *Acres of smooth lustrous jade.*
>
> *"Master Li breaks the silence.*
> *High on wine he lifts his flute,*
> *Playing into the mist.*
> *Strange music rises to the stars;*
> *Apes in the mountains*
> *Screaming at the moon,*
> *A stream rushing through a gorge.*
> *Ox accompanies on his sheepskin drum;*
> *Head held like a mountain peak,*
> *Fingers beating like raindrops.*
>
> *"A fish breaks the surface of the water*
> *And leaps ten feet into the air."**

When we got to land again we galloped through villages where children with huge dreaming eyes gathered to watch us pass (who

* Officially attributed to Yang Wan-li.

hasn't imagined himself as a legendary hero of the postal service?), and through narrow mountain passes where bandits with hyena faces snarled at the flag of the gyrfalcon and drew back in fear. That may give the impression that imperial control was total, but such was not the case.

"My children, there are corners of the empire where the emperor is little more than a figurehead, and we're approaching one of them," Master Li said. "In the Kingdom of Chao there is only one ruler, and his name is Shih Hu."

Master Li threw out his hands in an admiring gesture so wide he nearly fell from his horse.

"What a man! He's been on the throne for twenty-eight years without making a major mistake, which approaches the supernatural. He stands six feet seven and weighs more than four hundred pounds, and enemies who assume his bulk is blubber soon decorate pikes on his walls with their severed heads. He's loved by his people, feared by his rivals, adored by his women, and Grief of Dawn will have something to think about when she sees his bodyguards."

He winked at her. "They're beautiful young women who wear uniforms of sable and carry golden bows," he explained. "I'd rather go up against a pack of panthers than the Golden Girls. They worship their king, and perhaps he deserves it. Chao is the best-governed state in the civilized world, but you must never forget that the king himself is not civilized. Shih Hu was born a barbarian, and his soul remains barbarian. His violence can be sudden and extreme, and his palace is hard to get into and even harder to get out of."

He rode on in silence for a few minutes.

"So far as I know, the king has only one weakness," Master Li said thoughtfully. "He avidly collects people with unusual talents, and I rather think he might open his gates to a living legend. Somebody like the world's greatest master of the Wen-Wu lute."

Grief of Dawn and I looked at each other. The Wen-Wu is the hardest instrument in the world to play properly, and we shrugged our shoulders.

"Venerable Sir, can you play the thing?" I inquired.

He looked at us in surprise. "What does playing it have to do with being the world's greatest master?" he said.

石

10

The great banquet hall of King Shih Hu was hushed and expectant. Minutes passed. Then the doors flew open and flunkies in sumptuous attire marched inside and blew mighty blasts on trumpets. They were followed by a parade of priests chanting hymns in praise of a master whose genius had surely been bestowed by the hand of Heaven itself. Then an army of acolytes pranced prettily through the doors, strewing rose petals hither and yon. Then came two senior apprentices: a fabulously wealthy young man who had abandoned all worldly goods to sit at the feet of the master, and a princess of the royal blood who had abandoned a throne. The princess carried a small ivory stool, and the young man carried a simple unadorned lute upon a silken pillow.

Priests and acolytes continued their hymns. Minutes passed slowly. Just when the suspense had become unbearable, there was a soft shuffle of sandals, and several distinguished guests swooned when the world's greatest master of the Wen-Wu lute tottered through the doors.

He was at least a thousand years old and semidivine. A thick beard whiter than snow fell down and brushed his ankles, and his enormous white eyebrows lifted like the fierce tufts of a horned owl. His coarse peasant robe was woven from the cheapest cloth, and his sandals had been patched at least fifty times. Green leaves still sprouted from his freshly cut oak staff. Disdain for worldly matters was written all over him, and he was matted with mud from a hillside where he had slept beneath the stars.

The great man slowly shuffled across the floor to the ivory stool, and the princess reverently lowered him to a sitting position. The young man knelt and placed the lute upon the master's lap. For what appeared to be an eternity the saint gazed down, silently communing with the instrument, and then his head slowly lifted. Piercing black eyes burned holes through the audience. A wrinkled finger lifted, and the wrinkled voice that emerged from the beard was like the drone of a pedagogical bee, yet vibrant with authority.

"The Wen-Wu lute," the great man said, "was invented by Fu-hsi, who saw a meteor land in a tung tree. Soon afterward a phoenix landed beside the meteor, and when the meteor fizzled out with a melodic hiss and the phoenix flew away with a contrapuntal cry, Fu-hsi realized that he had been granted a sign from Heaven. He felled the tree, which was precisely thirty-three feet long, and cut it into three eleven-foot pieces. These pieces he soaked in running water for seventy-three days, one fifth of a year. He tapped the top piece, but the pitch was too high. He tapped the bottom piece, but the pitch was too low. He tapped the middle piece, and the pitch was just right."

One of the banqueters sneezed, and the master raised a white eyebrow. Flunkies, priests, acolytes, and apprentices descended upon the wretch and pitched him out the door. After two minutes of glowering silence, the master condescended to continue.

"Fu-hsi commissioned Liu Tzu-ch'i, the greatest artisan in China, to fashion the middle piece into a musical instrument. It was precisely thirty-six inches long, corresponding to the three hundred sixty degrees of a circle, four inches wide at the rear end, corresponding to the four seasons, eight inches wide at the front end, corresponding to the eight festivals, and its uniform height of two inches corresponded to yin and yang, the generative forces of the universe. Twelve stops were intended to correspond to the twelve moons of the year, but Fu-hsi later added a thirteenth stop to account for leap year."

One of the banqueters coughed, and the master raised the other eyebrow. Flunkies, priests, acolytes, and apprentices descended upon the wretch and pitched him out a window. It was three minutes before the ancient demigod condescended to continue.

"The five original strings," he wheezed, searing the cowering assembly with flaming eyes, "corresponded to the five elements:

metal, wood, water, earth, and fire; the five temperaments: quietude, nervousness, strength, hardness, and wisdom; and the five musical tones: kung, shang, chueh, cheng, and yu. When King Wen of Chou was imprisoned at Chiangli, his son, Prince Pai-yi-k'ao, was so grieved that he added a sixth string to express his sorrow. This is called the Wen string, and it produces a low melancholy sound. When King Wu launched a military campaign against King Cheo, he was so pleased at going to war that he added a seventh string to express his joy. This is called the Wu string, and it produces a high heroic sound. Thus the lute of seven strings is called the Wen-Wu lute, and in the hands of a performer of talent it can tame the most ferocious beast. In the hands of a performer of genius it can start or stop a war. In the hands of a performer such as myself it can raise the dead."

The great man paused. Flunkies, priests, acolytes, and apprentices peered around for sneezers or coughers. Nobody breathed. The great man continued.

"The proper tone possesses eight qualities: clarity, wonder, remoteness, sadness, eloquence, manliness, softness, and extensibility, but the tone will suffer under any of six conditions: bitter cold, extreme heat, strong wind, heavy storm, noisy thunder, or swirling snow, and the Wen-Wu lute must never be played under any of seven circumstances: mourning the dead, simultaneous playing with orchestra, preoccupation with worldly matters, uncleanliness of body, untidiness of costume, failure to burn incense in advance, and lack of an appreciative audience."

The audience held its collective breath as the demigod slowly raised the lute from his lap. He plucked a string: *plink!* He plucked a second string: *plonk!* He returned the lute to his lap.

"I," he announced, "am currently mourning my wife, secondary wives, concubines, children, grandchildren, great-grandchildren, and pet parakeet, all of whom perished during a typhoon. The snoring of those louts in the corner constitutes playing with orchestra. The leering moron in the blue robe is more interested in dancing girls than in art. Half of you haven't washed in a month, and the other half have spilled soup on your robes. I fail to perceive the slightest trace of incense, and to call this collection of oafs an appreciative audience would be to provoke the gods into howls of hysterical laughter."

The world's greatest master of the Wen-Wu lute slowly rose to his feet. The forefinger of his left hand lifted. *"However."* A divine nimbus appeared to envelop the awesome figure. Six more green leaves appeared to sprout from the staff as his fingers closed around it. "My period of mourning ends in two days, and if the other factors are rectified, I may possibly grant you a performance. In the meantime you may direct me to my suite. See that I am not disturbed, for I wish to contemplate the phenomenon of human fallibility."

The great man shuffled slowly from the room, accompanied by a series of dull thuds as distinguished guests fainted and toppled to the floor.

"Fraud, my children! Fraud and forgery. Dry rot covered with paint and gilded with lies," Master Li declaimed. He tossed the Wen-Wu lute to a hook on the wall: *plunk.* "A fool will study for twenty or thirty years and learn how to do something, but a wise man will study for twenty or thirty minutes and become an expert. In this world it isn't ability that counts, but authority."

"Sir, you're doing wonders for my education," I said.

"And mine," Grief of Dawn said admiringly.

"What do we do now?" I asked.

"Wait to be arrested," Master Li said matter-of-factly. "I didn't fool the king for a moment, of course, but I hope I entertained him. What did you think of the Golden Girls?"

Of the king I had seen only a vast shape looming in the shadows, but his bodyguards had been very visible.

"They're beautiful," Grief of Dawn said. "Beautiful and dangerous. Did you see the captain? She worships the king and can't wait to kill to prove it."

Master Li nodded. "Be very careful when we're summoned to his majesty's presence. Was Moon Boy there?"

"No, sir," said Grief of Dawn.

The suite was enormous, with a number of private bedchambers connected to bathing rooms that made my eyes bulge almost as wide as Grief of Dawn's. There were jade-tiled tubs that one could sit in while warm water poured from the mouths of nine-headed bronze dragons. There was soap made from perfumed Fenglai peas, and thick velvet towels, and the water exited through the mouths of nine-headed bronze tortoises. In the central suite were racks containing beautiful paintings in rich brocade cases with jade-tipped scroll unrollers, and an entire wall was covered with books. The inkstone on the desk had the most perfect purple eyespots I had ever seen, and Master Li said it was a genuine Tuan from Ling-lang Gorge. His nose led him to a cabinet that contained wines from every corner of the empire, and he selected a jar and moved to the windows.

He was studying the layout of the castle. A deep moat ran between two high parallel stone walls, and anyone crossing the drawbridge was stopped at three checkpoints. Getting out was not going to be easy, and I was not cheered by King Shih Hu's idea of decoration. The walls were lined with pikes holding severed heads, and a row of bare pikes had nameplates beneath them—bandit chiefs, I learned, who would sooner or later join the decorative scheme.

"They're here," Grief of Dawn whispered.

I hadn't heard a door open, but I turned to see six of the Golden Girls and the captain. The captain had the eyes of an eagle, fierce and pitiless, and she gestured commandingly. Master Li held up a hand.

"Would you mind if I remove this atrocious thing first? I'm either going to strangle in it or trip over it."

He removed his fake white beard, and then his huge eyebrows. The Golden Girls escorted us outside and down a maze of marble corridors. We approached a pair of very pretty lacquered doors that stood fourteen feet high, and they swung open to reveal the most beautiful room I had ever seen.

It was big enough for five village dances and a riot. Various sections were curtained off by shimmering screens of falling water that flowed into pools where brightly colored fish swam. Skylights let sunbeams play over magnificent rocks that had been left as nature had placed them, and the air was rich with the scent of growing flowers. In the center of the room was a boulder of bluish-green stone that needed only a cushion to become a throne, and upon it sat Shih-Hu, King of Chao.

The closer we came, the huger he grew. His eyes were small bright dots in the vast expanse of his face, and I was relieved to see a suggestion of a twinkle in them. We knelt and performed the three

obeisances and nine kowtows, and he signaled for us to rise. His
voice was soft, with thunder rumbling beneath it.

"We prefer you without the beard," he said to Master Li. "It was
rather overdone, although we cannot fault you for allowing artistry
to overpower reality. It was a superb performance."

Master Li bowed.

"Who are you and what do you want?"

"Your Majesty, my surname is Li and my personal name is Kao,
and there is a slight flaw in my character," Master Li said politely.
"This is my esteemed former client and current assistant, Number
Ten Ox, and the lovely young lady is Grief of Dawn. With your
permission, she would like to show Your Majesty her hair clasp."

Grief of Dawn removed the clasp and handed it to the Captain of
Bodyguards, who examined it for sharp points and poison before
passing it to the king. He examined the interlocking phoenix and
dragon and turned it over and read the names. He whispered to one
of the Golden Girls, who bowed and left the room.

"Grief of Dawn wishes to see Moon Boy again, and I saw no
reason why I should not help her enter the palace," Master Li said
smoothly. "As for my own interest, I am seeking a manuscript. I
wish only to read it, not take it, and I have heard that Your Majesty
is the greatest collector of rare things. I took the liberty of a harmless deceit to gain entrance, and I have a small fragment of the
manuscript in question."

He handed the fragment of the Ssu-ma to the captain, who
checked it over and handed it to the king. I began to warm to the
huge monarch when I saw the obvious incomprehension on his face.
He could no more read ancient scholar's shorthand than I could.
He shrugged and handed it back to the captain, who passed it to
Master Li.

"It means nothing to us," he said. "Your information is slightly
inaccurate. We do indeed collect the rare, but our interest is not in
things but in people. Here is the jewel of our collection."

The Golden Girl stepped from behind one of the screens of falling
water accompanied by a young man, and Grief of Dawn forgot
protocol completely and let out a squeal of joy and ran toward him.
The young man whooped happily and met her halfway, and the two
of them blended together in an embrace so tight that I had the
impression of a single body with two heads. I assume that my com-

plexion was bright green, and the grinding of my teeth was probably audible in Soochow.

Nobody had any right to look like Moon Boy, who was the handsomest man in the whole world. In addition, he would have put a peacock to shame. He wore a purple cap embroidered with gold and trimmed with jewels. Circling his forehead was a silver band with the same phoenix-dragon motif as Grief of Dawn's clasp, and the same names were probably interlocked on the back. Around his neck was a golden chain twisted in the form of coupling snakes, and his dark red tunic was embroidered with bright flowers and butterflies. The tunic was secured by a belt woven into a design of flower stems and ears of corn, and over the tunic he wore a blue satin cloak fringed with gold. His gold-embroidered shoes were also of blue satin, and the maddening thing was that none of the finery was overdone. Moon Boy was all of a *piece,* and the only thing missing was applause. The damned creature was destined to ride through the world in a shower of rose petals while Number Ten Ox pitched manure in a barnyard.

They finally broke apart. The king gestured. Moon Boy led Grief of Dawn up to the throne, and with great gentleness the King of Chao reached down and picked up first Moon Boy and then Grief of Dawn and placed them upon his vast lap.

"What charming children you are," he said. He kissed Moon Boy's cheek. "This is the most special of all my special people, and clearly he shares his soul with Grief of Dawn. Why should that be?" He gently tilted Grief of Dawn's chin and looked deep into her eyes. "Are you special too, my child?" For a long time he studied her, and then he said, almost whispering, "Yes. In you is something very like the strange inner core of Moon Boy, although he is not properly named. He is more like the sun, and it is you who are more like the moon. One cannot look directly at the sun without being blinded, so wise men study the sun by looking at the moon."

The king suddenly smiled, and it was breathtaking. His smile was as open and spontaneous as that of a child, but there was a strange hint of yearning and melancholy to it, and he delicately lifted her free hair and replaced the clasp.

"Would you like to wear a uniform of sable and carry a golden bow?" he asked softly. Then he chuckled. "That is not a fair question, of course, and you are not forced to reply. None of our girls has ever been forced. Grief of Dawn, we want you, but we shall court you as we have courted all the others, and the decision will be yours alone to make."

He effortlessly picked up both of them and placed them back upon the floor. His eyes moved to Master Li.

"Even this humble orphan has heard of the astonishing Li Kao, whose achievements are said to be without limit," the king said graciously. "There is much we would like to discuss with you, and we look forward to the enlightenment of your wisdom. One day you may even confide in us the real purpose of your visit, but there is no hurry. You have brought us Grief of Dawn, for which we are deeply grateful. She shall be our honored guest, and may your own visit be a long one."

A flick of a royal finger dismissed us. We bowed backward from the throne room. The chamberlain directed us back to our suite, where a splendid repast was waiting.

"Master Li, did he mean what I thought he meant?" I asked.

"That Grief of Dawn and I have just joined his collection of special people? I hope so," Master Li said cheerfully. "Well, my love, are you ready for gold and sable?"

Grief of Dawn blushed and lowered her eyes. "What an extraordinary man," she whispered.

I didn't realize just how extraordinary the king was until late that night. I awoke just after the third watch. Musical instruments were playing somewhere. I slipped into my tunic and stumbled out to the central room, yawning and rubbing my eyes, and I discovered that Grief of Dawn had heard it also and was standing at the window overlooking a garden.

It was the Golden Girls. Instead of bows they carried lutes and pipas, and they played very well. Then a great dark shape moved from the shadows, and the King of Chao stepped out into the bright moonlight. He was absolute monarch. He could take whatever he wanted, but that wasn't his way. Even at a distance I could sense that he was enjoying himself immensely, and he bowed deeply toward Grief of Dawn's bedchamber and then turned to face the moon. The king placed the big toe of his right foot upon the big toe of his left foot and began to sing a love charm from the barbaric country of his birth.

I can't explain it, but it was one of the most impressive things I
have ever seen and heard in my life.

> *"I loose my arrow and the moon clouds over,*
> *I loose it and the sun is extinguished,*
> *I loose it and the stars burn dim,*
> *But it is not the moon, sun, and stars I shoot at.*
> *It is the heart of Grief of Dawn."*

His majesty flapped his arms, imitating some sort of bird, and
began to dance with grace that was accentuated by his huge bulk.
There was nothing funny about it. He was like a vast force of nature, totally incapable of making a fool of himself.

> *"Cluck-cluck! Grief of Dawn, come and walk with me,*
> *Come and sit with me,*
> *Come and sleep and share my pillow.*
> *Cluck-cluck! Grief of Dawn,*
> *When thunder rumbles remember me,*
> *When wind whistles remember me,*
> *When the Red Bird sings remember me,*
> *When you see the moon remember me,*
> *When you see the sun remember me,*
> *When you see the stars remember me.*
> *Cluck-cluck! Grief of Dawn,*
> *Come hither to me,*
> *Let your heart come hither to mine."*

Three times the song charm was repeated, and then his majesty
bowed again toward Grief of Dawn's bedchamber. The Golden
Girls also bowed. Then the king and his girls were gone, blending
into the shadows, and I suppose that my face was rather expressive.
How many young women are courted by a huge, powerful, infinitely
courteous and gentle, yet infinitely barbaric monarch? Sable and
gold awaited Grief of Dawn, not to mention an impossibly handsome young man named Moon Boy.

"Oh, Ox. Poor Ox," Grief of Dawn said softly.

Her hand slipped into mine. "Come and walk with me, come and
sit with me, come and sleep and share my pillow," she whispered.

"Cluck-cluck!" I said.

There are mornings one would prefer to forget.

This one began beautifully, with sunlight sliding through the window and dappling Grief of Dawn's lovely shoulder. I nuzzled her cheek and listened to the lethargic buzz of lazy flies, and a drowsy drone of bees, and the curtains gently rustling in a whispering breeze, and a happy voice that bellowed, *"Come back here, you little bugger!"*

I sat bolt upright.

"Oh, damn," Grief of Dawn sighed plaintively.

A naked boy, perhaps thirteen or fourteen, raced past the window on the veranda.

"Hey, bugger, don't you want the plugger snugger?" the happy voice yelled.

"Ten million curses," Grief of Dawn groaned, smothering a yawn.

A naked young man galloped past the window after the boy, stopped, trotted back, and stuck his head inside the room.

"Good morning, my love!" Moon Boy said cheerfully.

"Why must you waste that thing on boys?" she said.

He glanced down complacently at his crotch. "Waste? What do you mean waste? You know very well that some of the little darlings can't sit down for a month." Moon Boy climbed through the window and sauntered up to the bed. "My, you've certainly picked a splendid specimen this time. Congratulations!"

I hastily jerked the covers up to my shoulders.

"You're Number Ten Ox, aren't you? Where did you get that divine nose? Looks like a cow stepped on it," Moon Boy said.

"Er . . . A slight disagreement with Big Hong the blacksmith," I mumbled.

"I trust he received a decent funeral," Moon Boy said, and then he sat down on the side of the bed and began caressing Grief of Dawn's right thigh. "Speaking of funerals, I once saw Master Li during one of his black periods," he said. "He wouldn't remember me. I was in the back row at court waiting to give my first imperial performance, and this wicked old man kowtowed to the emperor, got to his feet, whipped a knife from his sleeve, and cut the throat of the Minister of Trade. Blood all over the place."

"Moon Boy, is that true?" Grief of Dawn said skeptically.

"Every word. When the emperor learned the motive for the may-

hem, he couldn't decide whether to boil Master Li in oil or make
him a duke, but it was academic because the old man had already
escaped to Turkestan. Shortly thereafter the High Priest of Samarkand was found with his nose caressing the sole of his left foot,
which says something about the condition of his spine, and when
the bailiffs paid a call on Master Li, they found he'd suddenly been
called to the sickbed of a great-granddaughter in Serendip."

I was used to Master Li stories, only a tiny fraction of which are
even marginally true, but I was not used to hearing one from a
revoltingly beautiful young man who climbed stark naked through
the bedroom window and began stroking my girl's bare leg. Now he
was stroking her left breast, and taking her into his arms.

"I've missed you," he said softly.

"How I love you," she whispered.

The king was wrong about Moon Boy's name. He was perfectly
named, I decided, because the moon is inhabited by a large white
rabbit, and everybody knows that rabbits are notorious perverts.

"Why not give up boys for a week and try me?" Grief of Dawn
whispered.

In addition, I decided, he moved like a cat, and Master Li once
said that certain Egyptians say that a cat lives in the moon, and
everybody knows that the soul of a cat is formed from the compos-
ite souls of nine debauched nuns who failed in their vows.

"Come away with me," Grief of Dawn whispered.

"Darling, I'd like nothing better, but his majesty is a wee bit
possessive," he said.

"Master Li will take care of that. He has a job for you, and that
boy you were chasing resembles a Swatow sea slug."

"Tell the wicked old man I accept. I shall pack a few essential
clothes and jewels—you must *see* the emerald the king gave me—
and kiss the lads farewell."

The lad on the balcony had realized he was no longer being
chased, and was coughing self-consciously outside the window.
Moon Boy was up with a smooth feline motion.

"Work, work, work," he complained. "Why must one's responsi-
bilities always interfere with one's pleasures? Still, duty is duty."

With a catlike bound he was at the window, and with another he
was out of it. *"Come back here, you little bugger!"* he yelled, and he
was gone.

Grief of Dawn smiled and settled back in my arms. "Well, now you've met Moon Boy," she said. "Slightly larger than life, isn't he?"

"Will he come to visit after we're married?" I asked apprehensively.

She looked at me gravely. "Ox, I can never get married," she said. "Moon Boy and I think that we were part of the same soul, and somehow it was split on the Great Wheel of Incarnations, and a piece of it is still missing. Apart we're nothing, and even when we're together we aren't complete. We wander the world, Ox, searching for the missing piece, and I can never settle down until I find it."

I wanted to argue about that, but Grief of Dawn had a better idea. We were getting back to where we started before the interruption, and things warmed up nicely, and it appeared that the morning would be saved after all.

"Good morning, my children!" Master Li said happily as he trotted into the room. "Why is it that the most delightful of physical positions to the participants is an aesthetic abomination to onlookers?"

We managed to get separated, and Master Li took Moon Boy's position on the side of the bed.

"Your absurdly good-looking young man just galloped lewdly past my window," he said to Grief of Dawn. "I've never been much for hopping into bed with boys, but if I could be ninety again, I'd be delighted to make an exception with him. Buddha, what a creature! Has he agreed?"

"Yes, sir," she said.

"Good. I want to get out of here as fast as possible. Ox, Grief of Dawn, I want you to find the highest point in the castle you can reach, with the best view of the courtyards and walls."

"Yes, sir," I said.

"This evening Moon Boy is scheduled to perform, and after that the Golden Girls will put on a show. Nobody will pay attention to young lovers walking by the lakes in the gardens. How long would it take you to get a sackful of toads and two sackfuls of lanternflies?"

"Not long," I said. "An hour or two."

"Splendid," said Master Li. "Plan to slip out and collect them just after Moon Boy's performance, and with any luck we'll be out of here before midnight. In the meantime, enjoy yourselves."

Grief of Dawn and I lay back. Dogs were barking and cats were yowling and roosters were crowing and grooms were swearing and cooks were screaming. We got up and dressed and went out to find the highest vantage point.

石

11

About an hour later we were able to report to Master Li that there were two accessible turrets with good views of the castle and walls, and he explained to us that bandit gangs crossed through Chao at this time of the year to reach their mountain hideouts before the rainy season made the roads impassable, and Shih Hu's favorite sport was massacring bandit gangs.

"He leads his troops personally, and he's renowned for being out of his castle and on the attack within minutes," Master Li explained. "The drawbridges are slow and cumbersome. I want to know whether or not he uses them, and my bet is that he has some other exit."

We had nothing to do until evening except mingle with the distinguished guests. Master Li huddled with Grief of Dawn and sent her out wearing her dusty travel clothes, with a wicked dagger in her belt and her bow over her shoulder and her hair bound by a leather cord apparently jerked from a broken bridle. Her hair clasp was polished like an emperor's adornment and pinned to the front of her sweat-stained tunic, and if ever there was a wild warrior princess, it was Grief of Dawn. She was besieged by admirers. I got close enough to hear her explain—apparently Master Li's suggestion—that she was searching for her brother, who had been transformed by an evil shaman and was wandering through the woods in the form of a tiger, with his matching clasp around his furry neck. After that I couldn't get within forty feet of her, so I wandered off.

King Shih Hu's special people were all over, and Master Li got into a furious argument with the world's greatest astronomer about the direction of currents in the Great River of Stars during the rainy season: "neo-Chang Hengian epicycles" and "Phalguni asterisms" and "reverse *ch'i* concentrations"—I couldn't understand a word of it. I fled to the company of the most beautiful woman in the world and had a very interesting conversation.

She had blond hair and green eyes and said she was a Greek from Bactria. She also said she was sick and tired of being kidnapped by one king after another ever since she had been ten years old, and she would insist upon being buried standing up because she never wanted to see another bed throughout eternity. I liked her very much, although there was a certain tightness at the corners of her eyes and mouth that argued against a close relationship.

I wandered off again and talked with an old man who had a very interesting story to tell, because he had once urinated over the statue of a local Place God when he was drunk, and apparantly the God of Walls and Ditches had been passing by, because the next thing he knew, he was encased in bronze and standing on a pedestal as a *T'u-ti* himself, and there was a terrible drought and the peasants demanded that he bring rain to the fields, and when no rain came, they brought out the ceremonial cudgels and beat him black and blue. He still had some very impressive welts to display. I was pressing him for more details when I heard the drawbridge lower, and then a courier came galloping across it and jumped from his horse and dashed into the palace to report to the king.

Master Li was nodding at me. Grief of Dawn was buried in admirers and couldn't get away, so I made hasty apologies to the former T'u-ti and ran for the stairs. I arrived at my lookout spot just as the king and his Golden Girls came from a side door into a courtyard and entered the stables. I knew that Master Li had been right when I heard the drawbridge raise and slam shut, and several minutes later I blinked at the sight of Shih Hu outside the walls. He was riding on a revolving couch on a great war chariot. He had racks of bows and mountains of arrows within easy reach, and Master Li had told me that he was one of the great archers of the world and would whirl around and around on his couch firing arrows so fast they looked like a waterfall. The Golden Girls rode on horses, and they were followed by foot soldiers jogging in disciplined ranks.

I went back down to report that the king had some kind of exit through the stables. Master Li was delighted.

The afternoon festivities continued with the chamberlain playing host. There were actors and acrobats and Sogdian spin-dance girls who wore crimson pantaloons and performed on top of huge rolling balls. Great mounds of food were brought out. It was half-civilized and half-barbarian. A perfectly traditional dish of ducks' feet and ham steamed with Peking dates and black tree fungus was followed by an exotic Mongolian stew: venison, rabbit, chicken, fish, figs, apples, peaches, curds, butter, spices, and herbs, all boiled together with mounds of sugar candy. I thought it was quite good, but I noticed that both Master Li and Grief of Dawn spat out the sugar candy.

The king and his bodyguards and soldiers returned just as the sun was setting. They were in high spirits, and the soldiers were carrying a new collection of severed heads mounted upon pikes. When the king and the Golden Girls had bathed and changed, it was time for the high point of the festivities: Moon Boy.

I will admit I was skeptical. A person who looked like Moon Boy could announce, "The song of the lark," and then go "quack-quack-quack" and get a standing ovation.

We entered a great stone hall. The chamberlain made a great show of rapping walls and floors to show that there was no trickery involved, and then some servants placed a simple wooden table at one corner of the room. More servants brought in two paper fans, a small jar of water, and four cups, which they placed upon the table. Then Moon Boy appeared. He was carrying a simple sounding board like the ones used by girls in my village, and his eyes searched the audience until he found Grief of Dawn. He gave her a wink, and I assumed he was going to perform something especially for her. The servants unfolded a large screen, blocking out the table, and the lanterns were extinguished until the room was almost dark. There was a buzz of conversation while Moon Boy warmed up, and then there were three sharp raps from behind the screen and the room was hushed.

All I know about sound-masters is that the greatest produce sounds that don't actually exist. Somehow they manage to suggest a sound to the ears of the audience, and the minds of the listeners fill in the rest. Master Li, who had heard the great ones for nearly a

century, later said that Moon Boy would become a legend that
would live ten thousand years, and I had no inclination to argue
with him.

I remember hearing a small soft wind blow and looking around to
see who had opened a window, and then flushing because I realized
it was Moon Boy behind the screen, waving the paper fans. After
that I listened with growing wonder and awe as Moon Boy performed a peasant song for Grief of Dawn. I cannot possibly describe
something that must be heard, but I made quick notes later on, and
I might as well include them here.

Soft breeze carrying night sounds, village sounds . . . Dog
barks loudly, sound seems to be coming in through a window . . .
Man grunts right at my ear, rolls over in bed . . . Barking fades
away, two pairs of sandals passing by window, a laugh and a hiccup
. . . In distance a wine seller calls goodnight and closes his doors
. . . Wind is shifting, blowing from a river . . . Water sounds,
barge poles splashing . . . Faint laughter, a man begins a bawdy
song, words carried away on shifting breeze . . . Dog begins barking again, right in ears, deafening . . . Man swears, gets out of
bed, stumbles toward window . . . Sharp yelp and sound of wood
scraping across floor as he bangs his knee against a table . . . Dog
even louder . . . Man fumbling for something, grunts as he
throws, barks change into yelps and howls, echoing from cottage
walls as dog races away, sound fades . . . Man yelps as hits table
again, crawls back into bed.

Woman sighs and rolls over, whispers to man . . . Man laughs
softly, woman giggles . . . Find myself blushing as soft lovemaking sounds come from bed . . . Lovemaking louder, rhythmic
. . . Baby wakes up and begins to cry, man curses, woman groans
. . . Woman gets up and begins nursing baby, man gets up and
relieves self in chamber pot . . . Boy wakes up and says something
sleepily, man curses and tells boy to get up and relieve self if needs
to . . . Mixture of sounds: man and boy relieving selves, woman
singing softly to baby, baby sucking and cooing, crickets, hoot of
owl, breeze through leaves . . . Boy back to bed, baby back to
sleep, man and woman back to bed, woman whispers, man begins to
snore.

Fire! Voice shouts outside window, other voices join in, every-

body out of bed, baby crying . . . Man yelps as hits table, shouts
out window . . . Voices say something about a barn . . . Feet
milling around outside, sounds of doors opening and closing, clank
of buckets, creak of windlass, man yelps as hits table again . . .
Sandals on, runs outside . . . Clanks and splashes from bucket brigade, flames hissing and roaring . . . Incredible confusion of
sounds: people shouting, horses neighing, donkeys braying, cattle
and oxen lowing, chickens squawking . . . Gates open and thunder of hooves as animals gallop out . . . Old man shouting, "My
hay! My grain!" . . . Woman screams about sparks on her roof.

Something very strange. All sounds of the village seem to be
lifting slowly into the air . . . Twisting, turning . . . As though
August Personage of Jade has reached down to China and picked
up the village and is turning it this way and that in his hand . . . A
slow, quiet, vast puff of breath as though blowing the fire out . . .
Animal sounds die down, bucket and water and fire sounds die
down, shouting and screaming die down . . . Village settling back
down to earth, one sound after another fading away . . . Boy's
sounds fade away, woman's sounds fade away, man's sounds fade
away . . . Baby cooing happily . . . Baby gradually fades away
. . . Silence.

Three sharp raps. The lanterns are lit, the screen is pulled away.
There is nothing but a table and a sounding board and two fans and
a jar of water and four cups, and Moon Boy, who clasps his hands
together and bows.

Grief of Dawn and I slipped away easily while the audience besieged Moon Boy. I had the sacks and sticks and lanterns ready,
and while we caught toads and lanternflies she told me that it was a
good thing we were getting Moon Boy out of there because the soft
life was causing him to lose his voice, particularly in the high regis-
ters, and unless he could find some pretty boys who would give him
a good run across the hills he was going to be nothing but the best,
as opposed to being supernatural.

"Well, he still seems to have a certain ability," I said weakly.

She laughed and kicked me in the shins, and we made our way
back with our bulging sacks. Master Li was waiting for us at the
stables, which was a pity because we couldn't stay and watch the
Golden Girls. It was their turn to perform. The great lawn was as

bright as day with thousands of lanterns, and they were entertaining the guests with a hair-raising game of polo, which I had never seen before. (It had been the rage at court ever since it had been imported from India, but I was not exactly an ornament of the court.) The Captain of Bodyguards was particularly spectacular, because she thought nothing of crashing her horse into another one at forty miles an hour, and as Grief of Dawn watched them I could see that she was yearning for a sable uniform and a polo mallet. I dragged her away.

We had time to decorate toad faces with a little white paint while we waited for Moon Boy. At last he managed to pry himself away from the adoring mob, and he slipped through the shrubbery carrying a large backpack of clothes and jewels.

The toad, as everybody knows, is one of the five poisonous animals, and is the Beast of Moon and Night, and it spits Vermilion Dust that causes malaria, and is the confidant of the tortoise, the most devious and inscrutable of all living things. When toads have feasted upon Chinese lanternflies their bellies swell to grotesque proportions, and since the lanternflies are swallowed whole they continue to produce greenish flashes of light at twenty-six pulses per minute. The effect is quite startling. The effect is particularly startling when the green pulsing bellies are highlighting white-painted demon-toad faces. If one adds ghastly ghost screeches from Moon Boy, the result can be an experience that will remain with you for life.

One hundred of the hideous things hopped through the doors of the stables, and the screams of the soldiers and grooms were drowned out by the howls from the audience at the polo match. We stepped aside to avoid being trampled to death, and inside of a minute the stables contained nothing but toads and horses. We raced inside.

The exit was easy to find, because it was directly across from the king's war chariot. It was a wide tunnel, sloping downward, and we grabbed torches. Master Li hopped up on my back and we ran down the dark passage. The king would scarcely allow an open path for his enemies, of course, so the problem was going to be getting through the doors. The tunnel leveled as it started to run beneath the moat. Ahead of us was a huge iron door, and Master Li told me to stop. His eyes moved slowly over the walls.

Rows of iron shields hung there. The centers of the shields bore strange emblems, and they protruded from the smooth surfaces. The emblems seemed to concern every subject from agriculture to the zodiac, and Master Li thoughtfully chewed on his beard.

"I suspect sequence locks," he said. "The king rides down this passage on his couch on the chariot and punches shields that form the code to open the door. It's almost certainly set up so that the wrong code will cause an unfortunate result, which means that the king can remember it even if he's drunk or half-asleep. Probably a personal horoscope, or his lucky stars. Does anyone happen to know when he was born?"

Nobody did, but Grief of Dawn said, "When he picked me up and put me on his lap I noticed the amulet around his neck. It had the planetary symbol of Mercury."

"Good girl!" Master Li rubbed his hands happily. "If the amulet means enough to him that he wears it permanently, the code may simply be characteristics of his guiding planet. Let's see if they're all here."

He had me walk up and down the line while he hummed through his nose and studied weird symbols. Then he had me go back to the beginning.

"We must hope he's used the Chinese system. If he's used a barbarian one we can expect a twenty-ton spike-studded iron plate to fall on our heads," Master Li said matter-of-factly. "The organ associated with Mercury is the spleen."

I closed my eyes. Master Li reached out and punched the spleen symbol. Nothing happened, so I timidly made my way down the line of shields while Master Li punched symbols.

"The taste associated with Mercury is salt . . .

"The color is black . . .

"The element is water . . .

"The parent element is metal . . .

"The child element is wood . . .

"The friend element is fire . . .

"The enemy is earth . . .

"The earthly analogue is a stream . . .

"The celestial analogue is a bear . . ."

As he punched the ninth symbol, the iron door slid open. We

stepped through the opening to the other side, and Master Li reached out to another shield.

"And the musical note of Mercury is sixth on the scale," he said complacently, and the iron door slid shut behind us.

"Education is a wonderful thing," Moon Boy said admiringly. "I should have paid more attention in school."

"Master Li knows everything," I said proudly.

Even Master Li was baffled when we reached the next row of shields. The tunnel was sloping up to an exit outside the walls, and another iron door confronted us. I could see no pattern at all to the symbols, and Master Li was clearly puzzled.

"Strange," he muttered. "All but three of the emblems are symbolic of nature, and those three form no pattern at all: a sandal, a fan made of feathers, and an incense burner."

We could be of no use to him. He had me walk back and forth along the shields. "This passage is his war route," the old man muttered. "Logically he would use symbols that would concentrate his mind on battle, but what is militant about symbols for rain and sunlight and a variety of animals?" He muttered to himself for a while. "Visualize him," he muttered. "Shih Hu, King of Chao, riding in his war chariot upon a revolving couch with his Golden Girls behind him."

He suddenly let out a whoop. "Ox, back to the beginning," he said happily. I trotted back to the first shield. "I should have seen it at once," said Master Li. "Shih Hu is remarkable in that his bulk requires him to fight while seated upon a couch, and has there ever been a mighty warrior before him who did the same thing? Yes, one. Shih Hu's idol is the great Chuko Liang, the legendary Sleeping Dragon of the wars of the Three Kingdoms, who charged the enemy while reposing upon a couch in a carriage. And how did he array his men? In the Eight Trigrams Battle Formation, which he signaled by languidly waving his white feather fan."

Master Li punched the fan symbol. No gaping pit opened beneath our feet, so I started up the line of shields.

"The first trigram is Heaven . . .

"The second trigram is earth . . .

"The third trigram is wind . . .

"The fourth trigram is cloud . . .

"The fifth trigram is dragon . . .

"The sixth trigram is tiger . . .

"The seventh trigram is bird . . ."

As he punched the seventh shield the door slid open. We stepped through and Master Li reached for another shield.

"And the eighth trigram is snake," he said, and the door slid shut behind us.

Moonlight had greeted us, and after a few more feet we were out on a hillside beneath the stars. Master Li gazed back at the huge walls of the castle.

"The grooms and guards will creep back to the stables and find nothing but indignant toads," he said thoughtfully. "If they do anything it will be to round up and spank the bottoms of any small boys who happen to be handy, and they certainly will not interrupt a banquet to tell their king that they deserted their post because they were attacked by awful amphibians. In the morning Shih Hu should have a royal hangover. I doubt that any of us will be missed until afternoon at the earliest, and then they'll search the palace and the grounds. Night will intervene, and not until the following morning should they realize we're gone. We should have nearly two days' head start, and we'll need every minute of it."

I started out at a fast pace. We couldn't use the horse stations of the postal service until we reached Loshan, and the rugged country was familiar to the king but not to us. I remembered the display of severed heads on pikes and lengthened my stride.

It was slow going, because no amount of effort can speed you through mountainous terrain when you don't know the shortcuts. The distant landmarks Master Li checked seemed to grow no closer, and on the morning of the third day we noticed some monks who were watching us from a hillside. The monks turned and vanished. A few hours later we reached a place where we could see the distant rooftop of the monastery. I thought I saw something lift from the roof and streak through the sky back toward Chao, but I couldn't be sure. Grief of Dawn's eyes were almost as sharp as Moon Boy's ears, and she had no doubt about it.

"Pigeons," she said softly. "Probably the king has sent messages to all the monasteries under his protection, and I think he's getting a reply."

I seemed to hear galloping hooves and the rumble of chariot wheels, and I picked up the pace even more, but it was still a long

way to Loshan. The following morning we stood on the crest of a
hill and looked down at a river that was very peculiar. Half of the
water was blue, and the other half was yellow.

"The Min," said Master Li. "Yellow clay washes into it from the
banks, and farther down it will be totally yellow. That's when it
joins the Yangtze, just above Five Misery Rapids. Past the rapids is
Loshan and the horse stations of the postal service."

His face was grim and remained grim as he told me to get to the
nearest village. There we bought a boat and a great deal of wine,
and I noticed that the peasant who sold us the boat was acting
rather peculiar when we climbed in and pushed off. He was smiling
and bowing at first, but then the smile faded as we went out farther
and farther toward the strong current in the center of the stream.
Then he began to shout and wave his arms, and he tried to run after
us as we reached the current and started rapidly downstream. The
last I saw of him, he was on his knees making shamanistic gestures
to release him from guilt.

"The perils of Five Misery Rapids are greatly overrated," Master
Li said calmly. "At least when you compare them to the perils of an
angry Shih Hu and his Golden Girls. We shall, however, take a few
precautions, and this is the first."

With that he tossed the oars overboard. I yelped in dismay, and
he tossed the pole overboard.

"Temptation," Master Li said. "If we had poles or oars, we'd be
tempted to use them, which would be suicidal. The second precau-
tion is to get stinking drunk, and that, my children, is an order."

Master Li opened wine jars. Moon Boy hoisted his enthusiastically, and Grief of Dawn and I did so dutifully. The water helped.
Blue and yellow were blending in dizzying patterns, and in no time
my head was spinning. Master Li and Moon Boy were quite mellow
when we heard the sound, and Grief of Dawn and I were reeling.
The sound was the roar of the Yangtze. Our little boat shot out into
the great river and hit a current like a brick wall and spun around
and began to race downstream. It was bouncing up and down like a
bucking pony, and I was drunk enough to giggle at first. Then I saw
what was coming at us and I stopped giggling and gaped in horror.

The water strikes Yenyu Rocks with enough force to send spray
like a woman's hair flying sixty feet into the air. I discovered that
my empty hands were frantically rowing imaginary oars, and Grief

of Dawn was shoving with a nonexistent pole. I watched a log float out to the safe water we were trying to reach. Then the current caught the log full force and drove it into jagged rocks just beneath the surface, and two splintered pieces shot out and flew through the air and smashed ten feet up a sheer cliff at the bank. Our little boat, meanwhile, dashed straight toward Yenyu, hit the backwash, skidded around the sharp stone corners, and plowed through the woman's-hair spray without suffering a scratch.

Grief of Dawn and I grabbed for fresh wine jars.

The speed was incredible as we raced straight at and then past Fairy Girl Peak, where the rocks are shaped like a nude nymph, and the Frog, where a forty-foot plume of water shoots from a stone bullfrog mouth. We passed through the Shiling and Chutang gorges without incident. Master Li and Moon Boy had their arms around each other's shoulders and were roaring a bawdy song, and I was foolish enough to think the worst of it was over. Then I saw what was coming and nearly fainted. Wu Gorge was looming through the spray.

Day turned into night. We had shot into a gorge so narrow that only at noon could one see the sun in a tiny ribbon of sky at the top of towering cliffs. The narrower the Yangtze became, the faster it ran. The noise was beyond belief. A stinging mist mercifully blocked out the rocks that reached like fangs to tear us to pieces. If our bodies had been rigid with sobriety there wouldn't have been an unbroken bone, but we were as limp as sacks of meal. I would have preferred being unconscious, because Five Misery Rapids was leaping toward us at a hundred miles an hour.

Master Li happily waved his wine flask. *"One!"* he bellowed, and suddenly we were airborne. The little boat turned completely around twice as we sailed over the falls, and we hit the surface again with a splash that sent spray fifty feet up the sides of the cliffs. I somehow got my stomach back in place just as Master Li bellowed, *"Two!"* We ascended toward Heaven again, practically grazing one of the walls as we shot through the air. It was a long way down to the level below the second falls, and Grief of Dawn and I clung to each other in terror. No sooner had we landed and scraped ourselves up from the deck than we felt our stomachs say farewell again. *"Three!"* Master Li yelled, and we sailed out into space. I don't even remember landing. *"Four!"* Master Li yelled, and I opened my eyes to discover we were headed somewhere in the direction of Venus. The boat spun around as we descended, and we landed backward, which allowed me to notice that we had missed a rock like a fifty-foot saw by two inches. The boat spun around. Now I could see that we were hurtling toward the narrowest part of the gorge, and I stared at a spume of water that was wrapped in rainbows as it shot a hundred feet out into nothingness. We joined the spume. *"Five!"* Master Li bellowed. I realized that we were flying from Wu Gorge, sailing into a million acres of bright blue sky, and then the spray settled around us and we soared down blindly. Down and down and down, while I prayed we were still right side up. We hit with a shock that nearly drove me through the bottom of the boat.

I think I was stunned, because it took some time for me to get my scrambled senses functioning, and then I wondered what was wrong. The noise had gone. The boat was peacefully floating upon placid water. I had the distinct sensation that I was about to be devoured by an enormous mouth, and I sat up and stared at the serene smile of the Great Stone Buddha of Loshan: three hundred sixty feet high, carved in the side of Yellow Buffalo Mountain at the safe end of Wu Gorge. Five Misery Rapids was behind us, and so was the King of Chao, and the only problems were Master Li and Moon Boy.

They wanted to go back and do it again, but Grief of Dawn and I sat on them until they regained their senses.

石

12

The next few days were rather interesting, although exhausting. I made a few notes, and perhaps I should include a couple of them.

Wake up, rub eyes, examine bug crawling into left nostril. Grief of Dawn sleeping, Master Li snoring, Moon Boy gone. Get up to gather firewood. Dogs barking, screams of rage in distance. Make tea, get more water for rice. Screams of rage closer, plus beautiful voice singing obscene song:

> *"There's a boy across the riiiiiiiiiver*
> *With a bottom like a peeeeeeeeeach!"*

Rest of it unprintable. Hear six hawk moths diving at my tea, look around for hawk moths, see Moon Boy doing something with his throat. Screams of rage very close, lynch mob gallops over hill. Leader has pitchfork, drags weeping boy. Moon Boy accepts tea. Leader screams accusations, Moon Boy sips tea. Leader charges with pitchfork. Moon Boy smiles—air turns sulphurous. Smiles wider—hills shimmer with heat waves. Moon Boy tickles leader beneath chin, purrs like cat: "Come here, sugar." Escorts leader behind large rock, boy stops weeping and starts laughing. Offer tea to lynch mob. Lewd sounds from behind rock, boy can't stop laughing. Offer rice to lynch mob. Leader emerges, adjusting clothing. Refuses tea and rice and drags boy away by ear. Moon Boy saunters from behind rock, whistling. Master Li awakes, regards Moon Boy and departing lynch mob, mutters, "If only I could be ninety again," goes back to sleep.

Our route back toward Ch'ang-an took us past the village of Moon Boy's birth, at which point I began to suspect that Moon Boy's moral turpitude resembled his art: almost supernatural.

Road past small temple, priest emerges. Stares at Moon Boy, lifts robe, races toward village: "Lock up the boys! Lock up the men! Lock up the goats and donkeys!" Moon Boy smiles proudly. Enter village, woman emerges from cottage: "My son!" Faints. Father emerges waving horsewhip: "Shame! Scandal! Infamy! Ignominy! Odium! Obliquity!" Father apparently fairly well educated. Priest runs up and sprinkles Moon Boy with holy water, begins beating with rod. Moon Boy tickles beneath chin: "Kitchy-koo." Priest faints. Mother revives: "Witness, O Heaven, that I was blameless!" Topples back to ground, Moon Boy smiles proudly. Neighbors gather, Moon Boy blows kisses. Father follows from village waving horsewhip: "Agony! Abasement! Depravity! Degradation!" Moon Boy blows kisses. Horses, goats, bulls, donkeys: whinnies, bleats, bellows, brays. Moon Boy blows kisses, Master Li mutters, "Rather an active childhood." Buy boat, push off into stream. Strange low hoarse sound, Moon Boy doing something with throat. Swans swim up. Great white glowing clouds of swans, canopy of wings lifting over Moon Boy, feathers shining in sunlight. Beautiful. Unreal.

If I am ever invited to take a ride on one of those tubes of Fire Drug that streaks up into the sky, goes *bang!* and hurls sparkling comets across the sky, I will bow politely and say, "A thousand pardons, but this humble one has already made the trip."

One of Moon Boy's most remarkable attributes was that he was completely without jealousy. When Grief of Dawn felt like climbing into my bedroll, which she did now and then, all Moon Boy did was lift his handsome head to the night sky and sing to the rabbit in the moon, asking for a soft silver blanket of moonbeams for Grief of Dawn and Number Ten Ox. Master Li would cry in mock agony, "Ah, if only I could be ninety again!" (actually, I think he was happy to be free from the tyranny of sexual desire), and it was clear that, for reasons of his own, he was becoming fascinated by the maid without a memory.

Grief of Dawn was a walking collection of contradictions. She was a simple peasant who spoke the *pai hua* of the people, like me, but at times she would unconsciously toss in *wen li* phrases that would have done credit to a courtier. She painted her forehead yellow but refused to pluck and paint her eyebrows: half-patrician, half-peasant. She was shameless enough to walk around with her hair uncovered, yet she was furious when she saw a man in mourning for his mother who carried a staff of oak rather than the appropriate mulberry. She was a prostitute who indignantly refused a fan Moon Boy bought because it was folding, and the symbolism was indecent, and ladies should always carry fixed fans.

Master Li's eyes lit up. "I haven't heard the fan taboo since I was a tad of six or seven!" he exclaimed.

"Little Miss Spotless Sandals," I teased.

"Everybody should dust his sandals now and then," she said demurely, and then she stepped behind me and dusted hers with two swift kicks to my rear end. *"Turtle Egg!"* she yelled.

Master Li collapsed with laughter. When he recovered he explained that people once believed turtles could conceive through thought alone, which made parentage impossible to establish, so "turtle egg" became a euphemism for bastard. Master Li swore that the insult had last been delivered during the Usurpation of Wang Mang, and he was willing to bet that at some point in her wanderings Grief of Dawn had found work in one of the moldy priories where antiquated old maids preserve ancient sayings and customs they learned from their great-great-grandmothers. Another time Grief of Dawn got mad at Moon Boy and called him "Forgetter of the Eight!" and even Master Li had to pause before connecting it to the corrupt courtiers whom Mencius swore had turned their backs on filial piety, politeness, decorum, integrity, fidelity, fraternal duty, loyalty, and sense of shame: the Eight Rules of Civilization.

Grief of Dawn was perfectly aware of Master Li's growing interest. She began to regard him with a speculative expression that had a hint of mirth in it, and I wondered if Moon Boy could read her mind, because he picked up the exact same expression. One scorching afternoon we reached a stream and in an instant Moon Boy had stripped and was gliding through the cool water like one of his

swans. Grief of Dawn had plenty of secluded places to use if she
liked, so Master Li and I undressed and dove in after Moon Boy.
There was another splash. Grief of Dawn swam like a seal, and
wasn't exactly shy about displaying her supple athlete's body. She
stood in a shallow spot, apparently to give Master Li a good view of
her lovely firm breasts.

"Venerable Sir, how many wives have you had?" she asked inno-
cently.

"Buddha, I started to lose count somewhere back toward the
beginning of the Sui Dynasty."

"And how many wives do you have now?"

"Not one," the old man said complacently. "They kept growing
old and dying on me, so when I reached the point where I could no
longer enjoy the Play of Clouds and Rain, I decided to settle for
selfishness and comfortable clutter, and I haven't had a wife since."

"But is that wise?" Grief of Dawn batted her eyes as though the
bright sunlight bothered her. (She had beautiful eyelashes.) "Wives
are useful for many things, and there are potions and incantations
that can do wonders with the Play of Clouds and Rain . . ."

I stopped listening and tried to make my clumsy mind come to
grips with Grief of Dawn's point of view. The more I thought of it,
the more sensible it became. Prostitutes are called "flowers of
smoke," and brothels are "smoke and blossom camps" because
worldly pleasures are transitory, and nothing is more transitory
than beauty. A whore's hopes can be measured in the distance between two wrinkles, and what could Grief of Dawn look forward
to? If she married me, it would mean a farm and children and
heartbreak when she was compelled to run off after Moon Boy and
resume her restless wanderings. But if she married an ancient sage?
Master Li would merely laugh if she ran off, and take the opportunity to smash up the shack with some old-fashioned drinking
brawls, and laugh some more when she returned, and when he died
she would become a respectable widow with a roof over her head.

". . . then you wash the dragon bones and grind them into a fine
powder, and put the powder into tiny silk bags and put the bags
into the body cavities of dead cleaned swallows and leave them
overnight . . ."

Master Li was smiling faintly as he listened to the innocent folk
remedy. He began whistling very softly. I felt my face turn red, and

Moon Boy had a hard time suppressing laughter, and Grief of Dawn flushed and began stumbling over words. The tune was "Hot Ashes," and for some peculiar reason the phrase "scraping hot ashes" refers to incest between in-laws—a young wife and her son-in-law, for example—and could it be said that I was something of a substitute son to Master Li? The arrangement that Grief of Dawn had in mind could become rather complicated, and Master Li held up a hand and cut her short.

"Forget about resurrecting erections," he said dryly. "At my age the last thing a man wants is one more petrified part. As for the rest of it, I'll think it over, and if I were you, I'd work on a young fellow who wears his peasant propriety like a suit of armor."

Grief of Dawn dove beneath the water and popped up in front of me like a dolphin. Her waving hand encompassed Master Li and Moon Boy and the water and the sunlight and the grass and the flowers and everything else we were sharing. "Oh, Ox, what fun we could have, and how happy we could be," she said pleadingly.

There was real yearning in her voice, and deep inside me it struck a sympathetic chord. My parents had died when I was nine. That had probably been the age of Moon Boy when he was first disowned, and Master Li hadn't experienced family life for years, and Grief of Dawn couldn't even remember if she had a family, and somehow I found myself thinking of the little shack in the alley in the coming winter, warm in the wind and snow, and I could smell the good food and fresh-scrubbed cleanliness that a young wife would bring, and I could hear the easy jokes and laughter, and I could see Moon Boy suddenly appearing like an exotic tropical bird —besides, if Master Li wasn't worried about who slept where, why should I be?

Grief of Dawn started a water fight. We said no more about her hope. It was Master Li's decision, and he would let her know in due course.

We didn't want to be sidetracked by several years in jail. Grief of Dawn made Moon Boy promise to be on his best behavior when we arrived in Ch'ang-an, and Master Li was in high spirits when he entered the Academy of Divination and Alchemic Research to get the report on the soil and plant samples. When he came out he was spitting nails.

"According to the finest minds in China, there is no trace of acid or poison or any other harmful substance," he snarled. "The only thing wrong with Princes' Path is that parts of it are stone-cold dead, and some oaf has scribbled on the bottom: 'Extinction through natural decay.' "

Master Li swore without repeating himself all the way down the hill to Serpentine Park, where he said he wanted to try something.

"I'm reduced to grasping at straws," he said sourly. "One straw concerns the last meal of the late librarian, Brother Squint-Eyes. I've been assuming that he paid for it with the down payment for Ssu-ma Ch'ien's manuscript, and that his tracing copy was stolen during the crooks' second visit to the monastery, but there could be another explanation. Let's go to the exhibits."

Bored schoolmasters were guiding classes around. Master Li found one with weak watery eyes and a nose covered with crimson veins. Money changed hands, and the delighted schoolmaster dove into the nearest wineshop. Master Li took over the class, and after huddling with the brats he started off toward the Boar Pavilion. The boys, I saw with surprise, were marching behind the old man with the precision of the Imperial Guard. It really was quite impressive —an ancient gentleman of the old school and his beautifully behaved charges—and a crowd began to follow Confucius and sons.

"The hope of the empire!" exclaimed an emotional matron.

Master Li lined the boys up and gave the downbeat, and they honored the exhibits of past glories with the most perfect rendition of "Evening Lake Scenes" I have ever heard. The applause was deafening. Vendors were mobbed, and the lads disappeared behind mounds of gooey sweets. Master Li lined them up again and marched off to the Gallery of Beautitude, and there the lads delivered a flawless "Shadows on the Eastern Window." Then they actually performed obeisances and kowtows.

"The hope of the empire!" the matron bawled, and a fierce old fellow with a floppy mustache told one and all that he had planned to return his medals to the General Staff in protest against the decline of standards, but now he wasn't so sure about the decline.

The Temple of Immaculate Illumination was next, and the boys' performance of "The Twin Pagodas of Orchid Stream" was so superb that every vendor in sight was cleaned out, and candy and crystalized fruit and honey cakes by the ton vanished into the boys' gaping maws.

"The hope of the empire!" cried Moon Boy and Grief of Dawn, beating the matron to it, and the fierce old gentleman with the medals vowed to move Heaven and earth to get his great-grandsons enrolled with Master Li.

The most sacred of all exhibits is the Confucian Stones (a row of stones engraved with all two hundred thousand characters of the master's writings). A low railing surrounds them, and the rule is, look but don't touch. Master Li lined up the little angels for a tribute worthy of the Ultimate, and the rendition of "The Tower of Floating Blue-Green" brought tears to every eye, including mine.

"The hope of the empire!" I bellowed, along with Moon Boy, Grief of Dawn, the matron, and the gentleman with the medals.

The vendors were cleaned out within minutes. The boys, I noticed, were beginning to turn green. They turned as one and groped for support, which happened to be a low rail, and leaned over it and began heaving their cherubic little guts out. All over the sacred Confucian Stones.

"One million miseries!" howled Master Li.

A gentleman of the old school is prepared for any emergency, however, and Master Li swiftly joined forces with the fierce old fellow with the medals to recruit a bucket brigade to dump cleansing water over the stones. Thoroughness is also a mark of the old school, and Master Li would not rest until he extracted some large sheets of paper from his tunic and pressed them down firmly over every indentation of the sacred text. Fortunately he also happened to be carrying a huge blue sponge, and he rubbed it over the surface so vigorously that the outside of the paper turned blue. When he lifted the sheets, the stones were nearly dry, and as good as new.

The audience, meanwhile, explained to the furious guards that it was all their fault for stuffing the little angels with goo, and the matron and the bemedaled gentleman took up a collection to pay the fine. There wasn't a dry eye as Master Li marched the lads away, and behind us I heard a chorus bawling, "The hope of the empire!"

Master Li led the boys into a secluded glade. "All right, brats, let it out," he said.

The boys collapsed on the grass, rolling around and pummeling each other and howling with laughter. "Please, sir, may we see?" one of them asked when he had regained his breath.

Master Li took out the pieces of paper. The ink from the sponge had settled in nicely, and the imprints were perfect. Genuine rubbings of the Confucian Stones are hard to come by. The boys begged to stay with Master Li and continue their lives of crime, but he advised them to remain in school and study hard so they could mastermind the mobs when they descended into depravity. Then he returned them to the schoolmaster and took the schoolmaster's place in the wineshop.

He ordered the stuff he had been named for, *kao-liang,* which is a terrible wine but a wonderful paint remover, and began using it to remove the peaks from every 丘 that was accompanied by 小 in the rubbings and replace them with flat lines: 且. Then he left the wineshop and we started up the Street of the Vermilion Sparrow to Dragon Head Plain.

"Brother Squint-Eye's forgery of the Ssu-ma was a crude tracing of a coded manuscript that contained the name of the historian's own father, and to a collector the monk's copy would have looked like the most obvious and inept fraud in history," he explained. "If the foolish monk brought it to Ch'ang-an and tried to sell it, it's a wonder he wasn't decapitated on the spot. There is, however, one place that might have bought the thing, and perhaps some pitying person told him where to go."

The Pavilion of the Blessings of Heaven is the greatest library in the world, and in addition to its collection of original manuscripts, it maintains a collection of forgeries. Both can be instructive to scholars, and some woefully inept forgeries are kept for pure entertainment value. Master Li made his way to the office of Liu Hsiang, the head librarian.

"Greetings, Hsiang," he said cheerfully.

"Lock up the manuscripts! Lock up the silver and incense burners! Lock up your wives and check your rings and purses!" the librarian screamed. "Hello, Kao. What brings you back to civilization?" he continued in a normal tone of voice.

"Shopping trip. My study lacks something, and I've decided I need a fake to hang on the wall."

"You know very well that our collection is not for sale," the librarian said primly.

"Who said anything about selling? I'm talking about trading," Master Li said, and he took out the rubbings and tossed them on the desk. "Think of the labor that went into that thing," he said with a chuckle.

"Who bothers to fake rubbings?" the librarian said skeptically. He glanced at them and then looked more closely, and after a few moments he began making small strangled sounds. I realized he was laughing. The librarian staggered to his feet and embraced Master Li, and the two old men clung together whooping and gasping with mirth. Moon Boy and Grief of Dawn and I pounded them on the back until they calmed down.

"Hilarious, isn't it?" Master Li said, wiping his eyes. "Think of the months it took the idiot to do this."

"Months? Say he did ten characters a day . . . That's seven years!" the librarian chortled.

Master Li waved us over to the desk. "My children, do you see the joke?" he asked.

We scratched our heads. "They look like genuine rubbings of the Confucian Stones to me," I said.

"Look at this character here—and here and here. Do you know what it means?"

"Yes, sir," Moon Boy said.

The librarian broke in. "Ah, but in the days of Confucius it wasn't written like that!" he exclaimed happily. "See the flat lines on top? In the old days it wasn't a flat line but a peak, like a rooftop"—he swiftly sketched 𡉈—"so the idiotic forger was saying that Confucius—"

Moon Boy's face lit up. "Confucius couldn't—"

Grief of Dawn's face lit up. "Confucius couldn't even—"

"Confucius couldn't even write 'ancestor'!" I howled.

The three of us clung together, whooping and hollering, and the librarian and Master Li very kindly pounded our backs until we regained control.

"Kao, this is truly a treasure of incompetence, and if you have something reasonable in mind, we might make a deal," the librarian said.

Master Li scratched the tip of his nose. "Well, I'm rather in the mood for mangled history. Anything new?"

"Not on this level. It isn't every day that—wait! How about a truly pathetic Ssu-ma Ch'ien?"

"Sounds promising," Master Li said casually.

The librarian rang a bell for his assistant. "Not long ago an idiotic monk showed up with the most inept Ssu-ma I've seen in years, and a tracing at that."

"Do tell," said Master Li.

It was as simple as that. A few minutes later we walked out of the Blessings of Heaven Pavilion, and Master Li had Brother Squint-Eyes' traced copy in his hands.

石

13

We found a pleasant little park and bought grasshopper pies and plum juice with vinegar from one of the vendors, and sat down on the grass beneath a pagoda tree. Master Li had already scanned Brother Squint-Eyes' forgery. He had also taken a detour through one of the scroll depositories, and he reached into his tunic and extracted an ancient scroll that was sealed with the stamp "Restricted Shelves: Authorized Staff Only." He placed the scroll, the forged manuscript, and the report on the soil and plant samples beside him on the grass, and concentrated on his grasshopper pie. Then he included all of us in a wave of his finger.

"Tell me the story of the emperor and the tangerines," he commanded.

We stared at him.

"Sir?" I said weakly.

"You heard me."

We looked at each other, and finally Moon Boy shrugged. "Long ago there was an emperor named Li Ling-chi," he said. "He was good. He was very good. In fact, he was so good that birds flew around his head singing songs of praise, and butterflies danced before him."

"He was so good that fish and frogs jumped from ponds to receive his blessing," said Grief of Dawn. "He was so good that on feast days a few of the gods always flew down from Heaven to have tea with him. Tea and tangerines, because his only weakness was a fondness for tangerines. His people were delighted that he wasn't fond of the things that usually entertain emperors, such as wars and massacres."

"Li Ling-chi got better and better," I said. "He became so good that he couldn't bear the sight of evil, so he had his craftsmen make him a headdress with a veil of two hundred eighty-eight jewels, and he couldn't bear to hear evil, so they added jeweled earflaps. That way he only saw pretty shining things and he only heard tinkle-tinkle-tinkle, except on feast days, when he took off his headdress to have tea with the gods."

"Tea and tangerines, except one day there were no tangerines," Moon Boy said. "The emperor was outraged. 'How can I have tea without tangerines?' he cried. 'O Son of Heaven,' said the chamberlain, 'it is winter, and in winter tangerines do not grow in your gardens.' The emperor was not to be fooled. 'I had tangerines last winter!' he yelled. 'O Son of Heaven,' said the chamberlain, 'last winter the roads were clear, but this winter there have been heavy snowstorms. Produce from the south, where tangerines still grow, cannot reach the capital.' The emperor turned purple. 'You mean to tell me that my subjects in the south are gorging themselves on tangerines when their emperor can't have any? We'll see about that!' he shouted."

"Emperor Li Ling-chi jumped up on top of his throne," said Grief of Dawn. "He had become so good that when he waved his hands to the south, all the green growing things tore loose from the earth and flew north to be blessed, and in no time tangerines were growing in the capital in the middle of winter. The gods who were coming to tea cried in horror, 'Stop! Stop!' But the emperor still had his headdress on, and all he heard was tinkle-tinkle-tinkle. They sent comets and apparitions and omens, but all he saw was pretty shining jewels. Meanwhile there was no food in the south, and the peasants began to starve, and bodies piled up in ditches just as if there had been wars and massacres."

"The August Personage of Jade gazed down from his throne," I said. "His roar of rage shook all the tangerines from the emperor's trees, and he flew down from Heaven and made Li Ling-chi eat every piece of the fallen fruit, and the emperor swelled up like the Transcendent Pig. Then the August Personage of Jade waved his hand and all the green growing things flew back south where they belonged, and he picked up the emperor and hurled him into the sky. But the emperor was lopsided because of all those tangerines, so he curved, and that's why we still see him to this day."

"Every seventy-five years," said Moon Boy, "peasants can gaze up at the sky and see a bright comet curving back toward earth. The orange color is all those tangerines inside the emperor, and the sparkling tail is his jeweled veil and earflaps, and if you listen very, very closely, you will hear the sound of an emperor with a tummy-ache."

"Waa! Waa! Waa!" we chanted in unison. "Ling-chi cries, candle dies, little children close their eyes—so!"

We sat there feeling like fools. Master Li polished off a few more grasshoppers and took a swig of wine from his flask.

"That bit of folklore has fascinated scholars for centuries," he said. "Part of it is based upon a real emperor, Huang Ti, who actually did attempt to block out reality with a jeweled veil and earflaps, but does the rest of it refer to an ancient invasion of the south by the north? A long-forgotten plague? There are some scholars who insist that it's a racial memory of a very rare phenomenon: a sudden shift in the *ch'i*, the life force, in various climatic areas. As for the suddenness, in theory there is no reason why the appearance of an overpowering concentration of ch'i couldn't draw less powerful life forces to it, destroying anything in its path, whether the intention behind it was as good as Li Ling-chi thought he was or as bad as the Laughing Prince knew he was."

He tossed the last of his grasshoppers to some fish in a pond and picked up the stolen scroll.

"Believe it or not, there's a point to this, but be patient," he said. "Am I correct in assuming that every one of you gave up on *Dream of the Red Chamber* after the first two paragraphs?"

Grief of Dawn and Moon Boy and I turned red. The problem with "the crown jewel of Chinese literature" is that it has two thousand pages and an equal number of characters, and the hero is an effeminate ass who should have either been spanked or decapitated, both ends being equally objectionable.

"No matter," Master Li said. "The book has been revised countless times, by Kao Ngoh and lesser talents, and the later versions bear little resemblance to the original. This happens to be the original, and it contains a rather peculiar story. Listen carefully."

He opened the scroll and searched for the place and began to read one of the strangest and most unsatisfactorily incomplete fairy tales I have ever heard.

" 'Of the 36,501 stones selected by the goddess Nu Kua for the Wall of Heaven, there was one she was forced to reject because of a serious flaw. The flaw was an evil one. Contact with the goddess had enabled the stone to acquire a soul, but its soul was evil. The stone had also learned to move around at will, and it wandered through Heaven causing much malicious harm, and at last the emperor was forced to intervene.

" 'The ways of the August Personage of Jade are subtle indeed. In Heaven there was also a flower named Purple Pearl, and Purple Pearl was even more flawed and evil than the stone. The emperor planted the flower in a barren spot beside the River of Spirits, and there it was discovered by the wandering stone. Evil attracts evil, and the stone began to bring moisture to nourish the flower. Purple Pearl bloomed and became beautiful, and her evil was exorcised by the dew and raindrops of Heaven, and she fell in love with the stone. She vowed that if ever she were reborn upon earth she would shun the Sphere of Banished Sufferings and seek the Source of Drenching Grief, and tears would build up inside her, and if the opportunity arose, she would repay her debt to the stone by shedding every tear in her body.

" 'The strange vow of a flower is of the utmost importance. The stone has been returned to earth, where it passed into the hands of Lao Tzu, who cried, "Evil!" and hurled it away. It passed to Chuang Tzu, who also cried, "Evil!" and hurled it away. The stone now lurks in darkness, waiting for the hand that will not hurl it away, and he who possesses the stone will be himself possessed. The stone is the Stone of Evil, and its malignancy will spread unchecked unless drowned in the tears of Purple Pearl.

" 'Let no man interfere with the destiny of the flower, for the outcome is awaited by both the goddess Nu Kua and the August Personage of Jade.' "

Master Li tossed the scroll on the grass. I choked on a grasshopper. "That's all?" I said incredulously.

"Not according to Ssu-ma Ch'ien," said Master Li. He picked up

Brother Squint-Eyes' copy and began rapidly decoding the complete hidden text.

" 'Red Chamber story correct about stone, tablet from Cave of Yu . . . Confirmation of reactions of Lao Tzu and Chuang Tzu . . . Have traced stone to Prince Liu Sheng . . . Consumed by evil, has become Laughing Prince . . . Secret hiding place . . . Down stairs . . . Cold room . . . Tunnel to construction site . . . Stone in sacristy . . . Plain appearance . . . Flat smooth area rising to round concave bowl shape . . . Found axe . . . Blow broke flat area from bowl area . . . Second blow broke off small chip . . . Soldiers seized, could not destroy . . . Imprisoned . . . Terrible sentence . . . Scholars, seek Stone of Evil! . . . Destroy it! . . . Evil that consumes men can consume world.' "

Master Li placed the copy beside the scroll.

"Ssu-ma Ch'ien was a very brave man," he said. "The question is whether or not he was correct about the mysterious stone, and he suggests that Tsao Hsueh Chin, the author of *Red Chamber,* may have taken the stone story from a tablet from the Cave of Yu. Do you know what that means?"

We shook our heads negatively.

"The legendary Emperor Yu is said to have received certain tablets from Heaven, which he concealed in a cave," Master Li explained. "They're called 'Annals of Heaven and Earth' because they supposedly deal with matter affecting men and gods alike. Now and then somebody produces an old clay tablet said to have come from the Cave of Yu. Usually the message involves something lucrative for the discoverer, but one or two of the tablets have contained prophecies that proved to be astonishingly correct."

He picked up the soil and plant report and waved it in my direction. The expression on his face made me very uneasy.

"Number Ten Ox, according to this, there isn't one damn thing wrong with Princes' Path, just as there wasn't one damn thing wrong with the green growing things in the south until Emperor Li Ling-chi waved his hand," Master Li growled. "If one allows for tale-telling embellishment, there's nothing impossible about the tangerine story. A tremendous concentration of ch'i would draw lesser life forces to it like iron filings to a magnet." The old man's eyes bored toward my brain. "Just after a section of Princes' Path was destroyed, you had a dream. In it you sensed an extraordinary ch'i, a pulsing life force, coming from a small round piece of clay that was colored orange. Was your sleeping mind guiding you to the story of the emperor and the tangerines?"

My mind was as blank and opaque as a pool of mud. I automatically swallowed my plum juice with vinegar.

"A stone touched by Heaven?" Master Li wondered out loud. "A stone worshipped by the Laughing Prince? All we know for sure is that something destroyed sections of Princes' Path, and a strange sound seems to be associated with it."

Moon Boy gulped. His eyes were wide and wondering. "I think I can tell you what the sound is," he said in a small hushed voice.

Confucian temples have no priests or formal worship, but they have a regular congregation of makers of bells. That's because of the *pien-chung,* a row of sixteen stone bells hanging in a wooden rack. The bells have no clappers and are struck by wooden beams swinging on ropes, and to most people the sound is dull and uninteresting, but bell makers view them differently. On the wooden frame is the inscription "When the bell speaks, the stone answers," because a perfectly tuned metal bell will produce a matching echo from a similar stone bell, and it's the most accurate tuning device known.

A Confucian temple wasn't far away. Moon Boy ran his hands lovingly over the stone bells. He was in his professional element, and he was all business.

"The ancients separated musical instruments into categories corresponding to the trigrams of Fu Hsi," he said, and for a mad moment I thought I was going to hear another lecture on the Wen-Wu lute. "Each instrument is defined by four qualities: the material it's made from, the cardinal point of its greatest strength, the season it suggests, and the related sound phenomenon."

He began fashioning a framework from pieces of bamboo.

"The mouth organ is classified as gourd, northeast, winter/spring, and the sound of thunder. The zither is silk, south, summer, and the sound of fire. All instruments were easily classified until they came to the sonorous stone, and then the ancients became entangled in an argument that lasted nearly six centuries. They easily provided stone, northwest, and autumn/winter. The problem was the related sound phenomenon, and their final decision is still fiercely debated. It won't be easy, but I'll try to show you why they chose as they did."

He lifted two of the stone bells to the bamboo frame and arranged them so the mouths were almost touching. He took two of the striking beams and swung them over so the ends were almost touching the sides of the bells.

"Ox has tried to describe the strange sound in Princes' Path to me," he said. "Now Master Li has spoken of a stone that might have been touched by Heaven, and which might be possessed of an overpowering ch'i. All I know is that stone produces two different sounds, and most people have only heard the sound from the surface. The other sound comes from the soul."

He began to tap the beams against the bells, very lightly and rapidly. A dull stone sound filled the temple. His hands moved faster and faster. A vibration made my stomach feel queasy. Moon Boy's hands were blurs and the vibration became a humming sound that made the temple shake. His head bent down and his mouth almost touched the narrow crack between the two bells. Moon Boy's throat began to vibrate like a lark's. I realized that he was somehow pitching his voice into the two bell mouths simultaneously, but all I heard was the hum. Sweat was pouring down Moon Boy's face. His throat vibrated faster and faster. "When the bell speaks, the stone answers," and the stones were beginning to answer. It was a nearly inaudible echo beneath the vibrating hum, gradually growing louder. Then the echo broke through, and my heart nearly broke loose from its moorings.

Kung . . . shang . . . chueeeeeeeeeeh . . .

Master Li had not been able to hear the sound on Princes' Path, but now he looked as though somebody had smacked him with a barge pole. Grief of Dawn was weeping. "That's it!" I cried. "The sound I heard was a thousand times as pure and strong, but that's it!"

Kung . . . shang . . . chueeeeeeeeeeh . . .

Moon boy stepped back, drenched in perspiration.

"The ancients," he said, panting, "decided that the related phenomenon of the soul-sound of stone was nothing less than the Voice of Heaven."

"Well, well, well," said Master Li.

All the way back to the Valley of Sorrows Master Li kept it up. "Well, well, well . . . Well, well, well . . . Well, well, well . . ." I hadn't seen him so happy in months.

Prince Liu Pao was delighted to see us. At first I was delighted to see him too, but then Master Li introduced Grief of Dawn. The prince jumped a foot into the air and his complexion switched back and forth from pink to white and the conversation went something like this.

"Would you care for tea?"

"No, thank you, Your Highness," said Grief of Dawn.

"Wine, perhaps?"

"No, thank you, Your Highness," said Grief of Dawn.

"Cakes? Fruit?"

"No, thank you, Your Highness," said Grief of Dawn.

"How about a few swans?" the prince said hopefully. "Cash? Lambs? Silk?"

Since those were the classic wedding gifts, I decided I was in trouble. The prince's reaction to Moon Boy was almost as strong, and within minutes the three of them were so close that I began to think deep thoughts about Grief of Dawn's belief that part of the soul she shared with Moon Boy had been lost on the Great Wheel of Transmigrations. Had the wandering soul settled inside Prince Liu Pao? I asked Master Li about it, but he only grunted noncommittally.

He had something else to think about. Now all his attention was focused upon the mysterious stone of the Laughing Prince, and he settled down in the library at the monastery and began poring over ancient records in search of any mention of an unusual stone. He asked the prince to do the same with family papers, and I was sent out to see what I could find in peasant tales and legends.

It was something to keep my mind off the prince and Grief of Dawn. The stone stories of the old women in the village were the same ones I had heard all my life, so I tried a different kind of folk tale. Blacksmiths are surrounded by boys as flowers are surrounded by bees, so I decided to lend the village smith a hand. After I had lifted the anvil a few times and bent a few iron bars in my hands I had all the boys I needed, and within two days I was able to race into the library at the monastery.

"A stone! A magical stone!" I shouted. Master Li looked up from the scrolls and blinked at me. "It's a boys' story, and very ancient," I said excitedly. "So far I've only heard a vague description, but I know it deals with a hero who sneaks into a secret cavern and finds a magical stone. Know what he's trying to do with it?" I said rhetorically. "Kill the Laughing Prince, that's what."

Master Li leaned back and pressed the tips of his fingers together. "Well, well, well," he said.

石

14

Adult visitors were rarely allowed to attend meetings of the Sacred
and Solemn Order of Wolf, but Prince Liu Pao was not the normal
kind of visitor. The moon was very bright. I listened for a treble owl
hoot and replied with two cat yowls, and a boy slipped from the
shadows and led us through a maze of thick brush to the side of a
low cliff. The prince and Master Li and Moon Boy and Grief of
Dawn and I got down on our knees and crawled through an opening, and when we stood up we were inside a small cave. Thirteen
boys, eleven to fourteen years old, greeted us formally. The occasion
was the induction of the thirteenth, Little Skinhead, into the elite
boys' gang of the Valley of Sorrows, and we would be allowed to
stay until they got to matters like codes and passwords.

A single torch burned at the back of the cave. Lying on the floor
beneath it was the skeleton of a boy who had been about the same
age as the members of the gang. It was a very ancient skeleton, and
the boy's death had been dramatic. The rib cage was crushed, and
inside it lay the iron head of an old spear. We followed the gang's
example and bowed to the bones.

The leader was called Deer Ears. "We bow to Wolf, as have our
fathers and grandfathers before us," Deer Ears formally announced.
"We gather in his honor, and our distinguished guests will be allowed to add one detail to his story."

The boys sat in a semicircle facing the skeleton. We sat just behind them, and Deer Ears picked up an ancient ring from the skele-

ton's separated finger bones. He handed it politely to the prince, who examined it and passed it around. The ring was black iron, and engraved on the front was the head of a wolf. Master Li studied the inside of the ring with interest. There were faint lines and markings that made no sense to me. We handed the ring back to Deer Ears, and he reverently replaced it.

There was a brief ceremony for the purification of the boy to be inducted, Little Skinhead, but sacred matters would be saved for later, after we had gone. When Deer Ears began the story of Wolf I was disappointed. It was like a thousand such stories, and I could almost predict what would happen next.

A woodcutter finds a baby in a basket at his doorstep. Around the baby's neck is a cord holding a ring and a small clay tablet. Neither the woodcutter nor his wife can read, so they take the tablet to a priest, who reads to them: "When the finger fits the ring, take the boy to Temple Spring." They have no children themselves, so they decide to raise the child as their own, and since the ring has the head of a wolf on it they name him Wolf.

When the boy is twelve years old the ring fits his finger, so the woodcutter takes him to the Temple of the Spring of the Master, which is renowned for handling all sorts of strange matters. A priest searches the records and says that according to instructions left twelve years before, Wolf is now old enough to be told that he has a cousin living in Ling-chou Valley, a very clever fellow known as Ah the Artificer. Wolf is to go to his cousin, but no other information has been left to guide him. The priest also hands Wolf a simple wooden bow, which seems to be his only inheritance except for the ring, and with many tears Wolf parts with his foster parents and sets off to seek his destiny.

Ah the Artificer is a classic villain. The greedy mean fellow accepts the boy as slave labor and works him half to death, but Wolf at least discovers that his mother died in childbirth, and his father was named Li Tan and was perhaps the greatest artificer of them all. Wolf's father then fell under the spell of a concubine of the lord of the neighboring valley, the Valley of Sorrows. The concubine was a witch. She was a barbarian called Crown of Fire, because of her bright red hair, and she had a daughter called Fire Girl, who was Wolf's age. The witch and Wolf's father had attempted to assassinate the lord, the Laughing Prince, and had been put to death, but their infant children had vanished and thus were spared.

"One day," said Deer Ears, "a mysterious stranger appeared at Ah the Artificer's door. They talked in low voices for many hours, and then Wolf was called in. When he saw the stranger's face, Wolf felt a shudder of fear, because—"

"Wolf wasn't afraid of anything!" Little Skinhead said indignantly. He had the right spirit for a recruit.

"Wolf felt a shudder of fear because the stranger's face was as white as death," Deer Ears hissed. "Sick, slimy, fish-belly white, and the stranger's heart was so cold that his eyes had turned blue, and a red beard crawled over his face like a hairy spider, and he was—"

"He was drunk," Little Skinhead said matter-of-factly. "My father took me to Soochow, where there are lots of barbarians, and barbarians are always drunk."

"He hadn't hit the wine jars yet, and don't interrupt!" Deer Ears yelled. "He told Wolf he was a trader with a caravan on its way to Samarkand with a cargo of . . ."

Deer Ears paused and looked thoughtfully at the guests. We could add one unimportant detail to the story, and nobody had yet bothered with the cargo. He bowed to the prince, who deferred to Master Li.

"Slavonian squirrels," Master Li said, intoning the words like a priestly chant. "Undressed vairs and vair bellies and backs. Martins and finches, goatskins and ram skins, dates, filberts, walnuts, salted sturgeon tails, round pepper, ginger, saffron, cloves, nutmegs, spike, cardamoms, scammony, manna, lac, zedoary, incense, quicksilver, copper, amber, pounding pearls, borax, gum arabic, sweetmeats, gold wire, wines, dragon's blood rubies, loaded dice, and beautiful dancing girls."

Only Master Li would have tossed in loaded dice and beautiful dancing girls, and the boys sat in reverent silence while they absorbed it. For the next ten or twelve centuries Master Li's cargo would be part of the tale of Wolf.

Deer Ears' voice changed to a nasty wheedling whine. " 'What a fine boy,' the stranger said. 'What a clever and manly boy. I have just the task for such a boy, and he who performed it would receive

six shiny copper coins.' Wolf looked at him silently. The stranger's
face contorted with terrible pain. 'All right, *seven!*' he shrieked.
'You see, I have a niece—a wild and ungrateful girl!—who has
stolen a gem and swallowed it to conceal the theft, and she has
slipped into a small cave at the end of the valley. The entrance is too
small for a man, but a clever boy could squeeze inside and bring my
niece back."

Wolf wants no part of it, but Ah the Artificer insists, so he takes
his ring and his bow and a torch and squeezes through a small
opening into a dark cave.

Then the story got very interesting indeed, at least so far as I was
concerned, and since it proved to be of use to Master Li, I will set
down as much of the important parts as I can remember.

WOLF BOY AND FIRE GIRL

Wolf lit the torch and looked around. There was nobody in the cave,
but there was a dark corner and when he walked over he stared in
astonishment at a smooth flight of stone steps leading down. Wolf's
eyes gleamed, and he thought of buried treasure, and he strung his
bow and made sure he could quickly reach his knife and started
down the stairs. The steps led on and on, winding sharply downward, and Wolf began to hear the sound of running water. Finally
something sparkled in his torchlight, and he realized it was an underground river in the center of an immense cavern. The water was
jet black, the color of the stone bed it ran through. To his right was
a glow, and he moved cautiously toward it and came to the first of a
long line of torches set in brackets on the stone walls.

The light was good enough for Wolf to extinguish his own torch.
A small crimson boat was tied to a post. There was another post
beside it, and it was stained with drops of water. The stain was still
damp, and Wolf untied the little boat and climbed in and pushed off
into the current.

Enormous statues carved in stone lined the banks. Wolf gazed in
wonder at images with the bodies of humans but the heads of animals or birds. What could they mean? The cavern was silent except
for the hiss of torches and the lapping of water. Nothing stirred.
The boat drifted on and on. Everything was black or white or gray,

except for the orange glow of the torches, but then Wolf saw a flash of crimson. He steered the boat over to a shelf of rock overhanging the side of the river, and beneath it was a crimson boat just like his. He tied his boat beside it and swam to the bank and climbed out, and he saw a trail of sandal prints, still damp, leading up over a mound of tumbled rocks. Wolf began to climb, following the prints, and he reached a small level area.

Something landed on his back and knocked him to the ground. A knife flashed in front of his face, and a small arm tried to jerk his head back. Wolf kicked and rolled over, pinning the knife beneath him, and managed to get to the top position. He was looking at a girl about his own age, and she was half-Chinese and half-barbarian, and her hair was the color of fire. She hissed like a cat and fought furiously, but Wolf was stronger and he managed to pin both arms, and then the boy and the girl stopped fighting.

Men were approaching, down at the riverbank. They heard coarse laughter and the clash of weapons, and something in the voices made Wolf and the girl break apart and crawl to the edge of the rocks and peer down. The soldiers had cruel brutish faces and they wore the uniform of the Laughing Prince, and Wolf realized that the cavern must run all the way to the Valley of Sorrows. The soldiers marched away and disappeared in shadows, and Wolf and the girl sat up.

Something was very strange. They should be in darkness, but they were silhouetted against light, and they realized that each of them had something on their backs that glowed. It was Wolf's bow and one of the arrows in the girl's quiver, and they held them out and stared in wonder. Writing had appeared on the bow and the arrow—writing in fire. Wolf glanced at the girl and blushed.

"I don't know how to read," he whispered.

"I can read, a little." The girl took Wolf's bow and scratched her head and wrinkled her nose and read, slowly and hesitantly:

> *"In darkness languishes the precious stone.*
> *When will its excellence enchant the world?"*

She took her arrow and scratched her head some more and wrinkled her nose some more and read:

*"The precious stone, hidden away,
Longs to fulfill its destiny."*

They stared at each other. Finally Wolf said, "I am called Wolf, and my father was Li Tan the artificer. I never knew him, and he left me this bow and a ring."

"I am called Fire Girl, and my mother was Crown of Fire the witch," the girl said. "I never knew her, and she left me this arrow."

"They say that my father and your mother tried to kill the Laughing Prince," Wolf said. "Is that barbarian trader really your uncle? He said you stole something, but I don't believe him."

"Stole something?" The girl turned and spat furiously. "He is called Brushbeard the Barbarian, and he was taking me to sell as a concubine to the Laughing Prince, just as he once sold my mother, and when I get a chance, I'm going to kill him."

As they talked, the glowing letters on the bow and arrow faded away, but now a third glowing light had appeared. It came from the ring on Wolf's finger, and he slipped it off. No writing had appeared, but the strange lines and marks on the inside were shining brightly. Wolf examined the markings closely, and saw that not all of the lines were glowing. The shining lines were running between parallel rows of dark ones, twisting and turning through openings.

"Could it be a map through a maze?" Fire Girl whispered.

Wolf turned the ring to display more scratchy lines on the front. "Look, these lines start at the wolf head and run to the edge, and then around and inside the ring, like going into a hole or a tunnel, and the shining lines twist through all these little openings to a circular mark, and stop there."

The girl grabbed his arm. "There's a statue farther on that has a wolf head just like this one!" she said excitedly.

Without another word they slid back down to the riverbank and ran until they came to the huge stone wolf statue. They looked for some mark or sign but found nothing. The eyes of the wolf head were fixed on a shadowed section of the stone wall, and when they followed the direction of the eyes they found a tiny side tunnel that was almost invisible. Wolf and Fire Girl managed to squeeze through the opening.

The ring was shining even brighter, and the eyes of the wolf were like small lanterns. There were many side passages, but Wolf followed the pattern of the lines inside the ring, and to be on the safe side they used their knives to scratch marks at the entrances when they turned into different passages. They twisted and turned through a maze, and ahead of them was a light, and finally they stepped into a small round cave. The light came from a natural chimney that ran up through stone to a patch of blue sky and a shaft of sunbeams.

The cave had a table and two benches. On the floor was a stack of torches, and across from them were two sleeping pallets. Between the pallets was a natural stone shelf. On the shelf were three bronze caskets, and the same legend was carved in the stone above the two end ones. The caskets had sliding lids carved in fish shapes, and Fire Girl studied the legends above the end ones and read:

> *"Pull not the scales*
> *Till all else fails."*

The casket in the center had two lids that folded together, with the yin symbol on the left and the yang symbol on the right, and above it on the wall were the four ideographs *tung ling pao-yu.*

"Stone of penetrating spiritual power," Fire Girl read.

Wolf opened the center casket. Inside was a piece of stone. It was small and slim and as sharp as a razor, and it was shaped like the head of an arrow. Fire Girl picked it up. On each side were two written lines, and after much scratching and nose wrinkling, she read the four lines together:

> *"When evil is taken for wisdom, wisdom becomes evil.*
> *When cruelty is taken for virtue, virtue becomes cruelty.*
> *The stone defeats cruelty and evil*
> *And flies to the heart of Liu Sheng."*

"Fire Girl, Liu Sheng is the name of the Laughing Prince," Wolf said.

When Fire Girl held up the tip of the arrow her mother had left her he realized it had no head. There was a groove for one. She slowly took the stone and slid it into the groove, and it stuck there as though it had been bound with rawhide. She lifted the arrow and placed the center of the shaft on her finger. It was perfectly balanced.

"What do you think we should do?" she asked quietly.

Wolf looked around. The chimney that ran up to the surface was against a wall, and he walked over and found foot- and handholds. He jumped and grabbed, and began to climb. It was a long way up, but the holds were good, and finally he stuck his head from the hole and saw that he had come up at the bottom of a deep gorge. Across from the hole he saw a good landmark—strange red and emerald-colored rocks in the side of the cliff—and he began climbing back down.

"You can climb that," he said, panting. "If we have to, we can get out quick. Fire Girl, I think that my father and your mother wanted us to try to kill the Laughing Prince if they failed, but I don't know anything about him. Why should he be killed?"

She shook her head. "I don't know, but I think we had better find out," she said.

They held hands and began retracing their steps through the maze to see what they could see.

(Here I will summarize, since the details were not important to Master Li. They discover the terrible destruction of the Valley of Sorrows, and the awful torture chamber in the grotto. They also discover that the instruments of torture are made by Ah the Artificer, and that the girls who please the Laughing Prince before being sent to the grotto are sold to him by Brushbeard the Barbarian. They are chased by soldiers, and find out from a cricket how to steal food. The wolf head statue can talk a few words and warns them of a geyser of poisonous steam. It also tries to warn them about bats, but "bats" can mean forty other things unless pronounced with the proper inflection, and since the statue can't move its lips, they don't understand the warning. Each is captured and saved by the other and they discover the throne room that the Laughing Prince has built in the cavern. They make traps by placing sharpened stakes in pits and covering the tops with mats that look like rock, and digging beneath boulders high on the slopes of rock piles. They agree that the Laughing Prince must be killed, and the only chance is when he holds court in the cavern. They crawl up a tunnel that overlooks the throne room, and discover that both Ah the Artificer and Brushbeard the Barbarian are among the dignitaries. The Laughing Prince appears and sits on his throne.)

"Can you reach him?" Wolf whispered.

Fire Girl shook her head and handed the bow and arrow to Wolf. The Laughing Prince wore a monk's robe, like the Monks of Mirth who flanked the throne, except that his robe was not motley. His face was in the shadows of the cowl, but evil glittering eyes pierced through the shadows like pinpoints of cold fire. He reached back and fed what might have been human liver to the seven black bats that perched upon the back of the throne, and he laughed with the sound of icicles breaking.

Wolf notched the arrow and slowly drew it back. His muscles strained to hold the feathers steady beside his right ear. Carefully he lifted the bow to the best elevation for a long shot. The sharp stone tip glittered in torchlight, and the seven bats flapped up into the air, the high shrieking squeals echoed through the cavern.

> *"Master, O Master, an arrow is near!*
> *Shining bright on the tip is the stone that you fear!"*

The glittering eyes of the Laughing Prince swept over the cavern. Icicles seemed to rush into the tunnel. Wolf tried to release the arrow, but his fingers were frozen. His arm was frozen. He felt ice enter his body and crawl toward his heart.

Fire Girl grabbed the bow and arrow and pulled back with all her might. The icicle eyes shifted and she was frozen. Seven black bats were streaking toward them.

> *"Master, O Master, a boy and a girl!*
> *With a wolf on a ring and fire in each curl!"*

"My thieving niece! Four gold pieces to the man who brings her to me! All right, *five!*" screamed Brushbeard the Barbarian, leading a platoon of soldiers across the cavern.

"Bring me my ungrateful little cousin, dead or alive!" howled Ah the Artificer, leading another platoon of soldiers.

The Laughing Prince shifted his eyes to his Monks of Mirth, and Wolf and Fire Girl fell back as though icy chains had snapped. Now there was no hope of a clear shot, and they turned and ran back down the tunnel. They reached the central cavern just ahead of the soldiers. Arrows whistled past their ears as they dove into the river, and spears probed the water as they swam beneath the black surface to the other side. They climbed out and raced toward a side tunnel, but Brushbeard the Barbarian and his men were right behind them, shouting in triumph.

Wolf and Fire Girl began counting silently: ten yaks and one, ten yaks and two, ten yaks and three . . . They leaped as far as they could. Ten yaks and one, ten yaks and two, ten yaks and three . . . They leaped again, and behind them came terrible screams, and seven black bats flew shrieking through the cavern.

"Master, O Master, your brave soldiers die!
In deep hidden pits where sharpened stakes lie!"

Where was Fire Girl? Wolf stopped and turned back and saw her standing calmly in the center of the tunnel. The sacred arrow was back in her quiver. A plain one was fixed in the bow, and the feathers held steadily beside her ear. A gross figure was moving forward, clinging to the wall and sobbing with terror.

"Dear Uncle, a gift from my mother," Fire Girl said softly.

The arrow whined like a wasp and Brushbeard the Barbarian clutched his throat and tried to pull the shaft out. Blood spurted, and he collapsed to the floor, writhing and gurgling. Fire Girl turned and ran back to Wolf, and they raced on. The tunnel exit was high on the cavern wall, at the top of rock mounds, and soldiers below at the riverbank looked up and pointed and yelled in triumph. Wolf and Fire Girl dodged arrows as they raced along a narrow path, pulling wooden braces from beneath the traps they had set. Seven black bats shrieked toward the ceiling.

"Master, O Master, to a trap have we rushed!
Beneath falling boulders your soldiers are crushed!"

Where was Wolf? Fire Girl stopped and looked around and saw him sliding down the rock slope with his knife between his teeth. Ah the Artificer shrieked in fear and swung his sword. Wolf ducked beneath it. Ah the Artificer screamed and fell, trying to pull the hilt of the knife from his stomach. Blood gushed from his mouth, and he jerked over the floor. Wolf turned and scrambled back up the rocks to Fire Girl, and they raced on. There were no more side passages until they reached their secret tunnel. They were in the open, and seven black bats were flapping above their heads.

"Master, O Master, the quarry runs here!
No escape to the front, and none to the rear!"

A cold wind whistled through the cavern. Wolf and Fire Girl turned and gazed in horror at the spectre of evil incarnate. A great black bat was flying toward them. The wings spanned at least forty feet, and the fangs glittered like huge spears, and a royal crown was on its head, and the eyes were the eyes of the Laughing Prince.

They had almost reached the wolf statue, and there was one last trap. It had been intended for soldiers who might pursue on a barge, and Wolf dove for a rope and pulled. A great boulder broke free and rolled like thunder down the slope and shot out into the air, and the splash as it hit the river sent up a blinding curtain of spray. Hidden by water, they dashed to the wall and slipped into the tiny entrance, and then followed the maze back to their cave. Behind them they could faintly hear the shrieks of seven black bats.

> *"Master, O Master, the quarry has fled!*
> *We shall search every crack till their bodies lie dead!"*

Fire Girl sat on the floor, exhausted. Her eyes were closed. When she finally opened them, she saw Wolf standing at the chimney looking up at the shaft of sunlight. Sounds of soldiers were coming down the chimney as the army of the Laughing Prince searched outside the cavern as well as in.

"I'm going to take a look," he said. His eyes were large and grave as he looked at her. "Wait for me, Fire Girl."

He scrambled up the chimney and paused at the top. Then he was gone. Fire Girl closed her eyes again. Then they opened wide.

"There's the boy!" a soldier shouted from above.

"Red hair! There's the girl too! They're both outside!" yelled another soldier.

Fire Girl jumped to her feet. Red hair? A girl up with Wolf? Her eyes fell on the stone shelf between the sleeping pallets, and widened even farther when she saw that the casket on the left was open. She walked over and looked solemnly at the legend above it: "Pull not the scales till all else fails." The casket was empty, except for a tiny strand of something red. On the bottom of the casket was writing, and Fire Girl scratched her head and wrinkled her nose.

> *"A boy who dies, dies not in vain;*
> *The Great Wheel turns, he comes again."*

Wolf had taken something red to pretend he had red hair, and he was leading the soldiers away from Fire Girl. They would catch him, of course, but she might escape.

Fire Girl walked to the last casket on the right. The fish scale lid slid down. She reached inside and lifted a small vial of pale liquid. On the bottom of the casket was writing.

> *"A girl who grieves and drinks of this,*
> *Will be awakened with a kiss."*

Fire Girl walked over and lay down on her pallet. She brushed her hair with her fingers and straightened her tunic. She carefully placed the bow and the arrow with the stone top on the floor beside her, and opened the vial. The liquid smelled fresh and clean, like forest herbs after a rain.

"Yes, Wolf, I will wait," she said softly, and she lifted the vial and drank. Her eyes closed, and she slept.

> *The Great Wheel turns, a boy will grow,*
> *His cave is kept for him to know;*
> *Again the ring of Wolf will glow,*
> *And the secret passage show.*
> *A touch of lips will open eyes,*
> *A girl of fire will thus arise;*
> *Then the sacred arrow flies,*
> *And the Heart of Evil dies.*

"The poetry is atrocious, but there's real merit in parts of the tale," Master Li said as we walked back down the hill in the moonlight.

"Yes indeed!" the prince said enthusiastically. "I always knew my ancestor had icicle eyes and the soul of a forty-foot bat."

"I think it's a glorious story," said Grief of Dawn.

"I even liked the poetry," Moon Boy confessed.

"It's sheer genius!" I cried. "Any one of those boys could be the reborn Wolf, so they have to spend endless hours looking for omens. Even if they aren't Wolf, they'll be officers in his army, so they have to prove themselves through ordeals—spending the night alone in the Forest of Sobbing Ghosts, for example, or packing Fire Drug into a hole beneath Terrible Tempered Wu's bad luck jar, so when Wu explodes it during the spring festival he'll return to earth somewhere in Tibet. And bats! They'll have to figure out how to handle those bats, and that means secret dark places. Lots and lots of cobwebs and spiders. They'll practice setting nasty traps, and learn spells to ward off the evil eye—I used to think my old gang was special, but the Seven Bloody Bandits of the Dragon Bones Cave shouldn't be allowed to *bow* to the Sacred and Solemn Order of Wolf."

Master Li was regarding me with rather cool eyes.

"Perhaps the extraordinary references to a stone are worthy of minor mention," he said wryly.

The example of Wolf and Fire Girl gave me backbone. "Damn it, it's *genius.* Centuries ago the boys who found the cave realized that if they chose as their hero a skeleton with a spearhead inside the crushed rib cage, it would be a hero who had somehow failed. So they pieced together bits and pieces from old heroic stories and—"

"Produced a tale that I admire, except for the poetry," said Master Li. "The poetry is abominable. The most admirable thing about the tale is its folk-epic nature, meaning that the words take on a quasi-religious significance. Did anyone notice Deer Ears' delivery?"

I hadn't, but Grief of Dawn had.

"His head was thrown back and his eyes were closed," she said. "Once he said 'which' and hastily changed it to 'that.' He was like my dear old Tai-tai, preserving the exact wording of an ancient story just as her parents and grandparents had preserved it."

Master Li gazed at her fondly. "Let me know if you can use some extra adoration between visits from these three gentlemen," he said. "That's the point about the references to the stone. Deer Ears came very close to the inscription above the sacristies, and two of the lines were exact: 'In darkness languishes the precious stone. When will its excellence enchant the world?' "

Prince Liu Pao threw his hands wide apart.

"Yes, but what *is* the stone?" he asked plaintively. "According to the boys' story, it's a magical thing that slays evil. But my ancestor kept and worshipped it, which scarcely makes sense unless he was in love with the idea of suicide. According to Ssu-ma and the author of *Red Chamber,* it's the embodiment of all evil. According to Ox's dream, it's an overpowering life force. Is it good? Is it evil? Is it anything more than a legend? I hate to say this, but much as I enjoyed the story of Wolf, it leads us nowhere."

"Prince, I must respectfully disagree," said Master Li. Somehow he gave me the impression of a conjurer who intended to reach into a two-inch pillbox and pull out a twenty-foot pole. "Remember those mysterious fellows in robes of motley who are somehow able to pop up out of nowhere and disappear the same way? Well, I strongly suspect that the cavern in the story is actually the tomb of the Laughing Prince, which means that the tomb is far larger then we had imagined. With daylight, we'll put the theory to the test."

石

15

The sun had just lifted over Dragon's Right Horn when Master Li led the way down the hill to the bottom of the gorge between the two peaks. I was carrying an armload of tools, and the others had torches.

"Thousands of peasants labored on the Laughing Prince's tomb," Master Li said. "Could he have murdered every one of them? Some details of the tomb were certain to be preserved in the folk memory of the Valley of Sorrows, and one form of preservation may be the fanciful tale of Wolf, who comes to a cave with Fire Girl and climbs up a natural stone chimney. He sticks his head from the hole and discovers he's at the bottom of a deep gorge. Dear Ears, head back, eyes closed, chants the exact words preserved through the centuries: 'Across from the hole he saw a good landmark—strange red and emerald-colored rocks in the side of the cliff.' "

The old man walked over to one of the sheer cliffs.

"I came down here to try to figure out how Ox had been able to climb down one side and back up the other," he said. "I didn't find a climbing path, but I did find this."

He bent some thick thistles, and we gazed at strange red and emerald rocks, almost like gemstones, set in the middle of plain granite. "Prince, is there anything like this formation in some other part of the valley?" he asked.

Without a word the prince began looking for the hole of a natural stone chimney, and the rest of us fanned out and followed his example. An hour passed before Moon Boy shouted. He was about twenty feet up the side of a cliff, at the only place where the slope allowed easy climbing, and he was pointing down at a thick clump of furze. We ran up to him. I chopped through the furze, and a black hole appeared. I had brought a long bamboo pole, and I thrust it down but couldn't reach bottom. I tossed the pole back to the other tools, and the prince helped me secure a rope ladder. Master Li handed me a torch, and I began climbing down with my knife between my teeth, feeling very much like a pirate.

The ladder was just long enough. I stepped into a small round cave with a narrow passage leading from it. My torchlight revealed an ancient wooden table and two benches. A natural stone shelf was set in the wall. I closed my eyes tightly and prayed, and then I began swinging the torch slowly around the room.

I will confess that I had prayed to find a thirteen-year-old girl with hair of fire, who had been sleeping for seven and a half centuries. I was very disappointed when she wasn't there.

"Come on down!" I yelled.

Master Li and the prince and Grief of Dawn and Moon Boy joined me. They lit their torches, and now it was bright enough to see that nobody had disturbed the dust on the floor for years. We cautiously made our way down the passage and found ourselves in a much larger cave. This one had been used for target practice, and I was willing to bet that the archer had been a boy—or a girl. Arrows were stuck all over, including the ceiling where ancient scaffolding held supporting beams. There was an old desk. To the left of the desk was a long wood table, and to the right was a row of brass-bound chests. The chests were empty. Directly in front of the desk was a large metal plate set in the stone floor, and Master Li scratched his nose thoughtfully as he looked at it.

"This looks like a paymaster's office," he said. "Engineers and overseers would stand in front of the desk to receive their wages, and the Laughing Prince was renowned for his playful pranks."

He walked behind the desk and searched for something, and then he pulled some kind of lever. I jumped backward. There was a screeching metallic sound, and then the plate split into two halves that dropped down on hinges. Where an overseer might have been standing was nothing but a black hole, and I cautiously knelt at the side and thrust my torch down. The light couldn't reach far enough to touch bottom. I found a splintered piece of old scaffolding and lit it from the torch and dropped it into the pit. It almost went out, but then it flared up again and we caught our breaths.

It had landed on sharp jutting rocks far below, right between two broken bodies. It took me a moment to realize that they weren't ancient skeletons like the ones piled in the tunnel. Hair still clung to them, and patches of dried flesh, and their clothes were almost intact.

"No more than twenty or thirty years ago," Master Li muttered.

"Thirty-three," the prince whispered. His face was white and strained. "I used to play with them. Ah Cheng and Wu Yi, gardeners at the estate. They let me ride the water buffalo and shovel manure and do all sorts of interesting things I wasn't supposed to, and one day they vanished and we never found them."

Master Li tested a bench at the table and sat down in a puff of dust.

He gazed moodily into the pit. "A stolen manuscript," he said softly, perhaps to himself. "Two dead monks, a weird sound, trees and plants destroyed—did the murder of two gardeners thirty-three years ago also play a part? Did they find the entrance in the gorge and come down here? If so, what did they see or hear that led to their deaths? If the unpleasant people dressed up in motley were involved back then, it strengthens the theory that some kind of religious cult may be behind this, worshipping the stone of the Laughing Prince and possibly continuing a line that goes back to his original Monks of Mirth."

Master Li jumped up. "This is just a preliminary look around," he said. "The next time we come down here we'd better be heavily armed. Fortunately, the dust will tell us if anyone has used a passage. Let's do a bit of exploring."

There were side passages leading from three walls of the cave. All of them had been heavily braced against rockslides. Scaffolding and posts and cross beams were everywhere, so old that the wood might snap from a loud sneeze, and we moved very carefully. The first passage ended in a rockslide that had blocked it completely, and so did the second. The third passage was so dangerous that nobody in his right mind would enter it. It was a miracle that the ceiling hadn't collapsed years ago. In the fourth we reached another dead end of fallen rocks, and so it went in all the passages. Whatever they led to couldn't be reached from the cave, and if we were going to explore a cavern that might be part of the Laughing Prince's tomb, we were going to have to find another entrance.

It was a terrible disappointment. Master Li swore without a pause after the sixth passage, and he was still swearing as we climbed gloomily back up the ladder and blinked in the sunlight. We walked back down to the center of the gorge, and suddenly Moon Boy stopped and held up a warning hand. His ears were incredibly keen.

"Horses," he said. "Lots of them, and the sound of wheels. Also jangling weapons. They're coming right at us, and if it's your monks in motley, they mean business."

We had no place to go and no time to do it in. Galloping horses and a huge chariot dashed into the narrow gorge, and mysterious monks in motley would have been far preferable to the grim-faced people we stared at. King Shih Hu of Chao reined up his horses and regarded us from his great war chariot, and his Golden Girls licked their lovely lips.

"We regret that we will be denied the enlightenment of your wisdom, Li Kao," the king said softly. "A man who can so easily spirit special people from our castle is worth listening to, but our chariot will hold only Moon Boy and Grief of Dawn."

I thought, he's going to kill us. To his way of thinking we're common thieves who have stolen valuable things from his treasury, and he's going to kill us. I decided I had better fall on my knees and do some abject kowtowing, and I had better do it fast.

"Surely Your Majesty does not claim ownership of people?" Master Li said, in the tone of a gentleman opening an interesting line of conversation. "Moon Boy and Grief of Dawn are not even your subjects, and perhaps they would prefer to make their own decisions."

I was on my knees banging my chin against the bamboo pole, the far end of which was gradually sliding toward a rake I had brought with the other tools. Only two more feet, I thought, and I tried another six kowtows.

"Neo-Confucians, of course, would argue that since Grief of Dawn and Moon Boy come from peasant stock, they should have no legal rights whatsoever," Master Li said judiciously. "Your Majesty is far too intelligent to be neo anything, and far too just to arbitrarily decide destinies without first hearing the wishes of the people involved."

"It is, Li Kao, the ability of a ruler to be arbitrary that determines his hold upon his throne," said Shih Hu.

A faint and oddly sad smile was on his lips. His eyes moved to the Golden Girls, who were fixing arrows to their bowstrings. I banged my chin one more time. The pole moved forward, and the handle of the rake slid into the hollow end. The rake was directly in front of the lead chariot horses. I grabbed the pole, lunged forward, and whipped it up. The rake plunged into the tender belly of a horse, and it reared and whinnied and pawed the air. I got the next horse. The plunging horses were in the Golden Girls' line of fire, and I felt Master Li's hand grab my belt, and I dove forward and crawled between the hooves until I was beneath the chariot. Master Li fell back out of the way. I tried to take the weight on my shoulders and legs as I heaved upward. My spine made nasty cracking noises, but I was trying to lift the chariot from one side, and the great bulk of the king helped to unbalance it. With a crash it toppled over, and the horses fell in a tangle of kicking legs, and I crawled between them while the Golden Girls maneuvered for a clear shot. It was a matter of getting a royal hostage before the girls got me, and Shih Hu was waiting for me. He even managed to keep his natural dignity as he sat on the ground like a great Buddha, and his dagger was in his hand, and he was smiling.

I heard the sharp click of the coil of rattan inside Master Li's sleeve as it shot the throwing knife from the sheath up to his hand, and a whine was almost simultaneous with the click as the blade shot past my ear. The king swore as the blade sank into his hand, and his dagger fell to the ground. I was on him in an instant, with an arm around his throat and his dagger pressed to the back of his neck.

The Golden Girls growled like panthers. They maneuvered their horses with perfect discipline, edging around and behind me. The king was paying no more attention to me than to a mildly annoying mosquito. He casually pulled Master Li's knife from the palm of his hand and tossed it away, and then, with one sweep of a massive arm, he sent me flying ten feet backward. He didn't look at me at all. The arrows drew back, pointed at my heart.

"Stop," the king said. Authority rumbled beneath the quiet tone, and the arrows lowered. He lumbered to his feet and walked over and knelt beside Moon Boy, who was holding Grief of Dawn in his arms. The shaft of an arrow protruded from her chest.

The golden shaft was aimed right at her heart, and with a shock that paralyzed emotion, I realized that Grief of Dawn was dead.

"Who could have done this?" the king whispered. "None of my girls shoots wildly." His huge head lifted. The Golden Girls bowed before his gaze, all but the captain. Her eagle eyes were defiant, but it was like trying to stare down the sun. Her eyes fell and her lips quivered. A tear slid down her cheek.

"Meng Chang, were you in so much pain?" the king said gently. "You should have come to us, my child. Jealousy is a terrible emotion. It transforms pinpricks into great gaping wounds, but there was no need for jealousy. That we loved Grief of Dawn did not mean we loved you less."

Master Li had knelt beside Grief of Dawn. His head jerked up in astonishment. "I don't believe it, but she's still breathing," he said.

My heart jumped like a speckled trout.

"If she survives this, she'll last until Mount Yun-t'ai falls on her," Master Li muttered.

His hand moved to the arrow shaft as though to pull it out. "No," the king said sharply. For the first time he was looking at me, and for the first time I realized that one of the girls' arrows had hit the fleshy part of my left thigh. The point was sticking out in the air. It was wide and flaring, and to pull an arrowhead like that back through the body is to kill the wounded person.

I snapped the head from my arrow and drew out the shaft and tossed it away, and then I ran up to Grief of Dawn and snapped off the feathered end of the arrow in her chest. I held my breath as Master Li slowly pushed the shaft down. My hand was beneath Grief of Dawn's back, and finally I felt the point bulge against the flesh. The head broke through, and I pulled the arrow completely out.

Grief of Dawn still breathed. Master Li neatly bandaged the wound. I thought Grief of Dawn was making muffled sobbing sounds, but then I realized they were coming from Meng Chang, the Captain of Bodyguards. Grief of Dawn tried to open her eyes, but couldn't.

"Tai-tai, are you ill?" she whispered. "Shall I sing to you, Tai-tai? Sometimes the pain gets better if I sing."

What happened next left all of us stunned and shaken. We had heard Grief of Dawn sing many times, but never as she sang then. She was singing to soothe the pain of the old lady who had taken her in and given her a home and a name, and what came from her lips and her heart was a miracle.

I can't describe it, other than to say it was like Moon Boy's sound magic mixed into the glorious glowing paintings of Prince Liu Pao. There were no words.

I heard pure notes climbing into the sky, brushing clouds aside, shooting past the moon, joining and singing with the brilliant glows of the stars in the Great River, and then lifting to Heaven itself to dance among the gods. The last note hovered, subtly changing pitch and color, and then began to descend to earth. The pure voice drifted among the wonders to be found in the raindrops and rippling streams of spring, and the soft drowsy sounds of summer, and the crisp clean noises of fall. Wind howled and snow fell, but Grief of Dawn was singing of a steaming kettle and boiling pot in a safe snug cottage where an old woman lay warm in her bed. The notes drifted down lower and softer, dissolving into whispering lullaby sounds, and then the last note sank into silence.

"I'm sorry, Tai-tai," Grief of Dawn whispered. "I can sing no more. It hurts to sing like that. It's beautiful but it's wrong, like stealing."

Her head fell back. Her heart was still beating, but she was unconscious.

We looked at each other in silence. Then the King of Chao got to his feet and walked back to his chariot. His huge hands separated the pawing horses and brought them to their feet, and he calmed them with pats and soft words. The Golden Girls parted to let him pass to the captain.

Meng Chang was dead. She lay on her face with her hands beneath her and the point of her sword thrusting out through her back. The king pulled the sword out and stopped the blood with his cloak. He picked her up and climbed into his carriage and sat on his couch with the girl's body on his lap. The Golden Girls opened a small chest and took out a white cloth of mourning and draped it over the king's head, and one of them took the reins. King Shih Hu and his Golden Girls rode away without a backward glance, and I never saw them again.

Grief of Dawn was tougher than the Kehsi steel of Hsingchou. Master Li was able to avert infection by making poultices from nasty-looking tree mold, and she clung ferociously to life, but fever made her hallucinate, and I decided that perhaps she was mixing the story of Wolf into something from her own life. In her private closed world she was running with somebody, and it was a desperate race.

"Faster . . . must run faster," she panted. "Where is the turn? . . . Past the goat statue . . . There's the raven and the river . . . Faster . . . Faster . . . *This way! Hurry!* . . . Soldiers . . . Hide until they pass . . . Now run! *Run!*"

She didn't always hallucinate about running for her life, and I remember the startled expression on Master Li's face when she moved restlessly in her bed and said, "Please, Mistress, must I go to Chien's?" She wrinkled her nose in disgust. "It smells so bad, and the bargemen make rude jokes about ladies, and that old man with one leg always tries to pinch me."

"Eh?" said Master Li. He walked over and began wiping the perspiration from her forehead. "Darling, what does your mistress want you to get at Chien's?" he asked gently.

She wrinkled her nose again. "Rhinoceros hides."

"And where is Chien's?" he asked.

"Halfway between the canal and Little Ch'ing-hu Lake," said Grief of Dawn.

Master Li whistled and paced around the room, and then he returned to her bedside.

"Darling, does your mistress ever send you to Kang Number Eight's?" he asked coaxingly.

Grief of Dawn smiled. "I like Kang Number Eight's," she said.

"Where is it?"

"On the Street of the Worn Cash-Coin," she said.

"What do you buy there?"

"Hats."

"Hats. Yes, of course. And where do you buy your mistress's painted fans?" Master Li asked.

"The Coal Bridge."

"I suppose she also sends you to buy the famous boiled pork at
. . . What's the name of that place?"

"Wei-the-Big-Knife," she said.

"Of course. Do you remember where it is?"

"Right beside the Cat Bridge," she replied.

Master Li took another six laps around the room. When he returned to the bed, he had his hands behind him and the fingers were
tightly crossed.

"Darling, when your mistress plays cards, what kind does she
use?" he asked.

"Peach-blend," Grief of Dawn said drowsily.

"And where do her dice come from?"

"Chuanchu Alley."

"And what do you buy from Yao-chih?"

"Cosmetics."

"And where do you get rare herbs?"

"Fenglai."

"What does your mistress get from Chingshan?"

"Writing brushes."

"Of course," said Master Li. "And what's-his-name personally
blends her ink?"

"Yes. Li Tinghuei."

"And that lovely courtesan makes pink paper for her?"

"Shieh Tao. Yes, she is lovely," Grief of Dawn said.

The fever was returning. Grief of Dawn tossed and turned while
Moon Boy and the prince tried to soothe her.

"Faster . . . faster . . . Where is the passage? *Hurry!* . . .
More soldiers . . . Faster . . . faster . . . *Hurry, darling!* . . .
There's the ibis statue . . ."

Master Li walked over to the desk and sat down and pulled out
his wine flask and swallowed about a quart.

"Pink paper from the hands of Shieh Tao," he snarled when he
came up for air. "Painted fans from the Coal Bridge and hats from
Kang Number Eight's on the Street of the Worn Cash-Coin. Li
Tinghuei personally blends the ink. Moon Boy! Can Grief of Dawn
read?"

"About as well as I do, which is not very well," he said frankly.
"Number Ten Ox reads ten times better than either of us."

Master Li swallowed another quart. "I don't even know what I'm talking about anymore," he muttered. "She'd have to be able to read Flying White shorthand."

He jumped to his feet and turned to the prince. "Your Highness, that damned fever will kill her unless we get rid of it, and the only medicine I know of that will do the trick requires the seeds of the Bombay thorn apple. Moon Boy and Ox and I are going out to find one, and in the process we will probably get killed."

Moon Boy looked at me, and then at Master Li.

"What shall we pack?" he asked.

石

16

There is no point in dwelling on my emotions regarding Grief of Dawn, but when I lay awake at night I passed the hours by planning for the day when she would be well and Master Li would take her for his wife. The Mings had quite a large shed at the rear of their house. Would they need it now that Great-grandfather was dead? We could buy it, and I knew how to lever it up and move it over to the shack, and I could fix it up as quarters for me and any guests—it was a great comfort to work out every last detail of such things, and eventually I would drift off and dream about it.

We made one stop before reaching Master Li's destination. It was at Unicorn Hall, which is a rather sad commentary upon earthly glory. The proud dignitaries of the Han Dynasty had posed for portraits that were intended to be worshipped throughout eternity, but Unicorn Hall is now in ruins. Weeds grow everywhere. Nobody has bothered to repair the roof for a century, and rain pours in. People have taken the doors and the wooden floor, and the only reason any portraits remain is that nobody can find a use for them.

Emperor Wu-ti's portrait was still intact, and even a flattering artist couldn't disguise the fact that he looked more like a bull than a man. The Laughing Prince's portrait was like the one at the estate, with the same strangely unfocused eyes. Master Li wasn't interested in the prince, however. He had come to take a close look at the prince's wife, Tou Wan.

"A friend of mine—dead for at least sixty years—once told me something interesting about Tou Wan," Master Li said. "He said that she may have been the only aristocrat to wear a hairpin that had a point fashioned from simple stone, in the style of poor peasants, and yet in all other matters she had been a spendthrift of classic proportions."

The young lady who gazed from the portrait was very beautiful, although I couldn't tell how much was real and how much was flattery. Her hair was secured by a single long pin, and the tip of it was just visible. Master Li studied it with his nose no more than an inch from the surface.

"That's what he meant," he muttered. "It's stone, all right, and the artist wouldn't have dared to toss in a sarcastic touch."

He turned and started back down the path. "Remember the words of Ssu-ma Ch'ien? The second blow of the axe broke a small sliver from the stone of the Laughing Prince, and it appears that a small sliver of stone decorated the hairpin of the Laughing Prince's wife. I'll have to remember to ask her about it."

We stared at him, but he said no more about it.

Where Grief of Dawn was concerned, Moon Boy was all business. He didn't once slip away in search of pretty boys, and we made good time. In a few days we stopped at the crest of a hill and gazed down at the roof of a small temple, and Master Li said it was our destination.

"The Temple of Liu Ling," he said. "Ever hear of him?"

We said we hadn't.

"We were quite a group, I suppose, but Ling was miles ahead of any of us," Master Li said, smiling at ancient memories. "I can see him now in his cart pulled by two deer, followed by a couple of servants. One carried enough wine to kill Liu Ling, and the other carried a spade to bury him on the spot—so much for Confucian ceremony. When I came to call he'd greet me stark naked, and I can still hear him scream, 'The universe is my dwelling place and my house is my only clothes! Why are you entering into my pants?'"

Master Li pointed to the temple. "Ling decided that men listen only to lies, so he founded the Temple of Illusion and arranged for the order to continue after his death. Moon Boy, can illusion of and by itself kill a man?"

Moon Boy shrugged. "My teacher, Lin Tsening, once deafened a

bandit by persuading him that he was hearing two monstrous dragons in the next room. There were no dragons. The actual sound was
scarcely loud enough to frighten sparrows, but the bandit was still
deaf."

"Ox?"

"Granny Ho once got mad at her son-in-law," I said. "She put
him into some sort of trance, and told him he had fallen downstairs
and hurt his left leg. When he woke up he laughed at her, and a day
later his left leg turned black and blue and began to swell, and he
was so lame he couldn't work for a week."

"Excellent," said Master Li. "My young friends, I need to recall
something. Years and years ago on a walking trip I saw a Bombay
thorn apple, but I've long forgotten where it was. In addition, I
need to take a totally fresh look at things I have seen or guessed at,
but not fully understood. In short, I need to take a trip into the
inner recesses of my mind, and I want to take you with me. Nothing
is more dangerous than a voyage inward. If your mind and senses
tell you that a spear has plunged into your heart, does it matter
whether the spear is real or imaginary?"

I thought about it. "It seems to me that either way, you'd be
dead," I said, and Moon Boy nodded agreement.

"Keep that in mind," Master Li said grimly. "The Temple of
Illusion is Liu Ling's masterpiece, and a great many people who
have ridden up to it in carriages have departed in coffins."

With those cheering words he started down the hill. The temple
was small and bare, and a small courtyard led to a plain room
where a priest sat behind a desk reading a scroll. He didn't bother
to look up when we entered. Master Li slid quite a lot of money
across the desk. "One," he said. He added another pile. "Two." He
added a third pile. "Three," he said. Still the priest didn't look up,
but he rang a bell, and another priest entered and led us to a small
room that contained only a row of pallets on the floor and a single
plaque on the wall.

I was rather surprised. I had expected mysterious music and
thick incense and all the other trappings of mumbo jumbo, but
apparently the illusions of Liu Ling didn't need any embellishment.
The plaque was in simple script I could read, and I studied it with
interest.

Butterfly Dreams

Chuang Tzu said, "Once I dreamed myself to be a butterfly, floating like petals in the air, happy to be doing as I pleased, no longer aware of myself. But soon enough I woke, and then, frantically clutching myself, Chuang Tzu I was. I wonder: Was Chuang Tzu dreaming himself to be the butterfly, or was the butterfly dreaming itself to be Chuang Tzu? Of course, if you take Chuang Tzu and the butterfly together, there is a difference between them, but is not the difference only the illusion of material form?"

The silent priest reappeared with three cups of wine and three small bowls, and he gestured that we should eat and drink. Master Li ate the stuff in his bowl with the air of a connoisseur. "I don't know what they put in the wine, but this is Devil's Ears, the most powerful of hallucinatory mushrooms," he said nonchalantly. Then he turned and pointed to the plaque.

"Chuang Tzu once made a meal of Devil's Ears. Then he had a vision that explained all the perplexing problems of mankind, and he wrote it down. When he came to himself he eagerly grabbed the paper and this is what he read. 'Sheep's Groom couples with bamboo that has not sprouted for a long while and produces Green Peace plants. Green Peace plants produce leopards, and leopards produce horses, and horses produce men. Men in time return to Sheep's Groom.' Wraps it all up rather neatly, don't you think?"

I choked on my mushroom. Moon Boy managed to eat his, so I followed suit, and then I clapped one hand to the top of my head and the other to my toes and waited for my hands to either spread apart or slam together. Nothing happened, and I began to breathe more easily. The silent priest came back in and gestured for us to follow, and walked through a door into a garden. I gazed with disbelieving eyes at the shadows.

The angle of the sun told me that it was at least the double hour of the horse. It had been early morning when we entered. Somehow nearly four hours had vanished. What had happened to them? Master Li didn't seem to be perturbed. He was trotting toward a small round pool of water in the center of the garden, and there was a happy smile on his face. As I came closer I saw something white at the bottom, and then I realized that a human skull was grinning up at us.

"Ling, dear old friend! My, you're certainly looking splendid today," Master Li said.

Moon Boy and I very nearly toppled over. There wasn't a breath of wind, yet a tall patch of reeds at the back of the pool suddenly sprang into motion: bending, arching, jabbing, thrusting—it was calligraphy; the reeds were writing in the air.

"Li Kao, you were born to be hung!"

"You mean 'hanged,' " Master Li said sweetly.

"I mean the gallows!"

The reeds began moving so fast I had trouble keeping up, but I gathered that the late Liu Ling was saying that the flaw in Master Li's character couldn't be explained by loathsome percentage alone, and in a previous incarnation Master Li must have been a hyena or a scorpion or even the East Idiot Ruler of South Tsi. The reeds became quite agitated as they reviewed that gentleman's career.

"—and cut off their hands and feet!"

"No, I couldn't have been the East Idiot Ruler of South Tsi," Master Li said thoughtfully. "I would have cut off their noses as well."

". . . burned right down to the ground!"

"If you must do something, do a thorough job," Master Li said.

". . . every last man, woman, and child!"

"Wasteful. Some of the girls must have been pretty. Ling, old friend, I hate to be overly critical, but was it wise to surround yourself with nothing but water?" said Master Li.

He pulled out his flask and splashed wine into the pool, and Moon Boy and I clung together for support. The dark stain of wine had gathered itself into a spinning whirlpool, and the spout was reaching down through the water to the grinning mouth of the skull. The reeds were still. Then one moved.

"Burp."

"This stuff is since your time," Master Li said. "It's called Haining Mountain Dew. What do you think of it?"

The reeds went into action again. *"Haining? Those clodhoppers make this excellent wine? I suppose even dung beetles have their talents. Speaking of dung beetles, has Belly Draft finished drinking himself to death?"*

"He's still working at it," said Master Li. "I tell his landlords that his liver is constructed from some kind of crystallized carbon, but they keep throwing him out because of the danger of spontaneous combustion."

He poured more wine into the pool and had some himself. The reeds went waving again.

"Who's the raving beauty and the carnival wrestler?"

"This is my esteemed former client and current assistant, Number Ten Ox," Master Li said. "This is Moon Boy, the world's foremost authority on sounds and bottoms like peaches."

We stepped forward and bowed to the skull. The reeds moved.

"Moon Boy makes me wish I still had a bottom, but why bring young heroes to an old quack lying at the bottom of a pool?"

Master Li took another sip of wine. "For one thing, I want Moon Boy to look into a mirror," he said casually.

Was it my imagination or were the reeds moving warily?

"What kind of mirror did you have in mind?"

"The only one that matters," Master Li said.

"Take care, Li Kao!"

"Others have made the trip," Master Li said. "I even hear that the emperor came to you for a passport, and he's still in one piece."

The reeds were quite agitated. *"T'ang needed both divine intervention and an enormous bribe to get out! Can you count on that kind of help? I can open the door, but once inside, you'd be on your own, and have the boys consented to such a journey?"*

Master Li glanced at us. I bowed to the skull. "Illustrious Sir, where Master Li goes, I go," I said.

"Most Noble Sage, the life of a girl named Grief of Dawn is involved, and I will go where I must," Moon Boy said.

The reeds were still, and when they moved, it was reluctantly.

"So be it. Li Kao, give my love to Queen Feiyen if you see her— gods, her breath was like an orchid!—and thank Li Po for leaving me his loaded dice."

The water in the pool began to revolve. It swirled faster and faster, moving in concentric circles toward the center, and my eyes were drawn to the skull. A strange light was shining in the empty eye sockets, beckoning to me, and it seemed that the skull was growing larger and larger. White bones appeared to fill the sky, and the light pulled me forward, and I found myself walking through a huge eye socket. Master Li and Moon Boy walked through the other one, and we were standing on a rocky ledge high on a mountain. Cold wind whistled around my ears, and in the distance an eagle screamed.

"Marvelous effects," said Master Li.

In front of us, set in the rock, was a bronze door. Master Li pushed it open and we walked through to a landing and placed our feet upon the first step of a long winding staircase that would take us down to Hell.

石

17

Barbarian readers, no matter how illustrious, will have but a rudimentary concept of Hell. This is not their fault but the fault of ignorant priests and sages who cling to two incredible fallacies: that Hell is reserved for the damned, and that the world is flat.

The world is a cube measuring 233,575 paces across. The center of the cube is occupied by the Kingdom of Hell, and it is the judging place for *all* mortals, saint and sinner alike. That is why people on the wrong sides of the cube don't fall off: We are all drawn toward our ultimate destination so no matter where one stands, Hell is always "down" and Heaven is always "up," and that's all there is to it.

The kingdom is enormous. There are one hundred thirty-five lesser Hells and ten principal ones: one for judgment by the God of Walls and Ditches, one for the Great Wheel of Transmigrations, and eight for the punishment of sinners. The lesser Hells contain people waiting to be judged, other people awaiting transportation to the Land of Extreme Felicity in the West, where they will sit at the feet of Buddha, extremely blessed people who await transportation to K'un-lun Mountain, where they will sit at the feet of the August Personage of Jade, and so many others that I will not try to list them.

It is strictly illegal for the living to enter Hell, with rare exceptions involving official delegations from the Emperor of China. Outside of Emperor T'ang, I knew of only two others who had illegally entered Hell and managed to return. One was Chou the Rogue, who was a crook so audacious that he once blackmailed the sun, and the other was Crazy Ch'i, who has become a demigod and has many temples dedicated to him. I would back Master Li against either of them, which is why I wasn't totally paralyzed with fear as we descended to the Land of Shadows. Master Li, however, had a few doubts.

"Our first task will be to evaluate the new regime," he said worriedly. "It is said that the former First Lord of Hell, Yen-wang-yeh, has been judged to have been too lenient and has been demoted, but no signs have been received to indicate who's currently in charge. If Legalists have won out, we could be in real trouble."

We were floating downward rather than walking—a blessing, since it is a terrible task to climb down 116,787½ steps—and a small circle of pale cold light was appearing before us. We came to rest in front of a doorway and cautiously peered out across a flat gray plain toward the walls of the principal city of Feng-tu. There was no sun, only a pearly glow in the gray sky. Even the trees and flowers were gray, and sounds seemed to be muted.

The demons weren't gray. Some had bright blue faces and fiery red eyes and long yellow tusks, and others had green fangs and crimson noses and black ears. They were every bit as horrible as the demons one sees in dreams, and they were herding the dead into long lines that slowly shuffled toward the city gates. The social hierarchy was absolute. Aristocrats formed one line, tradesmen another, scholars another—bureaucrats and soldiers and farmers all had their assigned line and priority of entrance, with the nobility taking precedence and actors bringing up the rear. The ceremony was formal and painstaking. Demons bowed to trolls, who bowed to ogres, who bowed to devils, and Master Li drew his head back and spat disgustedly.

"Bat shit," he growled. "The Neo-Confucians have taken over." He thought about it and cheered up. "Actually, this makes our task much easier," he said. "Moon Boy, put on your best jewels and costliest clothes. Ox, you want the garb and facial expression of an ideal peasant, and I'll take a few liberties with current reality."

We opened our packs. I put on a pair of sandals that were falling apart and a hat that resembled a rat's nest, and ripped an old tunic in the back to resemble lash strokes. When I had plastered an expression of meek animal resignation across my homely face, I was a peasant to warm the heart of the most demanding mandarin. Moon Boy dazzled the eyes. It would take four pages to do his clothes justice, and his jewels would have bankrupted some kingdoms.

Master Li was awesome. Never before had I seen him in full academic regalia, and it was magnificent. He had finished his examinations as *chuang yuan,* the number one scholar in all China, and he proudly wore the emblem of the rose. In addition, he had a breast emblem of imperial axes and dragons: *chien-kuan,* the dreaded censor who is empowered to promote or decapitate on the spot. (Years ago he had been entitled to wear it.) His lacquered cap bore all nine buttons of rank, and he handed me his state umbrella. I put it together and raised it above the heads of the scholar and the handsome peacock.

"Arrogance, lads!" said Master Li. "Never forget that the flames of Hell exist for the privilege of brewing tea for noble Neo-Confucians like us."

We took deep breaths and marched out into the cold gray landscape of Hell. Demon nostrils twitched in disgust at the aroma of living flesh, and fiery eyes turned toward us.

"Make a note of that fat fellow with the purple eyes and lumps of flesh hanging from his fangs! Ten lashes for slovenliness," said Master Li, and Moon Boy scribbled in a ledger. "Look at these lines! Mired in molasses and not even straight! Isn't that the corpse of the fellow who called himself Duke of Chou? Since when does a pimp take a place in the aristocrats' line? A good housecleaning is what this place needs, along with a few hundred decapitations."

The fierce old fellow appeared to be the type of person one passes on to superiors, and fangs and talons hovered but did not strike. We marched rapidly toward the gates. Moon Boy had the natural assurance of beautiful people. He graciously inclined his head right and left as though acknowledging applause, and a faint frown indicated that the least the ogres could do was line his path with incense and flower petals. Meanwhile, I was discovering why so many of my humble class take pride in their servility and lash marks.

I held a state umbrella on high, which meant that I too was marching beneath the yellowish-black gauze cover, red raw silk linings, three tiers and silver spires that signified an official of the highest rank. I belonged. What is a great official without a peasant to lash? A sense of power passed from the handle to my hand, and I discovered that the most natural expression in the world was a lofty sneer. Slavery is a marvelous refuge from uncertainty.

The fiends who guarded the gates held up their claws: halt! "Look at those filthy nails! Twenty lashes!" Master Li screamed furiously, and he marched right between them. I clutched the umbrella for dear life, and the next thing I knew we were through the gates and inside the city. Master Li marched past the vast basilica of the God of Walls and Ditches toward the palace of the First Yama King, and as we approached the doors, I knew we were in trouble. None could pass without the permission of a very senior devil who had a black face, crimson eyes, steel fangs, iron wings, and a head covered with writhing vipers instead of hair. Puffs of smoke came from its ears and nostrils. I wondered if the knocking sound came from my knees or Moon Boy's, and decided we were playing a duet.

Master Li tapped his imperial censor's emblem and regarded the terrible creature with the scientific detachment of a butcher examining a chunk of meat. "Lord Li of Kao, emissary of the Son of Heaven, to see the Recorder of Past Existences. Immediately!" Master Li snapped.

The demon glared. Flames spurted from its mouth.

"Do I detect insolence?" Master Li said coldly. He plucked an emerald broach from Moon Boy's tunic and tossed it into the river of molten iron that ran beside the walls of the palace. "It would be regrettable should I be forced to report that an insolent doorkeeper stole a valuable broach and attempted to conceal the crime by swallowing it." His cold eyes moved to the creature's belly. "Although it might be entertaining to watch your superiors recover the evidence," he added.

Without another word he turned and marched straight toward the great steel doors. I hastened to catch up, and I was so blinded by sweat and terror that I didn't realize the doors had opened until my sandals began to slap across a marble floor.

Even Master Li had a thin line of perspiration on his forehead. Moon Boy alone seemed unperturbed. He continued to acknowledge imaginary applause, although he appeared to be slightly annoyed at the lack of welcoming trumpets, and I stiffened my spine and raised the state umbrella a bit higher. We walked down a long hallway to a large room where an army of clerks shuffled papers.

Hell is staffed by ordinary spirits as well as demons. (Demons aren't evil, incidentally. To be reborn as a servant of Hell is one of the incarnations of the Great Wheel, and blood lust is simply part of the process, like becoming a tiger.) The head clerk must surely have been a banker in his last incarnation. He had thin straight hair, thin straight eyebrows, thin straight eyes, thin straight nostrils, thin straight lips, thin straight shoulders, thin straight hands placed precisely parallel upon the desk, thin straight knees pressed primly together, and thin straight feet planted firmly on the floor. Moon Boy regarded him thoughtfully.

"Mine," he said.

"You have him," said Master Li. "We need to get into the Recorder's office."

It was like one of those dances in opera that tell more than words are capable of. My cheeks burned as Moon Boy undulated gracefully toward the desk—I had never seen him do that before—and the clerk's eyes glazed. Moon Boy smiled. The clerk's eyes bulged, and beads of sweat appeared on his forehead. Moon Boy cooed soft words. The thin knees jerked beneath the desk. Moon Boy cooed some more. The thin hands twisted together and the thin feet pawed the floor. The poor fellow managed to say something, and Moon Boy's hand behind his back pointed a finger at one of the side doors. Master Li and I moved unobtrusively over to it. Moon Boy gestured and accidentally brushed the clerk's hand, and the clerk shot to his feet and wobbled shakily to the door and deferentially knocked and opened it.

We were through the door before the clerk knew what was happening, and Moon Boy rewarded him with a pat on the cheek before slamming the door in his face.

I expected another army of clerks, but the Recorder of Past Existences was seated alone at a huge desk almost buried beneath ledgers. The face that lifted to us reminded me of paintings of Hengchiang, the Sniffing General. His eyebrows were vertical and his eyes bulged like a frog's and his nose was wrinkled as though he permanently sniffed something unpleasant. Master Li bowed as to a social equal, and Moon Boy's bow perfectly matched courtesy and condescension.

"Eh?" said the Recorder.

"Lord Li of Kao, emissary of the Son of Heaven, and the Son of Heaven is furious," said Master Li.

"Eh?" said the Recorder.

"Such an unseemly intrusion would be intolerable were not serious matters involved, and what could be more serious than failure to adequately apply the Broth of Oblivion?" Master Li said gravely.

"Eh?" said the Recorder.

Master Li whirled around and glared at me. "Look at this witless and lice-ridden representative of the lower classes!" he said angrily. "By rights his knowledge should be limited to fields, fealty, and flatulence, yet he claims to recall every detail of a previous existence in which he was the great-great-grandfather of *this* jewel of the current court!"

Moon Boy took his cue and bowed gracefully.

"Not only that, this drooling crotch-scratching clod insists he was tutor to the princes of the Sui Dynasty!" Master Li yelled. "He tells tales of Emperor Yang's debauches that would curl your hair, if you had any, and every time he opens his silly mouth, he substantiates his claim to have been Lord Tsing!"

(That gave me my cue. Tsing was the name of the dear old assistant abbot in the monastery near my village, who taught the village boys when they finished working in the fields. He was a sweet kindly fellow who suffered from terminal pedantry, and I used to amuse Master Li by imitating him.)

"Step forward, oaf!" I drooled and scratched my crotch and stepped forward. Master Li looked around and pointed to an ornate bronze bowl. "What decorative motif is that?" he snarled.

I tried to make my eyes film over, and my jaws creaked like unoiled hinges as they relentlessly spread apart.

"T'sao-t'ieh, or 'glutton mask,' is a distinctive motif of the Shang and early Chou dynasties," I droned in a dull monotone. "It is an animal face seen from the front, sometimes recognizable and sometimes stylized to resemble a fabulous monster. It is flattened on a side surface or bent around a corner; in either case a flange is likely to split it into symmetrical halves, each having a protruding eyeball. From each side of the face, sometimes in proper proportion and sometimes not, extends a body in perfect symmetry with its opposite, as if the carcass had been cut through along the backbone and the two halves had been folded out like wing attachments to the head. The bodies have serpentine dragonlike qualities, coiling in spirals or geometric twists and turns, and are themselves covered

with spiral or geometric designs, sometimes including smaller t'sao-
t'ieh. The same glutton mask usually appears many times on a ves-
sel. It is a striking, powerful, and unique design, and what it represents . . . (pause, slowly count to ten) . . . is not known."

Moon Boy's eyes had glazed, and he was teetering on his feet.
The Recorder of Past Existences was slumping at his desk. He
jerked his head up when his chin bounced against his inkstone. I
picked my nose. Moon Boy woke up and fell at my feet and began
kissing my sandals. *"Great-great-grandfather!"* he howled.

My rheumy eyes creaked toward a vase of gray flowers. My re-
lentless jaws creaked open.

"The following plants and flowers," I droned, "each create a
mood. The plum flower goes with poetry, the orchid with seclusion,
the chrysanthemum with rustic flavor, the lotus with simplicity of
heart, the cherry apple with glamour, the peony with success, the
banana and bamboo with gentlemanly charm, the begonia with seductive beauty, the pine tree with retirement, the plane tree with
absence of worry, the willow with sentimentality, the—"

"For the love of Buddha, stop!" the Recorder howled.

"Awe-inspiring, isn't it?" Master Li said. "How can one doubt
that this worm was tutor to princes when he can put an entire
regiment to sleep in two minutes flat? Failure to remove all memory
of previous existences is an extremely grave matter!"

"I can't understand it," the Recorder whispered. "Hundreds of
such cases have been reported in the past, but we have been very
careful during the past few centuries."

"It could be fraud," Master Li pointed out. "The Son of Heaven
has proposed an infallible test, which is the reason for this visit. We
shall simply make this revolting creature stand before *Nieh-ching-
t'ai,* and the truth shall be revealed."

"It is strictly illegal for the living to stand before the Mirror of
Past Existences!" the Recorder snapped.

"The gods look the other way when the cause is just and wise,"
Master Li said smoothly. "Besides, this preening peacock claims to
be the great-great-grandson, and fraud is so often a matter of con-
spiracy."

Moon Boy did a good job of turning pale and trembling, and the
Recorder's eyes gleamed. Bureaucrats and courtiers do not love one
another, and a few minutes later we were walking down a maze of

corridors. A great black door swung open to reveal a dark tunnel at the end of which was a glow of greenish light. As we came closer I realized it was a natural mirror formed by an immense crystal set in the stone wall.

A sense of sacred awe surrounded the Mirror of Past Existences. I found that I was on my knees, kowtowing, and the others were kowtowing in front of me. We got back to our feet. The marks of two sandals were drawn on the floor in front of the mirror, and Master Li shoved me forward. I placed my feet on the marks and slowly raised my eyes. The green light from the mirror was pulsing like a heartbeat. I could see my own reflection clearly, but there was no reflection of the others. A strange sense of peace had entered my heart. I was not frightened when a soft voice spoke in my ear.

"Why does a living person stand before me?"

I had no idea what to reply, so I said the first thing that came to my mind.

"Master Li seeks truth."

The green light pulsed silently. Then the voice spoke again. "So be it. Look straight at me, Number Ten Ox."

Two columns appeared at the sides of the mirror. One was headed "Virtues," and the other was headed "Sins." Then my image dissolved and reformed, and I realized that I was looking at my first existence upon the earth.

I was a blob of something I couldn't identify, something like a tiny jellyfish. The blob combined with other blobs to form larger jellyfish. Then I became something with tendrils, and then something that crawled, and finally I was delighted to recognize one of my existences: a flatworm. The virtues and sins columns remained empty.

I was reborn as a fish. Then I became some sort of plant, and then some fungus, and then an insect. I was reborn as a hawk moth, a cockroach, a cow, and a tortoiseshell cat. I was quite proud of myself as I moved up the scale of existences.

I frowned. I appeared to be backsliding. I became a piece of kelp, a patch of pond scum, six kinds of rock, four trees, and a number of plants. Then I began moving up the scale again: a snapdragon, a black grouse, a gecko, and a bowlegged mongrel with one eye, chewed ears, and a body bearing the scars of a thousand back-alley battles. The virtues and sins columns remained as empty as the minds of the General Staff. I eagerly awaited my first human existence.

Here it was. I was reforming as a human being. I gaped at the familiar ugly face of Number Ten Ox, and when I felt my body, I watched the reflected hands move in the mirror. The virtues and sins columns disappeared.

"I'll be damned," said Master Li.

"We don't say that down here, but I know what you mean," the Recorder said. "Extraordinary! This boy is as innocent as an apricot."

"Not quite," Master Li said grimly. "We now know that he was never a tutor to princes, and one wonders about the nature of his accomplice. Peacock, step forward!"

Moon Boy took my place in front of the mirror. That was what Master Li had wanted from the start, and I admired the neat way he had arranged it.

"Virtue" and "Sin" columns appeared. Moon Boy's image began to dissolve, and he too became some kind of blob. Again I saw the procession of other blobs and things with tendrils, but then things turned dramatically different. In rapid order Moon Boy became poison ivy, a patch of deadly nightshade, and a clump of red berries I wouldn't have approached with a barge pole. He was moving up the scale at great speed, and he dissolved into a tarantula, a cobra, and a horrible thing with twenty writhing tentacles. The thing dissolved into the image of a sweet little old lady with twinkling eyes.

The little old lady was bustling about her kitchen adding green and purple powders to a pot. Purple smoke lifted from it, and black liquid boiled over the side, and the sweet little old lady cackled with delight as a kitten lapped at the stuff, turned blue, and dropped over dead. The sins column began to show activity, and apparently the Great Wheel of Incarnations decided to go back and try again.

The little old lady dissolved into something I couldn't identify, but Master Li muttered that it looked like a case of leprosy. The leprosy dissolved into a misshapen worm, a vulture, a poisonous toad, a sow bug, a patch of spleenwort, and then a happy laughing little boy who was torturing a gecko. The sins column went to work again, and Moon Boy's next incarnation was the stuff of legend: Mad Monk Mu of Midnight Marsh.

The goulish monk dissolved into a patch of quicksand as the

Great Wheel of Incarnations tried again. The quicksand dissolved into feverish swamp vapor, a series of spiders, a vampire bat, a hyena, and finally into Moon Boy—but Moon Boy dressed as a girl and playing with a cat. I was relieved to see that he wasn't torturing it. Then I slowly realized that Moon Boy was training the cat to scratch the eyes from the rival's baby, and the mirror appeared to shudder as though gathering forces for one final effort.

Light formed around Moon Boy's beautiful face. The nimbus grew brighter and brighter, shimmering like tongues of fire. Moon Boy was changing and yet not changing, rearranging in a way that was both familiar and strange. His face lifted. His arms rose as though reaching for the sun. Brilliant colors moved around and through him. The sins column had overflowed and was stretching down the wall, and the virtues column remained empty.

Suddenly the columns disappeared. The image disappeared. Words formed in the mirror. *"Judgment is beyond the jurisdiction of lower courts, and is reserved for the Supreme Deity."* Then the words vanished and Moon Boy was staring back at his own image.

"Heaven preserve us," the Recorder whispered.

"Incredible," Master Li said. "We must thank the gods that this fellow is not under our jurisdiction! The Son of Heaven will assign temporal punishment to him and his oafish accomplice, but I had best glance at the Register of Souls to ensure that an earthly sentence will not conflict with a divine one."

I doubt that the Recorder of Past Existences would normally have allowed such a thing, but he was a shaken man. He meekly allowed Master Li to spend a minute in the room where the register was kept, and then he hastily escorted us back through the maze, opened a door, shoved us outside to a courtyard, and slammed the door behind us.

Master Li doubled over with laughter. "What a pair you are!" he chortled. "It's an honor to travel with such distinguished young gentlemen, so let's travel to see a friend of mine, and then on to see Tou Wan, the wife of the Laughing Prince."

I had to admire Moon Boy. He had just discovered that his previous existences broke the world record for wickedness, but he preened himself as though nothing had happened and kept his voice steady.

"At the risk of sounding stupid, why don't we go see the aristocratic assassin himself?" he asked reasonably.

Master Li started off in silence. Finally he cleared his throat and said, "That would be a bit difficult. You see, according to the Register of Souls, the Laughing Prince managed to elude the bailiffs, and he has never arrived in Hell."

石

18

Looking back at it, I think it was fortunate that Moon Boy and I were preoccupied with images of a mad mummy creeping up from a tomb to the room where Grief of Dawn lay helpless in bed. It distracted us from the details of Hell, and some of them were very unpleasant. We were approaching the river How Nai-ho, which is the boundary between the First and Second Hells. It is spanned by three bridges: One is gold and is used by visiting gods and their emissaries, one is silver and is used by the virtuous, and the third is a ramshackle bamboo bridge with no handrails that is used by sinners. The sinners scream in terror as they try to cross the river. Inevitably they fall off, and horrible bronze dogs and snakes splash through the water with jaws gaping wide. The water bubbles with blood, but it's merely a foretaste of what is to come, because the mangled bodies wash up on the far bank and are miraculously healed, and laughing demons lead the sinners to places where torment begins in earnest.

Master Li marched toward the gold bridge while Moon Boy bellowed, "Make way for Lord Li of Kao, emissary of the Son of Heaven!" and we proceeded past glaring demons and over the golden span as though we owned it. The Second Hell punishes dishonest male and female intermediaries and ignorant or unscrupulous doctors. The torment is not one of the terrible ones, but the smell is revolting, and Moon Boy and Master Li clapped handkerchiefs to their noses. I was used to barnyards, so I wasn't bothered very much. We made our way down long lines of pits, and finally

Master Li stopped at one where a fat fellow with a mournful flabby face was buried in soft manure up to his chin. Even through the reek he could smell living flesh, and his eyes slowly lifted.

"Now, look here, Li Kao, if it's about that land I sold you—"

"Nothing like that," said Master Li.

"I had no idea there was alkali in the soil! May Heaven judge if I . . . er . . . may Heaven judge . . . er . . . oh, shit."

"Well, you should be an expert on the subject," Master Li said cheerfully. "Actually, the Yama Kings were quite lenient, considering the fact that you sold some of the same land to your own father."

The fat fellow began to weep, and tears made pale furrows in the brown goo that covered most of his face. "You wouldn't bring that to their attention, would you?" he sobbed. "You can't imagine what the Neo-Confucians are doing to this place! They'd send me to the Eighth Hell, and that's horror beyond belief."

"You should see what the same fellows are doing to China," Master Li said gloomily. "The other night I dreamed you had returned as court physician, and I hadn't been so happy in years."

It was difficult to draw oneself up with dignity under the circumstances, but the fat fellow tried.

"Not all of my patients died," he said huffily. "Some even managed to walk again, and one or two didn't even need crutches!"

"The ones you treated for colds?"

"Colds or pimples. It is not the physician's fault if a patient is lunatic enough to come in with a case of hangnails," the fellow said reasonably.

"You were a doctor in a million," Master Li said warmly. "Who else would have prescribed arsenic oxide for hiccups?"

"It worked!"

"No patient is in a position to dispute it," Master Li said somewhat ambiguously. "Medical expertise is not what I've come to see you about, however. Do you remember the walking trip we took in Tungan? It must have been eighty or ninety years ago, and I've reached the point where my brain resembles the stuff you're buried in. All I can remember is a girl in a scarlet sampan."

The transformation was amazing. Flab appeared to melt from the fat fellow's face, and I realized that he had once been a lighthearted and rather handsome young man.

"You remember her too?" he said softly. "Li Kao, not a day has passed in which I haven't thought of that girl. Wasn't that a time? She sang 'Autumn Nights' and tossed rice cakes into the water and laughed as we dove for them like ducks. By all the gods, I hope she made it to Heaven."

"Wasn't there a festival?" Master Li asked.

"A wild village one. Masks and drums and monkey-dances, and that big farmer picked you up after you'd blackened his eye and crowned you King of Fleas. We stayed drunk for a week, and they gave us gifts of food and flowers when we left."

He gazed sadly down at his manure pit. "What a wonderful thing it was to be young," he whispered.

Master Li told us to keep our eyes peeled for demons while he leaned down and tilted his wine flask at the fellow's lips. It had been a long time between drinks, and he gulped a quart.

"Buddha, that's wonderful stuff! Haining Mountain Dew?"

"The best," Master Li said. "You were an avid botanist in those days, and I seem to remember that after we left the girl in the sampan we set out cross-country. We passed a temple or a convent, and when we climbed into the hills, you discovered—"

"The Bombay thorn apple!" the fellow cried. "How could I forget it? The find of a lifetime, and I always planned to go back, but somehow the world closed in on me and I never did."

"Could you find it now?" Master Li asked.

The fellow looked up with sudden intelligence in his eyes. "So that's it. You need a Bombay thorn apple, do you? Dangerous stuff, Li Kao. You always did get involved in the damnedest things, and how you manage to keep alive is one of the great mysteries of the empire."

Master Li leaned down with the flask again.

"What a pair we are," the fellow said when he stopped coughing. "I'm damned and you're demented. I may be a sinner, but at least I know it isn't nice to deprive children or lunatics of their toys, and if I wanted the only Bombay thorn apple I've ever seen in China I'd go about two miles past the White Cloud Convent to the point where the hills are closest to the road. I'd turn east and start climbing. Shale followed by granite followed by some kind of black rock, and past the black rock I'd come to a clearing in front of a cliff. Tunnel through the brush, and right against the cliff is another tiny

clearing, and in the center is a Bombay thorn apple—unless somebody's cut it down for firewood and massacred his family and
neighbors in the process."

His eyes moved to Moon Boy and me. "Something to do with
Beauty and the Beast, eh? Take care, Li Kao. This is the soft area of
hell. Later on you'll need a better passport than a state umbrella."

Master Li bowed and turned to go. "You know, the Yama Kings
are stern but just," he said. "Good intentions can at least partially
mitigate bad results, and the Great Wheel waits patiently. Who
knows? After a couple of insect and animal incarnations, you might
find yourself poling down the Yangtze in a crimson sampan."

The fellow looked up with desperate hope in his eyes. "You
couldn't possibly have sneaked a look at the Register of Souls," he
whispered.

Master Li winked. We started off down the path, and the last I
saw of the fellow he was weeping with joy at the thought of being
reborn as a sampan singsong girl, and the last I heard of him he was
practicing "Autumn Nights."

The torments of the Third and Fourth Hells are also relatively
light, and are designed for such sinners as bad bureaucrats, backbit-
ers, forgers, coiners, misers, dishonest tradesmen, and blasphemers.
Serious torment begins in the Fifth Hell, where murderers, unbe-
lievers, and the lustful are punished. I will make no attempt to
describe the caldrons of boiling oil, the pits of molten lead, the
beams of hollow iron, the Hill of Knives, and the Sawmill. Master
Li told me that such things are utilized by most cultures with the
exception of the Tibetan, and that the Yama Kings had no intention
of instituting the unspeakable atrocities of the Tibetan World of
Darkness.

According to the Register of Souls, Tou Wan had been damned
not for murder and torture but for wanton carnality, and the Fifth
Hell provides such sinners with beds in which to cool down. We
marched down rows of beds formed from sheets of ice to which
sinners were held by frozen iron chains, and naked bodies shuddered unceasingly and the air was loud with the sound of cracking
joints. We came to the wife of the Laughing Prince in the fiftieth
row.

I was not prepared for her youth and beauty. Like the others, she
shuddered and jerked in her chains, but she made not a whimper

and her eyes were open instead of being fastened shut by eyelids thick with frozen tears. Master Li bowed deeply.

"Princess, I hope you will forgive the intrusion," he said. "We had hoped to interview your noble husband, but he appears to be unavailable."

Her lips parted with the sound of cracking ice. "Unavailable?"

"Somehow he managed to dodge the bailiffs. Do you have any idea how he managed it?"

She managed an ironic laugh, and I decided she was the toughest person I had ever met. "They should have searched for his soul inside the stone," she said.

"The stone!" Master Li exclaimed. "Wherever we go, we keep running into references to that stone. Would you be kind enough to enlighten me on the subject?"

Tou Wan's voice was as cold as the ice she lay on. "Guess, if you like. If you guess right, I may answer one or two questions."

"I shall guess that the stone was broken into three pieces, and the largest piece was placed in a sacristy, and the second largest was used by your husband as an amulet, and the last sliver became the tip of your hairpin," said Master Li.

"You guess well, old man," the princess said. "Ssu-ma Ch'ien broke it, the meddling fool, and he wasn't even half-right about it. He called it the Stone of Evil, and his mistake cost him his balls. What would you call the stone, old man?"

Master Li looked thoughtfully at her. "I would not call it evil, and I would not call it good," he said slowly. "I would call it a concentrated life force that in the hands of a saint could heal all wounds, but in the hands of your husband could wound all heals, if you will forgive the sophistry."

"Better and better, old man," Tou Wan said. Her eyes closed. Ice began to form over her lips. I thought she had ended the interview, but then her body shuddered and jerked, and the ice over her mouth cracked.

"It was not his, it was never his, it was mine . . . A lover gave it to me . . . Lovers always gave things to me . . . I was ten when I let a boy think he had seduced me; he gave me his mother's rings . . . A pretty boy, so easy to train, like a dog . . . Lie down! Sit up! . . . His father came for the rings and I trained him too . . . Roll over! Beg! . . . I led him around on a leash that only women could see; how they hated me, the sluts . . . He made me his number seven wife, and I persuaded him and his pretty son to go to a war where they were sure to be killed . . . Hsu was the lawyer and Kung-sun was the magistrate . . . Lie down! Sit up! Roll over! Beg! . . . I threw the other wives out into the street, and then Yi Shou the merchant with his jewels and carriages, Governor Kuo with his houses and land, wriggling like good little dogs begging to be petted . . . I could not train Prince Liu Sheng, but he gave me a crown . . . It was his steward who gave me the stone . . . The stone . . . Holding it against my skin, feeling the pulse . . . My husband stole it from me and it drove him mad, madder than I believed possible . . . The Little Tour, the Big Tour, one thousand seconds, the Embryonic Pearl, kill, kill, kill, kill, kill! . . . Ssu-ma broke the stone, and all I had was the sliver for my hairpin . . . That maid, always looking at it, always wanting it, trying to steal it . . . I stabbed her, but she ran away with my stone . . . My maid and that concubine with the ring of Upuaut my husband gave her . . . The soldiers killed them, but they could not find the stone . . . It was mine, all of it was mine . . . My husband refused to give me a second piece . . . He laughed and showed me a tender poem for my coffin, and then he made me drink poison . . . Mad monks in motley dancing and laughing around my bed . . . Cold . . . Colder . . . Mist, sounds of water, bailiffs pulling me into a gray world, Yama Kings, freezing, freezing, freezing . . ."

Tou Wan's eyes opened. She looked at me. "Peasant boy, you would have made a good little dog." Her eyes were deep and wondering as they moved to Moon Boy. "You I would have worshipped." Her eyes moved to Master Li.

"You I could neither have worshipped nor broken and trained," said the princess. "Old man, I fear you. Go away."

Master Li bowed, and Moon Boy and I followed his example. Tou Wan's eyes closed and her mouth shut with a sound like the click of a lock. I raised the state umbrella and we marched on down the path.

"What an extraordinary young woman," Master Li said admiringly. "The phrase 'tougher than Tou Wan' must enter the language, and we should try to do something about her bed of ice."

石

19

We walked across a long gray plain that led to the great gray walls of the Sixth Hell. Gray grass bent beneath a cold gray breeze, and the gray sky seemed to press down upon us.

"Master Li, I don't understand about the stone," I said. "Isn't it evil? Ssu-ma thought so, and he wrote that the author of *Dream of the Red Chamber* had been quoting from the Annals of Heaven and Earth."

Master Li walked on in silence for some time. Then he said, "Ox, we can't be sure that the legendary annals were actually involved, but we do know that both Ssu-ma and Tsao Hsueh Chin accepted as proof the reactions of two great men who possessed the stone. Both Lao Tzu and Chuang Tzu cried, 'Evil!' and hurled it away, but did they really mean that the *stone* was evil? Could they have meant something else? There's at least one other possibility, and it has to do with the shape of the stone."

The shape? I tried to recall the words of Ssu-ma. "Flat smooth area rising to round concave bowl shape." What did that have to do with evil?

"But Tou Wan said that it drove her husband mad," Moon Boy pointed out. "Doesn't that imply the stone was evil?"

"No," Master Li said flatly. "Her words make it perfectly clear. The inner power of the stone tempted the Laughing Prince to use it in the ridiculously dangerous discipline called Taoist Ideal Breathing. The goal is personal immortality, which is always an invitation to disaster. You lie on your back with your tongue pressed against the roof of your mouth to catch brain dew, which is what Taoists call saliva. Normally you press the middle finger of each hand against the opposite palm, but I suspect that the Laughing Prince pressed his fingers against the ch'i pulse of the stone. You suck in air and hold it for thirty seconds, and then purify it by releasing drops of brain dew and send it through your chest and heart. That's called the Little Tour. Every lunar month you increase the time you hold your breath by five seconds, and when you can do so for one hundred fifty seconds, you're ready for the Big Tour."

"Holding your breath for two and a half minutes can be dangerous," Moon Boy pointed out.

"You get dizzy and disoriented," I said. "If you keep it up, you might damage your brain."

"You might indeed," said Master Li. "That's only the beginning. The Big Tour is to send purified air through your chest, heart, abdomen, liver, kidneys, and sexual organs, and every lunar month you continue to hold your breath five seconds longer. When you reach one thousand seconds you will supposedly produce inside your body something called the Embryonic Pearl, which is a divine Elixir of Life."

"Of life? You'd be dead!" I exclaimed.

"Not necessarily. The body is capable of amazing things," said Master Li. "The problem is the brain. It must have a steady supply of fresh air, and the Laughing Prince went mad."

I saw the Laughing Prince clutching the stone, holding his breath longer and longer, holding it until the physicians shook their heads and ordered the Cloud Gong to sound the death knell; I saw a mad prince wrapped in darkness, clutching the stone and holding his breath as the centuries passed; I saw his eyes open, and the lid of his coffin lifting up, and a lunatic encased in jade stalking from his tomb; I saw a shadow in the moonlight, and Grief of Dawn on her sickbed—

"Ox, this is your department," Master Li said.

I snapped back to reality. I had thought that the gray plain was smooth and unbroken, but I was wrong.

"Did either of you happen to glance back after we first stepped out into Hell?" Master Li asked.

Neither of us had.

"The door closed behind us and vanished. Nothing but the blank wall of a cliff," he said. "That means we have only one exit from the underworld, the Great Wheel, which means we must reach the Tenth Hell."

Ahead of us was Yin-Yang Gorge, which is spanned by a swinging rope no more than two inches wide. We stood at the edge and peered down, but there seemed to be no bottom.

"What do you think?" Master Li asked.

I looked around. Demons have lowly servants called raksha. Some of them carried huge water buckets on the ends of long wooden yokes, and I said, "Sir, I think the two aristocrats should beat the insolent peasant, and punish him by slapping a yoke on his stupid shoulders."

The demons appeared to approve as Master Li and Moon Boy whacked me, and they made no objection when the fierce old dignitary commandeered a raksha and took his yoke. I dumped the water from the oversize buckets and told Master Li and Moon Boy to climb in. Master Li added rocks to his bucket until the weight was balanced, and I fixed the yoke on my shoulders and approached the rope bridge.

Anyone who has seen rope-walkers at festivals knows they balance themselves with long poles, and peasants spend a great deal of time carrying heavy things balanced on the ends of a yoke. I knew it wouldn't be difficult so long as I didn't panic. Besides, I had an umbrella far better than any rope-walker's.

I placed my left sandal upon the rope and started slowly across, using the state umbrella for added balance. The rope was swinging, but that was no problem so long as I didn't fight it. I quickly gained confidence. There was nothing to it, and I got to the center of the gorge with no difficulty. Then from the black depths came a sound so horrible that I knew whatever lurked down there was far worse than anything we had yet seen.

"Buddha! Moon Boy, what was that?" Master Li called from his bucket.

The sound came again, louder and even more horrible, and the hair on the back of my neck lifted so stiffly that it stretched the skin of my face back, and my teeth involuntarily bared in a wide mirthless grin.

"The evil minister!" Moon Boy yelled in terror. *"It's the lips of Ch'in Kuei, moving over a sinner who fell!"*

I very nearly toppled off the rope. Ch'in Kuei is the prime minister who assassinated the great Yueh Fei, and has been punished by being given the body that reflects his soul. He's made of nothing but huge slimy lips. They have jagged little teeth set in them, and the minister eats and eats, sucking the flesh from sinners, starting with the eyeballs, and the sickening sound was like a great wind that sucked the rope back and forth, swinging wildly over the gorge.

Sweat was blinding me. I wiped it away and tried to concentrate on the rope beneath my feet, but I kept imagining that fat drooling lips were lifting over my toes. In a moment I was going to fall. The only thing I could do was lean forward and start to run. The state umbrella was a lifesaver, catching air and pulling up, but the problem was keeping my shoulders straight so the buckets didn't swing, and I had to use short rapid steps because the rope kept moving. Sooner or later I was going to miss.

I knew from the moment that my right sandal started down that I would miss the moving rope, and if I leaned to the left to catch up to it, I would be completely unbalanced. A smacking slobbering sound from below helped me to push off with my left foot and leap ahead. My hands reached out as far as they could, and as I fell, my fingers just reached the edge of the cliff at the far side of Yin-Yang Gorge. I dangled there, kicking wildly for a foothold, and my right foot hit a jutting rock. In half a minute I had made it over the edge, and Master Li and Moon Boy tumbled from the buckets to the gray grass. We crawled forward while the sickening sounds of Ch'in Kuei feeding on flesh gradually faded away.

"Ox, I wondered when things were going to get exciting," Moon Boy said, and then he leaned over and threw up.

Now we were in the Sixth Hell, where sacrilege is punished, and the torments we stared at didn't make it easier to control our stomachs. Finally we made it to our feet, and I picked up the state umbrella, which had fallen in front of me. We took deep breaths and started out again, marching arrogantly in our armor of Neo-Confucian superiority. Master Li avoided confrontations as we reached boundaries. The Seventh Hell punishes those who violate graves or sell or eat human flesh, and the Eighth Hell is for those lacking in filial piety, and I have no intention of describing the terrible things we saw. (I will, however, strongly advise against winding up in the Eighth Hell so long as Neo-Confucians are in charge.) Master Li could no longer avoid confrontations at the border of the Ninth Hell. The only way to get to the Tenth and the Great Wheel was to go right through the palace of the Ninth Yama King, and Master Li was thinking deeply as we approached the walls where long lines of sinners shuffled toward their doom, weeping gray tears.

"*Goo-goo-goo.*"

"Ox, did you hear that?"

"*Goo-goo-goo.*"

"Yes, sir."

"*Goo-goo-goo.*"

"Great Buddha! It's the entire congregation from the Eye of Tranquility," Master Li exclaimed.

Indeed it was, and he walked up the line peering at faces.

"Hello, Hsiang!"

"Hello, Li Kao. What are you doing here?" the toad asked mournfully.

"I was about to ask the same of you," said Master Li.

The toad shook his fist in the general direction of Peking. "Those cursed vendors!" he yelled. "Kao, it occurred to the greedy bastards that gentlemen in search of salvation should mortify the flesh, so along with worms they began selling cheese."

I shuddered. Like most Chinese I find cheese disgusting, and I could well imagine that eating the stuff would be mortification of the first order.

"Cheese killed all of you?" Master Li asked skeptically.

"Well, no," the toad said. "Competing vendors began selling raw sea slugs."

Master Li shrugged. "I prefer them minced and steamed with eels, but they shouldn't have done much more than make you throw up when they squirmed in your stomach."

"Well, you see, Li Kao, they came from the bay where the boys deposit the night soil," the toad said sadly.

"You didn't eat them!" Master Li exclaimed in horror.

"We lived through that, but then the vendors began stuffing the sea slugs with the cheese."

Master Li turned pale, and Moon Boy and I turned green.

"I remember it precisely," the toad groaned. "It was the double hour of the cock on the third day of the eighth moon when a homicidal vendor came up with the idea of peddling all his wares at the same time, so he began stuffing the worms into the cheese inside the sea slugs."

"Jade Emperor, preserve us," Master Li said. "I assume that the next thing you knew, you were shuffling toward the basilica of the God of Walls and Ditches."

"The god was furious," the toad sniffled. "Nothing in the Register of Life and Death covered the combination of worms, cheese, and sea slugs, and since we had prematurely departed from the red dust of earth, we were sentenced to the Ninth Hell."

"Goo-goo-goo," the codgers chanted, hoping that Heaven could still see them release worms from jars.

"Look at the bright side," Master Li said soothingly. "In three years you'll be allowed to return in ghost form, and you can haunt the vendors as much as you like."

The toad turned purple. "You don't know those vendors!" he shouted. "They'll stuff our ghosts inside the worms inside the cheese inside the sea slugs and call it the Four Fetid Flavors of Suffering Serenity and make a goddamn fortune!"

Master Li's eyes moved to the gate ahead. The demons were the most ferocious we had seen, and the devils were obviously high officials, and we weren't going to get very far with a badge of office and a state umbrella. A side gate led to a garden of gray flowers, and Master Li bent down and slipped his lock picks from the false heel of his left sandal.

"Hsiang, are you going to give up this easily? No, by all the gods!" Master Li exclaimed. "You've been treated most unfairly, and surely Heaven will hear your plea if you all put your hearts into it. Where's His Holiness? There you are! Come on, men. One last grand effort!"

"Goo-goo-goo," the codgers chanted timidly, but the saintliest of them all was made from stronger stuff.

"I pray to the Heavenly Master of the First Origin!" he bellowed. *"I pray to the Heavenly Master of the Dawn of Jade of the Golden Door! I pray to the Queen Mother Wang! I pray to Chang-o and the Hare! I pray to Mother Lightning and the Master of Rain and My Lord Thunder and the Earl of Wind and the Little Boy of the Clouds!"*

"Goo-goo-goo-goo-goo!" cried the codgers, gaining a little backbone.

Master Li bent to the lock of the side gate, hidden by the crowd. His Holiness obligingly drowned out the scrape of the pick.

"I pray to the Great Emperor of the Eastern Peak! I pray to the Princess of Streaked Clouds! I pray to Kuan-yin and Kuan-ti and the Eight Immortals! I pray to Lady Horsehead and King-of-Oxen and the Transcendent Pig and Prince Millet and Hun-po Chao, patron deity of the armpits!"

"Goo-goo-goo-goo-goo!"

The lock snapped open and we slipped through the gate and closed it behind us. The noise faded as the line shuffled on toward the palace. We saw that there was a series of small gardens, each secured by a locked gate, and we would have to get through seven of them to reach the side of the palace. Master Li swore under his breath as he tackled the next lock. None of the picks was the right size, and he had to work with infinite care and patience. At last it opened and we raced through the next garden. The lock on the second gate was easier, but the third one was almost impossible. Master Li broke two picks and was trying to get leverage with a third when we heard footsteps crunching over gray gravel. It sounded like the approach of an elephant, and Moon Boy slipped back through the shrubbery to take a look.

"Got it," Master Li whispered.

The gate swung open. We left it ajar for Moon Boy and ran through the next garden to the fourth gate. The crunching footsteps had stopped. Then I heard a noise that made the hair lift on my head.

A demon was angrily sniffing the scent of living flesh. The sound indicated something huge and horrible, and we heard a growl like muffled thunder. Master Li worked furiously on the lock, but it was another difficult one and when the footsteps started toward us I knew we'd never make it through in time. I picked up a large gray rock as a weapon and slipped back through the bushes, and when I parted some branches and peered out I had to stifle a howl of horror.

This demon was enough to terrify the great Ehr-lang. It stood at least ten feet tall. Its muscles looked like rolls of steel piled together, and its talons could rip tigers apart, and its fangs might have come from one of those creatures found frozen in Mongolian glaciers, and its nostrils were sniffing furiously, and its red eyes were blazing with blood lust. I was paralyzed. As I stood there like a statue, I suddenly realized I wasn't alone. Moon Boy stood across from me, mostly hidden by gray leaves, and he took a deep breath and squared his shoulders. In ten more steps the monster would reach a clearing where it could see the gate and Master Li, but Moon Boy was sauntering out to the path. The demon stared. Fangs glittered; talons lifted to strike.

Moon Boy smiled—the gray sky blurred and produced a patch of blue. Moon Boy smiled wider—two gray flowers strained to produce pink blossoms. Moon Boy reached high up and tickled the terrible creature beneath its chin.

"Come here, sugar," Moon Boy purred, and he led the demon back into the bushes.

石

20

Master Li had to spend a great deal of time on the fourth and fifth locks. He was working on the sixth when we heard a sound behind us and a handsome young man came limping up the path. He was pale and weak and shaky, but he managed an elegant wave of a hand.

"Hell," he said, "is grossly maligned. I must come here often."

I honored him with the three obeisances and nine kowtows.

"Buddha, the thing on that divine creature reminded me of the imperial flagpole at the funeral of General Ching!" Moon Boy said happily. "Better hurry. Any moment now the darling boy will catch his second wind and come looking for an encore."

"Moon Boy, designing your medal will be one of the great challenges of the millennium," said Master Li. "We'll have to acquire the services of Deng the Debauched, and even Deng will be hard put to do you justice without landing all of us in jail."

The lock snapped open and we hurried through the garden to the seventh and last gate. Fortunately, it had an easy lock. We slipped through just as heavy crunching footsteps approached, and we reached the palace wall as a huge hoarse voice cooed, "Yoo-hoo?" I found a likely window and a moment later we were inside.

Down a corridor ahead of us was a huge room where endless rows of clerks scribbled in enormous ledgers, and above the doorway was the inscription "Tribunal of the Ninth Realm of Darkness." We straightened our clothing and brushed off gray leaves and dirt. I raised the state umbrella proudly, and Master Li marched beneath it into the anteroom. Bureaucrats were dashing in and out of a doorway, and I actually got a glimpse of a Yama King: a dark crowned shape seated upon a throne, surrounded by clerks and courtiers. In all great bureaucracies the clerks are too busy and important to look up, so Master Li simply marched past rows of doors until he came to one with the title "Treasurer of the Ninth Realm of Darkness." He shoved the door open and we walked inside. We marched past more busy clerks to a great desk where a spirit who resembled a shark was clicking like mad on two abacuses at once, and the nine buttons on his gauze cap indicated that we had reached the treasurer himself. Cold shark eyes lifted to Master Li's emblems and state umbrella.

"No inspection has been scheduled," he snapped.

"Of course not," Master Li said with equal coldness. "One who raids an illegal cricket-fighting parlor does not announce his plans in advance."

The treasurer shot to his feet. "You dare to compare this office to a cricket-fighting parlor?" he said furiously.

Master Li shrugged. "In such establishments peculiar things happen to the odds, and it has come to the attention of the Son of Heaven that peculiar things have happened to the odds in this office."

"Explain yourself, sir!"

"The emperor," Master Li said, "has been informed that the fee which purchased his own release from Hell has been unaccountably increased, which makes it virtually impossible for those unfairly imprisoned to be saved."

"A lie! A vicious and unfounded slander!" the treasurer yelled. "Emperor T'ang purchased his passage for thirteen casks of silver and gold, and thirteen casks remains the price!"

"I sincerely hope so. We are here to ensure that the system works smoothly and equitably, and there is but one way of doing so," said Master Li. "The Son of Heaven, you will recall, had no funds with him but was able to borrow on the credit account of the saintly Hsiang Liang."

The treasurer sat down. A smile was on his face and malice was in his eyes.

"The emperor indeed did so, but only on the authority of Minister Ts'ui," he said softly. "It so happens that I currently occupy the ministerial position, and do you have my authority to borrow on the account of Hsiang Liang?"

Master Li wrinkled his nose. "Who said anything about using the same account? Since there are three of us we shall require three times the amount, and I doubt that even Hsiang Liang's good deeds have deposited that much."

"Less than twenty mortals in all history have amassed thirty-nine casks of silver and gold in their credit accounts," the treasurer said with a malicious laugh. "I sincerely hope for your sake that you are in a position to borrow from T'su T'sin, the priest of the Temple of Lepers."

"Nothing so grand," said Master Li, bowing reverently at the name. One hand was behind his back and the fingers were tightly crossed. "We request you to check the credit balance of—"

Moon Boy and I stared at each other. Who could possibly have that much virtue on deposit?

"—a common singsong girl and prostitute named Grief of Dawn," Master Li said calmly.

We smothered yelps of astonishment. The treasurer grabbed ledgers and ran his finger down rows of names and numbers, and when the finger stopped I thought he had suffered a stroke. "You have proof of permission to borrow on this account?" he said in a choked whisper.

Master Li took the interlocking phoenix/dragon headband from Moon Boy and handed it across the desk. The treasurer's finger moved to the fine print, and his voice took on a weak whine. "Well, why didn't you *say* it was a joint account? Of course you can borrow the money. As much as you like! Sign here, here, and here."

Moon Boy signed there, there, and there, and in about as much time as it takes to tell it, I was hauling a cart upon which were piled thirty-nine casks of silver and gold. Master Li and Moon Boy sat on a couple of the casks, and the state umbrella rose grandly above them. The treasurer led the way to a side door and clapped a perfumed handkerchief to his nose.

"Get out quickly," he hissed.

The door opened, I pulled the cart through, and the treasurer hastily slammed the door shut behind us. We were in the Ninth Hell, and I hope I may be allowed to pause for a brief tirade.

The Ninth Hell is the delight of theologians and the despair of

everyone else. Technically it houses *wang-ssu-ch'eng,* those who
died in accidents, but it is also the destination for suicides, those
who died without proper prayers and ceremonies, and all who died
before the official date set down in the Register of Life and Death—
like the toad and his goo-goo friends. In the Ninth Hell there are no
torments, which is the worst torment of all. Without punishment
there can be no repentance and purification and rebirth, and the
poor lost souls of the Ninth Hell must serve the sentence of impris-
onment for all eternity.

Mind you, no crime is involved. Many of the damned are innocent children. After three years the damned are allowed to occasionally return to earth in ghost form (which is the reason for the
Feast of Hungry Ghosts), and it is theoretically possible for a ghost
to be saved by finding someone to take his place. That is why it is so
dangerous to linger where a child has drowned or a man has hanged
himself. The spirit will try to seize you and drag you down to the
Ninth Hell, and only by doing so can it earn a place on the Great
Wheel of Transmigrations. In practical terms the chances of reaching the Wheel are almost nonexistent.

All one hundred thirty-five lesser Hells and all but one of the
major ones are dedicated to justice. The Ninth Hell alone is unjust.
None but a theologian could love it. How can I forget a little girl I
saw weeping beside the road, damned for eternity because she
slipped and fell into a stream? It is my sincere belief that priests
could deal a death blow to atheism by destroying the Ninth Hell,
and the proper petitions should be submitted to Heaven at once.

The moment we stepped outside we were assaulted by the stench
of unwashed bodies. Venality is rampant in the Ninth Hell, where
the lowest of demons sell food and drink at ruinous prices, and an
army of lost souls besieged us, screaming for coins. We would surely
have been crushed had not Master Li and Moon Boy been able to
scoop handfuls of gold and silver from the casks and hurl them into
the mob. The poor souls fought for coins like animals, and the weak
and the young had no chance at all.

Each chest was nicely calculated to get us so far across the long
gray plain. Master Li and Moon Boy hurled coins until their arms
were falling from the sockets, and as the cart grew lighter, I was
able to pull it faster. Ahead was the great gray wall of the Tenth
Hell, rising at the top of a hill. I puffed and panted as I hauled the

cart up the steep slope. The howling wretches began to dwindle behind us. One determined band kept up, but Moon Boy had one last cask, and he tilted it and a shower of silver fell down the hill. At last we were rid of the mob and could start worrying about reaching the Great Wheel.

A demon army patrols the walls of the Tenth Hell. Master Li wasted little time. By ripping the canopy from the state umbrella he was able to fashion an acceptable ceremonial wreath, and the handle passed for a wand, and Moon Boy's jewels produced a pearl that could pass for the sacred one. Moon Boy and I were naturally suited to be the Disciples of Wealth and Poverty, and Master Li's venerable wrinkles formed a passport of their own. He started toward the walls waving blessings right and left, and the cry went up: *"Ti-tsang Wang-p'u-sa! The God of Mercy arrives for his annual inspection!"*

The wall was not difficult. There were many foot- and handholds, and Master Li hopped up on my back and Moon Boy grabbed my belt. I was halfway up the side before the soldiers began to wonder why the God of Mercy simply didn't fly over the thing, and the alarm wasn't sounded until I was almost at the top. Arrows flew harmlessly over our heads as I started down the other side, but I almost fell nonetheless. I simply wasn't prepared for my first view of the Great Wheel of Transmigrations.

The immensity of it cannot be described. Some phenomenon made the lower spokes move slowly even while higher ones were lifting with blinding speed. The wheel lifted up and up and up, and it wasn't even halfway visible. It vanished in gray clouds, and I realized that it had to reach the surface of the earth and then keep lifting until it could deposit newborn yaks upon the highest mountains of Tibet.

Endless lines of the dead were converging upon a humble cottage where Lady Meng brewed and served the Broth of Oblivion. When the dead were herded back into lines their minds were as empty as the eyes of politicians, and demons tossed the trappings of their next existences over their heads: animal skins, bird feathers, and so on. It took a little while for the soldiers inside the wall to be alerted to our presence, and by that time we were shuffling in a line with sheepskins over our heads. Master Li's nimble fingers had snatched them so quickly the attendant didn't know they were gone, and the soldiers passed us by.

We were getting very close to the Great Wheel. The dead were climbing inside to swinging platforms. "Ox, if we get inside we'll never be able to get out," Master Li whispered. I nodded and he prepared to hop on my back, and Moon Boy prepared to grab my belt.

"Now," I whispered.

Master Li hopped and Moon Boy grabbed and I jumped and caught a spoke. I managed to get my feet on the outer edge of the rim just as the soldiers spotted us. Demons screamed with rage, and arrows and spears flew, but we were rising with great speed. An arrow missed Moon Boy's nose by half an inch and a spear grazed my arm, and then we were too high for missiles to reach, and a moment later we were shooting up into the clouds. We rose with incredible speed that made tears blur my eyes, and Master Li began to swear quite foully.

We had left the demons below, but we would be lost if we couldn't see where to get off, and the clouds obscured everything. Long minutes passed as we whirled into infinity, and still the clouds billowed around us. Then I began to see pinpricks of light like tiny stars, and Master Li scanned the sky.

"There! The perfectly round one. See it?"

"Yes, sir," I said.

"Don't miss."

"No, sir," I said.

The small round spot of light appeared to be zooming toward us at an unbelievable speed. I crouched, trying to judge the trajectory. "Ready," I said. My heart stopped when a thick cloud blinded me, but then we shot through it. "Set," I said. The light was crossing my imaginary target point and I jumped with all the strength I had. We shot across the sky like a projectile from a catapult, and the light grew brighter and brighter, and then we plunged straight into the center of it and hit a wall of water.

The breath was knocked out of me and I almost choked to death as I floated upward, and then my head broke through the surface and I gasped and gulped fresh air. I hauled Master Li and Moon Boy to a bank and dragged them up. We were lying on green grass, and a yellow sun was shining, and bright birds were chirping, and a white skull was grinning up at us from the bottom of a pool.

Master Li crawled over and tilted his wine flask over the pool, and Moon Boy and I watched the wine whirl in a spout that disappeared into the grinning jaws.

"Ling, old friend, you are a truly great artist," Master Li said admiringly.

The reeds moved. *"Burp."* They moved again. *"No, but I am not a bad quack."*

Moon Boy was probing sensitive areas that might or might not have come into contact with an oversize demon. I stared at a long bleeding scratch where a spear might or might not have grazed my arm. Master Li grinned at us.

"Moon Boy, have you forgotten your teacher and the bandit he deafened? Ox, have you forgotten Granny Ho and her son-in-law? If Moon Boy hadn't handled that demon we would have been killed, and if Ox had missed the target just now we would also have been killed. We have been treated to the artistry of the great Liu Ling, which makes questions of literal truth immaterial, if not absurd. Was Chuang Tzu imagining himself to be the butterfly, or was the butterfly imagining itself to be Chuang Tzu?"

He turned back to the pool and poured more wine in, and the old man and the skull drank in comfortable silence like old friends.

"Ling," Master Li finally said, "your priests did a marvelous job of probing our minds while we lay in mushroom stupors, and they were not blinded—as I am—by subjective experience. Is it permissible to ask for an opinion?"

The reeds remained still.

"Let's put it this way. If you were to entertain somebody with the story of Li Kao and Number Ten Ox and Grief of Dawn and Moon Boy and Prince Liu Pao and so on, what would you call it?"

The reeds remained quiet, but then, slowly, they moved.

"Shi tou chi."

"The Story of the Stone?" Master Li nodded. "Yes, I vaguely perceive what you mean. It's a question of priorities, of course, and I haven't quite sorted them out. But I'm almost there, I think."

He got to his feet. Moon Boy and I followed his example, and we bowed to the skull.

"Ling," Master Li said, "I still say you're a very great artist."

The reeds moved for the last time. *"Kao, I still say you were born to be hung."*

A priest was holding a gate open for us. We walked out to a green hillside, and the last I saw of the Temple of Illusion was a window in a small tower with shutters half-closed. A winking eye.

石

21

A few miles past the White Cloud Convent we turned off the path and climbed shale and granite and black rock and crossed a clearing. We burrowed through brush to another clearing at the side of a cliff, and Master Li gazed happily at a strange and rather unimpressive plant.

"The mind is a miser," he said. "Nothing is ever thrown away, and it's amazing what you can find if you dig deep enough." He began stripping thorny little seedlike things. "Don't play with thorn apples unless you know what you're doing," he cautioned. "They're of the nightshade family, like mandrake and henbane and belladonna, and their principal product is poison. From the Bombay thorn apple comes the legendary potion of India, dhatura, which can stupify, paralyze, or kill, depending upon the dosage, but which can also produce a medicine with remarkable effect upon internal bleeding and fever. With any luck we'll have Grief of Dawn on her feet in no time."

Our trip back to the Valley of Sorrows was fast and uneventful, although Moon Boy and I grew ever more apprehensive as we approached, and we were weak with relief when the feather duster head of Prince Liu Pao thrust from a studio window and called cheerfully to us.

"Hurray! Grief of Dawn is as good as cured!" the prince yelled optimistically. "She's been unchanged! No weird sounds while you were gone, no more murdered monks, and no mad mummies crawling up from tombs!"

Moon Boy and I ran inside. Grief of Dawn looked very lovely and very vulnerable as she tossed in fever. She seemed to sense our presence and tried to sit up, and fell back, and Master Li stepped up and took her pulse. Since he used the right wrist I assumed he was checking on the condition of her lungs, stomach, large intestine, spleen, and parta ulta. He grunted with satisfaction.

"She can take the potion in full strength," he said confidently, and at once he set to work with the thorn apple: boiling, distilling, blending with herbs and mysterious ingredients, and finally testing it on a cat, who seemed to enjoy it.

I don't know whether or not the stuff could be called miraculous, but I do know that Master Li added a final ingredient that no other physician could have managed. Moon Boy and I propped up Grief of Dawn, and Master Li managed to get a good dose of the portion down her throat. Within a minute she was stirring restlessly, and then her eyes opened. At first she saw nothing. Her eyes cleared and focused and her head moved forward and her lips brushed Moon Boy's cheek. "Darling," she whispered. I leaned forward. "Dear Ox," she said, and she kissed me too, and even managed to blush when Prince Liu Pao grinned and presented his cheek for a kiss.

"What happened?" she whispered. "It was dark and damp and I was running and running and running, and something terrible was behind me."

"Well, it's gone now," Master Li said comfortingly. "You have nothing to worry about except how in hell Ox is going to add enough space to our shack."

The sick girl sat up straight.

"I've already figured it out, and there'll even be space for Moon Boy when he pops up," I said happily.

"How about the prince?" said Master Li. "Let's include all of the family. Your Highness, do you object to sleeping three to a bed when you wander into our alley in Peking?"

"Not at all!" the prince said cheerfully.

Grief of Dawn was looking at Master Li with wide glistening eyes. The old sage shook his head ruefully.

"A man my age starting one more family. Sheer idiocy! At least," he added, "I'll have the most fascinating young wife in all Peking, and that is the understatement of the century."

I didn't fully understand what he meant until Grief of Dawn had completely recovered. Both she and the prince had us recount our adventures in Hell over and over, and Grief of Dawn gazed in wonder at the scar where the arrow had entered her chest and said she wished she could remember what it was like to be stone-cold dead. Master Li paced the floor, obviously yearning for action. His excitement was catching, and I think it helped speed Grief of Dawn's recovery, and then she was as fit as she had ever been and Master Li got us up with the sun. He said it was time to try something, and we had best be heavily armed. I chose an axe and stuck a short sword in my belt. Moon Boy and the prince both selected spears and daggers. Master Li lined his belt with throwing knives. Grief of Dawn was far and away the best archer among us, and she selected a bow from the pile and added a quiver of arrows and a knife in her belt. Master Li climbed up on my back.

"Start down the hill, and go across the valley to the hill beside the monastery," he said. "Along the way I'll entertain you with some fascinating notes I've taken."

Master Li pulled out a sheaf of notes and told Grief of Dawn to walk beside me. It had rained during the night, and the morning was very beautiful. Raindrops like tiny pearls glowed on each leaf, and damp grass sparkled like diamonds in the sunlight.

"My pet, according to the inner recesses of my mind, you have a credit account in Hell that could buy one or two of the lesser kingdoms. The reason lies in a lullaby to old Tai-tai that you sang when you were delirious, and that was only the beginning of an incredible performance. You're packed with more marvels than the Puzzle Book of Lu Pan!" he said enthusiastically. "Let's start with one of the most astounding conversations I've ever experienced."

He flipped through his notes and began to read aloud.

GRIEF OF DAWN: Mistress, must I go to Chien's? It smells so bad, and the bargemen make rude jokes about ladies, and that old man with one leg always tries to pinch me.

MASTER LI: Darling, what does your mistress want you to buy at Chien's?

GRIEF OF DAWN: Rhinoceros hides.

MASTER LI: And where is Chien's?

GRIEF OF DAWN: Halfway between the canal and Little Ch'ing-hu Lake.

MASTER LI: Darling, does your mistress ever send you to Kang Number Eight's?

GRIEF OF DAWN: I like Kang Number Eight's.

MASTER LI: Where is it?

GRIEF OF DAWN: On the Street of Worn Cash-Coin.

MASTER LI: What do you buy there?

GRIEF OF DAWN: Hats.

MASTER LI: Hats. Yes, of course. And where do you buy your mistress's painted fans?

GRIEF OF DAWN: The Coal Bridge.

MASTER LI: I suppose she also sends you to buy the famous boiled pork at . . . What's the name of that place?

GRIEF OF DAWN: Wei-the-Big-Knife.

MASTER LI: Of course. Do you remember where it is?

GRIEF OF DAWN: Right beside the Cat Bridge.

Master Li lowered his notes, and regarded Grief of Dawn with the fondness of a connoisseur examining a rare orchid. "My pet," he said, "you were describing a shopping trip that the personal maid of an aristocratic lady might have taken in Hangchow."

"Hangchow?" the prince said with a startled expression on his face.

"Indeed yes, but you're right. No such establishments exist today, and the only reason I know about them is because they were often mentioned in the casual journals of classical writers," said Master Li. "Both one-legged Ch'ien and his famous rhinoceros hides disappeared during a fire that destroyed the entire neighborhood during the late Han Dynasty. The Coal Bridge and Kang Number Eight's were razed to make way for a new canal more than three centuries ago. Wei-the-Big-Knife's was destroyed during the turmoil of the Three Kingdoms, and so it goes with every single reference."

Grief of Dawn's eyes were like soup bowls. "I don't remember saying any of that, and the names mean nothing to me," she protested.

Master Li shrugged. "You were delirious. At first I thought you were citing the same journals I'd read, but they're written in ancient scholarly shorthand that none but academics can decipher. I started asking loaded questions to pin down the exact date of this marvelous shopping trip, and I found it in two references."

He went back to his notes.

MASTER LI: And what's-his-name personally blends her ink?

GRIEF OF DAWN: Yes. Li Tinghuei.

MASTER LI: And that lovely courtesan makes pink paper for her?

GRIEF OF DAWN: Shieh Tao. Yes, she is lovely.

"Li Tinghuei and Shieh Tao are mentioned again and again in classical journals," said Master Li. "Since Tinghuei was senior by more than forty years, there could have been only a brief period when it was possible to patronize both of them. I checked the dates, and the amazing shopping trip took place between 765 and 771 years ago."

Moon Boy and I were gaping at Grief of Dawn, who was gaping at Master Li. Prince Liu Pao looked like he was mentally counting on his fingers, and Master Li read his mind.

"Precisely! That was when the Laughing Prince and Tou Wan kept a palace in Hangchow, and Tou Wan's maid would have accompanied her between Hangchow and the Valley of Sorrows."

Occasionally a moderately intelligent thought misses a turn and accidentally enters my mind, and I said, "Sir, in Hell you confirmed from the Recorder of Past Existences that the Broth of Oblivion isn't always properly administered, and Grief of Dawn had come to the Valley of Sorrows, but perhaps she was *returning* to the valley, because when she was wounded and hallucinating—"

"Good boy!" said Master Li. "I had begun to suspect that Grief of Dawn had been Tou Wan's maid in a previous incarnation. Fever allowed deep-buried memories to rise to the surface, stimulated by the familiar surroundings. I wasn't just guessing wildly, of course. An absolutely delightful pattern was beginning to emerge, and we'll get to it in a few minutes."

We began to climb again. Master Li led the way along a twisting path, and then we got down on our knees and crawled through the opening of a cave where the angle of the sun sent a flow of warm light over a small pile of bones. We sat in a semicircle around the skeleton of Wolf, and Master Li patted Grief of Dawn's knee reassuringly.

"A thought kept returning to my mind," he said. "Was it merely the familiar landscape of the Valley of Sorrows that released memories of a long-forgotten existence, or was something more dramatic involved? The night before you were wounded, you sat here and heard the story of Wolf and Fire Girl. Folk epics of the heroic quest are almost always based upon historical fact and then embellished beyond recognition. Was there fact behind the flight of Wolf and Fire Girl? They were running beside an underground river that was lined with statues bearing heads of animals and birds. During your fever you relived parts of a terrible experience. Here's some of it."

He picked up his notes and found the place.

GRIEF OF DAWN: Faster . . . Must run faster . . . Where is the turn? . . . Past the goat statue . . . There's the raven and the river . . . Faster . . . Faster . . . *This way! Hurry!* . . . Soldiers . . . Hide until they pass . . . Now run! *Run!*

"Interesting," Master Li said thoughtfully. "Here's how my subconscious mind reacted in Hell."

TOU WAN: All I had was the sliver for my hairpin . . . That maid, always looking at it, always wanting it, trying to steal it . . . I stabbed her, but she ran away with the stone . . . My maid and that concubine with the ring of Upuaut my husband gave her . . . The soldiers killed them, but they could not find the stone.

Master Li shrugged. "I have no idea why I tossed in the bit about the maid having been stabbed, but other parts are clear enough. Anyone ever hear of Asyut?"

The sudden change of subject startled us. We shook our heads negatively.

"It's a city in Egypt, or used to be," he explained. "The patron deity was called Upuaut, and when the barbarian Greeks conquered the place, they retained the deity but renamed the city Lycopolis. Prince, can you provide a literal translation?"

The prince was obviously pleased to be able to contribute something. "City of the Wolf," he said promptly.

"Exactly. The head of Upuaut is that of a wolf, and the artisans of the city are renowned for amulets and bracelets and rings with wolf heads." Master Li carefully lifted the ring from the skeleton's finger bones. He displayed the faint inner markings. "Hieroglyphs. It means 'He Who Rules the West,' which is one of Upuaut's many titles."

Master Li gently replaced the ring. "Did you know that it is virtually impossible to distinguish between male and female skeletons? All one had to go on is size. A fairly large boy and a small young lady would look precisely the same. You see, one of Upuaut's duties was guarding women through pregnancy, and that is why his rings were strictly for females. Nobody would give such a ring to a man or a boy, but he would give it to a concubine." He turned to his notes.

GRIEF OF DAWN: Faster . . . faster . . . Where is the passage? . . . *Hurry!* . . . More soldiers . . . Faster . . . faster . . . *Hurry, darling!* . . . There's the ibis statue . . .

Master Li put his notes away. "I strongly suspect that more than seven and a half centuries ago a maid and a concubine were forced to run for their lives from the construction site of the tomb of the Laughing Prince," he said. "Over the years the boys of the valley transformed them into Wolf and Fire Girl, but many details of the story are still accurate history. Here in this cave the concubine was caught and killed. The maid was no doubt also killed, and if I may borrow an atrocious poetic style: The Great Wheel turns, the lives roll on, the maid returns as Grief of Dawn."

She was stunned and shaken, and Master Li patted her shoulder.

"Dear girl, we need more than this delightful hypothesis to go on," he said quietly. "May I have your permission to try to bring buried memories of a previous incarnation up to the surface?"

"You have my permission," she whispered.

I had seen him do it before, but it always fascinated me. Master Li took his business card from his pocket and attached it to a leather thong. (The card is a seashell, and the half-closed eye painted upon it seems to say: "Part of the truth revealed; some things I see, but some I don't.") Slowly the shell swung before Grief of Dawn's eyes, back and forth, back and forth, while his soft voice told her she was getting sleepy. Her eyes closed. Grief of Dawn slept yet didn't sleep, and when she awoke she wasn't Grief of Dawn. She was Hyacinth Bud, the personal maid of Tou Wan.

"We're your friends, darling," Master Li said soothingly. "We're going to help you. Do you remember running up to this cave?"

"I think so," she whispered.

"Soldiers were chasing you?"

"Yes."

"You and your friend?"

"Yes, Golden Belt. We ran and ran, but the soldiers were getting closer, and then we saw a small hole in the hillside and hid in here." She looked around puzzledly and frowned. "I don't remember a skeleton."

"Can you remember the path you took up here?"

"I think so."

"Darling, it is very important for you to show us how you got up here to the surface. You were underground, weren't you?"

"Yes."

"Will you lead us to the exit you took?"

She moved like a sleepwalker. The altered landscape frightened her, but Master Li told her to concentrate on the unchanged landmarks, like the old monastery and Dragon's Head, and she began to walk straight toward the area of Princes' Path that had been destroyed at the death of Brother Squint-Eyes. Her hands were out in front of her, and she stopped with both of them pressed against a huge boulder.

"The door is closed! It's closed!" she whispered.

She was becoming increasingly agitated. Master Li thought it might be dangerous for her to continue to relive the experience, and he brought her out of her trance.

Again she was Grief of Dawn, and Moon Boy held and soothed her. We could have searched for a lifetime and not found the secret door. The workmanship was nearly supernatural. I finally found the lever, but it wasn't until the door in the boulder swung open that I saw the shape in the intricate patterns of apparently natural cracks.

It opened silently, which meant recently oiled hinges. Inside was a rack of new torches, and a flight of steps leading down toward the bowels of the earth.

Now we knew how nasty people in motley appeared and disappeared, and somewhere down there—almost certainly—was the mysterious stone that lay behind all of this. I led the way with my axe and a torch. Master Li followed with a throwing knife ready.

Prince Liu Pao had his spear in one hand and his dagger in the other. Moon Boy held a spear and Grief of Dawn's belt.

Grief of Dawn was a born fighter, and the job of an archer in close quarters is to guard the exposed rear. She walked backward, totally secure at the touch of Moon Boy's guiding hand, and she was surefooted as a mountain goat. I placed my foot on the first step and we started down.

石

22

Recent torch cinders marked the steps, and there were smoke stains on the ceiling. The steps were smooth and regular and steep, and we came to four landings. The air was fresh but rather moist, and Moon Boy said he could hear water. Finally I could too, and as we arrived at the last step our torchlight reached out to an underground river.

The story of Wolf flashed through my mind. The water was jet black because of the rock bed it ran through, and on the other side was something huge and dark. It made no movement or sound. I bent down and swung my torch until I found the right angle, and light bounced across the water to an enormous stone statue. It was of a man, and the features were rather familiar.

"Yen-wang-yeh, the former First Lord of Hell," Master Li said in a normal tone of voice. "There's no need to whisper, you know. Our torchlight will have already announced our presence."

He studied the statue thoughtfully. "The representation of a guardian of the dead suggests that this cavern actually is an extension of the tomb of the Laughing Prince, as we had assumed. Considering the fact that the bastard tunneled under most of the valley, he may have built the largest tomb in history."

The cavern was immense. Our torchlight barely reached the ceiling. The slap of our sandals echoed away in the darkness and came bouncing back in a distorted manner, as though filtering through a maze of side tunnels. Master Li started off upstream, while I clutched my axe and glared ferociously at the shadows. Grief of

Dawn's bow swung back and forth behind us, with a notched arrow ready.

Spaced at about two-hundred-foot intervals were more huge stone statues. Master Li identified the strangely named Emma-hoo, the Japanese King of the Dead, and muttered something about the Laughing Prince having enlisted deities from every culture he could think of. Many of the figures Master Li couldn't identify, but he bowed deeply to a strong young hero who was holding a captured lion, and as he walked on he began chanting under his breath. I caught part of it.

> *"In the house of dust*
> *Lives lord and prophet,*
> *Wizard and priest,*
> *And Gilgamesh whom gods*
> *Have anointed in death.*
> *Great was his glory.*
> *Great was his pride.*
> *Dust is his nourishment,*
> *And his food is mud."*

"Doesn't sound very heroic to me," I muttered.

"Dear boy, the story of Gilgamesh makes our epics of the heroic quest look like scribblings of half-witted children," Master Li said sternly.

I was in no position to argue with him. The next statues were Egyptian underworld deities, and there were an extraordinary number of them. I nearly jumped out of my sandals when the torchlight picked up a huge threatening mummy holding some kind of hideous creature, but Master Li said it wasn't intended to represent the Laughing Prince, but Osiris and the monster Amemait. He identified a god with the head of a jackal as Anubis and a lady with a feather as Ament, but he seemed to be looking for something else. Finally he stopped and pointed.

"Toth," he said. "Grief of Dawn, in your delirium you said, 'There's the ibis statue,' and here he is. What we're looking for, incidentally, is a statue with the head of a raven."

The only sounds were the lapping of water and the slapping of sandals and the hiss of torches. The shadowed emptiness seemed infinite. I felt the cold chill of eternity pressing down on me and I clutched my axe tighter; statue after statue, secretive, monstrous, eternally guarding the mummy of a laughing madman whose coffin was empty; I would not have been surprised to hear deadly shrieking squeals and see seven black bats flapping overhead.

Master Li grunted with satisfaction. Moon Boy had bounced torchlight across the water to another statue. It was a woman whose head was that of a raven. "I have no idea what she represents, but Grief of Dawn said, 'There's the raven and the river,' and just before that she said, 'There's the goat statue.' We can assume that she had just come in sight of the river, so start looking for a side passage. If we don't find one here, we'll try the other bank."

We were on the right side. Sixty feet farther on we found a side passage with steps leading up, and on the first landing was a statue of a deity with a goat's head and horns. We reached countless landings, and I was willing to bet that we had climbed far above the level of the valley and were inside one of the hills. Finally the steps came to an end. We had reached a semicircular marble floor like that of an anteroom. Four iron doors were set into the stone wall, and beside each one was a stone statue with a porcelain jar in its hands.

"Back to Egypt," said Master Li. "These represent the four sons of Horus, whose jars hold organs removed during embalming. The one with the human head is Imstey, who protects the liver. Dog-head Hapi protects the lungs, jackal-head Duamure protects the stomach, and hawk-head Qebsnuf protects the intestines." He scratched his nose thoughtfully. "The style isn't Egyptian but Chinese, and I wonder if the Laughing Prince had a different symbolism in mind. Hapi's head resembles that of the Celestial Dog, and perhaps the Laughing Prince felt he deserved a bodyguard equal to that of the Emperor of Heaven."

Not everything was stone and rigid, so Master Li reached out and lifted the jar from the statue's hands. The rest of us jumped backward as the door beside the statue slid open. The prince jammed his spear in the frame to keep the door from accidentally closing. We lifted our torches and stepped inside, and Grief of Dawn and Moon Boy cried out in wonder.

They hadn't seen it before, but we had. We were back inside the formal tomb, and the door was so neatly hidden in the wall that we would never have found it. Now we knew how fresh air could get in and a mummy in a jade suit could be carried out. There was no sign or sound of merry fellows dressed up in motley.

Nothing had been taken since we had been there. When we looked into the room where the skeletons of poisoned concubines lay in their beds I saw tears trickle down the cheeks of Grief of Dawn. Once she had laughed and cried with these girls, and one terrible day she had run away with one of them. What must it have been like to live in the shadow of Tou Wan, and to be at the command of a lunatic torturer and murderer like the Laughing Prince? Looming over all of them had been the strange power of a mysterious stone, and Master Li had the stone in mind as he led the way to the burial chamber and the exposed mummy of Tou Wan.

"Ox, see if you can get the jade plates away from the skull," he said.

It was a slow process, but finally I managed to break the gold wire at the corners of one of the plates, and after that it went more quickly. White bones appeared, and then I let out a howl of terror and jumped four feet backward. I know nothing of embalming, but somehow the hair had survived. I thought it was a living creature as it bulged out between cracks. I got hold of myself and removed the last plates. Master Li reached out and withdrew the hairpin, and a lustrous black lock, shocking against the bare white bone, slid over my hand like a snake. Master Li swore. The tip of the hairpin had been snapped clean off.

"The sliver is gone, the piece of stone from the sacristy is gone, and if the Laughing Prince used the third piece for an amulet—hell, *he's* gone," Master Li snarled. He scratched his head and frowned. "Odd. Something deep inside my mind had expected this," he muttered. "In Hell I had Tou Wan say that the stone from her pin had been stolen, possibly by her maid. Why did I suspect the sliver was gone?"

We had no answer, of course, and Master Li finally shrugged and started back to the exit. "At any rate, we know for certain that the stone was taken before she was encased in jade, which leads us back to the Monks of Mirth who very probably provided perverted prayers at her deathbed. If the order has continued to this day, hidden down here in a cavern, they've had all three pieces of the stone for more than seven hundred fifty years. What in the name of Buddha have they been doing with it?"

It was another unanswerable question. We went back out to the semicircular anteroom, and Master Li replaced the jar in the hands of the statue and the door slid shut. The next statue was the one with the head of a jackal. Master Li said that jackals meant many things to ancient Egyptians but that the symbolism here was probably Chinese and we should keep tight hold on our stomachs. He lifted the second jar and the second door slid open, and when we walked inside his warning wasn't good enough. Both Moon Boy and Grief of Dawn threw up, and the prince and I were close to it.

It was another medical research center, but even worse than the grotto. The dry air had better preserved the graphically illustrated experiments painted on the walls, and it was harder than ever to believe that any man could do such things to human beings. Prince Liu Pao couldn't take his eyes from the iron cages. Skeletons of peasants lay there, patiently awaiting their turn to entertain the Laughing Prince. Master Li's attention was drawn to the charts and formulas that annotated the experiments.

"Ch'i and shih, the life and motion forces that animate the universe," he said matter-of-factly. "He was using an extraordinary stone to chart the energy patterns of life as it slowly drained from the bodies of dying peasants. The man who could master the flow of energy would become a god, of course, and if he had also used Ideal Breathing to create the Embryonic Pearl, he would be immortal. Show me a quest for personal immortality and I'll show you a path through a slaughterhouse, and the incense of personal divinity is the stench of other people's corpses. Ox, when I decay to the point where I start dabbling with potency potions and the Elixir of Life, lead me to the Eye of Tranquility and hand me a fishing pole and a jar of worms."

He led the way back out and closed the door behind us. The third door was guarded by Quebhsnuf the hawk-headed, and the hawk is the hunter. The Monks of Mirth would have to go out to grab more peasants, and Master Li said it would be a good idea to see if there were other exits in case we had to get out fast. The door slid open and we walked into a long tunnel, lined with side passages.

Master Li ignored the side passages and continued down the tunnel until we reached a dead end. Then he started back to check the passages one by one. When we turned around, Prince Liu Pao took the lead and confidently stepped into the first dark opening. He disappeared.

"*Aaaarrrrgghh . . .*"

The scream of terror dropped down and down, echoing ever deeper in the depths of the earth, and then it faded away. The silence was more frightening than the scream.

I forced my feet to move. Apparently the prince hadn't been paying attention to his sandals, because a black pit opened in the floor just inside the entrance. I knelt and thrust my torch down. The drop wasn't vertical. A smooth stone chimney sloped down through solid rock, as slick and even as packed snow. I remembered how the prince had nursed Grief of Dawn, and I saw his warm glorious paintings glowing before my eyes. I sat down and slid my legs over the edge.

"Can you see him?" Master Li asked.

"No, sir, but I will," I said grimly.

I pushed off before anyone could stop me. Moon Boy yelled, and then all I heard was the air whistling past my ears as I picked up speed. The slick stone was faster than the ice on Boar's Head Hill behind my village. The flame of my torch was streaking behind me like the flags on racing boats during the Dragon Boat Festival, and I shot around another curve, sailed up the smooth wall almost to the ceiling, and skidded back to the center groove at ninety miles an hour. Even in my terror I felt the thrill of excitement. I shot around another curve and sailed up the smooth bank and back down to the center again, and the wild exhilaration of the ride was furthered by the fact that I was racing into pitch blackness, and for all I knew, the chimney was going to branch into a pair of six-inch holes with a jagged fanged rock in the center. The speed was incredible. I careened like a comet around three more curves, and then the slope leveled and lifted, and I was shooting upward when the chimney came to an abrupt end. The next thing I knew I was flying out into the air, and water was rushing beneath me, and I just had the wit to hurl my torch ahead before I plunged down and splashed into a river.

I came to the surface spouting water, and paddled to the bank. Pitch is hard to put out, and my torch lay there still burning. I had come back to the central cavern and the black river, and I lifted the torch and jumped back in and paddled to the other bank. I walked up and down peering upward, and finally I saw the black hole I had come flying out of.

"*I'm all right!*" I yelled. "*I don't see the prince, but I'll find him!*"

I began slowly walking along the bank looking for wet marks where the prince had climbed out—or been carried out. I didn't want to think of him landing on the back of his neck or striking a submerged rock. A sound made me whirl around, raising my axe.

I should have expected it. Master Li was flying through the air. He hit the water like a cormorant, and Grief of Dawn came flying after him and landed like a swan. Moon Boy couldn't do anything that wasn't graceful, and he reminded me of a great dancer at the opera as he turned a somersault, touched his toes, and split the water as cleanly as a knife blade. I helped drag them out, and collected their torches and relit them from mine.

"Buddha, what a toy!" Master Li said, pounding the side of his head to force water from his ears. "The man who could duplicate that ride in the public parks would be a mandarin inside of a month."

"Mandarin? Emperor!" Moon Boy said enthusiastically.

"I only hope the prince enjoyed it as much as I did," Grief of Dawn said somberly.

Master Li was looking for something, and he found it. Ancient iron brackets were set in the wall leading up to the hole of the chimney. "Nature rarely produces something that smooth, and I suspect that nature had some help," he said. "The river was used to transport heavy objects to this point. They were hoisted to the hole, and windlasses hauled them on sleds up through the rock to the higher levels of the tomb. There should be a staircase very close."

We soon found it. Master Li wanted only to be sure there were steps if we needed them, and then we began to search for Prince Liu Pao. We walked up and down the bank, and were about to cross to the far bank when Grief of Dawn's sharp eyes found what we had missed. It was a small scarlet tassel.

"The prince's tunic has scarlet tassels at the bottom," she said excitedly.

We widened the search, and sixty or seventy feet upstream we found another tassel.

"They've got him," Master Li said flatly. "If he were free, he would have yelled as Ox did, and he would have immediately looked for a way back up and found that staircase. We have to assume that he's been grabbed by our friends in the funny robes, but has enough movement to leave a trail."

At regular intervals we continued to find the tassels that the prince had surreptitiously torn off. Then they stopped. We doubled back, and finally found a side passage that was almost invisible behind a jutting shelf of rock. Another tassel lay just inside the entrance, but Master Li brought us to a halt. His eyes were bleak as he examined the tunnel. Ancient wooden supports and scaffolding were everywhere, and the floor was littered with rocks that had fallen from the ceiling. It was a death trap, and the prince wouldn't conceivably have entered it unless he was being carried. Master Li lowered his voice.

"Moon Boy, this is your department," he whispered. "Rather nasty gentlemen may be back in there, and I'd like them to hear us enter without us actually entering."

Moon Boy nodded. He sat down at the entrance and took off his sandals and placed his spear so he could scrape it against the wall with his shoulder.

"Sssshh, quiet!" Master Li whispered—except it wasn't Master Li, but Moon Boy pitching his voice into the tunnel. The sandals in his hands moved rapidly and lightly, and four pairs of feet seemed to move into the tunnel.

"I don't see anything," my voice whispered.

"I don't either," Grief of Dawn's voice whispered.

"All clear this way," Moon Boy whispered in his own voice.

The sandals were gradually hitting the floor harder, as though the people wearing them were coming closer. Moon Boy moved his shoulder and produced a metallic scrape from the spear, followed by a muffled curse in the voice of Master Li.

"Is that another tassel?" my voice whispered, louder.

Deep in the darkness of the tunnel was a sharp snapping sound, followed by the screech of splintering wood. We heard a great crash. The floor shook and waves rippled across the river, and dust and wood splinters billowed from the tunnel mouth. Crash followed crash as though the entire ceiling was collapsing, and it was a long time before the noise stopped and the echoes faded away.

"Good," Master Li said quietly. "Officially we're dead, pulverized like corn beneath a grindstone, and they won't be looking for us when we pay them a call. Fortunately, they shouldn't be hard to find."

石

23

Master Li rode on my back. The staircase was very steep, with innumerable landings, and I was ready to stop and catch my breath when we reached a large cave that had other side passages branching from it. Master Li climbed off and wandered around the cave while Moon Boy and Grief of Dawn and I sat down and rested. Suddenly he made a sharp exclamation, and we got up and ran over to him.

He had accidentally pushed against a part of the wall that moved. A doorway had opened into another room. All of us had been there before, and we walked inside and looked around at the paymaster's office and the pit where the two dead gardeners lay. The arrows were still stuck in every available piece of wood, and Grief of Dawn bent down and looked closely at one. Her eyes were puzzled when she lifted them.

"I know, I saw it before," Master Li said. "Those aren't ancient arrows but relatively modern ones, yet it would have been absolutely impossible for a local boy or girl to have found this place and played here without somebody finding out about it. No youngster could keep such a secret, unless he had been born with the secret. Happy home life with the Monks of Mirth?"

He walked over and looked gloomily down into the darkness of the pit in front of the paymaster's desk.

"I wonder," he said as though talking to himself. "Were you paid to carry a boy or a girl up steep steps as Ox just carried me? Did you stop at this level to rest, and did the boy or girl pause to play around with a bow and arrows? Did you then carry him up the rest of the way, and did he take another wonderful ride down that slide to the river? And then up for more archery, and up farther for another slide, and so forth? Did you hear or see more than you should, and then stand in front of the desk to receive your pay?"

The pit was silent. Master Li shrugged and led the way back to the cavern. He got on my back and I began to climb again, and the final steps up from the fourth landing brought us back into the tunnel where we had begun, right beside the passage with the pit and the marvelous stone slide. I had a sudden clear vision of a gardener setting down a laughing child, who ran to the slide and vanished down into darkness.

Master Li walked rapidly back down the tunnel and out to the little anteroom. One more door remained, and beside it stood the last of the sons of Horus.

"Imstey, who alone bears a human head," Master Li said grimly. "We're looking for humans, very unpleasant ones, and we have to hope they didn't leave the prince tied up in that tunnel when they sprang the trap to crush us."

He lifted the last jar, and the door swung open. This time we didn't need torches, because a long row of them was already burning in brackets spaced along a tunnel wall. The air was fresh and foul at the same time, and Moon Boy grimaced disgustedly and said something about the virtues of bathing at least every seven years.

The tunnel sloped sharply downward. Again I took the lead with my axe, and Master Li followed with his throwing knives, and Moon Boy held a spear in one hand and Grief of Dawn's belt with the other, and Grief of Dawn walked backward swinging her bow to cover our rear. We tried to be quieter than mice. The tunnel kept going downward, and gradually the air grew moister as though we were again approaching the river, and I saw two small rocks lying on the tunnel floor. I remembered the rockfall that had supposedly killed us, and glanced nervously at the ceiling. I couldn't see any serious cracks, but a few feet farther on there was a sign that this passage had at least shaken when the other one collapsed. Dust covered the floor, and Master Li grunted with satisfaction. Recent sandal prints were marked in the dust.

We moved faster. I had to smother a yelp, and I grabbed Master Li's arm and pointed. A crimson tassel lay on the floor. Moon Boy whispered to Grief of Dawn, and she turned and looked and her eyes lit up.

"He's alive," Master Li whispered. "The prince is a lot tougher than he looks, and when he runs out of tassels, he'll find a way to cut himself and leave a trail of blood."

Moon Boy began to hear sounds we couldn't. He whispered that people were laughing somewhere in the distance, and finally we came close enough for the rest of us to hear it; coarse and merry, with other sounds of celebration.

"A good sign," Master Li whispered. "They're celebrating our demise, and if they were in the process of sacrificing the prince to the stone—or whatever they do—the ritual would have a somber religious sound."

Ahead of us was light, and we passed a number of empty side passages. The laughter was right in front of us when we came to a passage that wasn't empty. It was a dressing room, with a row of monkish robes in motley hanging upon pegs, and at the end of it there seemed to be a ledge looking down over the area where the light came from. We slipped inside and dropped to our stomachs and crawled to the ledge and cautiously peered over it.

The cavern below reminded me of the courtyard of a large monastery. It was illuminated by a thousand blazing torches in brackets on the walls. The scene was very strange: Monks in motley laughed uproariously as they danced with stiff awkward movements in concentric circles. They were capering around a throne upon which sat a monk who wore a smiling paper mask with a curling beard. A large urn stood beside the throne, and a monk who appeared to be some kind of dignitary stood about ten feet away. There was no sign of the prince.

Master Li signaled for us to slide back. "It's an ancient ceremony called the Festival of Laughter," he whispered. "The one on the throne is the leader, wearing the mask of Fu-hsing, God of Happiness. The monks will dance up to the throne and embrace the leader and take a paper scroll from the urn, which they will bring to the assistant, and he will open it and read aloud a comical wish for happiness. When everyone has his wish, the assistant will cry, *'Tienkuan-ssu-fu,'* beginning the festival, and they'll release flocks of bats, since both bat and happiness are pronounced *fu*. The leader will be carried on the annual tour of inspection, and that should lead us right to the prince, and then they'll get stinking drunk at a banquet."

Master Li crawled back and selected a robe that fit him. He helped us hide our weapons on our backs, beneath robes, and the huge cowls neatly covered our faces.

"Aesthetically the ceremony leaves much to be desired, but it's marvelous for murder," Master Li said grimly. "I'm not going to wait for the tour of inspection. Too risky. That fellow and his happy friends tried to kill us, and it's time to return the favor. If we can get right in the middle of them and they're suddenly without a leader we should have an easy time of it, but don't forget to leave one or two alive to tell us where the prince is."

He bent down to the sandal that didn't contain lock picks and slipped off the rounded end of the false sole. It had a small threaded hole in it. He reached father into the hollow sandal and took out a slim rounded blade not much thicker than a large needle, and screwed the base of it into the hole. The piece of sole fit neatly into the palm of his hand.

"Ox should bring up the rear in case I miss," he said. "I should be right in front of him. Any volunteers to go first?"

"Me," Grief of Dawn and Moon Boy said simultaneously.

Master Li chose Moon Boy to go first and Grief of Dawn to follow, and we slid back to the ledge. The ceremony was going exactly as he had predicted, and the laughing monks were slowly circling in toward the throne. Each formally embraced the leader and took a scroll from the urn and danced up to the assistant, who opened the scroll and read a happiness wish in a loud braying voice. They were crude jests without wit or imagination—to be eternally pickled in a cask of strong wine, for example, or to be reborn as a pillow in a brothel. Each stupid joke was greeted by howls of laughter.

All eyes were on the throne and the assistant. We easily slipped down the side of a sloping cliff and fell in at the end of the procession. The only problem was matching the awkward dance steps of the monks, who seemed to be woefully uncoordinated. The line moved steadily toward the leader.

"Brother Pimple-Puss, who shall be granted his wish to be buggered by the Transcendent Pig!" the assistant bellowed.

Even that was greeted with laughter. The last line was circling in, and my heart was in my mouth as Moon Boy danced toward the throne. I had never known anyone braver, but his complexion was becoming sickly green. He managed the brief formal embrace without incident, however, and took his scroll to the assistant, who read another idiotic happiness wish. Grief of Dawn was next, and she too had turned green, but she also made it safely. Now it was Master Li's turn.

I could swear I saw a greenish tinge on his wrinkled skin as well. He danced up and extended his hands for the embrace, and his right hand slapped suddenly against the leader's heart. A swift flick of the wrist unscrewed the sandal sole. He collected his scroll and danced on to the assistant, and now it was my turn. I soon realized what caused the green complexions. The leader hadn't washed in six months. A step closer I changed it to six years, and then sixty.

Master Li hadn't missed. The head behind the paper mask lolled lifelessly against the back of the throne. The tiny blade had drawn almost no blood, and with the sole gone, it was nearly invisible. I was relieved that I wouldn't have to strangle the bastard. I took my scroll and danced on, and for the first time the assistant changed the ritual. Apparently the last in line served a ceremonial function.

"The last shall be first!" the assistant bellowed. "Our belated brother is granted the wish to carry our leader on the tour of inspection!"

I looked around for a carriage or a litter, and realized that in the ancient ritual one carried the leader on one's back. Master Li and Moon Boy and Grief of Dawn were so closely squeezed between laughing monks that it would be difficult for them to get to their weapons, and all Master Li could do was raise both eyebrows heavenward as two large monks approached the throne and picked up the leader.

Luck was with us. The flickering torchlight didn't permit a clear view, and the paper mask stayed in place, and it occurred to me that they might not be surprised if the leader got a head start and was already stinking drunk. Swiftly I found myself with a corpse on my back, his head lolling over my shoulder and his arms hanging down on either side of my neck. The only thing I could do was hold the lifeless legs and hope the tour of inspection would do what Master Li first surmised: lead us to the prince.

"T'ien-kuan-ssu-fu!" the assistant shouted. *"The Agent of Heaven*

Brings Happiness! Ring the bells! Beat the gongs! Release the bats! Let there be dancing and merrymaking, for the Festival of Laughter has begun!"

"Ha, ha, ha! Ho, ho ho!" the monks laughed, and off we went.

Bells and gongs were banging so loudly they hurt my ears, and cages were opened and thousands of terrified bats flapped frantically through the torchlight.

"Dance! Dance! Dance! Let joy reign supreme in the Festival of Laughter!" the assistant howled.

I managed to glance back and saw that Master Li and Moon Boy and Grief of Dawn were each so tightly hemmed in by capering monks that they could do little but dance along with them. The harsh cacophony of bells and gongs was completely disorienting the bats. They were crashing against the walls and up against the roof, and small furry bodies were dropping down all around us.

"More laughter! More dancing! More bells and more bats!" the assistant screamed.

The corpse I carried was growing rigid with astonishing swiftness. The dangling arms were pressing uncomfortably against the sides of my neck, and I was finding it difficult to breathe. I tried shifting the weight, but nothing is harder to move properly than a corpse. It's like a sack of meal equipped with awkwardly positioned arms and legs.

"Joy!" the assistant howled. *"Joy! Joy! Joy!"*

The arms were squeezing tighter and tighter. I had no choice but to drop the corpse's legs and reach up and wrench at the arms, and we staggered forward with his feet bouncing against the ground. It was like trying to pry thick iron bars apart . . .

Iron bars. A vision of the library at the monastery flashed before my eyes, and iron bars squeezed like soft candles. I wrenched with everything I had. The arms simply squeezed tighter.

"Let joy be unconfined, for our Lord of Happiness greets his honored guest!" the assistant screamed.

The cowl of the corpse's robe fell back. The mask was slipping off. The head slowly lifted. One eye popped open and winked at me, and carrion breath made me gag as the mouth opened. Now I knew why two monks lay dead with horror stamped on their faces.

"How kind of you to carry this humble one on the tour of inspection," said the Laughing Prince.

I could not be mistaken. Half of the face was the face of the portrait in the tomb. The other half was also the Laughing Prince, but like an effigy molded in wax and placed beside a fire. The flesh had partially decomposed, and his voice was also half-decomposed: thick and slurred and clotted and foul. The other eye popped open and winked at me. Both eyes were totally mad.

"You shall enjoy yourself in my kingdom," the Laughing Prince snickered.

"*Dance! Dance! More joy and merriment!*" howled the assistant.

"See how my monks enjoy themselves," said the Laughing Prince. "What delightful additions you and your friends will make to our company."

Cowls were falling from the faces of capering monks, and I saw that they were corpses. Patches of flesh still stuck to white bones, and empty eye sockets stared in eternal horror.

"*More bats and more bells! Ring more gongs!*" the assistant screamed.

The Laughing Prince had sought godhood, and he had found eternity as *chiang shih,* the corpse who crawls from the grave and strangles wayfarers and steals their souls. Never in history had anyone escaped the embrace of a rigid corpse.

"Oh, yes, you and your companions shall enjoy yourselves so much that you will never want to leave," the Laughing Prince hissed in my ear. "Such joy. Such unending laughter. And you will dance for me forever and ever and ever."

"*All praise to our Lord of Happiness!*" howled the assistant. "*All praise to the Stone!*"

"The Stone!" the corpses cried. "All praise to the Stone!"

I frantically looked back and saw that the assistant was lashing Master Li and Grief of Dawn and Moon Boy with a whip, while corpses crowded in to squeeze their arms tightly against their sides. I looked to the side. I could barely breathe now, and my vision was blurred, but I could make out the destination we seemed to be circling toward. A sacrificial altar stood at one side of the cavern. Beside it was a huge stone basin filled with ceremonial oil, and behind it was a pillar, where sacrificial axes hung on hooks.

"*More bats!*" howled the assistant! "*More dancing and laughter!*"

Better now than later, I thought, and I knocked over a row of corpses as I made a detour. The bodies of bats crunched beneath my feet as I staggered toward the altar. More bats were shrieking in fear as they collided with the skulls of capering monks, and crawled into empty mouths and eye sockets for shelter. My neck was breaking. Black and red spots danced in front of my eyes. The basin of ceremonial oil suddenly loomed in front of me, and with the last of my strength I lunged forward and carried my body and the corpse's over the edge and into the oil.

I came to the surface, gasping, and grabbed the oily arms and shoved upward. Slowly they began to slide. They stopped at my ears, and I reached down with one hand and scooped up more oil, and finally the deadly arms shot up over my head with a loud popping sound. I lurched to the rim of the basin and toppled over it to the ground, and the Laughing Prince stood up in the oil and extended his arms lovingly.

"Come back, dear boy. We haven't finished our dance," he chuckled.

I crawled to the pillar and hauled myself upright and grabbed one of the sacrificial axes. The rigid corpse was out of the basin and walking toward me, arms extended. Both mad eyes were winking. I let the thing get within range, and then I chopped the legs off at the knees. The Laughing Prince tumbled over backward.

"The Stone and the Lord of Happiness crave more merriment!" the assistant howled.

I chopped the hands from the arms, and the arms from the torso, and raised the axe high and brought it down on the decomposing face. The head split apart, and as it did, the eyes winked in sequence.

"Quite," said the left half of the mouth.

"Useless," said the right half of the mouth.

I dropped the axe and staggered away and fell. I lay there, gasping for breath and unable to move.

"Sing the great Hymn of Joy, for our Lord of Happiness prepares the sacrifice!" screamed the assistant.

I managed to turn my head. The severed hands of the Laughing Prince were scuttling toward me like crabs. They crawled up my legs and over my chest, and clamped viciously around my throat.

"Ha, ha, ha!" laughed the capering corpses. "Ho, ho, ho!"

I staggered to my feet, futilely wrenching at the strangling hands, and lurched back toward the basin. I ducked my head into the oil and pried the oily fingers free, one by one. I hurled the hands back into the oil and stumbled to the pillar and wrenched a torch free. I hurled it blindly. It almost missed, but it teetered for a moment on the rim and then fell into the basin. I fell on my face, unable to move.

A pillar of flame shot toward the roof. Two balls of fire crawled over the rim and down to the ground, and all I could do was watch as the flaming hands crawled toward me. They were hissing and popping. Bones were separating. Fingers spurted greasy smoke and fire and detached from the hands and fell off. Black clouds were crawling toward my legs. They stopped and I jerked in pain as hissing stuff spattered my ankles. Then the clouds cleared, and where the hands had been were two piles of smoking charcoal.

The bells stopped. The gongs stopped. The corpses stood frozen in awkward dancing positions. Only the bats still continued to fly through the torchlight.

Something moved, and tears welled in my eyes and trickled down my nose as I saw Master Li crawl toward me. He was alive, and so were Grief of Dawn and Moon Boy, and I was alive too, and we weren't waking up to eternity as merry monks in motley.

石

24

Moon Boy propped my head up, and Master Li took out his flask and poured wine down my throat until I choked and coughed and sat up and spewed alcohol over my tunic. It helped to clear my head, which Master Li patted in grandfatherly fashion. "When traveling, always bring an ox with you," he said.

Moon Boy planted a kiss on my left cheek, but it wasn't Moon Boy I wanted, and I was still so weak that I felt my eyes fill with tears. Grief of Dawn hadn't bothered to come to me, and I was about to drown in self-pity until I realized that, alone among us, Grief of Dawn had kept her head. She had finally been able to free her bow, and we had no idea what other horrors might be down there, and she was crouched behind the basin of oil sweeping the cavern with a drawn arrow. Nothing stirred except bats. Finally she released the tension of the string and crawled back.

"Ox," she said, giving me a kiss, "the boys will have to add you to the story of Wolf. Never before has anyone broken the grip of a chiang shih."

The rigid corpse lay in pieces, but could it somehow rise again? I shuddered, and so did Moon Boy, and Grief of Dawn's hands slid slowly up her body to her shoulders, and she hugged herself protectively.

"Master Li, I hate and fear that horrible thing, but why am I drawn to it?" she whispered. "It's almost as I am drawn to Moon Boy, or even to the prince."

Moon Boy looked at her with somber eyes and turned to Master

Li. "I too feel the attraction," he said. "When I danced behind that creature, it was only partly because I was forced to. I also wanted to."

The old man looked at me. "Ox?"

I shook my head. "No, sir," I said. "All I feel is fear and loathing."

"It's the same with me, and I think we're deficient in sensibility," he said. He walked over and bent down to the severed torso. His knife glittered in the torchlight. "More than seven centuries ago the Laughing Prince died, and during the forty-nine days while the Bailiffs of Hell waited to ensure there had been no mistake in the Register of Life and Death, the flesh began to decay. The Laughing Prince wore an amulet of stone on a chain around his neck, and the stone sank into his body. Before the bailiffs arrived, the stone had entered his heart and he had arisen from the dead; mad, almost mindless, totally evil—but does that mean the stone was evil? My children, the attraction you feel would make far more sense if the opposite were true."

The flesh was so rotten that he scarcely needed the knife, and he scooped more than cut and came up with a smooth flat piece of stone. He carefully washed it in the oil and dried it on his robe, and I was quite frightened when he walked back with the stone in his bare hands. I suppose I expected his fingernails to grow a foot and coarse black hair to crawl over his flesh, and when he lifted his eyes from the stone I looked for the flow of lunacy. Instead I saw a film of tears, and his voice was soft and gentle.

"Is the stone evil? Here, Ox, judge for yourself."

He handed me the stone. It happened so quickly that I took it without thinking, but then I let out a yelp and would have dropped it if his fingers had not closed around mine.

"Don't be afraid," he said quietly.

The stone was warm. It was living, and I could feel a flow of energy like a heartbeat. A tingle entered my fingers and spread throughout my body. It spread through every nerve like a miraculous tonic, and my weariness vanished, and I had the distinct sensation that at any moment I might begin to bloom like a flower. Master Li gestured for me to pass it around, and I handed it to Grief of Dawn. She began to weep, even while a smile came to her lips, and when Moon Boy received it he turned white as a ghost and pressed it to his chest as though he wanted to join the stone with his body.

Master Li took it back and held it up to the torchlight. "The author of *Dream of the Red Chamber* never saw the stone, but I'm willing to bet he did indeed see one of the Annals of Heaven and Earth, and that it simply said the stone was flawed. It was the flower that was evil, but Tsao Hsueh Chin imputed evil to the stone because of the peculiar reaction of two great men who once possessed it. Ssu-ma Ch'ien never touched the stone with his hands, and he too imputed evil because of the reactions of Lao Tzu and Chuang Tzu. If Ssu-ma had not been under such a strain he might have paid closer attention to the shape of the stone, and reached a different conclusion."

Master Li grinned at us and quoted Ssu-ma. " 'Smooth flat area rising to round concave bowl shape.' What does that suggest to you?"

It suggested nothing at all to me or Moon Boy, but Grief of Dawn's eyes lit up.

"A place to grind an ink stick and a bowl to dip the brush into. It was a natural ink stone," she said.

"Good girl! Natural ink stones are highly prized, and this one was presented first to Lao Tzu and then to Chuang Tzu. I would give almost anything to have been there when the great men first used it," Master Li said. "Their writing brushes dipped into the well and moved over the flat area, coming into contact with a stone that carried the touch of Heaven, and they gaped with stunned eyes when the calligraphy that flowed from their brushes was that of the gods. They could keep quiet about the stone and claim such genius as their own, and the temptation must have been terrible, and they yelled, 'Evil!' and hurled the stone away. Anyone who heard them would assume they were referring to the stone, not the temptation that came with it."

He placed the piece of stone into his purse and secured it with a leather thong.

"This is only one piece. There are two to go," he said grimly. "When the Laughing Prince rose from the dead he was totally mad and almost totally mindless, and he couldn't possibly have planned rational actions. Somebody else has been doing the thinking, and somewhere down here is the ringleader who has his hands on Prince Liu Pao. Unless . . ."

His voice trailed off. We knew what he was thinking, and our faces were white and strained as we methodically moved among the Monks of Mirth. We pulled back cowl after cowl. All we found were white skulls, or recent ones with patches of skin and hair still clinging to them. Moon Boy nearly had a heart attack when both empty eye sockets of a skull suddenly winked at him, but then a frightened bat flew from the hollow skull. Something terrible might have happened to the prince, but at least he wasn't one of the monks.

We took torches and bent close to the floor. It took nearly an hour to find it, but Moon Boy suddenly whooped happily. A scarlet tassel lay at the entrance of one of the side passages. Again we clutched our weapons and started off, with me in front and Grief of Dawn covering the rear.

If the prince hadn't managed to leave that trail we would have been hopelessly lost in a matter of minutes. It was a maze inside a labyrinth that was inside another maze, and tunnels branched off in all directions. Everywhere we saw heavy wooden braces holding the ceilings together. We had to move carefully to avoid touching scaffolding, and we found ourselves whispering, as though a loud word could bring the tomb down on our heads. Tomb it was: room after room, some finished and some incomplete, designed for every conceivable function and pleasure. The Laughing Prince had decided to take his whole world with him, and I even expected a polo field until I realized that in his day we had imported the marvelous horses from India (left by the mad Greek invader) but not the game that went with them.

The scarlet tassels continued to show us the way. Moon Boy whispered that he could hear water, and a few minutes later we stepped into a beautiful cave. From what we could see in torchlight, the stone was blue and green and very beautiful, and a marble floor led to a pool fed by a small trickle of water falling from a ledge nearly forty feet above it. Marble steps led up to jutting rock shelves, and I had a weird vision of a parade of skeletons and mummies climbing up to dive.

Moon Boy held up a hand. "Something moving," he whispered. "It's coming this way. Up there," he whispered, pointing to one of the rock shelves above the pool. Then we all froze like statues, because a high screeching voice began to shriek.

"*Master, O Master, the game nears your bow!*
An old stag, two young bucks, and a lovely young doe!"

The echoes bounced back and forth between the walls and vibrated into endless passageways. Something moved. A small graceful figure wrapped in a robe of motley was standing on the shelf looking down at us. I stopped breathing when I saw the cowl was pulled back just far enough for the top of the head to be seen above dark shadows. The hair was the color of fire. I heard a clear lilting laugh, and then the pure lovely voice of a girl.

"I hope I didn't frighten anybody. Who are you?"

Master Li's eyes were slits so narrow I wondered how he could see anything, and his cool voice was sardonic.

"Tourists," he said. "Who are you?"

The girl shyly plucked at her robe. "My friend calls me Fire Girl," she said. "Have you seen him?"

"Possibly," Master Li said. "Is your friend the happy fellow who cavorts with monks who wear robes like yours?"

"Yes. He's my friend until my real friend comes, but I haven't seen him for the longest time." Her pure voice was puzzled. "He promised to come back, I know he did, but I can't remember when it was."

Master Li heaved a sigh and reached for his wine flask.

"His name, no doubt, is Wolf."

"Yes!" the girl cried delightedly. "Have you seen him? I've been waiting and waiting and I know we have something important to do, but my head isn't very clear and I can't remember what it is."

She had the most beautiful young voice I had ever heard, but there was a strange discordant note behind it. Something was off center, and it came not from the vocal chords but the mind.

Master Li swallowed some wine, and for once he didn't seem to enjoy the taste. "We also have a friend," he said. "He has funny hair that sticks out all over, and ink stains on his nose. He may have gone with your other friend, the one with the monks."

"Yes, I saw him." She gestured vaguely behind her. "Back there. Maybe he's sick, because they were carrying him."

"Then we'd better go to him with some medicine," Master Li

said reasonably. "Do the monks call your friend the Lord of Laughter?"

"Yes, but I don't like it when he laughs," she said gravely. "He smells bad too, but when I woke up I was all alone, and I was alone for the longest time, and I was glad when I found him."

"That was when you learned how to open the doors and get into the burial chamber," Master Li said matter-of-factly. "Was he out of his coffin when you found him?"

She plucked her robe nervously and was silent for a long time.

"Yes," she whispered. "But he wasn't really awake, and it took me the longest time to learn how to wake him up."

"With the stone from the sacristy?"

"Yes, but then he wasn't any fun," the girl said petulantly. "He wasn't any good at games, and he got nasty unless I made the stone sing and calm him down, and when I asked him to find more friends, he came back with those monks, and they weren't any fun either."

"Aren't you forgetting something?" Master Li said coaxingly. "You had two other friends, didn't you? Two men who came down from outside? They carried you up the steps so you could slide, and then you shot a few arrows, and then you went back to the slide, and one day you found out how to get into the burial chamber."

She plucked her robe more nervously. "Yes," she whispered.

"And your other friend wasn't out of his coffin then, remember?" Master Li said gently. "You had the men lift the lid, didn't you? And you'd already found out about that iron plate in front of the desk, and the men stood there so you could pay them. It must have been hard to pull the lever."

Tears were trickling through her lovely voice, pearls slowly drifting down through nectar.

"I didn't want to do it, but they would have told everybody about the room of gold and the suit of jade, and I knew I had to keep it secret. I have to keep everything secret. I can't remember why, but I know it's important, and one day Wolf will come back and remind me of the reason."

"Secrets can be very hard to keep," Master Li said sympathetically. "At night you went into the world above and listened at windows and heard things, and one night you came back to the cavern and told your friend who smells so bad that a monk from the monastery had a manuscript by somebody named Ssu-ma Ch'ien, and your friend told you that Ssu-ma had found an entrance to the tomb. Isn't that how it happened?"

"Yes," she whispered.

"And after that you listened at another window and learned that the monk had made a copy, and your friend who smells so bad had to deal with that too."

"Yes," she whispered. "You were there! You and your friend with the hair and ink spots." She threw back her head and laughed like a peal of lovely bells. "Your friend's hair is really very funny. Do you want to see where they carried him?"

Master Li swallowed more wine and put his flask away. "That might be a nice idea," he said dryly. "Lead on, Girl of Fire."

My head was hurting, and words slipped like sly lizards through cracks in my solid granite brain, darting, stopping motionless, creeping cautiously toward meanings: "You told your friend who smells so bad that a monk from the monastery had a manuscript by somebody named Ssu-ma Ch'ien, and your friend told you . . ." The girl had said yes, and that her smelly friend had also planned the second burglary and murder, but how could the Laughing Prince have planned anything? He hadn't been rational! Suddenly I realized that Master Li had led the girl to confirm that the only two people who could have been responsible for the murders of the monks were the Laughing Prince and the girl herself, and the girl had certainly killed the two gardeners.

But was *she* rational? She kept her distance as we climbed to the rock shelf, moving like a timid fawn as she turned into one of the side tunnels. Her beautiful voice reached back through the darkness, singing.

> *"The boy who dies, dies not in vain;*
> *The Great Wheel turns, he comes again.*
> *The girl who grieves and drinks of this,*
> *Will be awakened with a kiss."*

Master Li grunted and flicked a finger downward, and I saw why he was following the girl wherever she led. One more scarlet tassel lay on the tunnel floor. She might be crazy, but she was leading us in the right direction.

> *"A touch of lips will open eyes,*
> *A girl of fire will thus arise;*
> *Then the sacred arrow flies,*
> *And the Heart of Evil dies."*

The sweet notes echoed away into the distance, and the girl's voice spoke from the darkness ahead. "I don't remember what that means, but Wolf will tell me when he comes," she said trustingly.

We turned and twisted through tunnels, all braced with rickety old wood. Four more scarlet tassels told us we were going in the right direction, and finally the small dim figure ahead of us turned into one more entrance, and her voice drifted back: "They took him in here."

When we reached the opening and stepped inside to a small cave, the girl was gone, but I saw another passageway in the far wall. The cave had once been a storeroom, and old metal tool racks lined a wall. Ancient posts lifted to crossbeams that held up the shaky ceiling. One of the posts had cracked, and somebody had tied coils of rope around the split.

Something was wrong. My gut told me that, not my mind, and I forced my eyes to move slowly around the cave. Suddenly they jerked back. A rope? A rope that had survived seven centuries and wasn't even frayed? I strode forward so I could see the other side of the thick post. The rope extended to a hole in the wall, and it was lifting and tightening. I swore and swung with my axe, but I was too late. Just before the blade reached it, the rope jerked taut and the flimsy old post snapped right in half.

Other posts groaned in protest. They bent, and the entire ceiling suddenly dropped two feet. The tortured posts screamed, and then they snapped with deafening sharp cracking sounds. Splinters of wood shot around the cave like vicious spears, and rocks tumbled down, and the entire framework supporting the ceiling began to bulge in the center. I dove forward as the bulge bent toward the floor and got beneath the center beam and heaved upward with all my might. I couldn't lift it, of course, but it temporarily stayed where it was.

"Get out!" I yelled.

I glanced back. My mind refused to believe what my eyes were telling me. It couldn't be. *It couldn't be.* Surely a shack in Peking would echo with happy laughter, and an old sage would whistle "Hot Ashes" and open another wine jar when his young wife slipped into the shed in back to visit Number Ten Ox, and Moon Boy and the prince would come every few months, and . . .

And my heart believed what my eyes said, and turned to ice. Moon Boy was cradling Grief of Dawn in his arms, and this time no medicine on earth would help her. A shaft of splintered wood at least three inches thick had struck her square in the chest like a bolt from a catapult, and she was as dead as Tou Wan. Moon Boy was not going to leave her body to be crushed. He picked her up and carried her back toward the tunnel, and then I saw no more as my eyes blurred with tears. The ceiling sounded as though it was groaning with grief as it pressed down upon me. I couldn't move or the whole works would collapse.

Master Li's hand was on my shoulder. "Is the weight distributed evenly?" he asked.

"No," I panted. "It's tilted forward."

Master Li scuttled to the old iron tool racks. Some were very thick and strong, and he began walking one toward me. He got it beneath the beam, and then he wrestled with another one. When they were placed on both sides of me I bent my knees, lowering the center beam as slowly as possible. It was shuddering like a living thing, and it wouldn't remain in one piece much longer. It touched the tool racks.

Master Li had moved back to the tunnel opening. I let go, dropped to the floor, pushed back, and did a back flip to the opening. I just made it to the tunnel before the beam snapped in half, and Master Li hopped up on my back and I began to run. The crash of the falling ceiling nearly deafened us. The whole tunnel was shaking and dust billowed and rocks and wood splinters flew. I was running blind, but then I saw a glow of light through the darkness and dust. Moon Boy had the body of Grief of Dawn over his shoulder, and he was waving his torch.

Once before I had seen Master Li use his incredible memory to find the way back through a labyrinth, and now he did it again. He took the second opening on the right, then the third on the left, then the first on the left, and kept it up without hesitation even though rocks were falling and stones were screaming like tigers as they scraped together. We ran through one more opening and found we were back at the pool. In a minute we were back at the tunnel we had taken before, and then we came to a halt.

The vibration had shuddered through the entire cavern, and some ceilings were weaker than others. The tunnel that would have taken us back to the Monks of Mirth was completely blocked by a rockslide.

"Master Li, I can hear water that way!" Moon Boy shouted. "It sounds like the river!"

Now Moon Boy took the lead, groping through passage after passage, moving ever closer to the sound. At last Master Li and I could hear it too, and we stumbled from a hole to the bank of the black river in the huge central cavern. Moon Boy's torchlight bounced across the water and revealed the features of the first statue we had seen: Yen-wang-yeh, the former First Lord of Hell. We were only a few feet from the stairs that led up to Princes' Path and safety.

Master Li hopped down from my back and trotted back into the tunnel we had come from. He told Moon Boy to raise his torch, and he studied the vast structure of scaffolding with the eyes of an engineer. He walked over to the central supporting post near the left-hand wall. There was a crack in the center of it.

"Ox, can you break this thing?" he asked.

"It's old and fragile," I said. "Sir, it might break, but if a tunnel collapsed here, after the collapse back there, wouldn't that put a tremendous strain on the entire structure? That crazy girl is still in there, and the prince may still be alive."

"Do it," Master Li commanded.

"Venerable Sir—"

I shut my mouth. Master Li was glaring at me, and it was not for Number Ten Ox to contradict the great man. I put my shoulder to the post, but I had underestimated how rotten it was. It snapped at the first pressure, and I very nearly fell and impaled myself on the stump. Master Li hopped up on my back and Moon Boy lifted the body of Grief of Dawn and we began to run. We could hear nothing but the scream of splintering wood and the thunder of falling rocks, but I saw Moon Boy's lips opening and closing and his finger frantically pointing up.

Just ahead of us a huge crack was spreading across the ceiling of the cavern. With an enormous roar, about a hundred tons of rock crashed down and blocked all possible paths to the staircase. The river heaved, and a tidal wave raced back against the current. Master Li was pounding my shoulder and pointing, and I realized our only hope was to get back to the staircase that led up to the formal tomb. Moon Boy was very strong, and he would rather have died than leave Grief of Dawn's body down there, and he carried her while I carried Master Li as we ran for our lives. The face of the cavern ceiling was spreading into a succession of wide smiles. Rocks fell like hailstones and the black river turned white with foam. The walls shuddered and the floor bucked like a wild horse, and chunks of shattered wood and clouds of dust burst from every side passage.

I climbed into an enormous extended hand, and then up and over the torso of the fallen Japanese King of the Dead. We raced on past fallen statues. Gilgamesh still stood in his pride, holding the lion, but Anubis had fallen. Screeching grinding sounds hurt our ears. A huge crack opened in the floor, and Toth and Ament dropped into the pit and disappeared. We just made it past the enormous mummy of Osiris before it toppled over and smashed, and inside my head and heart I was listening to a beloved voice:

"Faster . . . faster . . . There's the raven and the river . . ."

There was the raven. We panted past it and lunged into the side passageway. The stairs were still intact. The walls appeared to be squeezing together as we bounded up the stairs, and it wasn't my imagination. The sound was indescribable. We finally reached the marble landing and the doors, and the statues still stood, and Master Li reached out and lifted the jar from the hawk-headed deity. The framework was beginning to twist and the door screeched in protest, but it opened enough for us to squeeze through. The tunnel was choked with dust and fallen rocks, and I had to feel to find a side passage.

The only passages we knew were the slide and stairs that led back down to the river, which would have been suicide, but if Master Li was right about the hawk symbolism, a number of side passages should lead out to the valley where monks in motley could hunt peasants. Luck was with us. I tripped over a staircase and began to climb, but then I ran smack into the stone wall of a dead end.

Master Li hopped off my back and began probing the wall, and then the side walls, and he pulled something and a crack of light appeared. I saw a patch of blue and a bright sun and white clouds, and we toppled out upon green grass. Dust was billowing behind us and I managed to shut the door, which was perfectly disguised in the face of a cliff. The thundering sounds faded, but the ground continued to heave beneath our feet. We were on Dragon's Right Horn, looking across the deep gorge to the matching peak and cliff and the estate of Prince Liu Pao.

The entire range of hills was shuddering, and muffled roaring sounds came from the bowels of the earth. The tomb of the Laughing Prince was like a cancer eating at the insides, but then the hills took charge. A billion tiny cracks appeared across the Valley of Sorrows as the earth squeezed down and pressed empty spaces together. Caverns and caves and tunnels were crushed out of existence, and great spouts of dust whistled up from holes and spread across the sky. The earth gave one last shudder and then was still.

Moon Boy straightened Grief of Dawn's body upon the grass and gently combed her hair with his fingers, and I sat down beside her and wept. Master Li lifted his eyes and watched tiny puffs of dust form a pattern on the matching cliff across the gorge, and then a door burst open and a small figure tumbled out. Dust covered everything. When it cleared I saw a robe of motley, and a cowl that revealed a glimpse of bright red hair. The head turned toward us.

"Oh!"

"Somehow I knew you'd make it," Master Li said.

The girl sat up and smacked billows of dust from her robe. "I'm so glad you're safe," she said in her beautiful off-center voice. "I'm afraid for my friend, though, and his monks, even though I don't like the monks very much. Did you find your friend with the funny hair?"

Master Li snorted and reached for his wine flask. His eyes and voice were cold and angry.

"We will just as soon as you pull that wig from your silly head and take your lips away from the stone. Prince, the time for games has ended. You and I are going to have a serious talk."

石

25

Moon Boy and I stared. I suppose that the pupils of our eyes were swimming around the whites like drunken dolphins when a red wig lifted and a feather duster mop of black hair appeared. The cowl fell back and Prince Liu Pao winked at us. In his hands was a piece of stone, round and concave like a bowl. "Yang," he said in a deep masculine voice. He moved his lips to the other side of the stone. "Yin," he said in the sweet feminine voice of the girl. "Needless to say, the sound from the center is quite extraordinary," he said cheerfully in his own voice. "I didn't dare use it underground because of the vibration, which shows how ill-equipped I was to take on the great Master Li. You didn't hesitate to bring the whole works down, and you very nearly squashed me like a bug."

The prince bowed deeply. Master Li grunted and emptied the contents of his purse upon the grass. The lining was waterproof, and he filled it with wine and sealed it. He still had plenty of spring in his right arm, and the purse sailed across the gorge to the prince. They toasted each other politely, and drank thirstily.

"As a matter of minor curiosity, how old were you when you first discovered the entrance in the gorge?" Master Li asked.

"Twelve," the prince replied. "I was thirteen when I learned how to open the doors and enter the burial chamber, and your reconstruction of the tragic affair with the gardeners was so accurate it chilled my blood." He heaved a melancholy sigh. "I hated to kill them. They were my friends, but as you yourself have pointed out, I was faced with the possibility of having every greedy bureaucrat and bandit in the empire at my doorstep. How could I trust those fellows to keep such a secret?"

"How indeed?" said Master Li.

I can't speak for Moon Boy, but I was convinced I was hallucinating. In fact, I was wondering where and when I had eaten some weird mushrooms.

"The manuscript of Ssu-ma Ch'ien posed a similar problem," the prince said. "I thought the secret would last as long as I would, but Brother Squint-Eyes came to me with a sample page. The idiot thought it was genuine. I knew it was forged, but two days later it dawned on me that the idiot was right. It had to be in code, and how could I be sure Brother Squint-Eyes wasn't playing stupid? For all I knew, he could even have deciphered it, but not yet put two and two together. I had to send my abominable ancestor to deal with him."

The prince flushed angrily. "I was being forced to take actions that made me ill," he said. "You revealed there might be a copy, and I had to try to get it, and that other idiotic monk had to stick his head into the library and commit suicide."

The two of them sipped wine and moodily watched butterflies dance through sunlight that was beginning to filter through a golden haze. The breeze carried a faint smell of rain, and black clouds were gathering in the distance. Far below us the Valley of Shadows was wrapped in deep purple shadows.

"In the tomb I always used the softest possible sound from the stone to control my ancestor," the prince said. "When I sent him and his merry companions to the monastery he wanted to linger and strangle a few more people. I had to make a loud sound to bring him back, and it was exactly like the emperor and the tangerines. The incredible ch'i of the stone overpowered weaker ones in its path, and when I pulled my ancestor back, I also pulled the life force from parts of Princes' Path. I was absolutely appalled! In fact, I felt like a character in a fairy tale who waves a magic wand to cure his wife's one blemish, and does so, except she's now a flawless yak. What had been so simple was becoming terrifyingly complex, and the immediate result was that the abbot was so frightened he rushed off to Peking to seek the legendary Li Kao. Even then I was idiotic enough to think you would weary of reaching dead ends and give up."

Master Li spat disgustedly. "The legendary Li Kao had better buy a bucket of worms and start practicing his goo-goo-goos," he said sourly. "It was the sheer simplicity of it that baffled me. If I hadn't been enchanted by complexity, I might have realized what was going on the moment I saw your studio."

"Oh, but you were magnificent!" the prince protested. "I simply couldn't believe it when you worked through one blind alley after another, knocking walls down if necessary, and you never really went off course. You were moving like doom itself straight toward the truth, and finally I had no choice but to try to kill you."

He threw his head back and laughed with all the old warmth and charm.

"I should have known that a man who would dare a mind trip to Hell would be harder to kill than the Stone Monkey." He inclined his head in my direction. "You too, Ox. You were a dead man the moment I led you to my unspeakable ancestor, and instead you will most certainly earn a place in the annals of P'u Sung-ling, the Recorder of Things Strange."

"Speaking of the Laughing Prince, how did he acquire his happy companions?" Master Li asked.

"My fault entirely." The prince grimaced and fined himself a slap on the cheek. "I may have been slightly precocious when I found my ancestor, but I was still a boy. One day I forgot to lock him back inside the burial chamber, and to make matters worse, I went off on a long trip. When I returned I discovered he had taken the opportunity to creep through the moonlight strangling wayfarers, and now he had companions to share his merriment. Ox, I'm deeply indebted to you for finishing him off. I was going to have to do so, but I wasn't at all sure of how to go about it."

I decided that Prince Liu Pao had been the most eerily precocious boy in history. Thirteen years old, killing two gardener friends when they opened a coffin for him and found a priceless suit of jade, carefully removing jade plates to gaze at a mummy, and gazing instead at the half-decomposed face of a monster that still breathed, learning to control the creature with sounds from a stone—thirteen going on ninety, with the heart of a hangman.

The hangman's eyes softened as they slowly moved to Grief of Dawn. He spread his hands helplessly. "I would like you to know that I really did love her," the prince said quietly. "I was pinned into a corner, and I had to make a difficult decision."

"It was a decision you made long ago when you first decided to sell your soul for gifts from a stone," Master Li said matter-of-factly. "Grief of Dawn made exactly the opposite decision—incidentally, Moon Boy, could you bring the soul-sound from this one piece?"

He picked up the piece of stone he had taken from the Laughing Prince and tossed it to Moon Boy, who shook his head and said, "No, not from a flat piece. I'd need two of them." From the tone of Moon Boy's voice, I assumed he had decided this was all a bad dream.

Master Li nodded. He got to his feet and walked over to the body of Grief of Dawn and pulled out his knife. Her life had drained away down in the tomb, and there was only a trickle of blood when he removed the ugly wooden shaft from her chest. He probed the wound and washed something in wine and dried it on his tunic. When he tossed it to Moon Boy, I saw that it was a small sharp sliver of stone.

"I was wrong about Grief of Dawn," Master Li said. "I thought she had been Tou Wan's maid in a previous incarnation. The truth is that she never left that incarnation. Tou Wan stabbed her with the hairpin. The top broke off inside her heart and kept her alive, and she fled and was hit on the head by soldiers who left her for dead. Again the stone brought her back to life, and the maid wandered into the world without a memory. A cruel and dangerous world for a pretty girl, and she was bleeding and unconscious when old Tai-tai took her in and gave her a home and a new name."

Master Li squeezed Moon Boy's shoulder, and walked back and squeezed mine and sat down beside his wine flask.

"Do not mourn Grief of Dawn," he said quietly. "Remember how she sang in her delirium when she thought she would ease the pain of an old lady she loved? Inside her heart she carried a gift from Heaven that was not rightfully hers. She could have become the most honored and celebrated woman in history, but she would not be party to stealing. I have no idea what her strange wandering life was like, nor how and why she moved from one existence to another without awakening her memory, but I do know that for seven and a half centuries she refused to steal from Heaven, and she is being greeted with the highest honors in Hell where her credit account could buy half the kingdom, and surely she will be allowed to ascend to K'un-lun and sit at the feet of the August Personage of Jade. Which is a good deal more than Prince Liu Pao will be able to do."

His eyes were cold and contemptuous as they moved across the gorge to the prince.

"He's already killed five people in order to dip his brush into the well of the stone and steal the touch of Heaven, and then paint pretty pictures and pass them off as his own." Master Li rinsed his mouth with wine and spat it out. "Fraud and forgery," he growled. "Paint slapped over dry rot and gilded with lies."

The prince turned white.

"Is that what you think, old man?" he whispered. "Is that what you really think?" Now he was turning red. "My paintings are private! I do not show them! What sort of fraud is that?"

"Masturbation," Master Li said. "In your circumstances, that still qualifies as rape."

"My paintings are for the purpose of learning the paths of universal energy!" the prince shouted furiously. "My loathsome ancestor sought truth in rivers of blood; I seek it in harmless paint, and even the Laughing Prince could claim that his was the proper goal of philosophy! You, on the other hand, waste your time with unimportant puzzles, which is the occupation of a child!"

Master Li raised his flask and drank deeply, and wiped his lips with his beard.

"Oh, I wouldn't call the puzzle of the stone unimportant," he said mildly. "I will, however, plead guilty to holding a certain childlike view of the universe."

The prince's color was returning to normal. He raised the purse and drank, and leaned back comfortably.

"Childlike? No, but very old-fashioned," he said with a chuckle. "In fact, everything you do is old-fashioned. Who in this day and age would charge all over China, even to the pits of Hell, trusting to the immediacy of experience rather than the trained objectivity of an army of investigators? You appear to take seriously the anthropomorphic folk concepts of gods and goddesses, and your concern for the stone appears to spring from a literal acceptance of fairy tales from the spurious Annals of Heaven and Earth. Li Kao, you

are a very great man, but—and I say this with the greatest respect—
an antique memorial to long dead concepts and practices and values."

The prince was laughing as he lifted his stone. I realized that it
was attached to a cord around his neck, and the silver cup for his
painting brush that had encased and concealed it was slipped down.
Master Li leaned over and whispered to me, and I surreptitiously
whispered to Moon Boy.

"He says you're to prepare to bring the soul-sound from the
stone. He'll yell when he wants it."

Moon Boy's eyes were glazed and he tried to focus them. His
fingers trembled as he lifted the two pieces in his cupped hands.

"Still, there are certain pleasures denied to an antique with a
slight flaw in his character," the prince said. "Such as being able to
hear the simple sound of total innocence. To be fair, half the villagers and monks couldn't hear the stone either. I would think, however, that at this distance, and with the acoustic effect of the cliffs
behind us—"

"*Now!*" Master Li yelled.

Moon Boy's lips moved to his cupped hands. His throat vibrated
rapidly, and my heart leaped as indescribable beauty and yearning
and hope and sadness bounced back and forth between the cliffs.

Kung . . . shang . . . chueeeeeeeeeeh . . .

Master Li reeled, but his reaction was as nothing compared to the
stone of Prince Liu Pao. It tore loose from the prince's hands and
literally flew toward Moon Boy, and the cord jerked tight around
the prince's neck and pulled him forward.

I am so stupid that it wasn't until then that I realized what the
prince had been planning to do to us. The gorge was only a few feet
away, two hundred feet straight down to jagged rocks. Prince Liu
Pao teetered at the edge, waving his arms for balance, and then he
fell. I closed my eyes, and when I opened them I was looking at a
miracle.

The prince was standing upon thin air. He walked across nothingness, intent only upon hauling the stone back and regaining control of it. Then he looked at us and smiled.

"Really, Li Kao, didn't you think I would expect that?" he said
mockingly. "And didn't you think I would learn something from
the stone and my ancestor's charts and formulas? I hate to brag, but

I rather suspect I know more about the energy forces of the universe than any other man alive."

He pointed to his sandals, resting upon a void.

"That, for example, is a path of energy strong enough to support ten elephants, if the elephants could learn to see and adjust to it. I have, and I sincerely hope you are similarly capable."

"One of us is," Master Li said calmly.

"You mean Number Ten Ox?" the prince said. "I agree that no man alive could climb down one side of the gorge and back up the other without the proper gear, and when Ox carried you from one peak to the other, he was crossing as I am now, upon a path of energy."

Master Li hopped up on my back, and the prince's smile grew wider.

"That's why in Hell you imagined him to show in the mirror that he was a firstborn, since walking on air can only result from absolute awareness or absolute innocence, but has it occurred to you that Ox was blinded by mist? He isn't now, and innocence cannot bear very much awareness."

His lips touched the rim of the stone in his hands, and the sound that came from the well was so pure and powerful that I heard not suggestive notes but the actual words from the soul of a stone.

"*Come . . . to . . . meeeeeeeeee! . . . Come . . . to . . . meeeeeeeeee!*"

Moon Boy and I were dragged to the edge. I saw no path of energy. All I saw were rocks rising like shark's teeth two hundred feet below, and terror shook me like a rag doll. I had no choice. I must obey the call or die, and my foot reached out into nothingness.

Moon Boy teetered on the edge. His throat was vibrating faster than a throat could, and sweat was pouring down his face, and something extraordinary was happening. He was projecting the sound of the stone, but at the same time he was blending another sound into it. It was wind and sunlight and rain and snow and a comfortable snug cottage—it was the song that Grief of Dawn had sung for old Tai-tai, but now she was singing to me. Grief of Dawn was calling me, and I couldn't imagine how I had missed the path before. There it was, not six feet from the empty space in front of my sandal, and I turned and walked to it. I stepped confidently out into the air, opening my arms to embrace Grief of Dawn, and I was only vaguely aware of the prince's white terrified face, and the click of the rattan coil inside Master Li's sleeve and the flash of his knife as it slashed out.

The sound of Grief of Dawn had turned. Now she was behind me, calling me back, and I turned around like a sleepwalker and stepped back over a path of swirling energy that was as smooth as a carpet. Master Li rode on my back, chuckling, and he laughed out loud when my sandals came down on rock and grass. Moon Boy collapsed, gasping and rubbing his throat, and Master Li hopped off.

The sounds had gone. I came back to reality and whirled around and stared at Prince Liu Pao, who was still standing upon thin air in the center of the gorge. He no longer wore the stone, and the warmth and charm was gone, and all I saw was a sly and selfish little man who looked like a terrified monkey.

"Really, Prince, there's no need to be frightened. Did you think I was going to slit your silly throat?" Master Li detached the stone from the cord he had cut from the prince's neck. Why do people take me for a crude assassin?" he asked plaintively. "I'm not crude at all."

The torch that Moon Boy had carried from the tomb lay on the grass. It still burned. Master Li pointed to it, and then across the gorge.

"Ox, can you put this thing through that window?"

I had a lot of pent-up emotion, and I released some of it. The torch tumbled over and over as it sailed across the gorge and plunged down through the window of the prince's studio. I thought it had gone out, but it hadn't. Oil and turpentine catch easily, and flames sprang up.

"Nothing to worry about, Prince," Master Li said reassuringly. "To cherish perfection is to commit creative suicide, and every true artist knows that a masterpiece is an accident that should be burned. Besides, your pretty pictures aren't to revel in but learn from, and you've already learned."

He reclaimed his flask and helped himself to another pint. "Not that I entirely approve of the goal," he said. "One of the previous possessors of the stone was Chuang Tzu. He had a disciple who spent seven years studying universal energy and then demonstrated his wisdom by walking across the surface of a river and back again, and Chuang Tzu broke into tears. 'Oh, my boy!' he sobbed. 'My poor, poor, boy! You spent seven years of your life learning to do that, and all the while old Meng has been running a ferry not two miles from here, and he only charges two copper coins.' "

Master Li replaced his flask.

"Besides, levitation can be positively unhealthy when one is accustomed to the support of a stone," he added.

The studio was blazing. Prince Liu Pao was weeping, and he turned and ran toward his paintings with outstretched arms. Suddenly he yelped in fear and stopped. I saw that his feet were slowly spreading apart as though the path was splitting into two paths, and he turned uncertainly this way and that. His white strained face turned back to me.

"Ox! Which way? Which is the solid path?"

"Prince, I can't see it anymore!" I shouted. "All I see is empty air!"

His legs were spreading wider. At any moment he would fall, and he squealed and jumped to the left. His feet came down on a solid line of energy and he began to run. He made two steps but not the third, and sometimes in dreams I still see a screaming feather duster turn over and over as Prince Liu Pao falls into the gorge, and I hear mocking echoes from the walls of the cliffs, and then I hear the sickening sound of a body splattering upon rocks far below.

Master Li walked to the edge and peered down. "Pity," he said. "He had real talent. Just the man for decorating dinner invitations."

石

26

The bottom of the gorge was leaping up at me, and I sat with my head between my knees until my stomach stopped heaving. Moon Boy was sitting beside Grief of Dawn with her limp hand held in his. Master Li turned from the gorge shaking his head in disgust, but not at the prince.

"When somebody performs my autopsy, he'll open the skull and pull out a turnip that's been masquerading as a brain," he said sourly. "I still can't begin to come to grips with this weird case."

I stared at him. Even Moon Boy raised his eyes from Grief of Dawn.

Master Li shrugged. "We'd have to be mindless as millipedes not to guess that the human involvement has been almost incidental. What matters is a stone."

He began pacing back and forth with his hands clasped behind his back. He stopped and glared up at Heaven. "How the hell do you expect idiotic human beings to *understand?*" he shouted impiously, and then he resumed pacing.

"The ancients gave up trying to understand," Master Li muttered. "After a couple of thousand years of watching fire transform solid pieces of wood into insubstantial heat and light, they produced the First Law of Taoist science: There is no such thing as a solid object. Five centuries later they produced the Second Law: All matter consists of bundles of pure energy called ch'i, the life force, and shih, the motion force. Another five centuries passed, and with the Third Law they threw up their hands and quit."

He stopped pacing and grinned at us.

"Believe it or not, there's a point to this," he said. "Ox and our late friend gave a marvelous demonstration of the First and Second Laws by adjusting their ch'i and shih to that of seemingly empty air and taking a walk, and Ox's dream about an orange-colored piece of clay unconsciously echoed the Third Law: All energy is controlled by adherence to classical patterns."

Master Li resumed pacing.

"Ox dreamed that the clay had a pulse that followed an unusual pattern. The Third Law states that the humblest piece of clay must adjust its ch'i and shih to that of the perfect piece of clay, and the energy of stars must follow the patterns of the perfect star. Every plant, animal, insect, drop of water, mote of dust—everything in the universe has a classical model to guide it, and those perfect patterns are the building blocks in the barrier against anarchy called the Wall of Heaven. That's when the ancients said to hell with it and stopped. You see, the next step required understanding the nature of universal energy as a whole, and such a thing is completely past the capabilities of the human mind."

Master Li stopped and shook a finger at us for emphasis.

"This can be said. Nothing in all existence is more important than maintaining the Wall of Heaven. Nothing! The forces are so awesome that should the barrier fail and energy run amok, the universe itself wouldn't last a second. The task of maintaining the Wall is that of the goddess Nu Kua, and what the goddess wants, the goddess gets. For unfathomable reasons she wanted a stone that had a flaw in it, and then when she couldn't repair the flaw, she dropped it in our laps."

Master Li sat down between Moon Boy and me and took Moon Boy's pieces of the stone. He carefully fit them together with the piece from the prince and held the stone up to the light.

"There's the flaw. See? A tiny vein of gold ran through it. Gold is pretty stuff, but terrible for a stone. Particularly when you're building a wall."

I hadn't noticed it when the pieces were apart, but now I saw the faint yellow lines at the edges of the cracks.

"According to one of the Annals of Heaven and Earth, assuming it existed, the goddess finally had to reject the stone, but not until contact with her hand had given it a soul," Master Li muttered.

"Two great philosophers later used it for an ink stone, and the touch of Heaven produced divine calligraphy. Prince Liu Pao used it to steal from the gods in order to paint pretty pictures, and I wonder . . ."

He let the sentence die a natural death while he swiftly bound the stone together with the cord he had cut from the prince's neck. He opened his wine flask and dipped the stone inside. After a minute he lifted the stone back out and removed the cord and placed the stone upon the grass. He lifted the flask to his lips, and I saw a slow sensual shudder spread throughout his body, and when he raised his head, his eyes were shining with reverence.

"Jade Emperor, if this is what you serve in heaven, preserve me long enough to become a saint," he whispered.

Moon Boy and I took small sips. I have no words for it. The raw alcohol of Haining Mountain Dew had become the Nectar of the Gods, and to describe it I'd have to steal from mystical accounts of divine revelations.

"Talk about temptation!" Master Li exclaimed. "I could start making this stuff by the lakeful and be deified on the spot!"

The taste had the greatest effect upon Moon Boy, who turned pale as death and began rocking back and forth with powerful emotion. I thought he was going to weep until I realized he never did. Moon Boy did not cry, not even when Grief of Dawn lay dead. Master Li was looking speculatively at him.

"You know, it's quite possible that I'm making the same mistake twice," he said thoughtfully. "I didn't see the obvious about the prince because it was too simple, and now I may be straining to understand something that doesn't require understanding. Perhaps all we need to know is that the goddess Nu Kua is blowing on the dice for one last desperate roll, and all we can do is pray they come up with a pair of Blind Queens. After all, we must assume that the stone is one of the most important objects in all the universe. Why else would she go to the trouble of Moon Boy?"

Moon Boy stared at him. So did I, and the old man threw his head back and laughed until tears flowed.

"What a creation is Moon Boy!" he chortled. "My lad, on the one hand you're the apotheosis of beauty, irresponsibility, and unbridled sexuality on a rampage, and on the other hand there isn't an evil, unkind, or even unpleasant bone in your body." Master Li shook his head wonderingly. "We may be sure that art is involved, for such a combination of excess and innocence is not to be found in nature," he said. "You couldn't possibly have perfected guiltless sin without experimenting with the common garden variety, and when Ox and I watched you stand before the Mirror of Past Existences, our subconscious minds played a duet. Buddha, what a series of incarnations! From baseness to depravity to malignancy to monstrosity, culminating in an incarnation as the most dissolute and irresistible slut ever to shake her rear end across the pages of history."

Master Li wiped his eyes and winked at me.

"Come, Ox, surely you recognized her? I thought every boy in China had memorized the more indelicate passages of her biography."

I remembered having seen Moon Boy dressed as a girl, and then I realized he *had* been a girl, and then I turned bright red. Suddenly his incredible beauty made sense, and I recognized the lady in the mirror, all right.

"Golden Lotus," Master Li said happily. "Moon Boy once walked the earth as a man-eating seductress so spectacularly immoral that she was elevated to Heaven to become the greatest Patron of Prostitutes in history, and I suspect that the goddess Nu Kua began to think deep thoughts about peculiar combinations of ch'i and shih the moment Golden Lotus began jiggling down the pearly paths, causing havoc among the young gods. Golden Lotus was removed from her post and given a new form. Remember it?"

I remembered Moon Boy in the mirror, changing and yet not changing, still beautiful but blending with bright colors, lifting his face and arms toward the sun, almost like—

"A flower," Master Li said softly. "A beautiful flawed flower named Purple Pearl who was placed in the path of a flawed stone, and the stone brought dew and raindrops to wash the evil from the flower, and the flower fell in love and vowed to repay its debt by shedding every tear in its body. It might take centuries, or even millennia for the time to be right for a flower to be reborn, but the greatest virtue of stone is patience."

Moon Boy's eyes were wide and wondering. Master Li picked up the stone, pieces still pressed together, and placed it in Moon Boy's hands. Then he took his wine flask and stood up.

"This will seem very silly, but who cares?" he said. "Clasp the stone tightly, Moon Boy. Close your eyes. Try to imagine a place without water near the River of Spirits, and dryness and wilting, and then a faithful stone flying up with the morning dew of Heaven."

Moon Boy closed his eyes and clasped the stone. Master Li waited, and then he tilted the flask and sprinkled drops of Heavenly Nectar over Moon Boy's head. The effect wasn't silly at all. Moon Boy trembled all over, and squeezed the stone against his heart, and from his lips came an indescribably beautiful singing sound that gradually resolved itself into words.

"Love . . . love . . . but I have no tears . . . Not even as a child could I cry . . . How can I cry for a stone? . . . Love . . . love . . . love . . . but I cannot cry . . ."

Master Li motioned for me to follow him.

"We will leave you for a while," he said quietly. "A flower that vows to shed tears is making a very serious commitment, and neither gods nor men have the right to influence the decision."

He walked away. We went around the peak to the far side of Dragon's Left Horn, and Master Li sat down on a flat rock and gazed out at the valley. Peasants were scurrying around fearfully, but so far as I could see the damage from the earthquake was limited to fallen thatched roofs and a few collapsed barns. Soft blankets of shadows were sliding over the fields, and the birds were singing their last songs. Master Li tilted the flask and reverently rolled the liquid around his mouth before swallowing.

"Ox, I think Prince Liu Pao should be a hero," he said thoughtfully. "It's better that way, even though it may cause long-term problems for his heirs. We'll tell the abbot that the prince fell in the final triumphant battle against the forces of evil, and never again will his abominable ancestor threaten the Valley of Sorrows."

"Yes, sir," I said.

"The peasants will want a temple for him, but a shrine should do."

Master Li was beginning to warm to the subject. "Make that two shrines," he said enthusiastically. "We'll say he wished to be cleft in half, from top to bottom, and each half buried in one of the destroyed areas of Princes' Path to fertilize new plants."

"Yes, sir," I said.

"He'll be the Holy Half-Princes of the Valley of Sorrows, each half turning the seeing side to the peasants' good deeds and the blind side to their bad, and the legend of what will happen when danger threatens and the two halves are reunited should be very interesting. I hope the cave of Wolf survived, because the boys should get to work on it at once."

"Yes, sir," I said.

"His last words were that he longed to lie in his graves and listen to the innocent laughter of children and the blissful bleating of little lambs and the—"

"No, sir," I said.

"I suppose you're right," Master Li admitted. "Peasants will go only so far. You'd better handle that part of it."

"Yes, sir," I said. "His last words were instructions to his heirs to repair the damage from the earthquake and give the monastery a new roof."

"Good boy," Master Li said.

"And fix the dike at the intersection of paths between the monastery, village, and estate. One torrential rain and the melons will wind up in Soochow."

"Anything else?"

"No, sir," I said. "Anything else and the peasants will expect the prince's heirs to repair their sandals and empty the chamber pots."

We sat in silence. Master Li's wrinkles seemed to be older than the seams and cracks in the hills across from us, and his mood was turning melancholy.

"You know, the prince was right," he said. "I'm almost the last advocate of the old way of doing things. Perhaps it's just as well. If one leaves out the Neo-Confucians, there's much to be said for the modern style. Still, I hope you keep filling your notebooks as a record of an archaic approach to problems. There's a good deal of fun to be found in the old way, and a good deal of beauty, and the practitioners seldom expired from ennui."

"Yes, sir," I said.

He looked at me gravely, and then he nodded. We got up and started back. I tried to prepare for it, but still it was like a blow to the pit of my stomach, and tears blurred my eyes.

"Oh, Moon Boy," I sniffled.

He always did things neatly. Master Li's knife had been carefully cleaned, and he had built a small dam of earth so the blood from his slit wrist would build up around and over the stone without staining the grass unnecessarily. Moon Boy had placed Grief of Dawn's hand over his, with the stone beneath them, and Master Li walked up and gently lifted the hands and picked up the stone. He washed it in the wine it had produced and dried it on his tunic and held it up to the light.

"Oh, Ox, what a beautiful piece of work," he whispered.

A stone had once washed evil from a flower. Now the flower had shed the tears it had saved up to wash the flaw from the stone, and there wasn't a trace of a crack or a sign of soft gold. The three pieces were one, and it was as solid as a stone can be.

Master Li turned and raised his head toward Heaven and drew in great lungfuls of air. I covered my ears, but still the high harsh eagle screams that burst from the old man's throat hurt my eardrums. The screams lifted one after another, shooting to the crimson clouds, and the echoes bounced back and forth between the peaks.

He dropped to his knees. I followed his example. "It is Li Kao," he said simply. "I pray to be allowed to address the goddess Nu Kua."

We knelt there in silence while clouds began to cover the sky. I suppose it was my imagination, but I began to sense something else that stretched from horizon to horizon: a vast maternal presence.

"Goddess," Master Li said politely, "forgive me for beginning with a minor matter, but I have sworn a vow. The current Patron of Prostitutes is an incompetent disgrace, and the whores of China wish her to be replaced. Since the great Golden Lotus is scarcely available, they have nominated Empress Wu."

The air was growing sulphurous. Thunder rumbled.

"Well, perhaps it might not be a good idea to let a woman like that run around loose," Master Li hastily conceded. "I have been authorized to select a substitute, and I humbly nominate Tou Wan, wife of the late Laughing Prince. It is true that she attempted to murder her maid, but I have yet to meet a lady of quality who has not had the same urge now and then. So far as I know she took no part in her husband's massacres and tortures, and as for her qualifications, she was immoral, lecherous, seductive, avaricious, blessed with a heart of the purest granite, and as tough as a person can get without infringing upon the supernatural. She was intelligent and brooked no nonsense, and would surely be a first-class manager. I cannot imagine a better representative of prostitutes, and should she cause trouble, it would only be necessary to send her a cool drink with lots and lots of ice in it. May I be so bold as to hope that a formal petition would receive favorable omens?"

The smell of sulphur faded away and the thunder died down. Master Li bowed again.

"Goddess, the world of men is a world of incomprehension," he said softly. "Our senses are woefully limited. Our brains are but tiny candles flickering in an infinity of darkness. Our only wisdom is to admit that we cannot understand, and since we cannot understand we must do the best we can with faith, which is our only talent. The greatest act of faith we are capable of is that of loving another more than we love ourselves, and occasionally we can be quite good at it."

He reached out and placed the stone upon the grass.

"We thank you for hoping that the one tiny talent of man might achieve what other forces could not," he said. "We thank you for sending us a flawed stone that would call across the centuries to a flawed flower. We thank you for sending us the flower that would answer the call, and come with the greatest gift love is capable of. We thank you for bringing the pieces together, and we pray that a stone and a flower will finally be granted the acceptance of Heaven."

He bowed flat to the ground. So did I, but I peeked, and Master Li did too.

A slanting sunbeam slid through the clouds and glided across the grass to the stone. I had the feeling that it was probing and testing as it moved over the surface. Then everything stood still. The birds stopped singing and the insects stopped buzzing and the animals stopped rustling. Even the breeze stopped blowing while the stone slowly lifted from the grass and came to a halt about four feet up in the air.

I heard a humming sound. A light was glowing inside the stone, and a vibration made my head spin. The inner light began to pulse faster and faster and the stone began to shake. The hum was now a muted roar of incredible power, and a halo of light began to spin around the stone. Another halo crossed it, and another and another. The stone was glowing with blinding light, and the halos formed a dizzying pattern of interlocking rings, and I knew with absolute certainty that the full ch'i and shih of a simple stone was powerful enough to reduce the Valley of Sorrow to a tiny pile of ashes.

The vibration still accompanied the roar, and the stone still shook. The roar increased and the stone threatened to shake itself to pieces.

Moon Boy was turning transparent, shimmering and melting and fading into nothingness, and something was appearing upon the shuddering surface of the stone. Colors deepened, buds lifted and opened, and we gazed at a lovely flower. The roar of power stopped vibrating and the stone stopped shaking, but then the power level lifted again—unbelievable force!—and the shaking and vibrating reappeared.

Now Grief of Dawn turned transparent. Her body melted like mist, and only the bent grass testified to the fact that it had lain there, and something else was appearing upon the stone. A slim graceful green creeper moved around the circumference, wrapping a stone and a flower in an eternal embrace, and the roar stopped vibrating and the stone stopped shaking.

Again the roar of awesome power grew stronger and stronger. The spinning halos were now seamless, and nothing could withstand the force as the energy level approached the infinite—nothing —yet the stone remained absolutely steady and resolute, and I lost my fear that it would burst. Then the blinding light faded, and the roar faded, and the halos spun slower, and the stone began climbing to the clouds, picking up speed, streaking like a tiny comet toward the Great River of Stars and the goddess Nu Kua and the Wall of Heaven. The distant twinkle of light faded away and was gone.

Master Li stood up and stretched. "How would I know?" he said, answering the expression on my face. "I'm no more capable of understanding the universe than the ancients were, and I applaud their good sense in leaving Heavenly matters to the gods. All I know is that certain things seem to work and certain things don't."

He turned and gazed across the gorge.

"Well, Prince, fraud may rule the world, but classicism still packs a wallop when one removes the neo from it," he said to the embers of the studio. "Classical truths still apply, and classical values still define the limits, and classical standards still hold the universe together."

He turned to me. "Come on, Ox. Let's find a place where they still know how to get classically drunk."

"Yes, sir," I said.

I bent over and he hopped nimbly up on my back. I turned and began loping down the path toward the monastery, and then on to Peking, and Heaven's Bridge, and the Alley of Flies, and the Wineshop of One-Eyed Wong.